HIS TO KEEP

TERRI L. AUSTIN

sourcebooks casablanca

Published by Sourcebooks Casablanca, an imprint of Sourcebooks, Inc.
P.O. Box 4410, Naperville, Illinois 60567-4410
(630) 961-3900
Fax: (630) 961-2168
www.sourcebooks.com

Printed and bound in Canada.
MBP 10 9 8 7 6 5 4 3 2 1

To Tracey Gee. Thanks for translating corporate speak, answering all my questions, and helping me nail those little details that made Brynn's story come alive. But thank you most of all for your friendship. I heart you!

P.S. I am not the evil twin!

Chapter 1

Which is worse—a status report meeting or bra shopping? Brynn Campbell's gaze remained fixed on her boss as she feigned interest and nibbled at her pen, considering the question.

These meetings always took forever. Brynn and office manager Paige Adams played the Which Would You Rather? game every Monday morning, A) to entertain themselves and B) as a way to remain conscious.

Brynn glanced at the question again. Tough call. By the end of every status meeting, she walked out of the room a little dumber than when she'd entered. But since her boobs were the size of two clementines, bra shopping was its own particular form of hell.

Cassandra Delaney held court at the front of the room, and in the last thirty minutes, she'd wandered off topic no less than five times—mostly with stories about her Persian cat's wicked bladder infection.

Brynn wrote: *Definitely bra shopping. Members of the Itty Bitty Titty Committee unite! Fight the big boob power!* She covertly scanned the room to make sure no one was watching her—not likely, since she'd parked in the back row. Given a choice, Brynn would always cling to the fringes of a group rather than take center stage. She preferred the comfort of flying under the radar.

Brynn refolded the note and lobbed it to Paige, who began to shake with laughter as soon as she read the answer. Covering up the giggle with a pseudo cough, her hacking drew attention from everyone—even Cass stopped talking. With one hand over her mouth, Paige stood, brushed off looks of concern, and left the conference room.

That brilliant bitch. She was going to skip out on the rest of the meeting, leaving Brynn to fend for herself.

For the next forty-five minutes, Brynn half listened as members of the sales team gave their reports for the week, plus any new leads they'd picked up. But the boss didn't ask Brynn for an update on her current projects, and that could only mean one thing—Cassandra had another assignment for her.

Brynn often referred to the head of the Delaney Training Center (TDTC) as "scattered." In reality, Cassandra was a neurotic mess. Prone to bouts of high drama, wherever she went, chaos followed. She was perpetually in the middle of multiple crises, both personal and professional—usually of her own making. However, those same traits also meant Cass was easily distracted. If Brynn laid low for a few hours, stayed out of the boss's crosshairs, she could concentrate on the tasks already filling her inbox. By noon, Cass might forget all about this latest job.

Though normally Brynn had the stealth of a ninja and was a master at hiding in plain sight—strategies she'd honed over the years—Cass still had a knack for finding Brynn, no matter where she was. She'd even cornered Brynn in a bathroom stall once and trapped her there for twenty minutes. While Cass rambled on about her latest boyfriend and his inability to come in under an hour—"retarded ejaculation," she called it—Brynn had wished that Cass would read just *one* of the many manuals she'd written on a hostile work environment. Despite owning a corporate training company, Cass was a walking, talking lawsuit in the making. *Drown myself in the toilet or listen to Cass complain about a sore vadge?* Her boss's sex complaints won by a nose, but it was neck and neck for a while. In the end, Brynn had swallowed her discomfort, given Cass a big hug, and suggested numbing lube. That was Brynn to a T—ever the helper.

After another thirty minutes of rambling, Cass wrapped up the meeting, and immediately, her dark brown eyes scanned the room, searching. Brynn knew that look too well. It meant there was a target on her forehead. Hunching a little lower in her chair, she purposely dropped her pen. Bending over to retrieve it, she ducked behind Ted Benson, the burliest salesman on the team. When he stood, Brynn did too, with her nose practically glued to his back. At twice her size, Ted made great camouflage.

Did Brynn feel like a coward for going to such lengths? Yes. Would that stop her? Not even. At TDTC, Brynn wore many hats: artistic director (animator of rudimentary cartoon films), curriculum developer (writer of corporate educational materials), and all-around troubleshooter (taking on the shit no one else would). She couldn't add one more thing to her agenda. There were only twenty-four hours in a day.

When Ted walked toward the door, Brynn stayed right behind him. When he slowed to speak to Lori, office receptionist and his unrequited crush, Brynn slowed too. Then he was on the move again. Finally, her exit was only five feet away. *So close to freedom*. But

Ted halted abruptly, causing Brynn to plow her forehead into his shoulder blade.

He turned and glanced down. "Hey there, Brynn, you all right? Didn't see you back there."

"I'm fine." She rubbed the spot between her eyes.

From the doorway, Cass spied her. "Brynn, I've been looking for you. Grab a cup of coffee and meet me in my office. Oh God, this day. You would not believe." She turned and marched out of the conference room. That's when Brynn noticed a run creeping up Cass's pantyhose and a few baby-fine, ash-blond curls drooping from her lopsided bun. Cass looked less put together than usual. There was a story there, and Brynn would be forced to hear every harrowing detail.

"Hey," Ted said, "I've been meaning to ask you something."

All of Brynn's conversations usually started this way. When people sought her out, it was because they needed a favor, not because they wanted to chitchat or invite her to lunch. She tried not to let it bother her. "Do you have time to put together a proposal for me? It's for a statewide savings and loan. Could mean multiple contracts. You do such a great job of pitching it on paper."

Brynn opened her mouth to say, "I don't have time." But then she gazed up into Ted's round face—the hopeful half smile, the desperate eyes. She smiled back. "Sure, shoot me an email."

"Thanks, Brynn. I owe you one. This could make my salary for the quarter." He clapped her on the shoulder. "You're the best."

No, she wasn't the best. She was just a pushover. But what was one more proposal? It would probably take ten minutes, and Ted was a good guy. If she could help him out, why not?

With a sigh, Brynn headed to the break room, grabbed a cup of coffee, and then wended her way through the office to knock on Cassandra's door.

"*Entrez.*"

Refraining from a serious eye roll, Brynn walked in. As usual, Cass's desk was a mound of folders, papers, and blue stress balls bearing the TDTC logo. There was no room for a mug, so Brynn waited while Cass kicked off her shoes and wriggled out of the ripped hose. She dropped them on her cluttered desk before accepting the cup from Brynn. "Thanks. I was up with Nef all night. She's in misery, my poor angel."

"That's sad. Well, it looks like you're swamped, so I'll let you get back to it." Brynn retreated to the doorway. It wasn't that she didn't have sympathy for the cat, but Brynn couldn't stand one more tale of feline incontinence.

"No, sit." Cass waved to the chair by her desk. "Just put all that stuff on the floor. I'll get to it later."

Not likely. There was months' worth of paperwork filling the room. Brynn couldn't see how anyone functioned in this kind of disorganization.

From the chair, Brynn hoisted an armful of binders, placed them neatly on the floor, then watched as they tumbled over like dominoes. Brynn ignored the impulse to stack them all over again and sat. "What's up?"

Cass blew across the surface of the coffee. "Blue Moon Corp. contacted me last night. The company needs effective management training ASAP. All of my regular facilitators are busy."

"All of them? How is that possible?" *Facilitators*—corporate speak for teacher. *Educator* or *team leader*—those worked, too.

"I called a few I keep in reserve," Cass said with a shrug, "but everyone's booked. Lots of conventions this week, I guess."

Brynn settled more comfortably in her chair. She could be here awhile. Cassandra and her litany of complaints wasn't a pleasant way to spend an hour, but it was all part of the job. *Root canal or Cassandra griping about the lack of staff support?* Listening to Cass was far less painful, but on the other hand, no nitrous. Choices, choices.

"Which is why I need you to do it."

Brynn nodded, made eye contact, and gave every appearance that she'd been actively listening. She hadn't been. "What now?"

"You're going to have to facilitate." Cass placed the mug on a precarious stack of papers and began searching. "Where's my phone? Have you seen it?"

Wait. What?

"Cass, I don't teach. That's not one of my jobs." Brynn was the ultimate team player. Whatever Cass threw her way, Brynn took on without a peep—well, not an outward peep. She peeped plenty on the inside. But this? No way. Even though Brynn had taken numerous seminars on the subject of public speaking, she hadn't been able to put the principles into practice. Just the thought of standing in front of a group of people, being the center of attention, gave her a case of flop sweat.

Cassandra froze and batted her big brown eyes. "You'll have to, Brynn. There's no one else."

Panic made Brynn's hands clammy. "Why can't you do it?"

Cass's thin, plucked brows rose halfway up her forehead. "Do you see all this paperwork? I'm up to my neck. Besides, I make you sit through those seminars so that I can network. I'm not up-to-date on the latest information, and you are."

In the two years Brynn had worked here, she'd been perfectly content to sit in her converted supply closet office and write manuals. Facilitating? Out of the question. "You didn't hire me to educate, Cass. You hired me to write curriculum." And somehow, Brynn had managed to add a pile of other duties to her job description without ever seeing a pay raise. But that was a conversation for a different day. Right now, she needed to find a way out of this. In an effort to control the anxiety flooding her system, Brynn breathed deeply from her diaphragm and counted to six. Then she exhaled in a whoosh. She repeated the process—breathe, whoosh, breathe, whoosh. It didn't help.

"Calm down," Cass said. "You'll be fine. Besides, there's no one else. Tag—you're it."

Brynn's mouth went dry. Her eyes dashed around the room as she gripped the nubby, padded armrests. Clearing her throat, she stood. "Cassandra." Maybe she could get her point across using the "I phrase" technique. "While *I* understand your predicament, *I* don't feel *I'm* the right person for this job. *I* simply lack the skill set."

Cass tilted her head to the side. "Brynn, you wrote the manual, for crying out loud. No one knows the material better than you." Then she slipped to her knees and disappeared under the desk. "Where is that damned phone? Call it for me?"

"Yes, but *I'm* not the right person to teach it." Brynn tugged her own phone from her pocket and dialed Cass's number. Ringing sounded from the trash can.

Cassandra popped out from beneath the desk and knee-walked to the wastebasket, upending it on the floor. "How did it get in there? Anyway, you'll be fine with this. From what *I* understand, it's not even a group. It's a one-on-one training session. Get the details from Lori. I emailed her all the particulars."

Brynn tucked her phone away. "Cass, I have mounds of work to do. I finished evaluating the dry cleaning chain, but I need to plan their antitheft awareness program." A *hey employees, quit cribbing shit from customers' pockets* program might be a more accurate description. But the corporate training world wasn't about accurate. It was about diplomacy and covering an employer's ass. "There must be someone else who can do this. Anyone. Ted's really personable." She glanced down at her jeans and sandals. "I'm not even dressed to meet a client."

"You look great. A little, you know, hippy dippy, but cute. I know this isn't your thing, that you're happier staying in the background, but you, Brynn Campbell, are my most reliable employee. You know the standard course backward and forward. It'll take two days, tops. If you do this for me, I'll consider hiring you an assistant. Please, Brynn. I really need you."

Pressing her fingers to her eyes, Brynn nodded, giving in way too easily. She always did. How hard was one little word? Brynn practiced saying "no" over and over, but it never came out when she needed it to. And maybe a one-on-one situation wouldn't be *so* bad. At least she wouldn't have to face a crowd of people. "Okay, I'll do it."

Cass hopped up. "You're a lifesaver. In fact"—she bent over, reached into a cardboard box on the floor, and pulled out a roll of candy, thrusting it into Brynn's hand—"our latest promo item—Lifesavers with the TDTC logo. Cute?" Then Cass looked down at her bare feet. "I guess I should put on a new pair of hose. I have some in my purse, which is…where?" She glanced at her desk and began shuffling things around, which knocked over the full mug of coffee. Brown liquid trailed over reams of paper and onto the floor. "Damn it."

Brynn quickly wheeled around and sped through the door before Cass asked her to mop it up, because like the jellyfish she was, Brynn would have probably done that, too.

Iain Chapman listened as his lawyer explained about the new economic regulations, zoning details, and ecological classifications that had just been enacted. But as Stan droned on, Iain became more agitated. "For fuck's sake, Stan, cut to the chase and tell me how all this is going to impact the land we want to develop. Preferably in English." Iain couldn't take one more acronym—NEDA, CDBG, SBA, USGS. It was giving him a bloody headache, it was. In his right hand, he rubbed a pair of red dice back and forth. It was a habit Iain had acquired over the years, one he couldn't seem to shake.

Stan Daniels sighed deeply. He seemed to do that a

lot around Iain—who had probably paid for the three-thousand-dollar suit the prat was wearing. So he could save his sighs for other clients, because Iain wasn't having it.

"Cut the drama, mate. Just give me the highlights already."

"Let the man talk, Iain. It's why we're paying him, innit?" From the window overlooking the busy street, Marcus Atwell turned to face them, all the while stroking his chin—a sure sign he was worried. But that was nothing new. It was when Marc started playing with his floppy hair that Iain knew real trouble was brewing.

"What this means," Stan said, "is you'll pay more in taxes, shell out more for inspections, and have to jump through more governmental regulation hoops. Get used to it."

"How much more are we talking about here?" Iain asked.

"A couple million, give or take."

Iain pushed back his chair and stood, pocketing the dice as he walked across the room. "That sounds like pocket change to you, does it?" Stan came from money and had gone to a fancy Ivy League school—probably grew up using hundred-dollar bills to wipe his privileged ass.

"Do we really have to do this today?" Stan asked. "It's pocket change to you too, Iain. You have a multimillion-dollar project you want to implement. This is a drop in the bucket."

"He's right, Iain," Marc said. "We're not the poor lads from Manchester anymore. It's all a matter of perspective."

At the credenza in the corner, Iain poured coffee

from an antique silver pot. Drinking from the delicate china cups always made him feel faintly ridiculous, but it added to the traditional British decor. No sense in having four-thousand-dollar Chippendale chairs only to drink from a cheap ceramic mug. Presentation was important. And two million really wasn't much in the bigger scheme of things, but he didn't take any of it for granted, not a bloody penny.

"Send us copies detailing the changes, and cc my project manager, yeah?" Iain sipped his coffee—strong, black, bitter. He glanced over at Stan. "Was there something else? I'm getting billed for every moment you stand there looking like a twat."

The bald man smiled. "I don't charge for looking like a twat. That one's on the house." He bent to pick up his briefcase. "Always a pleasure, Iain."

"Fuck off."

"Nice seeing you, too." Stan nodded at both men and left the room.

Once he was gone, Marc paced the floor. "She's coming this morning?"

"Yeah. Should be here in a few."

"We don't need to do this," Marc said. "There are other investors. We could develop the properties slowly, take our time."

"And we may have to," Iain said with a shrug, "if this doesn't pan out."

"It probably won't. Brynn Campbell might hate you on sight—and I wouldn't blame her, because you're a bit of a blighter, truth be told. And if she finds out you set her up, she could turn Trevor Blake against us."

"It'll work, trust me. Hiring Brynn's firm is a stroke

of genius. We need a fresh partner for this project. One with deep pockets. Who better than Trevor Blake? If we're really lucky, Brynn's other brother-in-law, Cal Hughes, might throw in with us. Those two have loads to spare, good business sense, and Trevor's name carries weight in this town. I went over every other angle I could think of, and Brynn Campbell is the weak link."

A lovely one at that.

The first time he'd laid eyes on her had been at an evening garden party, a benefit for her family's cancer foundation. He'd paid a fortune for a ticket in hopes of meeting Trevor. While wandering through the garden, Iain had spotted Brynn, and he'd been struck immobile. It wasn't just her beauty or that delicate, graceful quality that captured his attention. No, it was the way she held herself apart from the crowd and observed everyone around her, as if, despite being who she was—the sister-in-law of the wealthiest man in Vegas—she didn't quite feel comfortable in her posh surroundings. It had reminded him, uncomfortably, of himself.

And he hadn't been able to look away.

He'd watched her for the better part of an hour. Though she tried to hide in plain sight, Iain couldn't take his eyes off her. *He* saw her clearly, so why couldn't anyone else? And when he'd begun to approach her, she'd turned on her heel and flitted away, into Trevor's monstrously large house. Trevor had also disappeared before Iain could introduce himself. Nevertheless, he'd stayed until the end of the party, hoping to catch another glimpse of Brynn, without any luck. She'd stuck in his head ever since, though he couldn't for the life of him say why. Now he was finally going to meet her properly.

About bloody time, too. All it took was an elaborate ruse and several thousand dollars to draw her out of her hidey-hole.

Not that this was about Brynn, he told himself. He had a goal. He was going to stay focused on that goal—she was just a bloody bonus.

"It feels wrong," Marc said, "using this girl to get to her relatives. Seedy, yeah?"

"It's called networking. No different than glad-handing at a cocktail party or going to a charity dinner in order to meet serious players. It's just business. You know we've tried every other avenue. Blake's lawyer won't return our calls. I even tried to play up the expat angle with him, but I couldn't get a meeting. Trevor Blake is a bloody fortress."

Marc stopped treading over the hand-loomed rug. "While I'm not convinced that this is our best solution, the course she's teaching might actually do you some good. Your leadership skills are a bit lacking, aren't they?"

Iain paused, the cup midway to his lips. "What the bloody hell are you on about?" Iain was leadership personified. He had the portfolio and bank balance to prove it. "There's nothing wrong with the way I lead, mate. I get results."

"You do," Marc agreed. "But you also hack off a lot of people. And those you don't offend are scared shitless of you."

"Good." He didn't give a damn if people feared him, as long as they did their jobs properly. This wasn't a popularity contest. No one got a prize for congeniality. "If they don't like working here, they're free to quit."

"Which explains our high turnover rate. You could stand to be a little nicer to people. Wouldn't kill you none, would it?"

"I expect people to show up and do their jobs. In return, we pay them very well at the end of each week. I'm not their mate. End of."

"The accounting department nearly piss themselves every time you walk into the room," Marc said.

"And?" Nothing wrong with that—at least his employees respected him.

"My gran used to say you catch more flies with honey than with vinegar."

"That's daft. Why would I want to catch flies?" Strolling to his chair, Iain carefully set the cup and saucer on his desk, then tugged on the bottom of his waistcoat before resuming his seat. "This scheme is going to work. Brynn Campbell will give me a pointless lesson, I'll be charming, she'll be charmed, and in turn, I'll ask her for an introduction to Trevor Blake. In the meantime, you make sure our proposal is sorted, yeah?"

"I'm on it, but I still say your management style could use an overhaul."

"Bugger off. By the way, how's Melanie? Haven't seen her in weeks."

"Fine." Marc combed his fingers through his hair, leaving it more disheveled than before. "Things are fine."

Something was definitely going on there, but if Marc didn't want to talk about it, Iain wouldn't pry—it was none of his concern as long as it didn't interfere with business. "We can't afford to have you distracted right now. I need you focused on this project."

Marc's blue eyes turned glacial. "Since when have I

ever cocked-up on a project? I'll do my bit, you do your part. But if we're relying on your *charm*, we could be in real trouble."

"Funny," Iain said to Marc's retreating back. The door shut with a click behind him.

Management training nonsense—Iain couldn't think of anything more useless. And his *management style* didn't need an overhaul. He and Marc had built this company from nothing, in spite of a crap economy. Fine, Iain was sometimes harsh with his employees, but if they couldn't handle it, they probably didn't belong there. Besides, he didn't get his jollies from being cruel. Everything he did, every decision he made, was for the benefit of Blue Moon.

A few moments later, Amelia knocked on the door and slipped into the room. "Iain, your appointment's here." Ames was a lovely woman—professional-looking in a conservative black dress. No one would have ever guessed that they'd met in a strip club.

Iain had been a bouncer, Ames a bartender. When the business started taking off, he'd brought her on board full time—steady hours, full bennies. With her disarming warmth and bright smile, Amelia made his visitors feel welcomed. In fact, they were so comfortable by the time they entered his office, they'd lowered their guard. And Iain took advantage of it. She was the honey, and he was the vinegar. Flies, indeed.

Until now, he hadn't realized he'd been fondling the dice once again. Shoving them into his pocket, he stood and donned his jacket. Then he smoothed his lapels and straightened his tie. When Amelia didn't move, he glanced up at her. "What's the problem?"

She shook her head. "No problem."

"Then why are you still here?"

"Iain, your trainer's a woman."

He hadn't told Amelia about his plans for Brynn Campbell. His assistant would disapprove, and then she'd nag. No, it was better that he and Marc keep this scheme to themselves. "So?"

"She's very pretty, and she seems so nice. Just for once…don't be yourself."

He reared his head back at her words. "What the bloody hell is wrong with everyone today?" Attacking his leadership skills, questioning his ability to be civil. Iain could do civil…when he put his mind to it. "I'll be myself, thank you. If you don't like it, sod off, Ames."

She wagged her finger. "Yeah. That's what I'm talking about. Do the opposite of that." When she disappeared through the door, he faced the window and looked out at his seven-million-dollar view. Seven-point-two-five, if one wanted to be technical. And when it came to money, Iain was always technical.

The morning sun slanted through the tinted window. If he stood at the right angle, he could catch a glimpse of jagged, brown mountains in the distance. The palm trees lining the street below swayed in the breeze, reminding him that he was in the middle of a desert. He never grew tired of seeing this. Nothing in Vegas was real—it was all a facade. The buildings, the people—all transitory. And Iain loved every bloody bit of it.

He heard the door open and, after a long pause, close. Her footsteps were hesitant and light across the gold onyx floor.

"Hello." Her voice was soft, feminine—young. The sound of it made his heart pound. She couldn't run from him today, couldn't hide in the shadows. He had her right where he wanted her.

Iain slowly turned, a smile fixed on his face. But as he once again locked eyes on Brynn, desire slammed into his gut like a sucker punch. The pictures in Iain's drawer, the ones he'd printed from the extensive background check, didn't do her justice. Ames had called her pretty, which was also inadequate. From his memory, he knew she was beautiful, but with the morning sun shining on her at an angle, she was the most bloody gorgeous woman he'd ever seen.

Iain thought he knew everything about Brynn Hope Campbell, from her shopping habits to her tax returns. He knew what hobbies she favored and the classes she'd taken in college. But nothing had prepared him for meeting her in the flesh.

His gaze moved over her, taking in her slight frame. Then his eyes swept over her again. And a third time. With every pass, he noticed something different. The color of her hair wasn't merely brown—it was tobacco brown with burnished-gold highlights. Her eyes weren't ordinary blue—they were navy. She wore leather flip-flops. Her toenails were varnished the same shade as her turquoise necklace. She carried a black binder in one hand, like a schoolgirl.

Lightly tanned, her skin glowed along high, smooth cheekbones. Her features were dainty, fragile—a lovely setting for those big, dark eyes. Her chin drew to a sharp point below a mouth that was too wide for such a delicate face. *Innocent*. The word floated through Iain's mind, but he immediately banished it. No one was innocent—not in this town.

Brynn was on the petite side, but her legs appeared long and slender. The white, loose blouse flowed over her torso, skimming her small tits. The V-shaped collar left her neck and throat bare. Iain's gaze fell to the wedge of visible golden skin. That sliver of flesh had his cock twitching. He wanted to see more. No, that wasn't true. Iain was a greedy bastard—he wanted to see everything.

She'd pulled her wavy hair into a low ponytail, but a lone curl refused to be confined and brushed against her squared jaw. She appeared almost fey—a wisp of a woman who might blow away with the gentlest breeze.

He moved toward her and buttoned his jacket, keeping his gaze trained on her. "I'm Iain Chapman." He saw no recognition in her eyes. To be fair, the lighting had been dim that night in the garden, and as soon as he'd been within five meters of her, she'd scampered off. Still, he recalled everything about her—her flowing ivory dress edged with frilly lace, the crystal necklace, the tiny flowers placed randomly throughout her curls. She didn't remember him. So he hadn't made the same impression on her that she had made on him. He shouldn't take it personally. And yet...

"You're British." She made it sound like an accusation.

"Observant, aren't you?"

She opened her mouth but didn't speak. Taking a breath, she tried again. "I try to be. Pleased to meet you, Mr. Chapman. My name's Brynn Campbell." She stared at his silver tie like it was the most fascinating thing she'd ever seen. She was timid, and he found that charming. For the first time, a hint of doubt robbed him of his certainty. Was this the right course of action? A simple introduction to Trevor Blake, that's all he was after. But now that he'd seen Brynn face-to-face again, Iain found himself wanting more. *That's all you want, is it, a meeting with Trevor? Then why have you stared at her picture* every day *for months?* Yeah, all right then. A meeting with Trevor was his priority, but getting close to Brynn was a definite plus.

"Call me Iain. I've been told I require a management makeover. Are you the woman to give me what I need?" He hadn't intended the innuendo, but he didn't apologize for it either.

Her gaze fluttered from his throat to his eyes. "I'm not sure. To be honest, I'm not really a teacher. I just write the curriculum."

He knew that, of course, had paid Cassandra Delaney a few thousand extra to have Brynn teach the class personally. "I'm not much of a student, so I'd say we're well matched." When her eyes swept over his face, he smiled. But Brynn didn't smile back, as most women would. In fact, she stared at him with a faint frown on her generous lips.

Well, that was new. Women generally flirted with him. And he wasn't foolish enough to believe they were attracted to his delightful personality. Although he did all right in the looks department, his face wasn't what lured them, either. No, Iain's main draw was his fat bank account. He was fine with that. Made things simpler. Everyone walked away happy. There were no expectations, no fuss. No emotional ties.

But Brynn didn't respond to him like other women, and he couldn't say why that intrigued him so much.

Brynn Campbell wasn't his usual type. Perhaps that's why he was utterly enchanted by her. She didn't wear her sexuality like armor. She was small, nearly flat-chested, and dressed as if she were attending a music festival rather than a business meeting. With copper bracelets stacked on her slender wrist, she wore tattered jeans and very little makeup. And the way she watched him with those wide, wary eyes…

When he took a step toward her, she tensed. What did she think? He was going to make a lunge for her? He never dreamed she'd be so skittish, at least not in a professional setting—or that he'd find it so compelling.

A knock sounded at the door and Amelia peered in. "Would you like some tea, Miss Campbell?"

Brynn glanced over her shoulder. "That would be nice, thank you."

While she was looking away, Iain took the opportunity to study her breasts. The blouse was deceptively sheer. Tilting his head, he tried to see through the crinkly material, but he couldn't even detect the outline of her bra. It was maddening and enticing at the same time. As soon as Ames shut the door, Brynn faced him again. And caught him staring.

Swallowing audibly, she raised the black binder, clutching it to her chest and blocking his view. "Why don't we get started?" she asked.

"Yes, why don't we?"

She stared at him for a beat, then squared her shoulders and stuck one hand in her purse. She pulled out a pen and opened her book to the front page.

Iain tried to get a peek at what she jotted down, but she snapped the notebook closed before he could read it. "Are you taking notes on me, love?"

Brynn angled her head to look up at him. "If I were your employee, your suggestive glances might be considered actionable."

"Actionable how? Like we'd clear the desk and have at it?"

Her brows drew together and formed a small *V*. "That comment would definitely qualify as actionable."

He leaned down, caught a whiff of perfume—vanilla and something floral. "Pretend you never heard it." Iain breathed her in. *Absolutely delicious*.

Her lips parted slightly, but she didn't move away. Brynn Campbell might be wary, but she was also interested.

"The key to running a successful business," she whispered, "is keeping a professional attitude. Sniffing me probably isn't professional."

"Depends on what your profession is, I suppose. And here I thought the key to running a successful business was making money. Shows how fucking little I know, eh?"

"Do you always use that language?" Brynn opened her notebook and scribbled again. "With employees, I mean."

"Yeah. I don't believe in censoring myself." He hadn't moved away, was still leaning toward her. Her shallow breaths caused her chest to rapidly rise and fall, and that became the focus of Iain's attention. Her breasts were so tiny, he'd be able to suck on the whole damned thing. The thought made his mouth water.

"Um, *I* don't feel very comfortable when you look at me like that."

Iain reached out, his finger grazing a red splotch on the side of her throat. "I wasn't trying to make you feel comfortable."

"Oh." She paused. "*I* feel that, together, we can create a work environment that is both productive and respectful. *I* don't feel respected as a colleague right now." She stepped back two paces, leaving Iain's hand dangling in the air before he let it fall to his side.

Blimey, she was serious. And so lovely it almost stole the breath out of his lungs. Iain felt an unwilling smile pull at the corners of his lips. "Are you quoting from a book or something?"

Brynn nodded and cleared her throat. "A manual, actually. *Leading by Example: A Partnership in Effectiveness*."

"Sounds boring enough to send me to sleep."

"I wrote it." She enunciated the words, pointing her chin upward. He'd pricked her ego a bit. It was always vital to know as much about one's opponent as possible, and Iain had just learned that Brynn Campbell took pride in her deadly dull work.

"Brilliant. Then we can dispense with the lessons. Give me the short version, and afterward, I'll take you to lunch." Iain really wanted to take Brynn to bed. He wasn't sure if she could teach him anything about leadership, but he was almost certain he could teach her a thing or two about pleasure.

Chapter 2

Short version? Brynn was thinking of adding a chapter or three based on Iain Chapman alone. His eyes kept roaming over her from head to toe, and with each glance, her skin tingled a little more. Her throat went dry. As he continued to stare at her, Brynn was aware of every breath she took, every beat of her thumping heart. Then he touched her neck.

How was she supposed to think clearly with his long finger brushing her heated skin? *Heated?* Damn, the splotches must be back. It happened every time Brynn got really flustered. She thought she'd outgrown them but apparently not. Awesome.

When she'd walked into this office, Brynn had been a nervous wreck. The thought of teaching a class, even to one person, made her stomach muscles seize up in fear. But after meeting Iain Chapman, after being inspected so thoroughly by those light brown eyes, seeing that dimple crease his right cheek—her anxiety had only gotten worse. Iain Chapman was attracted to her. No, not just attracted—he *wanted* her.

Brynn was a wallflower by choice. She didn't garner attention from men like Iain Chapman. Handsome men. Powerful men. He must treat all women as potential sex partners, because Brynn couldn't think of one reason why he'd single her out.

She put him somewhere in his early thirties. Tall,

with wide shoulders and narrow hips, the mere idea of what he must look like naked sent a little thrill shooting up her spine. Not that she'd ever find out. Still, Brynn's fingers itched to grab a pencil and start sketching based on her imagination alone.

Iain was stunning in a virile, hot, masculine way. With his short, black hair neatly combed away from his face, it tended toward wavy. One lock broke ranks and fell across the top of his forehead, where ghostly horizontal lines deepened when he frowned. Which he'd done a couple of times in the last five minutes. Shallow sunbursts radiated from the corners of his eyes—sharp eyes that missed nothing. Not her toenails or her bracelets…or her boobs—he'd checked those out more than once. It must have been a habitual reaction, because Brynn didn't have much to ogle. She wouldn't be able to hold the interest of a man who wore arrogance and self-assurance as casually as he wore an expensive designer suit. He even had one of those little pocket-square things that matched his silver tie.

And to top it off, he was British. Not that there was anything wrong with that—both of her brothers-in-law were Brits. Posh ones. But there was nothing posh about Iain Chapman, despite his clothes. The three-piece charcoal suit, the starched white shirt, the power tie—they smacked of wealth. This office, with its expensive furnishings, the outstanding view, and a floor so shiny she could see her reflection—it made a statement. Luxury. Success. Elegance. But that accent gave him away. Iáin didn't come from wealth—he'd earned it.

Now standing only a foot apart, he still leaned toward her. Brynn fought the urge to take another step backward, give herself a little breathing room. Somehow, she managed to keep her feet in place.

He was the antithesis of everything Brynn normally found attractive in a man—he was large, intimidating, cocky. She'd only had two relationships, and both had ended up the same way—in humiliation. But they had been boys, unsure of themselves. Iain Chapman was one hundred percent confident man.

Brynn felt a sharp tug of desire, a pull of sexual interest so strong it caused her breasts to feel prickly and sensitive. Caused her nipples to harden. Warmth spread through her body as he continued to size her up.

She'd never experienced anything like this, but she had to ignore it, because A) Iain Chapman was her client. Romance between coworkers was fraught with inherent drawbacks and inevitable embarrassing consequences—as outlined in the HR manual *Fraternization: Keep It Out of the Workplace*. B) He was simply too much. Not only was his physical presence overwhelming, but his personality also sucked up all the oxygen in the room. He filled the space, commandeered every square inch of it. And that intimidated the hell out of her. C) He was sexually intense. Brynn didn't do intense, and she was an abject failure in the sex department. She had a low-gasm problem that wouldn't be solved by a man like Iain Chapman. He'd only make her affliction worse—or at least more embarrassing. So…time to snuff out that sexual spark and get on with the business at hand.

Shoving the pen behind her ear, she once again tightened her arms around the binder, as if it could shield her from the inviting heat in his eyes. "*I* think you would be sabotaging your chance for personal development by not completing the course yourself." She tried to appear unaffected as she scuttled past him and moved to a large, tufted sofa near one window. She sat on the edge of the slick, brown leather. If she scooted back any farther, her feet wouldn't touch the floor.

He turned his head, his steady gaze following her. "Why do you say it that way?"

"Say what?"

"Stress the word 'I.' It's odd, yeah?"

First, she'd broken out in red splotches, and now he thought she was an oddball. Brynn ran her tongue over her front teeth, like she used to do when she had braces. It was like being in high school all over again. Because four years of hell wasn't enough, she needed to carry this shit into adulthood. "No, I'm simply stating the facts as *I*...I see them. And I'm taking ownership of my feelings."

He stalked toward her, but instead of taking the chair adjacent to the sofa, he sank down next to her—so close they were practically touching. Another few inches... "Ownership of your feelings? Who the fuck talks like that? In real life."

"We're not in real life. We're in the corporate world, where saying words like 'fuck' can get you into trouble." She opened her notebook and spread it across her lap. "Don't ever confuse the two."

"My business *is* my real life. I say what I want, and I don't give a *fuck* who hears it."

Brynn straightened and crossed her arms. "In my opinion, you need a long-term strategy. We're a litigious society. It's a wonder you haven't been sued for workplace incivility."

"A wonder," he murmured, and plucked the pen from behind her ear. He slid his finger along the length of it, stroking. That shouldn't have been sensual, but watching his finger work over that pen pushed all of Brynn's buttons. She gazed up into his eyes and found him staring at her, a smile playing on his firm, thin lips.

She wasn't sure how to respond to this seductive onslaught. It wasn't in Brynn's nature to tackle things head-on. Every instinct told her to get the hell out of there and never look back. In spite of her discomfort, she remained seated and tried to stick to the job at hand. She grabbed the pen back and forced herself to remain calm and professional. Hard to do with trembling hands, but she tried her best. "Tell me about your relationship with your employees."

Iain rolled his eyes and sat back, flicking a hand over the knife pleat running the length of his long, sturdy thigh. His shoes were as polished as the floor, and his gray socks matched the shade of his suit exactly. "Relationship? What the hell are you on about?" He nodded toward her list of questions. "And what is that?"

"An assessment on your leadership style."

"I can sum it up for you: an employee should do what I say, or I'll toss their ass out on the street and find someone who will." His eyes raked over her. "Is that what you call business attire? You're here to lecture me while wearing jeans and a see-through blouse?"

Embarrassment flooded her, making her whole body feel as if it were on fire. Brynn jerked her head downward, glancing at her shirt. Could he really see through it? She'd successfully performed the lightbulb test—holding her blouse in front of the light and placing her hand behind it to make sure it wasn't see-through. When she looked up and saw the gleam in his eyes, she realized he was trying to get a response out of her. Joke was on him—he didn't even have to try. She'd never reacted to a man like this in her entire life. Sitting close to him, smelling his delicious cologne with just a hint of bergamot—it distracted Brynn so much she was having a hard time stringing words into a coherent sentence.

A knock sounded at the door, dispelling some of the tension between them. Amelia walked in, bearing a tea tray. "How are you two getting along? Everything okay?" She set the tray on a side table and her gaze flew from Iain to Brynn.

"We're not in nursery school, are we?" Iain said. "I don't need to be patronized, Ames."

She didn't seem to take offense at his words but merely smiled. "Don't let him scare you, honey."

In her mid-forties, Amelia's look was classic. Her reddish-blond hair swung around her jawline in a chic bob. She had a few shallow lines around her blue eyes, model-worthy cheekbones, full lips, and a figure to die for—boobs, ass, the whole package. But Brynn didn't get the sense that Amelia and Iain had ever *bow chica bow-wow'ed*. Rather, his assistant seemed almost maternal toward him.

"His bark is worse than his bite." Amelia poured tea through a strainer and into a china cup.

"Actually, my bite is lethal," Iain said.

"Only to those who deserve it. Sugar or milk?"

"Neither, thanks," Brynn said. "How long have you worked for Mr. Chapman?"

"Iain," he corrected.

Amelia shot him a hasty glance but didn't respond. She poured a cup for Iain and handed them each a napkin—a heavy linen one, embroidered with a blue half-moon in one corner. She said nothing else, picked up the tray, and departed.

Iain and his assistant had been silently communicating. Brynn wondered what they'd been saying and why Amelia wouldn't answer a simple question. Being left out made Brynn feel awkward. She filled the silence by sipping her tea—oolong, the high-end stuff. An office with a view, the handmade suits, the expensive tea—Iain Chapman had some serious swagger. "What does Blue Moon do?" she asked.

He looked at ease, sipping tea, the linen napkin draped over his knee. "You mean you don't know? For someone who's here to teach me the ways of leadership, you seem to be caught flatfooted."

Swallowing, she made an effort to pull herself together. "I wasn't expecting to facilitate a course today."

"*Facilitate*—another useless word. And why weren't you prepared? That's the first official rule of business. *Always be prepared.*"

"Actually, that's the Boy Scout motto."

He lifted one shoulder. "It's a good one."

Brynn sighed and set her cup on the low coffee table. "I am unprepared. You're right, it's not very professional of me."

He glanced at her over the rim of his cup. After taking a sip, he set it next to hers. "You want to know about Blue Moon Corp.? My mate, Marc, and I are Blue Moon. We buy things. We own things."

"What do you own, exactly?"

"We invest in clubs and restaurants. We own stores, rental property, car parks, etcetera. If there's something we fancy, we buy it. If it doesn't exist, we create it."

Judging from the opulent office, he was very successful. Iain had a right to his healthy ego. Still, that arrogance could be toned down a notch or two—it might make him more relatable. Maybe Brynn could help him with that. "Let me ask you a few questions."

"Fine, then it's my turn to ask you questions."

"What kinds of questions?" The warmth in his honey-colored eyes told Brynn that he wasn't talking about business practices and management techniques. Those eyes looked right through her, like he could actually *see* her. Brynn had spent her twenty-four years staying on the sidelines of life, but there was no blending into the background when he looked at her like that. "*I* don't feel that's a good idea."

"I think it's bloody brilliant. I want to know everything about you, Brynn Campbell."

She cast her eyes downward, as though by not looking at him she could make herself invisible. "There's nothing to know. I'm probably the most boring person you've ever met."

He laughed then, and that caught her attention. Keeping her head lowered, she lifted her eyes. He had angled toward her, exposing that sexy dimple. In laughter, it deepened, lengthened. To see him smile like that, to watch his eyes crinkle in the corners and his face soften a bit…it left her dazed.

Robbed of breath, she became a statue when he reached out and fingered that stupid strand of hair that would never stay in a ponytail. He gently yanked on it and edged closer. That's when she noticed the tiny flecks of amber dotting his light brown irises. Frozen by his proximity, Brynn couldn't have moved away if she wanted to.

"I think you're fascinating, pet. And I believe in fair play, so I'm telling you now, right? You and I, Brynn—we're going to be lovers."

She was shocked at his frank words, and for one small moment, Brynn actually believed him. The mere thought of it sent a ripple of excitement coursing through her entire body. Then, as she gasped for air, sanity returned, reminding her of all the reasons why that could never happen. Lots of good, sound reasons. Leaning back as far as she could, Brynn pressed her spine into the armrest of the sofa. "I don't think so, Mr. Chapman." Her voice sounded warbley and uncertain, but Brynn had managed to say no. Kind of. It lacked conviction, but at least she'd refused. She considered that a victory.

"Fuck me, I do love a challenge."

Hell no. That wasn't her intention at all. Brynn didn't want him to see her as a challenge. She wasn't going to give in, either. She couldn't. Her self-esteem couldn't handle someone like him. If a man that powerful and aggressive discovered she couldn't orgasm with a partner, could rarely even orgasm on her own, he'd probably see it as his manly duty to fix her. And when he failed, it would be one more humiliation Brynn could add to the list. No thanks. Not interested.

She took a fortifying breath. All of this inappropriate sex talk had to stop. Now. Brynn needed to finish this job. Yet her brain kept screaming over and over: *Get out now, while you still can!*

But she couldn't leave. Brynn promised Cass she'd teach this course. There was no one else to do it. Time to get this train back on track. She glanced down at her questionnaire. "How would you describe your management style?"

"Authoritative."

She wrote it down, kept her eyes glued to the page, but she could feel him looking at her.

"How would your employees describe you?"

"Who cares?"

That response got her attention. "What kind of attitude is that?"

"One that's served me well."

"You don't care how your employees view you?"

He shrugged. "Couldn't give a shit, really."

Where was she supposed to go from there? "Do you ask your team members for input?"

Iain scoffed. "Do you want me to say, 'Hey, Frank, would you mind doing your job? I'd be ever so chuffed if you did, mate'? Is that it?"

"No, that's not it. But people need to feel heard. When people feel heard, when their opinions matter, they're happier. Happier employees are more productive employees."

Iain draped his arm along the back of the sofa and unbuttoned his suit jacket with the other hand. For one second, his fingers brushed a few strands at the bottom of her ponytail, making the hair on the back of Brynn's neck stand on end. She could feel the warmth coming off his arm. It was making her warm—in all the wrong places. "But I don't care if they're happy. And if I had to spend all day listening to other people's fucking ideas, I'd take a leap out this window."

"Mr. Chapman—"

"Iain, love. Best get used to saying it—well, shouting it, more like."

Whoa. Thoughts of Iain on top of her, inside her, made Brynn swallow convulsively. The fantasy was so damned erotic—no, not erotic. Unprofessional. That's what she meant, unprofessional.

Brynn shot out of her seat and threw herself into the armchair next to the sofa. Three feet wasn't as much distance between them as she'd like, but it was a start.

She should have set ground rules from the beginning. She'd let him get by with too much. "Mr. Chapman. *I* feel that you're being very inappropriate right now. You might benefit from a class in sexual harassment, which will take another two days of training."

"Oh God." He rubbed his eyes and exhaled a weary sigh.

"I'm sorry. I'm very confused about my role here. If you're not interested in being a better leader or taking this class seriously, why did you call us in the first place?"

As Iain placed a hand on his leg, his gaze slid to the window. "Right. You're here to train me." He stared out at the cloudless blue sky and said nothing. When he looked back at Brynn, something had changed. She couldn't put her finger on it, but his face was harder, his eyes cooler. Any sexual interest he'd shown earlier was now gone. "My mate, Marc, thinks I could use a little refining. Claims employees are afraid of me."

"What do you think?"

"I suppose he's right." He'd been so dismissive of

his employees a moment ago, but now all of the sudden, he acted compliant. It didn't add up. But as long as he stopped talking about sex, she wasn't going to question his change of heart.

"Okay then. Let's finish this questionnaire, and then I'd like you to show me around the office."

"How many questions are in that bloody thing?" He nodded at the binder.

"Seventy-five."

He muttered under his breath. "Fine. Let's just get on with it, eh?"

~

By question six, Iain's eyes began to cross. He answered more or less honestly, and given Brynn's tightening lips, he could tell she wasn't impressed with his so-called managerial skills. Honestly, though, how in the bloody hell was he meant to "honor people's need for creativity"? What did that even mean?

As Brynn added up his score, Iain's gaze kept tripping over her. He'd been so taken with her, he'd nearly forgotten that he'd arranged this entire scenario. All he could think about was seeing her naked, knowing what that petite, willowy body looked like without clothes. But getting her naked was a secondary goal. A vital one now, to be sure, but it needed to take a backseat. His cock was having a very hard time with that concept, however. It had been rock hard since she walked into the room.

When she glanced up from her notebook, she wore an expression of disappointment. "*I* believe that you could use improvement in several areas. If you practice and apply the techniques from this class, you'll see a real improvement in how you relate to your employees."

Iain didn't want to relate to his employees, but he had to at least pretend, if only to win her over. He stood and walked to the door. "There's no better time than now. Come on, I'll show you around."

Brynn stood and nabbed her purse, slinging it across her shoulder. "Great. Where should we start?"

Iain didn't have the slightest clue. "Why don't you tell me?"

"Could you introduce me to your staff and give me a few details about each department?"

Iain knew the names of his department heads, naturally. The workers? No. Not that he'd admit that to Brynn.

He took her to the numbers section first. "This is Tom, head of accounting. Tom, Brynn Campbell." She shook hands with him. Maybe it was because Tom was in his fifties and weighed no more than ten stone sopping wet, but Brynn didn't seem shy with him at all. She shook his hand and looked him squarely in the eye.

"Pleasure to meet you."

"Introduce her around, Tom, and tell her what you do."

Iain watched as Tom rattled off the names of the six accountants who worked under him. All of them avoided eye contact with Iain. Marc said they nearly pissed themselves at his presence. Iain had never noticed before, but it seemed like Marc was correct. Was he such an ogre, then?

Hardly. He paid more than the average salary, after all. So maybe he barked at people every once in a while.

That only happened when they cocked up. The rest of the time, Iain left them alone to do their work. That made him a boss, not a monster.

As Tom blathered on about tax structure and payroll, Iain allowed himself to stare at Brynn's tight little ass. It was compact, like the rest of her, but damned adorable. When she turned, he quickly shifted his eyes and tried to look as if he'd been listening to every number-crunching word. "Thank you, Tom. Carry on." He waited for Brynn to exit the room first.

"What's next?" she asked.

"Data research." He led her to a cubicle near the center of the room. "Paul, Brynn Campbell."

Paul leaped from his seat as if the chair had scorched his ass. "Sir."

"Please explain to Brynn what it is you do." Iain thrust his hands in his pockets and grabbed hold of the dice. He refrained from pulling them out, but just barely. Paul's nervousness was palpable.

"Our department both buys data and collects it. That's about it."

"For pitching your restaurants and clubs to tourists?" Brynn asked.

"Mostly. Every time someone uses a credit card or cell phone in one of our businesses..." He paused, his eyes straying to Iain. "I mean one of Mr. Chapman's businesses, we have access to that person. It helps us define who our customer is."

Brynn shuddered. "I know this is standard practice, but I find spying on people a little creepy."

If Brynn had any idea how much Iain really knew about her—the fact that she'd bought her house over a year ago, that she purchased mostly organic food and ate at a cheap Thai restaurant at least once a week—she'd be even more disturbed. Fortunately, she'd never find out. "Introduce her to your team, Paul."

He tapped on the side of his cubicle until a woman with straight hair peered over the partition. "This is Jane."

"Hello." Then she disappeared.

"That's it. That's our team. A team of two. More of a duo, really."

Iain held back a sigh. "Right, get back to it."

"Yes, sir." Paul dropped into his seat.

Iain took Brynn's elbow and steered her toward the sales department, then the development teams—property and business, IT, PR, legal—and the HR section. Finally at the end of the room, he stood in front of a closed door.

"This is Marc's office."

"And what does Marc do?"

"Everything. He's in charge of the day-to-day operations. I meet with investors, check the progress on our various sites, and make sure everything is running smoothly outside the office." He knocked on the door and opened it.

Marc sat behind his desk, his jacket off, shirtsleeves rolled up. Where Iain was fastidious about his suits, Marc was more casual, often foregoing a tie.

"Marc Atwell, this is Brynn Campbell, the corporate trainer."

Marc stepped out from behind his desk. "Nice to meet you. You have your hands full with this one, yeah?"

Brynn glanced up at Iain. "Would you mind if I had a few minutes alone with Marc?"

Hell yes he'd mind. "Why is that necessary?"

"I'd like to be thorough in my recommendations. If you're concerned about what Marc has to say, the three of us could dialogue about it afterward."

Dialogue. Rubbish. "No, it's fine. Meet me in my office after you're done, right?"

Iain longed to wipe the smirk off Marc's face. As he made his way back to his office, he wondered what his mate would say about him. He could give Brynn an earful, no doubt. They'd known each other since they were lads—the good, the bad, and the awful. Marc was the only person Iain really trusted. Well, besides Amelia, but she didn't know everything about him.

No, he told himself, Marc wouldn't tell tales. If for no other reason than the fact that Iain would retaliate—mutual destruction and all that.

He stepped into his office suite and Amelia glanced up from her computer screen, her mouth turned down at the corners. "Oh no. You scared her off, didn't you? Too bad. I liked her. Brynn had substance, I could tell."

Iain pulled the dice from his pocket, grounded by the familiar weight of them in his palm. "She's talking to Marc. She'll be back in a jiff."

Ames's brow cleared. "Good. Stay on your best behavior and try not to say *fuck* so much."

"I don't need you telling me how to win women, do I?"

"Mmm, you kind of do. The girls you usually date are little more than shallow gold diggers. It's time you settled down, don't you think?"

Iain stalked to his office. When he reached the door, he turned back. "When I want your sorry *fucking* advice,

I'll ask for it. I know you have work to do. If not, I'll give you some."

"Save it, Iain. You may terrify the minions out there, but you don't scare me."

Chapter 3

Marc Atwell was Iain's opposite in every way. Casually dressed, he wore a ready smile and a long mane of light brown hair that brushed the collar of his rumpled shirt. "Have a seat, Brynn. It's all right to call you Brynn, innit?"

"It is. Thank you." His office wasn't as opulently furnished as Iain's. While the desk and chairs were nice, they weren't antiques, and this space was a good deal smaller, with only two windows.

"How long have you known Iain?" Brynn crossed her legs. She felt at ease in Marc's presence. While he was an undeniably attractive man, with piercing blue eyes and a strong jaw, there was zero sexual attraction simmering between them. He gave off an older-brother vibe, and for the first time since entering the Blue Moon offices, Brynn felt herself relaxing.

"Can't remember a time when I didn't know him. We grew up together, back in Manchester."

"And you came to America together?"

He stared at his desk blotter and caressed it with his fingers. "That we did. Seems like a lifetime ago."

"Tell me the truth."

At her words, Marc's gaze returned to her. "What truth?"

"Iain doesn't know the name of a single employee out there, does he?"

He huffed out a laugh and ran a hand through his hair.

"You've pegged him, love. Tried to pretend otherwise, did he?"

"He had all of the department heads make the introductions. So what does he need from me?"

"That's a question. Iain's a complicated man. He demands a lot from people, himself more than anyone. He's not the friendliest bloke, even on a good day. Maybe you can help him warm up with that lot out there."

"I'll do my best. Anything else I should know?"

Marc opened his mouth, then snapped it shut and studied his hands.

Brynn waited, but when he remained silent, she stood and walked to the door. "Well, it was nice to meet you. Thanks for giving me some insight."

"Wait. Iain's not a bad sort. You'll remember that, yeah? But he has tunnel vision when it comes to the business."

"Okay, I'll remember."

"Just do your best, love. No one expects miracles, do they?"

Puzzled by that brief exchange, Brynn left. As she walked back through the office, she received more than a few worried glances. Several employees huddled around the development section. When she passed, they stopped talking. If Brynn had to guess, she'd say these people were scared for their jobs. They probably thought she was a corporate guillotine.

When she entered Iain's office, Amelia was talking on the phone and waved Brynn toward the door. Giving it a perfunctory knock, she walked inside.

Iain had his jacket off, but unlike Marc, he was still buttoned up to his chin, his tie perfectly knotted, his vest snugly fitting his impressive chest. He knocked the wind out of her sails every time she looked at him. Iain Chapman was a whole lot of hot man in one tempting package—more than Brynn could ever hope to handle.

"Well, did Marc tell you all of my misdeeds as a lad?"

"No. He only confirmed what I already knew."

Iain's sharp eyes became watchful. "What's that, then?"

"That you're out of touch with your employees." She walked to his desk and took a seat in the formal guest chair. "You don't know any of them. Did you think I wouldn't figure it out?"

"I'm bad with names. So what's next?"

"I'm going back to my office to set you up with an online class. You can choose videos or a written tutorial."

"I choose neither. I specifically told your employer I require personal, *hands-on* instruction." He made it sound *very* personal, his tone becoming throaty and suggestive.

"Um...*I* don't believe that's necessary. Usually a facilitator is only required in a group setting."

"Too bad. It's what I require."

"Well, maybe a real trainer will be available over the next few days." She stood and began backing away. "I'll have Cassandra call and let you know."

Iain stood too and began stalking her. He wasn't in a hurry about it either. He casually approached her until Brynn's back was plastered against the door.

When he flattened his hand on the wood, his wrist rested against Brynn's shoulder. She caught another waft of his delicious cologne as Iain lowered his head, his lips hovering just above hers. "I don't want another trainer. I want you, Brynn."

His words, the rich timbre of his voice—it made Brynn's panties the tiniest bit damp. Licking her lips, she stared at his mouth. All she had to do was angle her head upward, just a couple of inches, and they'd be kissing.

Her gaze slowly moved over his face. Iain's skin held a fading tan, as if he'd spent some time outdoors but not recently. His nose was a little pointed at the end and skewed a bit to the left. To Brynn, it made him even more attractive. Finally, she looked him in the eye. He stilled, waiting to see what she'd do. He could keep on waiting. If it were up to Brynn, she'd be halfway to the Strip by now, a streak of smoke trailing from her tires as she sped away as fast as possible.

"I told you," she said, her voice hushed. "I'm not an educator."

"You are now. I won't accept anyone else." When he pushed off the door and walked back a pace, Brynn had her chance to run. But oddly, her feet remained firmly in place, as if Iain held her there by some spell. "I'll expect you tomorrow morning. In fact, I'm very much looking forward to it, Brynn Campbell."

The next morning, Brynn stood outside Blue Moon Corp., debating with herself. She didn't want to go in. But she couldn't turn back. Iain Chapman must have been paying Cass an ass load of money, because her boss was adamant that Brynn, and only Brynn, was the right person for this job.

Yesterday, after getting back to her office, Brynn had tried, in her ineffectual way, to persuade Cassandra to let her off the hook. Brynn had recounted all of the work she had piled up, the clients who were waiting on their curricula, and the newsletter that was due in three days, but Cass refused to budge.

"There's no one else available, Brynn, and I'm not going to lose this client."

"Iain Chapman is very resistant. A more experienced educator—"

"Sorry, kid, but you're going to have to do this whether you like it or not."

Not.

Cass took her by the shoulders. "This is like that time in college when I ran my car into a stop sign in order to get out of my biology final. The doctor refused to sign a waiver saying I had a concussion, and I had to take the test anyway. I may have failed Biology 101, but I learned a valuable life lesson."

What the hell was she talking about? "I don't understand the correlation, Cass."

"I learned that sometimes in life, you have to face your fear. This is your fear, Brynn, and this is your time to shine. Go shine, girlfriend."

Brynn closed her eyes for a moment. "I don't want to shine. I just want to do my job."

"Maybe shining *is* your job, did you ever think of that?" Cass dropped her hands and stepped back. "Now, I have to take Nef to the vet. I probably won't be back today. Hold down the fort, okay?"

Brynn shuffled out the door, feeling like an utter failure. Why couldn't she just stand up for herself? *Because you want people to like you, jellyfish.* A conflict resolution specialist who avoided conflict at all costs. Oh, the irony.

So now, here Brynn stood this morning, staring at

the half-moon logo, telling herself to open the door. She hadn't gotten more than two hours of sleep last night, and when she had dozed off, she'd dreamed of Iain. She'd awakened in a sweat, her body heavy with need and not an orgasm to be had. So no, Brynn didn't want to go in there and be subjected to that hot piece of British ass. Not again.

But she had to.

When the office door opened, she jumped.

Marc Atwell stopped just shy of running into her. "Brynn, you all right? You look a little pale."

She nodded. "I'm good. Just getting ready to meet Iain."

"He's in his office. Go on in." He held the door for her.

No chance of backing out now. Brynn adjusted her purse strap and walked forward. She passed a few desks and smiled, trying to appear innocuous to the rattled employees.

Amelia beamed when she saw Brynn. "You're here. Yay, I'm so glad."

"Did I have a choice?" The assistant laughed as though Brynn had told a joke. She glanced down and spied a photo on Amelia's desk—a ginger-haired kid with bright blue eyes. "Your son?" Brynn asked, stalling for time.

"Yep, that's my Tyler. Too smart for his own good. Now go on, honey. Iain's waiting."

Grasping the doorknob, Brynn tried once again to get a grip on her nerves. She didn't have much success as she quietly stepped into Iain's office and took a second to study him as he sat behind his desk. He concentrated on the computer screen, and his brows dipped toward the bridge of his nose. He was just as gorgeous as she remembered. "Hey."

When he looked up and saw her, his expression cleared and a predatory glimmer dawned in his eyes. "Brynn, good to see you—although I'm surprised. To be honest, love, I thought you might bottle it."

She walked farther into the room. "What does that mean?"

"I thought you'd chicken out and refuse to come back." Boy, did he have her number. "Glad you made it. I'd hate to get you in trouble with your boss."

She let that slide without comment. "Are you ready to get started?"

He pushed away from the desk and stood, gathering his jacket. As he walked toward her, he slid it on and tugged at each cuff. "Absolutely. Shall we go?"

"Go? No, I brought you a binder." She held it up. "I even have a list of exercises."

Iain removed the notebook from her hands and tossed it in the chair. "No need for all that. We'll wing it."

"You mean ignore the lessons? But there are helpful worksheets in there, guided instructions."

"Look, Brynn, I don't do textbooks and exercises, right? I prefer a more realistic approach. So while we look at a few potential buildings I might be interested in buying, you can teach me how to be a smashing leader."

"How am I supposed to do that without the manual?"

"You wrote the manual." He circled her temple with his finger. "It's all up here, innit?"

"*I* don't believe this is a good idea."

"*I* happen to disagree. And the customer's always right."

"Not in this case."

"Especially in this case, as I happen to be the customer." Iain grabbed her hand and walked through the outer office, dragging Brynn behind him like a toy wagon.

Amelia pursed her lips in disapproval. "It's best to go along, honey. He always gets his way."

Employees in the front office watched in silence as Brynn tried to pull free from his grasp, but Iain's grip, while not tight, was unyielding. Keeping her head down, Brynn felt the rising tide of heat cover her neck. She hated this, hated being the focus of everyone's attention. If she'd just stood up to Cass in the first place, none of this would be happening.

Iain led her to the elevators. Once he punched the button, he finally let go of her hand. He hadn't been rough, but she flexed her fingers anyway. He glanced down at her. She wouldn't look at him.

When the doors opened, Iain gestured for Brynn to get in first. She did, her shoulders rigid, her back straight.

He climbed on and instead of facing the doors, he planted himself in front of her, his big, lean body demanding her attention. "You're angry."

"*I* don't appreciate being manhandled. And *I* don't like being made a spectacle of in your office." She refused to look at his face and kept her eyes trained on the numbers as they lit up on descent. "I'm here in a professional capacity."

He took a step closer, completely disregarding her personal space, blocking out the numbers, and forcing her to meet his gaze. "What do you think you can teach me, professionally speaking?"

"If your treatment of me is anything to go by, you

have a lot to learn. I'm surprised you haven't been sued a dozen times—for harassment, for assault."

"Assault?" He sounded shocked. "Brynn, I'd never hurt you. I was just trying to speed this along. I have an appointment in forty-five minutes. You'd have argued, politely, which takes even longer. I'd have countered. Ultimately, I'd have won." Iain unpocketed his hand and cupped her jaw, using his thumb to follow the curve of her cheek. "I'm sorry for embarrassing you. Yeah? Forgive me?"

At his grazing touch, Brynn's heart kicked into overdrive. It was so wrong, but she melted the moment he placed his warm hand on her. God, he smelled good—manly, earthy, with that hint of bergamot. Though he'd shaved, she could see the dark, shaded area on his cheeks and chin, hovering beneath the surface of his skin. His five o'clock shadow probably made an appearance around noon. His brows were sleek arches above warm, brown eyes. Iain Chapman was beautiful.

This shouldn't be happening. Brynn should put a stop to it, but she didn't want to. This wasn't like her at all. Cautious with her affections, Brynn usually had to warm up to people, but Iain steamrolled over her logical objections. She couldn't remember why mixing business with her personal feelings wasn't a good idea. Because at that moment, the thought of kissing him, feeling his body pressed against hers, seemed like the best idea she'd ever had.

He must have read everything in her eyes. Iain held her gaze as his head dipped lower. He moved his thumb across the bow of her upper lip. Then he leaned closer still. When his mouth finally touched hers, Brynn's eyes drifted shut. Lost to the sensation of his touch, his kiss, his scent, she grabbed on to his lapels to hold herself steady.

His lips were firm and talented. When he swept his tongue against hers, heat coursed its way through her body—scorching heat that caused her breasts to feel full and achy. She kissed him back, opening her mouth wider, allowing him better access. She brushed her own tongue against his tentatively. She'd never been a champion kisser, but Iain was. He slanted his mouth over hers, using just the right amount of pressure. Then he eased off a bit, leaving her hungry for more.

Taking advantage of her enthusiasm, he snaked an arm around her waist and walked them backward, until Brynn's shoulders met the elevator wall. Then his kiss became more aggressive, more demanding, a little rougher, sweeping her away in a tide of arousal.

When Iain took control, Brynn immediately surrendered, yielding to his will. She'd never been kissed like that in her life—with such forceful expertise. God, had she been missing out.

Though she shouldn't have been making out in an elevator, right then she was too caught up in Iain to care. His touch was decadent, his kiss addictive.

He bit down on her bottom lip, then sucked on it gently. That's when Brynn's brain shorted out. She didn't care about right or wrong or being professional. She just wanted more of him. Heat pooled in her belly and lower. Where Iain's body pressed against hers, every nerve ending tingled.

He wrapped his free hand around Brynn's nape, spreading his fingers across her hot skin. Skimming the edge of her collarbone with his thumb, he shifted his lips off of her mouth.

Brynn groaned in protest. She wasn't ready to stop. But once Iain started trailing his tongue along her jawline and down her throat, she quieted. Letting go of his jacket, she gripped the back of his neck where the starched edge of his collar rubbed her wrist. Brynn's hand drifted over his short hair. With her fingers, she sorted through the soft layers, then gently dragged her nails across his scalp. At her touch, Iain pressed his hips against Brynn, and his cock prodded her belly.

"Do that again," he said against her neck.

He didn't ask, he commanded, and without hesitating, she scraped her nails over him once more. He moaned against her skin, causing goose bumps to break out over her arms.

Somewhere in the distance, a bell dinged. Brynn ignored it, but when the doors slid open, she heard a shocked feminine gasp. All at once, Brynn remembered where she was, who she was with—Iain Chapman. In a public elevator. And he was still gently sucking that sensitive part of her neck, right below her ear.

What the hell had she been thinking? "Iain," she hissed, slapping her palm against his shoulder.

He lifted his head. His pupils were dilated, his cheeks flushed. "Wha'?" He thrust his hands into her hair. "God, you are fucking lovely."

Even though she was humiliated by being caught—in public no less—a little niggle of pride crept its way to the surface. Brynn Campbell, the invisible wallflower, had been kissed within an inch of her life by the sexiest man she'd ever met.

She placed a hand over her swollen lips. Wait, this was bad. She wasn't supposed to be kissing Iain while she was on duty. Actually, she shouldn't even be touching him. PDA in the workplace was a no-no. She'd violated so many of her own rules, she should force herself to take a seminar.

At the sound of a man clearing his throat, Iain grinned but continued to hold her. That dimple erased the harsh edges from his handsome face, made him seem more human, less arrogant. It was downright boyish.

"Got carried away, didn't we, pet?"

"Please let me go."

At once, Iain released her head and stepped back. Before turning around, his hand skipped down her spine until it rested above the curve of her ass. Their audience—two smirking men and a red-faced woman—moved aside and let them pass.

Brynn wanted to disappear for real right now—just close her eyes and whisk herself away from here, from this stupid, embarrassing situation she'd gotten herself into.

Iain didn't seem affected by it. From the corner of her eye, Brynn watched him as they walked down the hallway. His expression was impassive. He really didn't give a damn what anyone thought about him. They could have been screwing against the elevator wall, and he would have turned around and glared at the trio for interrupting. Brynn wished she had balls like that. Pure titanium.

Taking a deep breath, she tried to forget the whole damned experience as they walked through the lobby. With its twenty-foot windows, sunshine filled the vestibule, casting long shadows over the green-and-white marble floor.

But then Iain's fingers flexed over Brynn's hip, making it impossible to forget his kiss or the way he tasted—hot and yummy. She wanted to kiss him again. *Lips to yourself, Brynn. Leave the sexy British man alone.*

Then his fingers inched lower, toward the back pocket of her khakis, gliding over the raised, embroidered threads. Brynn's stomach fluttered at his touch.

Oh shit, she was in serious danger. Brynn had trouble saying no in the most benign circumstances. How was she going to say no to the raw, sexual force of nature that was Iain Chapman?

She didn't stand a chance.

Chapter 4

IAIN LED BRYNN TO THE BLACK SEDAN IDLING NEXT to the curb. He wanted another go at her. He planned on having it too, but he didn't think she was ready for another round quite yet. She seemed rather shell-shocked by it all. Right now, he needed to listen to her leadership blather.

Iain slid into the backseat. The closed partition and gray-tinted windows gave them a measure of privacy. "All right, let's get started."

Brynn's eyes widened. "What do you mean?"

"The lesson. We have approximately fifteen minutes until we arrive at the first building. I'm all ears."

Once again, Brynn brushed a hand over her lips. She'd enjoyed that kiss as much as he had, and if she denied it, Iain would call her a liar. "Right. How to validate your teammates."

Groping her in the lift had been a damned stupid idea. Their time traveling between floors was limited. Iain wanted much more than a quick snog. But he'd been acting on impulse. And she'd tasted ripe, with a hint of mint. Fucking delicious.

But what really had him gobsmacked was Brynn's wholehearted response. Unless he'd missed his guess, Brynn liked it when he took charge—that's when she'd really lost herself in the moment. She'd grabbed his jacket like it was a lifeline, stroked her fingers through his hair, and made those breathy little moaning sounds in the back of her throat. Iain found himself getting hard all over again just thinking about it.

God, the things he wanted to do to her. She'd love every minute of it—he'd make sure of that. Iain wanted to see Brynn look up at him with those big, blue eyes as she came. Wanted to hear his name wrenched from her in that moment of passion.

As she continued to lecture him on teamwork, Iain hardly heard a word—he simply sat back and watched her mouth move. He wanted that mouth sliding up and down his cock. Wanted her delicate hands trailing over his thighs, caressing his sac. Oh yes, he was so bloody hard right now it hurt.

"Agreed?" she asked.

"Yeah, naturally," he answered. "Who could argue with that?"

Brynn appeared relieved as she smiled. "Great. Then that's your first assignment."

"Wait, wha'?"

The smile slowly fell away from Brynn's face. "You weren't listening to a word I said."

Before he could deny it, the car slowed to a stop. "Oh good, we're here." Iain climbed out and waited for Brynn.

His estate agent, Patty, had already arrived. Iain made brief introductions, then followed on a quick tour through an office building. It had possibilities, but the location wasn't as central as he'd hoped. Iain put it on his short list and hustled Brynn back to the car.

Once they got on the road, she glanced at him. "Are you ready to try this again?"

Iain held up one finger when his phone vibrated. "Just a moment, love. Got to take this." He spent twenty minutes speaking on a conference call with his group of investors, which he continued even after they arrived at the next stop. Iain remained in the car while Brynn paced the parking lot and Patty texted. Once he hung up, he spent three minutes scouting the building before declaring, "Really, Patty? This is what you dragged me out here for? I need something that has a quick turn-around. This will take more money to fix up than what I can sell it for." And then it was back to the car.

Iain spent most of the drive time to the next three sites on the phone. He felt a bit guilty as far as Brynn was concerned. He was meant to be listening to her lessons about holding his employees' hands and patting them on the head for a job well done. But real business took precedence.

Since it was nearly lunchtime, after his last call, Iain lowered the partition and instructed the driver to take them to his new restaurant. Well, not his exclusively. He and Marc belonged to an investment group of nine other businessmen. They pooled together resources for various bars, clubs, and eateries. It was profitable for the most part, but with so many owners, seeing steady growth was sometimes a slow process. Which was why he needed Trevor Blake and all that lovely capital. By having just one partner, Iain and Marc would see a faster rate of return.

It felt wrong, maneuvering Brynn, manipulating her into this situation for his own selfish reasons. Iain's first instinct had been spot-on—she was an innocent. She was more than just lovely. There was something sweet and gentle about her. And though bashful by nature, during that kiss, Brynn had forgotten to be shy with him. He liked that.

"So, what were you telling me about this leadership thing?" His phone rang again. "Sorry, love," he whispered before answering.

As the driver navigated the Strip, Brynn crossed her legs and started bouncing her foot. Her blue toenails had him mesmerized. Along with those delicate ankles. Never before had Ian looked at a woman's feet with the slightest bit of interest, but everything about Brynn was compelling—from her vanilla scent down to her dainty, turquoise toenails.

Iain spoke with one of his property managers and watched Brynn's foot work faster and faster, causing her whole leg to vibrate. She stared straight ahead, giving him a good view of her profile. Classic—with a small, perfect nose and those prominent cheekbones. For the millionth time in the last few months, Iain imagined her naked. It was a distraction, wanting her this way.

"Yeah, I'm here," he said into the phone while he continued to study Brynn. "Delinquent tenants? Busted water pipes? Those all sound like problems I pay you to handle, Jim. If you're not up to the task, I'll find someone who is. You have one day to get your shit together." He ended the call.

Brynn turned to stare at him. "It's possible to speak to people with kindness and still get results. You catch more flies with honey than with vinegar."

Iain narrowed his eyes. "That's the second time I've heard that goddamned phrase in two days."

"Maybe the universe is trying to tell you something."

"I don't think the universe gives a damn." He brushed one finger across her shoulder and down the length of her arm. The light blue cotton shirt was soft. Brynn's forearm was even softer. Iain glided his fingertip down to her wrist and over the back of her hand, where it rested on the seat between them. He kept going, sweeping his forefinger over her middle one. "Even your hands are graceful."

She pulled away from him and placed her hand in her lap, while her tongue darted nervously across her lips. "We need to stay professional. What happened in the elevator can't happen again."

Before Iain could tell her that it would happen again, and frequently, his phone rang once more. *Marc*. Iain was torn. He wanted to continue flirting with Brynn, but he had a business to run. He hit the Call button. "Talk."

"I got the schematics for the downtown apartments. Still not sure about this one, Iain. It's an expensive gamble. I'm coming down on the side of letting it go, mate, or at least waiting until we can raise the capital ourselves. That way, we won't need a certain outside investor."

"I still say we move forward, stick to the plan. Big risks and big rewards. That's how we've always done it."

"We have more to lose now. The property's had two previous owners in the last five years. Getting buyers for luxe apartments right now, in that section of town, for the price we plan on asking—I'm not sure it's feasible."

Iain slid a glance at Brynn. "Let me worry about that. I have the situation under control." He hung up on Marc's protestations.

Brynn shifted to face him. "I couldn't help but overhear."

"I suppose not. Marc's a fucking loud talker."

"He disagrees about a property, but you're going through with it. Why?" Her eyes were serious. She wasn't feigning interest.

"The building is only two blocks from Fremont Street, which is transforming. I want to buy up as much land as I can. Twentysomethings will want to move there because it's just seedy enough to be cool and is in close proximity to the bars. Plus, it's historic, old Vegas. That will bring the hipsters. Marc's wrong on this one."

"Marc acts as your advisor?"

"He does."

"How often do you actually take his advice?"

"Over half the time."

"He seems to have a poor track record then."

"He's more than my advisor," Iain said with a tight frown. "He's my business partner and best mate."

Propping her elbow on the top of the backseat, Brynn watched him with those large eyes of hers. "But he's wrong so often. You're harsh with everyone else. I'm just trying to understand why you give Marc a pass."

Iain's body locked down. "You don't know what the bloody hell you're talking about. I don't give him a pass, yeah? He's brilliant. He gives good advice—sound advice. He's just not a risk taker."

"And you are?"

He understood then. She was assessing *him*, not attacking Marc. He rolled his shoulders forward and his muscles relaxed somewhat. "I am. Wouldn't be here today if I weren't."

"Maybe other people on your team have valid advice, too."

Iain plucked the end of her flowing sleeve. "You mean I should treat all of my employees as though they're the most important people in the world. Maybe I should start handing out gold stars. What do you think?"

"I think you're making fun of me."

"I am. A bit. How did you get into the manual writing business anyway?" He already knew the answer, of course. What else would someone do with a degree in literature?

"I have a degree in English lit," Brynn said, "and I minored in art history. At TDTC, I can put my skills to good use. I like my job."

"That didn't sound half-convincing, pet."

"I do like it."

He continued to stare at her.

"I'm just overloaded right now," she said, squirming. "Anyway, not everyone likes their job all the time."

"I do. I love my job."

"Why?"

"Why?" he repeated. "What's not to love? I'm my own boss. I shape my own world." Iain woke up every day with a challenge before him: let the naysayers win or take them down. He took them down with a vengeance. He'd done it time after time and it never got old.

Iain had opened his first business a year after coming to Vegas—a car wash and detailing shop. The bank wouldn't loan him a dime. A twenty-one-year-old foreigner with no track record and little education? They'd all but laughed in his face. So Iain had worked three jobs to rent the space. And when he and Marc had taken their shirts off one hot, summer afternoon, they discovered that Vegas mums enjoyed staring at muscular, half-naked men. Their Manc accents didn't hurt either. Within days, SUVs were lined up around the bloody block. Marc and Iain hired more buff employees to titillate the ladies. In six months, they'd purchased the facility. In a year, they'd opened their second location. By year three, they'd parlayed that money to buy a strip mall, and had kept building from there.

Through hard work, long hours, and a few lucky breaks, Iain had gotten to know some of Vegas's heavy hitters. He'd lost tens of thousands in friendly games of poker, all to win the trust of men who had deep pockets. Throwing away money damn near gutted him, but he'd done it with a shrug and a smile. He'd learned to play a decent round of golf, even though he despised the game. But the one thing Iain couldn't quite manage was kissing ass. Fortunately, Marc excelled at it. "Being polite," he called it. Together, they had grown their small business into a moneymaking enterprise.

Iain had created the world he'd envisioned as a lad, where he was the boss, where he called the shots, and where no one—except Marc—could question him. He'd come a long way from that frightened boy who cowered at the sound of his father's voice.

There was more to be done, more to create. In this ever-changing town, people would remember his name. *Iain Chapman was here, you fuckers. And you'll never be as good as I was.*

The car pulled up to the hotel. He climbed out and held the door for Brynn. "We opened a Southern bistro a few months back. I think you'll like it here." He reached down and offered her a helping hand. Brynn hesitated for the briefest second before placing her palm in his. He wanted those long, lovely fingers touching him, gripping his cock. His heart stuttered at the mental image—Brynn naked, her dark hair falling over one golden shoulder, her hand gripping him. Then she'd lower her head, take him in her mouth. Bloody hell. It was getting damned uncomfortable, having his cock this hard with no immediate chance of relief. Iain thrust his right hand into his trouser pockets, fumbled for the pair of dice, and escorted Brynn through the lobby.

Instead of going for a modern aesthetic, the hotel had used a timeless, traditional scheme for a quiet elegance, an air of refinement that one didn't usually find in Vegas. It reminded Iain of a castle he'd toured on a school trip. That was the day he'd realized there was a difference between old shit—like the saggy, tattered furniture stuffed in his parents' flat—and *really* old shit that only wealthy people could afford. His office was filled with the latter.

"Is the whole hotel yours?" Brynn openly glanced around, taking in the faded carpet beneath the chandelier.

"No." Although it was just a matter of time. Iain had ambitions he hadn't even begun to realize.

He kept hold of her hand and led her past the front desk and down a corridor. Wooden columns, polished to a high sheen, flanked either side of the restaurant doors.

Inside, the hostess greeted him with a wide, phony smile that looked more like a grimace. "Mr. Chapman. So good to see you." She moved toward them, but Iain held up a hand to stop her.

"I'm headed to a table in the back. Give us two lunch

specials and have the sommelier pair it with a couple of wines. Also, I'd like to see the manager before we leave." He moved past her, guiding Brynn through the dining room.

Iain looked around. The place wasn't quite half-full. Not bad for an early lunch, but he'd like to do better. Getting into the hotel itself had cost a bloody fortune. It would be worth it—eventually—but they needed to generate more customers during the day. He'd bring it up at the next meeting.

Iain stopped at the last booth, in the corner farthest from the kitchen. "What do you think?"

Sliding across the bench seat, Brynn ran her hand over the smooth wooden tabletop. "It's lovely."

"Pecan wood." He knocked on it three times for luck. Not that he needed it.

A waiter hustled to the table and filled their water glasses. The lad was obviously nervous. Hands shaking, he dribbled water across the table. "So sorry, Mr. Chapman." He mopped it up and shot a hasty glance in Iain's direction. "I'll bring out appetizers and the sommelier will be right over."

Brynn gave him a bright smile. "Thank you." Then she glanced at Iain. When he said nothing, she sighed.

"You're welcome," the waiter choked out and scurried away.

"These people are terrified of you," Brynn said. "So are your employees at the office."

"Why does everyone think that's a bad thing?" His phone rang again, and he glanced at the screen. His banker. Thirteen years ago, Iain couldn't get a loan. Now, he had his own personal banker. Success didn't suck. "I've got to take this one." As he chatted, the waiter came back and deposited a few nibbles on a tray. When the wine came, Brynn refused a glass. Her smile was open and friendly to the people who worked for him. But every time she looked at Iain, her expression became guarded.

Brynn put a few canapés on a plate and pushed it toward him. He nodded as he wrapped up his conversation. "What do you think of the food?" he asked once he'd ended the call.

"It's delicious. These tomato tarts are amazing."

"Heirloom tomatoes and goat cheese, I believe. You don't like wine?"

"I do. But not at lunch or when I'm supposed to be facilitating a class. Which is a little difficult when my sole participant won't participate."

"Business is booming, what can I say?" He took a sip of wine. Dry and crisp. He usually didn't indulge during the day either. Unless it was a working lunch, Iain ate a sandwich at his desk. But he'd wanted to be alone with Brynn, and if he could check on the restaurant at the same time...well, two birds and all that.

"Can you describe your process for problem solving?" she asked after polishing off the last bite of toasted corn bread.

"Oh God. Fine, I'll answer your questions on one condition."

"*I* don't feel that conditions are necessary. You called us, remember? You're paying for this course, Iain, and *I* don't feel you're getting your money's worth by talking on the phone all morning."

"So let's continue over dinner."

"That sounds suspiciously date-like. And besides, I have plans."

Iain's jaw tightened. She had a date? The background report specifically stated she didn't have a boyfriend. This bloke must be new. Iain had never been jealous in his life, but he felt it now, burning hot inside of him. Over his dead fucking body would she go out with another man. "What's his name?"

"What's your process for problem solving?" she countered.

"I see a problem and I fix it. What's. His. Name?"

"Can you describe a recent situation that called for immediate action?"

Iain shoved the plate aside and leaned his forearms on the table. "You think you can avoid my question, love. You're wrong."

"*I—*" She stopped talking as his frown deepened. "I don't think we should get into personal topics. They'll only cloud the issue."

"What issue is that?"

Brynn seemed to be choosing her words carefully.

"Just spit it out, pet. No need to spare my tender feelings. I don't have any."

"I'm here as your educator. I can't do my job if you're not willing to do yours. I need your attention and your cooperation. Will you give me your cooperation, Iain?"

"Gladly." Iain kept his eyes on hers, but extended his hand and trailed his fingers over the thin, copper bracelets lining her wrist. He twisted a couple back and forth. "How's this wanker you're dating going to feel when you start shagging me? He's going to feel like rubbish, yeah? You'd best break it off with him now."

Without looking, he turned her hand over and slid his finger across her palm. "A recent situation that called for immediate action? And we're not including our snog in the lift, right?"

Brynn opened her mouth, but no sound came out. Her eyes grew wide as he slipped his finger over the heel of her hand and through two bracelets. Caressing her inner wrist, Iain felt Brynn's pulse hammering against her skin. She liked it when he touched her. Her body's response gave her away.

"Every situation calls for action," he said. "It's a matter of degrees, innit? I look at the big picture, decide what I want, and hire people to handle the details. If there are situations that require immediate attention, I tend to those first, and I use all the resources at my disposal to fix a problem." Yeah, Iain could speak corporate bullshit when it suited him. However, blunt words were generally more effective.

She lifted one brow. "And you use threats to get the outcome you want, like that man with the busted water pipe? Are those the resources you're talking about?"

"I never threaten. Second rule of business: words are meaningless unless you can back them up. You make an example of one bloke"—he continued to softly rub her smooth skin—"and everyone else will fall in line."

"I don't think that's the best way to go about getting what you want. What if you could, um"—she glanced down, watched his fingers trace the lines along her palm—"get the most from your employees and have them, you know, feel invested in the process? Wouldn't that be a more satisfactory outcome?" Though she sounded winded, Brynn kept her hand in place and let him stroke her. Whoever this boyfriend was, he was yesterday's news.

"And what would satisfy you, love?" As Brynn studied him with those solemn eyes, the moment seemed to stretch out and crackle with tension. It was the same kind of sexually charged energy they'd shared in the lift. Her lips parted slightly. With dark waves framing her face, she looked so young and fresh.

"We're not talking about me," she finally said. "We're talking about your need for control."

"I do like to be in control—in the boardroom. In the bedroom. I think you'd like that too." She breathed in a little gasp and her eyes widened slightly. "So I ask again, what would satisfy you, Brynn Campbell?"

Seeing Iain Chapman buck-ass naked might do for starters. She wanted to watch him move, see the solid bands of muscle play over his body as he flexed. Brynn had taken a life drawing class in college. At first, she'd been so embarrassed when the guy dropped his robe that her strokes had been little more than squiggles. But once she got to work, the model ceased being a real person. He was like a bird or a bowl of fruit. Just another subject. Brynn couldn't imagine viewing Iain that way.

What would it feel like to have him inside of her? Amazing, that's what. To be held down and taken by this powerful, dominant man? That was her ultimate fantasy. Brynn's breathing became erratic and her heart rate sped up to a scary pace.

In her fantasy, having Iain call all the shots would feel incredible, but in reality, it would probably be a disappointment. Brynn had trouble bringing herself to orgasm. Though her hormones gave the green light—she could throb and ache and come so close to release it was nearly painful—it rarely happened. She could count the times on one hand. It was depressing.

His earlier kiss, and now his touch, left Brynn with pent-up desire and a restlessness she'd become used to. Except with Iain, the level of unfulfilled sexual hunger was amplified times ten.

His fingers were long and blunted at the tips. She watched as he continued to sneak his thumb beneath her bangles and skim the veins crisscrossing her wrist. His touch was electric, causing goose bumps to march up her arms.

What was it about this man? The accent? Although Brynn was accustomed to Brit speak because of her brothers-in-law, Iain's accent was different than what she was used to—rougher, sexier, with an edginess Trevor and Cal didn't possess. Then there was the aura of power that surrounded him, a level of unshakeable confidence on display with every move he made. The way he carried himself with purpose and determination. Iain Chapman knew where he was going, and God help the idiot who got in his way. Ruthlessness wasn't a great trait to have, and ordinarily it would have turned Brynn off, but Iain made it alluring. He was comfortable in his own skin, and that was appealing, too. Her pussy had been wet since that kiss, and now, with all these soft touches, he was keeping it that way. *Job well done, sir*. But there was no relief to be had. Not for Brynn.

She'd had two boyfriends in the past, each willing to try just about anything, but she was too shy to ask for what she really wanted—to be held down, controlled, subjugated by a strong man. After a while, her boyfriends had grown tired of working so damned hard and Brynn refused to fake it. The relationships fell apart.

Brynn resorted to watching porn—all flavors—and while it left her excited, she struggled to find a happy ending. She bought toys left and right, hoping one of them would unlock the mysterious, elusive puzzle that left her body in limbo. Brynn had even gone spelunking for her G-spot with zero results.

So now she was left with a duffel bag full of vibrators shoved in the back of her closet and sublimated energy she focused on work. Brynn knew she wouldn't be able to keep up with a sexually aggressive man like Iain Chapman.

But if he took control…

No, it was hopeless. And though Iain's touch felt crazy good, it wouldn't culminate in fireworks. She was wound too tight to find release with a partner. It just wasn't in the cards.

Time to put an end to all this flirting and touching and kissing. Taking a long pull of air, Brynn eased her hand away from his. "What I want is for you to take leadership training seriously."

Iain continued to stare into her eyes. The air surrounding him was electric, heated. He was still thinking about sex, she could tell. His dick was probably hard, too. Hard and long and thick.

"Is that all you want?" he asked. "Because I think you like it when I touch you. Kiss you. Imagine what it will feel like when I fu—"

"Whoa." When she held up her hand, the bracelets

slid toward her elbow and made a soft tinkling sound. "All of that is completely wrong. *I* feel we need to stay on point. Let's be honest, Iain, you have no intention of changing your attitude toward your employees. While that's up to you, I have a truckload of work back at the office. I know it's hard for you to believe, but there are companies who *want* my help."

His phone rang on her last two words. "Hold that thought, love." He pressed his cell to his ear and started an in-depth conversation about the cost of existing infrastructure and beam integrity.

Iain thought this course was a joke. He didn't respect her work. He had time to kiss her, touch her, and verbally bait her, but no time to listen. That part was particularly insulting.

With halting, angry movements, Brynn grabbed her bag and scooted out of the booth. She crossed the restaurant, smiled at the hostess, and walked at a fast clip out of the hotel without ever looking back.

Iain Chapman could find himself a new trainer, because Brynn was through.

Chapter 5

After the taxi dropped her off at the parking garage near Iain's office, Brynn hopped into her own car and called Paige Adams.

"How's life on the outside?" Paige answered.

"Not as pleasant as you might think." Since noonday traffic was a pain, with too many red lights and daring pedestrians darting into the middle of the road, Brynn hooked a left onto a side street. "How's Camp Cray Cray this morning?"

"Head Counselor Fucking Nutballs asked me to call her house and leave affirmation messages for her cat. Seriously, Brynn, I can't take much more of this. Keeping her on track is impossible. The woman's so disorganized, she lost her phone in the break room freezer today. Who does that?"

An insanely neurotic, disorganized mess of a boss. "Listen, I'm going to try and sneak into the office. I need to be out of there by six tonight, or I'll never hear the end of it." Tonight was a newly instituted SNO, otherwise known as Sisters Night Out. Allie and Monica would make her life hell if she missed it. Getting out of a SNO required an act of God or a doctor's note. Brynn had neither and deadlines didn't count. "Can you create a diversion?"

"What kind of diversion?" Paige asked. "Do you want me to whip out a Snickers bar and send Brandon to the emergency room? That would shake things up around here."

Recent hire, Brandon, and his peanut allergy had caused quite a stir. "Only if we want a lawsuit on our hands."

"Dude needs to get an EpiPen and deal with it. Why make the rest of us suffer?"

Brynn steered her Toyota toward the highway entrance ramp and floored it. "Perhaps if you step back from the situation and put things in perspective, you might find that your need for a midafternoon sugar rush isn't as imperative as Brandon's need to breathe. Maybe? Just a little bit?"

"Talk like a real person already. You've taken so many of those training courses, you sound like one of your own manuals."

That wasn't so terrible, was it? If there was one thing Brynn hated, it was confrontation, and by using neutral language, she could usually get her point across in a kind way. *The coward's way. You never say what you're really thinking*. So what? Brynn might temper her language, but that was hardly a fault. Take Iain Chapman for example—the man was blunt to the point of rudeness. If everyone went around spouting their true feelings, society would break down in a heartbeat. No, Brynn would stick to diplomacy. It was probably less satisfying than telling someone to fuck off, the way Iain would, but she'd have fewer regrets. "Just don't let Cass know I'm in the office this afternoon, okay? And if a man named Iain Chapman calls, play dumb."

"Cass totally takes advantage of you, Brynn. You could work in a normal place. A place where your boss doesn't cry about her broken vibrator or tell you about the time she lost her virginity to a second cousin. It's gross."

"Yes, her sex stories are a little creepy, but Cass would fall apart without me. I just need an assistant to run interference and things will get better." Besides, if Brynn ever tried to quit, Cass would only talk her into staying. Brynn had no illusions about her lack of spine—she'd fold like a card table the second Cass's brown eyes filled with tears. Besides, Brynn liked her work most days. True, she could be making more in a bigger firm, but she'd have less creative control. Money wasn't everything.

Iain Chapman thought it was, though. He was very caught up in the bottom line. The man was an autocratic, sexy, British, sexy—and fine, she'd already listed that, but he was so hot, it was worth repeating—tyrant. Which shouldn't turn her on and yet her nipples got hard at the thought of him getting all bossy in the bedroom.

"You're supposed to be an expert in conflict resolution, Brynn. Grow a set already."

"I'm working on it."

"Sure you are, and I'll finally lose those last ten pounds I've been trying to shift."

"Diversion?"

Paige sighed. "Fine, but you owe me. And I will collect."

Brynn turned into the office parking lot and grabbed a lone spot in the back row. Adjusting the hobo bag on her shoulder, she squinted against the sun as it glared off the reflective glass of the building. With the highway to her back, the hum of traffic roared until she stepped inside and took the stairs.

Sneaking into her own office—it was pathetic. The

same way she'd hauled ass out of the restaurant while Iain took yet another phone call. She should learn how to approach people in a straightforward manner, but it was so damned uncomfortable. Confronting Iain would be pointless anyway. Though she'd only known him for two days, Brynn had that much figured out. No, it was much easier to slink off, hide, and hope that a real facilitator would be available tomorrow. Then she'd never have to see Iain Chapman again. It would have all ended in disaster anyway, right? Low-gasm Brynn with Steamroller Iain? Not a good combo. *It felt good, though.* In fact, the touch of his hands, the way his tongue slid over her skin—it was better than good. It was ecstasy.

Brynn pushed Iain's kisses to the back of her mind and trudged up the stairs. When she reached the third floor, she heard screams behind the door. Easing it open, she peered inside and saw six salesmen rushing around, peeking under chairs. The only other people in the room were Paige and Lori, who stood atop of their desks. What the holy hell was going on?

When Paige caught Brynn's eye, she winked, then yelled, "Oh my God. The rat went toward the break room! Get him!" Lori looked as if she might faint, but the guys stampeded down the hallway and out of sight. Paige subtly waved Brynn on.

Brynn shot into her office and locked the door. Leaning against it, she sighed with relief, then dropped into her chair and booted up her prehistoric computer. As she waited, she saw the office phone light up. Iain would call here, demand to speak to her. Too bad. Brynn's time was valuable, too. *Big talk for a woman who fled like a rabbit.*

Instead of immediately opening a client folder, Brynn typed Iain Chapman's name into a search engine and spent the next half hour cyberstalking him. There wasn't much to find. For such a brash character, he seemed to be a private person. The official Blue Moon bio didn't have anything personal about him, except that he was from Manchester.

When Brynn looked up Blue Moon in conjunction with the city, she hit on a connection. "Blue Moon" was the unofficial song of the Manchester City Football Club. Brits were nutty for their soccer. But knowing Iain liked a sport didn't give her any insight into the man himself.

Realizing she'd been goofing off for too long, Brynn shut down the browser and got to work. Over the next few hours, she received eight texts from Cassandra, each more hysterical than the last. Brynn ignored them, along with numerous incoming calls and the three separate knocks on her office door.

Hunkering down, she worked steadily and pretended not to hear the howls coming from her empty stomach. She never had gotten lunch. By three, Brynn was hungry, cranky, and desperate for a hit of caffeine, but if she stepped foot outside her office, she'd be bombarded by requests. So she sucked it up and stayed put.

Finally at five, Paige texted: *Leaving now. That Chapman dude is an ass. Cass made me call every hospital in the city to see if you'd been in an accident. Ur buying me sushi for lunch.* That seemed fair. Brynn would throw in dessert, too. She'd actually gotten a lot accomplished that afternoon.

At six, she shut down her computer and bundled up

a few files. Time permitting, she'd slog through them tonight, but dinner with her sisters was more pressing.

Standing for the first time in hours, Brynn stretched her arms above her head. Then gathering her things, she left her hovel. In the main office, the overhead fluorescents had been turned off. Every desk was empty. But Brynn noticed light spilling from beneath Cassandra's closed door. They were the last two here—as usual.

As quietly as she could, Brynn opened the side door and held on to the handle so that it wouldn't close with a bang, alerting Cass to her presence. Looking over her shoulder, she walked down the hall.

"Where have you been all day, Brynn?"

She winced. Damn. She'd forgotten about the bathroom. Brynn faced forward and smiled at a narrow-eyed Cassandra Delaney.

"I was in my office."

"Huh." Cass placed her hands on both hips. "I was worried sick. Why didn't you answer any of my texts?"

Brynn smacked her forehead. "Shoot, I must have turned off my phone." She reached into her pocket and grabbed it. "Yeah, that's what happened all right. So sorry."

Brynn tried to edge her way past Cass. No luck. The other woman moved to block her exit.

"Well, I have some very troubling news. You'll be shocked to know that Michael and I broke up. He ended it this afternoon. I found out when he changed his status to single. He didn't even tell me to my face."

"No! Wow, that's terrible."

"I'm going to die alone, Brynn." Cassandra pulled a wad of Kleenex from inside her bra and rubbed at her eyes.

"No, you're not. You'll find someone. Probably when you least expect it." Poor Cass. Her life was one epic disaster after another. Yeah, it was mostly her own fault, but still, Brynn couldn't help but feel pity.

Cassandra grabbed Brynn's hand. "Promise me something. Swear it by all you hold dear."

"Okay." Brynn tried to tug her hand free. "But *swear* is such a strong word."

Cass ignored her. "Promise me that if I'm missing for more than a day, you'll check on me. I don't want to be one of those people who lays there, dead for weeks, with no one to notice until my body starts decomposing. I don't want maggots on my rotting corpse, Brynn." Tears began streaming down her face. "What happened to my life? No one cares about me."

Brynn finally pulled her hand loose and wrapped one arm around Cass's shoulders. "People care. I care. A lot." If Brynn didn't leave now, she was going to be late for dinner. *Stay and comfort Cass or be late for dinner and get grief from Allie and Monica?* She could handle her sisters—Brynn was used to that. "I'm really sorry about Michael. I know how much you love him. I have a dinner thing, but I can stay with you for a while. Maybe we can come up with a strategy to get you back on your feet."

"No, that's all right. You go on," Cass said, her voice rising to a dramatic crescendo, "go live your life to the fullest, Brynn. In fact"—she paused and tossed back her head—"live it for both of us, kid."

Oh God. "I will. Thanks." Brynn felt terrible, leaving Cass to sniffle into her soggy tissue. But she consoled herself with the fact that she'd been there for Cassandra through various crises. And Allie would probably serve chocolate cake for dessert. Shallow, yes. But Brynn was damned hungry.

Taking the highway home, she weaved in and out of traffic, switching lanes often. Brynn hated getting stuck behind slow drivers, and going for hours without any food hadn't helped her mood. When she finally arrived at her house—a midcentury ranch that had taken months to decorate and update—Brynn slammed into her driveway and rushed inside.

After shedding her clothes and dropping her bracelets on the dresser, she hopped in the tiny shower stall for a speedy rinse. As she reached for the towel, the doorbell rang. Actually, it was more of a continuous buzz, as if someone was leaning against it. Probably her neighbor, Natasha, here to vent after having another fight with her hubby.

Tash was from Belarus, and Zeke, a drummer for a mediocre eighties cover band, hailed from Wisconsin. The cultural gap couldn't be wider. Plus, he'd talked Tash into naming her toy Chihuahuas Moose and Squirrel, which he thought was hilarious. Brynn thought it showed an immature streak—unattractive in a fifty-year-old man.

She wrapped a towel around her wet torso, leaving the damp, wavy ends of her hair clinging to her back and shoulders. Hustling to the door, Brynn shivered and secured the towel before peering out the peephole.

Shit, that wasn't Natasha. It was *Iain Chapman*, standing on her porch with his hand pressed over the buzzer.

When she'd left the restaurant earlier that day, she never dreamed he'd chase her down. While Brynn dreaded the thought of confrontation, part of her was secretly thrilled that he had gone to the effort.

Suddenly, the noise stopped. "I know you're in there, Brynn. I can feel you staring, and I'm not going away." While he didn't yell, he said it loud enough to be heard through the door.

"Hang on a second," she called.

"I'll give you thirty. Then I'm coming in."

Brynn believed him. Racing to her bedroom, she tossed the towel in the sink and snatched her red kimono. No wait, she couldn't answer the door in a robe. That was too intimate. Too provocative. Brynn should be fully clothed for a standoff with Iain. Otherwise, he'd see it as an advantage. If only she owned a turtleneck.

Frozen by indecision, she jumped when the doorbell started buzzing again. Panicked, Brynn shrugged into the robe and cinched the tie tight around her waist. She gave herself a hasty once-over in the full-length mirror. Her cheeks were flushed and the goddamned splotches were back, climbing the sides of her neck like ivy up a brick wall. She brushed a hand down her throat and sped to the front door, flustered and out of breath. Taking two more seconds to try and pull herself together, Brynn reached for the handle, closed her eyes, and repeated a mantra she'd learned in a self-assertiveness seminar: "I have all the power I need. Today is the day I accept my possibilities."

She didn't feel any different or more powerful. That stupid mantra never worked.

Taking a deep breath, Brynn opened the door just a crack and, with one eye, peered up at Iain. His lips were compressed into a thin line and tiny creases underlined his narrowed eyes. The knot in his tie was crooked and his pocket square was MIA. She figured he'd be pissed off, but that might have been an understatement. Iain looked ready to go nuclear.

"Let me in, Brynn. Now."

Without hesitation, Brynn stepped aside. Once he'd entered and planted himself in front of the door, it occurred to Brynn that she didn't have to follow his orders. But he seemed so confident, she'd automatically obeyed. Brynn had just invited the wolf inside, and now she was trapped.

Fiddling with the edges of her robe, she stepped backward. "Now's not a great time, Iain. Perhaps we can discuss this over the phone tomorrow. Like two rational professionals."

He remained silent, glaring at her. Something wild and untamed moved behind his eyes, turning them from light brown to a darker, richer shade, reminding her of molasses rather than honey. This morning, his hair had been neat and tidy, except for that one wayward lock that fell onto his forehead. But now, deep grooves plowed across the short waves, like he'd thrust his fingers through them in frustration—or anger. Brynn placed her bet on anger. His five o'clock shadow was in full bloom, and the overall effect made him look like a well-dressed outlaw. He wasn't just handsome—he was magnificent. She wanted to sketch his likeness from every angle. Although she wouldn't do him justice, she longed to capture the proud jawline and the feral gleam in his eyes.

Despite Iain's mood, Brynn wasn't scared for her safety. No, she was afraid of *herself*, that she'd be putty in his hands. His strong, capable hands.

For the first time in her life, Brynn was *lusting* after a man. Not just any man—Iain Chapman, a man she didn't even know. Yet there was something unpredictable about him. Though Brynn's brain sent out a warning signal, reminding her this was a terrible idea, her body didn't receive the message. Her nipples puckered and her pussy started growing slick. Her body felt lush and ripe, ready for sex.

She wanted him to rip the kimono off her body and nail her right here against the pale blue wall. So what if she didn't have an orgasm? They were overrated. Getting pounded by a man like Iain would be enough.

Brynn's tongue flicked out over her lips, moistening them. Iain's gaze followed its trail and remained fixed on her mouth. Even though they were a foot apart, Brynn could feel carnal hunger coming off him in waves. It mingled with his temper. The combination felt almost tangible, as if his emotions were battering against her, searching for a way past her defenses.

Heat wove its way from her chest upward, past her already splotchy neck and into her cheeks, making her skin feel tight. One droplet of water slid from her collarbone and flowed down the center of her chest. With her skin on fire, Brynn was surprised it didn't sizzle on contact.

Iain's attention switched from her mouth to that lone trickle. His fierce eyes made Brynn's insides flip in nervous spasms.

She picked up her foot to take another step backward, but she didn't get the chance. With one stride, Iain stood in front of her, *looming*. Before Brynn could react, he lowered his head and slowly licked the droplet from her chest while simultaneously wrapping his arm around her waist.

Oh *God*. It was the most sensual thing she'd ever experienced. Brynn fisted the shoulders of his suit. He made her almost woozy with his nearness, the warmth of his tongue lapping across her breastbone. He remained bent over, his tongue licking up to her neck. Brynn angled it to one side in invitation.

"Brynn," he murmured, his voice husky. Pushing back the curtain of her hair, he sank his teeth into her earlobe, biting until it stung. That little bit of pain, along with the pleasure of his lips sucking the same spot a moment later, caused Brynn's breasts to tingle, to ache for attention.

Iain wasn't doing anything outrageous—licking her chest, nibbling her ear—but Brynn had never felt such a heightened sense of arousal before.

Loosening her grip on his shoulders, she stroked the back of his neck with one hand while grabbing his hair with the other. When Iain growled against the column of her throat, it made Brynn feel proud. She liked eliciting that kind of uninhibited response from him.

He continued to rain kisses along her neck. His stubble abraded the tender skin, but Brynn didn't care. The changes in sensation were delicious. She wanted to feel every texture, every part of him. The back of his neck was silky beneath her palm, and warm to the touch. Did he have hair on his chest or was it smooth? She needed to know these things. Right now.

Iain's hand tightened on Brynn's waist, his fingers digging into the space below her ribs. His cock pressed against her. With a twist of her hips, Brynn brushed against his erection, causing him to groan again, deep in his chest. Then he raised his head and stared into her eyes. His face was flushed, his lips bright red.

"Bedroom." It wasn't a question.

Brynn couldn't speak. The man took her breath away. She pointed one finger in the direction of the hallway.

Iain kept his hand clamped around her waist and straightened, lifting her up with one arm. "Which room?" His accent became thicker, his voice huskier.

Brynn had to think. Her senses were completely overwhelmed by Iain Chapman. She gave her head a little shake to clear it. "Last on the left."

Iain strode into her bedroom. He didn't notice the retro furniture or the pink, girly accents. His gaze never left Brynn.

Lowering her to her feet, he fumbled with the knotted kimono belt. Brynn brushed his hands aside. "Can we do you first?" All-encompassing need took precedence over her shyness. She wanted to see him. All of him.

"Undress me, Brynn."

Reaching up, she tugged at the knot in his red tie. While she worked on that, Iain shrugged out of his jacket and kicked off his shoes.

With little jerks, she pulled the tie from his collar. He still looked dapper in the navy vest, but less constrained. She placed her hands on his chest. The lightweight wool was a soft, fine weave. With deliberation, Brynn slowly slid her hands downward.

What the hell are you doing? That little thought tickled the back of her mind, but Brynn ignored it. She wasn't sure what she was doing, besides petting Iain's chest. Where did this boldness come from? Brynn didn't know and, frankly, didn't want to question it, because this new brazen Brynn wasn't thinking too clearly. Instead, she focused on what she was feeling. Tension coiled tight in her belly, sending little sparks straight to her pussy. Iain made her forget to be reticent, forget that she was supposed to be doing something else right now. Whatever it was, it seemed irrelevant when she was seconds away from seeing Iain naked.

"Brynn, stop groping me and take my clothes off. *Now*." So forceful. That bossy tone caused her pulse to quicken. What else would he make her do? The possibilities were titillating and endless.

Brynn started flicking open the buttons along his vest. It was double-breasted, so there were twice as many of them. While she was stripping him, Iain stroked his large hands up her wrists, delving into the wide sleeves of her robe to cup her elbows.

"Brynn."

She pushed aside the vest and began unbuttoning his shirt.

"Brynn. Look at me."

Her fingers didn't stop until she'd slipped the last button through the hole. "I am looking at you. You're something else." She flicked her finger over his nipple and it hardened. Then she tugged the shirttails from his slacks.

"You did a runner on me today. Never again. Understand?"

Instead of answering him, she separated the edges of his shirt and glanced at his torso. He had chest hair. Short, dark, and crisp—it wasn't too thick, wasn't too sparse, as it covered his pecs, leaving his well-defined stomach bare except for the happy trail that started below his belly button and disappeared into his waistband.

Brynn planted her hands on those pectorals and Iain's muscles leaped beneath her palms. As she moved her hands lower, he sucked in an audible breath, causing his abs to contract. They were a work of art—firm, rigid. Even his obliques were sculpted down to the hint of a V-cut peeking out of his pants. The bulge at his fly was even more impressive up close. She stared at it as she continued to feel him, gliding her hands over his hot skin. With each passing touch, Iain's breath became increasingly heavy and uneven.

Fingering his raised muscles, Brynn gave herself free rein to manhandle him as much as she wanted, exploring to her heart's content. She wasn't the kind of person who fucked someone after knowing him for two days, but she felt as if she'd fallen into some kind of trance.

Then Iain grabbed Brynn's hands, holding them away from his body. "I said look at me." His sharp tone whipped through her, snapping her out of that dreamy state.

Brynn gazed up into his eyes. She blinked a couple of times and tried to pull away. "What am I doing?"

"You're taking my clothes off. And I'm about to do the same to you."

She shook her head. "There's something I have to do tonight." If only she could remember what it was. She tried to break free, but he wouldn't let her go. "Is this a mistake?"

He thrust her hands to her sides, pinning her. "The only mistake you made was leaving me in the restaurant today. Who the bloody hell do you think you are? No one treats me that way."

Brynn opened her mouth to answer, but he swooped down and slanted his lips over hers. Unlike the kiss in the elevator, there was nothing soft or persuasive about this. This kiss was punishing, harsh. He didn't give her a chance to kiss him back, but took complete control.

And Brynn loved it. She tried to move her arms, but he kept them anchored to her sides as he swept his tongue into her mouth. This was possession, pure and simple.

Brynn's heart pounded. Allowing her head to fall backward, she submitted to his kiss, his branding. And she wanted more of it. His hard, demanding lips sent every one of her nerve endings into overdrive. Her tits throbbed, her nipples hurt, her pussy clenched, feeling empty, hungry.

Iain let go of Brynn's wrists and circled one arm around her hips, latching onto her ass, kneading it roughly while he thrust his other hand into her hair. He gripped it near the scalp and forced her head to one side.

Brynn slid her hands beneath his shirt and clung to his back. When he nipped her lower lip, her legs buckled. Fortunately, she was close to the bed, and with very little effort, Iain tipped her onto her back. He didn't let go but followed her down, stretching himself out on top of her.

The edges of Brynn's robe parted, and when Iain wedged his knee between her legs, the material of his slacks brushed against her bare pussy. Brynn ground her hips against him. The friction was amazing. Having Iain's weight on top of her, his tongue tangling with hers—so good.

When he rose to his knees and tugged off his shirt, Brynn reached out, unbuckling his belt. She wanted to see for herself just how big he was.

Iain fiddled with his cufflinks and tossed them to the floor before yanking the starched shirt from his arms. Brynn stopped working his belt and just stared up at him. His wide shoulders were perfection. The biceps were large and solid with veins running beneath the smooth skin. Her fingers itched to trace them.

She felt another wave of desire wash over her. That heady desire gave her license to ignore all her reservations and give in to temptation. Sitting, Brynn abandoned his belt and trailed her hands up his waist, past his sternum. Closing her eyes, she explored his shoulders and the shallow indentation where they met his arms.

When Iain pulled at her kimono sash, Brynn's eyes popped open. She found him staring at her, his eyes dark and hungry as he untangled the knotted belt. With deft fingers, he had it loose in no time, then peeled the robe off her body.

Completely exposed to the cool air, her nipples became tight points. She tried to cover herself.

"No," he ground out. That one word had Brynn lowering her hands. "Don't you dare cover up. I need to see you right now. Been thinking about it all bloody day."

Brynn had never felt this sexually attractive. Potent. Feminine. He placed both palms over her breasts, and his hands felt delicious, his warmth intoxicating. But when he abandoned her breasts a moment later, her body turned cold at the loss of contact.

Iain stepped back from the bed and removed his

pants. Now he stood in front of her wearing only silky, black boxers from which the head of his dick poked out of the waistband. A dot of moisture glistened along the slit. Brynn's need suppressed all the fear, the doubt, the worry that usually plagued her. She lowered her head to lick that drop—salty with a hint of sweetness. Then, darting her tongue out, she swirled it around the tip, like an ice cream cone.

"Brynn." Iain's rough voice demanded attention. Brynn lifted her head and looked up into his eyes. "Touch me, pet." He tugged the boxers down over his hips and his cock bobbed forward, longer and thicker than she'd imagined.

Instead of grasping him in her hand, Brynn gently tracked the length of him with one finger, all the way down to his sac. He shivered when she touched him there. So Brynn did it again, lightly scraping her nail across his skin. She smiled when his dick twitched. Before she could repeat the motion, Iain grabbed both of her hands and had her flat on her back. He stretched out beside her, forcing her arms above her head, keeping both of her wrists secured in his firm grip. When Brynn tried to pull away, she found herself captive. *Yes, finally.* This was what her body craved.

"Hold still." It did something to Brynn when Iain went all authoritative. It made her hot. Eager. All this time, she'd wondered what it would be like to be dominated by a strong man. The reality was more sensual, more provocative than she'd ever imagined.

Arousal flashed through her. Her body literally ached for him, but it was more than just physical. Iain stirred her emotions. She was all mixed up—vulnerable yet unashamed, submissive but powerful in her femininity. Brynn's thoughts were a jumble.

Once Iain cupped one of her breasts and flicked the nipple with his thumb, she quit trying to figure it all out. She tilted her chin toward the ceiling, reveling in the moment. He toyed with her breast, massaging it in rough, unhurried circles.

"Spread your legs."

Enthralled by his demanding words, she was powerless to do anything but obey, planting her heels on the bed and letting her knees fall open. Besides, Brynn wanted more of his expert touch. The man knew what he was doing. His caress wasn't hesitant, as she'd experienced in the past. Iain was self-assured and seemed to know just what she needed.

He increased the pressure on her breast, pinching her nipple, making her crazy. Each squeeze heightened her excitement until Brynn was breathless, wondering what he'd do next. Her heart beat erratically in anticipation.

Iain wasn't gentle when he dipped his head and took her other breast into his mouth. Then he began to suck—long, slow pulls. A hot tug of desire ran from her breast to her clit. She was throbbing now, as his teeth tightened against her budded nipple. It was glorious, being helpless to his whims. She was participant but restricted—her fantasy come to life. The one she'd played out so many times as she masturbated, though Brynn seldom made the leap and climaxed.

She tried to put that from her mind, to forget about the end game and just enjoy Iain's warm tongue circling her nipple. She tried to move her hands again but couldn't. That stimulated her more than she thought possible—being held down, ravished. Nothing in her daydreams had prepared her for the reality of being helpless and bound.

As he continued to suck, Iain's touch on her other breast relaxed and skimmed her sensitive skin. Brynn shivered. Oh, that was good too. His hand brushed down her body, lingering as he traced over her stomach. No matter what amount of pressure he used, his touch was powerfully erotic, leaving little tingles in its wake.

Brynn ground her hips into the mattress, desperate for some relief. Inside, that persistent tension rose and twisted, taking her right to the edge. If Iain would only touch her clit, she just might topple over. Her pussy was so heavy and swollen. Ready for him. Instead, his hands fluttered over her ribs, traced her belly button. She was going to lose her mind. Pressure ratcheted deep in her belly. With each graze of his hand, with each sharp sting of his teeth, it built. She needed...something. Anything. Brynn's moan sounded like a sob, a wordless plea.

Iain's hand drifted lower, rubbing her hip. With languid strokes he finally—God, *finally*—worked his way downward and cupped Brynn's mound. When he ground the heel of his hand against it, she bucked her hips.

Iain raised his mouth from her breast. "Hold still. Understand? Don't make me say it again."

She shivered at the command, her clit throbbing beneath Iain's palm. She wanted him to press down again, so she froze and prayed he'd continue. Desire made her almost dizzy. *Please don't stop*. She bit her lip to keep from crying out, but she would if he didn't start kneading her again. Soon. If he ignored her for too long, she wouldn't be able to keep the words from escaping.

She'd beg. She'd bargain. Brynn would promise him anything, if only he'd bear down on her pussy.

After a long moment, he placed his mouth over her breast once more and sucked hard, using his lips, his tongue. Brynn willed herself to remain motionless. Finally, Iain began to massage her mons in a circular motion. When he slid two fingers inside of her, Brynn stopped breathing altogether.

Then without warning, her body jerked and her hips leaped off the bed. Sharp, almost violent sensations flashed through her, causing her pussy to contract, her toes to curl. Oh hell. She closed her eyes and tried to hang on as her body tightened. But another spasm, strong and unexpected, tore her to pieces, robbing her brain of oxygen. His fingers pumped faster, not allowing her any relief. Iain Chapman manipulated her body, forcing her higher. When another surge hit, every thought in her head dissolved.

With her stomach muscles quaking, Brynn rode out the mind-numbing waves of pleasure. It seemed to go on forever; it didn't last long enough. Once her body stopped shaking, she opened her eyes.

She lay limp, exhausted. Exhilarated. It was the most intense experience of her life. Between the confident way Iain touched her and his bossy, domineering attitude, Brynn had shattered beneath his hands. His wonderful, talented hands. She *could* come—it just had to be under the right circumstances. *And the right partner*.

She realized that Iain was staring down at her, a bemused look on his face. "You all right, love? You seem a bit gobsmacked." He wiggled his fingers, which were still sheathed firmly inside of her.

She gasped. "No, I'm good." She tried to sound all casual and cool, as if having an orgasm were a daily occurrence, but Brynn's voice came out a little squeaky. Now, after the heat of the moment, her self-consciousness returned. She was lying there with a naked man, a client no less. *Who just rocked your world so hard you can't even move*. Yeah, he'd done that all right. "Really. I'm good."

He opened his hand, releasing her from his grasp, and Brynn rotated her wrists. "You like it when I take charge." Very carefully, he pulled his fingers out of her body.

Though he hadn't asked a question, she answered anyway. "Yes, I liked it," she said softly. Truthfully.

Iain moved to cover her with his big body. "I know," he murmured against her lips. "I liked it, too."

Brynn enjoyed the solid weight of him. His chest hair tickled her breasts. She wanted to experience all of him, every inch. But as she wrapped her arms around his back, the front door opened and slammed shut.

"Brynn?" an accented voice called from the entry-way. "Where are you?"

Chapter 6

Shit. "Get off me," Brynn hissed and slapped Iain's shoulder until he rolled over. She hopped off the bed and tripped over clothes as she ran to the bedroom door. A gold cufflink dug painfully into her heel. "Hang on, Tash. I'll be out in a sec."

She shut the door and locked it, then spun around in a blind panic. Bending down, she began gathering Iain's clothes and tossing them toward the bed. "You have to leave." Ice-cold reality doused her passion, chilling her naked body and bringing with it the realization that she was standing in her bedroom with a virtual stranger. She didn't even have any condoms on hand. Brynn hadn't had sex in ages. What in the hell had she been thinking?

You weren't thinking; you were too busy coming. Be grateful, jellyfish. She was grateful. And horrified. And embarrassed.

Her hands shaking, Brynn pulled at her robe, which was trapped beneath Iain's leg. "What the bloody hell is wrong with you?" He lifted his thigh, freeing the kimono.

Brynn backed away from him and yanked the robe over her shoulders. She held the edges together, covering herself.

Iain stood, still hard and ready to go. "Who is that out there?"

"My neighbor, Natasha."

"She just barges in, does she? Doesn't even bother to fucking knock? Go get rid of her." As he walked toward her, Brynn couldn't take her eyes off him.

"I can't. She's a steamroller, like you."

Iain stopped in front of her and, cupping her chin, forced her head up. "Get rid of her. I'm taking you out."

Brynn clutched the robe so tightly, her hand cramped. There was something about dinner, something she needed to do. Oh, crap. SNO. She was supposed to have dinner with her sisters. "I can't. I have plans."

Iain turned and grabbed his boxers. As he stepped into them, his butt flexed. Even his ass was stellar. He glanced back at her. "The boyfriend, yeah?"

Brynn shook her head. "I don't have a boyfriend."

He reached for his slacks. "Good. That makes things easier."

Brynn had made it too easy for him already. Just a few kisses and a couple of imperious commands, and she'd abandoned all of her common sense.

She pressed her lips together and gathered her courage. "Maybe it's a good thing we were interrupted. *I* don't feel that casually hooking up is right for me. I realize I gave that impression a few minutes ago. I apologize for sending mixed signals."

"No apologies necessary, pet. But you were going to fuck me, which you admit is out of character. Why is that?"

Brynn tried to think of a reasonable explanation but came up blank. Could she claim temporary insanity? Iain made her feel very reckless. Irrational, in fact. When she was near him, Brynn's senses were attuned to his every move. Her body responded to his voice, his smell. It was alarming. But she wasn't about to outwardly acknowledge any of that. Brynn pressed a hand to her stomach. "Out-of-control hormones? That's my best guess."

Iain laughed and that dimple appeared. "Try again." He fastened his pants, then grabbed his shirt, thrusting his arms into the sleeves. "This thing between us, love, it's inevitable. It might not happen this minute, but it will happen."

"No, I don't believe that. This was a onetime thing. I work for you. Personal and professional lines shouldn't cross." Brynn walked to the closet and yanked open the door, taking a second to secure the belt tightly around her waist. "Right now, I need to get ready, so if you could finish dressing, I'd really appreciate it."

"Are you trying to dismiss me? You won't get rid of me that easily. And I like crossing lines. I do it every chance I get." With his shirt still undone, his feet bare, Iain padded toward her. "I'll do things to your body that you've only dreamed about, Brynn Campbell. I can be your sexual facilitator." He rested his hands on her waist.

Brynn's fingers froze on the hanger, her mind spinning with possibilities. She'd done a whole lot of dreaming over the years. "Sex," her voice cracked on the word. "Sex is the most primitive form of communication. I hardly need an instructor to figure it out." He laughed again and pulled her backward, so that she rested against him. "What makes you think I'm not sexually experienced?" she asked. "Maybe I could teach you a few tricks." What the hell was she talking about? The only moves Brynn knew were the ones she'd seen in pornos, most of which required a serious lack of inhibition and a lot of muscle control. But Iain's arrogance had gotten the better of her.

"In spite of the fact that you were gagging for it five minutes ago," he said, "you have an innocence about you. I think you could use a little corrupting." He kissed her cheek, then moved away.

Brynn wanted to be corrupted. Just having Iain hold her down had been enough to let her fall over the edge into bliss. But she worked with him. For him. And he was too domineering outside the bedroom—which, if she were being honest, she kind of enjoyed—the rudeness, though, that she could live without.

While continuing this little encounter would be sexually gratifying, they weren't a good match. Brynn was too much of a pushover and Iain would tromp all over her, wipe his feet on her feelings, and then do it again. It was simply his nature, like it was Brynn's nature not to stand up for herself.

"When was the last time you had sex, Brynn? Are you taking precautions?"

She turned to find him completely dressed. Even his tie was knotted. Iain had something in his hand. It looked like a pair of dice.

Brynn didn't want to discuss sex or birth control or what they had done five minutes ago on the rumpled bed. "It's not going to happen again, so let's not talk about it."

"Are you embarrassed?"

"Yes. Extremely."

"I had my fingers inside of you, pet. The time for embarrassment is over. And it is going to happen again, so answer the question."

Brynn turned back to the closet, pulled a pink maxi dress off the hanger, and bit her tongue.

"You're not a virgin, at least not technically. You have been with a man before, haven't you, love?"

Brynn kept her back to him. "I'm not a virgin, but *I* don't feel comfortable with this conversation." She reached for a faded jean jacket when she felt his presence directly behind her once again.

Iain buried his face in her hair and breathed her in. "Brilliant. I want you so far out of your comfort zone, your head will spin. Now where do you want to eat?"

Brynn's eyes drifted shut and she fought the urge to lean her head back, letting it rest on Iain's solid chest. "I told you, I have plans."

"Cancel them. You disappeared at lunch, so you owe me dinner."

Turning, Brynn peered up at him. "Actually, I disappeared at lunch because we were supposed to be having a training session. You were so busy talking on the phone, I'm surprised you noticed I was gone."

"Oh, I noticed. When the hostess said you'd left, I fired her on the spot."

"What?" Brynn's jaw fell open. "Firing people on a whim is a really crappy thing to do. This is why you need a facilitator who knows what she's doing, one who's not personally involved with you. That poor woman is out of a job because you were pissed at me."

"She should have told me at once that you'd gone."

"Iain, that's not fair."

"You need to toughen up, pet. The world is a vicious place, and if getting fired from a hostessing job is the worst thing that happens to her, she'll get off lucky."

"You don't even know her name."

"No, I don't. As far as I'm concerned, they're all expendable."

That attitude right there—that was why they weren't a good match. Brynn had never met anyone so hard-hearted, so uncaring. Was this how he'd be after he grew tired of her, after the shiny newness had worn off? Would Brynn become expendable? "*I* find your attitude very disturbing."

"I'm gutted that I haven't fucked you yet. A disappointing day all around, wouldn't you say?"

It took a lot to make Brynn angry. She could simmer for days, months even, but once she reached a boil, that was it. Iain hadn't merely crossed that threshold—he'd sprinted over it. "I'm not having dinner with you, Iain Chapman. Leave. Now." Still holding the dress, she extended her arm and pointed at the door. "And don't be rude to Natasha on your way out. If you can't manage that, don't say anything to her at all." Brynn couldn't believe she'd just said all that, but she was glad she had. He deserved it.

Surprise flitted across Iain's features, quickly followed by amusement. "So the kitten has claws. Good to know." He clamped his hand around her nape and thrust his face near Brynn's, his lips so close their breaths mingled. Even as she steeled herself against him, Brynn closed her eyes in expectation as she waited. And waited. Her lips drifted apart and her eyes fluttered open to find Iain gazing down at her with a smug grin. Then he kissed her hard before letting go and strolling to the door. "I'll see you tomorrow, love."

Not likely. Brynn's new mission in life was avoiding

Iain Chapman. Cassandra would just have to find someone else to do the job. For once in her life, Brynn was going to have to stand tough.

Too bad she had no idea how to follow through on that.

Iain rolled the dice in his palm, caressing them with his thumb. He'd been in a foul mood all afternoon. When Brynn left the restaurant, he'd been angry. True, he could have been more considerate of her time, but to leave as she had, had irritated him. Then, to add salt to his wound, she'd ignored his phone calls all fucking day. It was simply unacceptable. So he'd come here to confront her. But when he'd found her in a red bathrobe, fresh from the shower, the smell of vanilla clinging to her tanned skin...all thoughts of taking her to task had flown out the window, and instead, Iain had taken her to bed.

He'd had her naked beneath him, had his fingers inside her, her breast in his mouth. It was even better than he'd imagined. Brynn Campbell was a stunner—long, slender limbs, a tiny waist, puffy, light pink areolas. He wanted her now more than ever.

But this woman sitting in Brynn's outdated living room had ruined it for him. With a tiny dog on either side of her, she wore a pink fuzzy tracksuit that clashed with her tangerine-toned skin. Her makeup was caked on—long, false eyelashes, trout pout lips glossed to a high shine, and tits the size of footballs. No way could they be real. This woman was full-on chavette, all the way down to her rhinestone-encrusted trainers.

"Who are you, strange man?" she asked in a heavy Slavic accent. "What are you doing in Brynn's bedroom?"

"None of your fucking business, and who the hell are you?"

"I am Natasha. I do not know you, Englishman." With a curled lip, she squinted at him.

Why did women work so hard to look unnatural? Perhaps that's why Iain found himself attracted to Brynn. She was a real woman—natural tits, golden skin that came from sunning herself. He'd seen her strapless bikini line. He'd prefer topless, but with Brynn, he suspected that kind of behavior would take some real persuasion on his part.

"Brynn," the woman yelled, never taking her eyes off him.

"Just a minute," came Brynn's muffled voice.

"You have Englishman in your living room. Do I call police?"

He heard the door open, but Brynn didn't appear. "No."

He lifted his shoulders. "See? I'm meant to be here. You, on the other hand, are an interloper. Do you do this often? Drop in uninvited, unannounced?"

"This is Brynn's house. She does not mind. What is your name?"

"Iain Chapman. Best get used to me, as I plan on being with Brynn."

"Being with. Another term for *fuck*, yes?"

"I reckon so." But Iain didn't want to just fuck Brynn. He wanted to know everything about her. Not just what he'd learned from the detailed report—those were dry facts and figures. There was so much more to Brynn. Why was she hesitant to stand up for herself? Why, if she had Trevor Blake and Cal Hughes as brothers-in-law, was she living in a dated house with old, hideous furniture? And why was she friends with this lunatic sitting across from him? Brynn intrigued him in ways he couldn't begin to understand, and not being a man who valued introspection, Iain didn't much care about the whys of it. He simply wanted Brynn Campbell.

She wasn't just a tool to get to Trevor Blake. In truth, he'd been a little obsessed since the first moment he'd seen her in that garden. So watchful. So cautious. So fucking beautiful he hadn't been able to banish her from his thoughts. Now that he'd seen firsthand how she fell apart in his arms, he wasn't sure he could ever let her go.

Natasha pointed a long, red-tipped finger at him and turned her inflated lips downward. "Here is deal, Iain Chapman—if you hurt my friend, I will beat you like dog and leave you in desert where animals will feast on your remains. Clear?"

"Yeah, abso-fucking-lutely." What a nutter.

As Tasha continued to give him the evil eye, Brynn stepped into the doorway, lingering there as if hesitant to come any closer. The low-cut dress she wore exposed her chest, which she tried, unsuccessfully, to cover with a well-worn denim jacket. Iain longed to part the frayed edges and get a better look. Maybe sneak another peek at those beautiful, upturned breasts.

He pocketed the dice and stepped behind the sofa, advancing toward her. Brynn's breath caught and held as he moved closer. When he reached her, he fingered a long, dark wave. "You look beautiful."

As she swallowed, his gaze was pulled to her graceful

neck. The red welts didn't appear. Iain chose to take that as a good sign. Perhaps she was getting used to him.

She raised her navy eyes upward. "You're still here."

"You're still observant."

"You met Natasha?"

Working his jaw from side to side, he nodded. "Yeah. She's mental," he whispered. "But she's fond of you, which means she can't be all bad." Bending, he brushed a soft kiss on her lips before releasing her hair. Then he stepped aside and allowed her to pass, but he placed his hand on her lower back. Her muscles tensed at his touch before relaxing.

Brynn smiled at Natasha. "Trouble with Zeke?"

"He is stubborn man."

"That's going around." Brynn moved away from Iain and gently picked up one of the sleeping dogs, placing it on the floor. "Do you think we could keep Moose and Squirrel off the furniture?"

Tasha huffed and relocated the other dog to her lap. "Whatever. Zeke the pig is on my list of shit. Can I watch your TV?"

"Of course. There's a veggie lasagna in the freezer."

Tash glared at Iain. "You remember what I say, Englishman."

"Don't know that I can forget it. As threats go, it was rather vivid."

Iain followed Brynn to the front door. On the way out of the house, he stopped and nodded at the grouping of framed black-and-white photos. Old Vegas—the Welcome to Vegas sign, the Fremont East District arch, the neon Silver Slipper.

"These are impressive," he said.

"Thanks. I took them."

"You're gifted." He hadn't seen photography listed as one of her hobbies. Why hadn't that been included, and what else was missing?

"Not really. I haven't picked up a camera since college." Brynn's eyes bounced away from him and she walked out the door.

Iain followed. "Why not? You're obviously good at it."

"I don't have time." She stood on the porch, and the setting sun bathed her face in orange and pink lights. The mountains behind her appeared hazy in the distance. "Why are you still here?"

Iain had been reluctant to leave while she was still cross with him. "Well, here's the thing, love—I don't like to get a girl naked, finger fuck her, and then just toddle off without saying good night. Unlike some people, who disappear without a word and then refuse to answer their phone all day, that's not my style."

Brynn closed her eyes for a moment and shook her head. "You're too much."

"Thank you."

"That might have sounded like a compliment, but I was just stating a fact."

"That's not the way I heard it. So what's her story, anyway? The mad Russian?"

"She's Belarusian, and she's only been in the country for eight months."

"A mail-order bride, then?" Iain had seen a lot of that in this town. Older, wealthy men. Poor, younger women desperate to leave their home country. Classic business model—supply and demand.

Brynn stepped off the porch and walked along the path to the driveway. "Sort of. But I wouldn't use that term around her if I were you. She doesn't like it. Tasha's settling in, getting to know her new husband. She's just lonely."

"You're a soft touch."

"Yeah, I am, but that doesn't mitigate the fact that she's my friend and she's in need."

"Fuck me," he muttered. "What's with you and the fancy words? Listen, my pet, the world is full of givers and takers. That woman in there, she's a taker. She may be your friend, but never forget that."

With a deep sigh, Brynn's shoulders rose and fell. "Have you considered that perhaps your view of the world is a tad rigid?"

"No, I haven't. I like my view of the world. Everything looks small from up here."

She reached the car and glanced at him. "Very funny. But life's not that black and white. You don't look for the good in people, Iain, or take into account their frailties. In fact, people are incidental to you, unless you can use them to your advantage."

That struck a bit too close to home. She wasn't wrong, though. If there was one thing Iain was good at—besides making piles of money—it was reading people, finding their weaknesses, and then exploiting them for his own gain. Brynn's was her soft heart. She let people step all over it, take advantage of her. *Aren't you doing the same thing?* Yes, he was, but he would never hurt her. Brynn brought out strange, protective instincts in Iain that he hadn't even been aware he possessed.

"You have a very low opinion of me." Accurate and

well deserved, but low just the same. Iain placed his hands on her shoulders, then moved them up under her thick waves of hair and beneath the collar of her jacket. He rubbed the pads of his fingers against her neck. Brynn's blind faith in people would end in tears. She needed saving from herself. Somehow, Iain was beginning to truly care about Brynn Campbell. And her *feelings*.

So where did that leave him? He couldn't give up on meeting Trevor Blake, pitching his ideas to the reclusive tycoon. The chance to make tens of millions was too great. And he wasn't going to stop chasing after Brynn either. Iain wanted Brynn in his bed and Trevor's money for his project. One had nothing to do with the other.

Brynn curled her hands around his wrists. The contact made Iain forget his train of thought for a moment.

He didn't stop touching her though, sliding his palms along her soft skin. Stray hairs at her nape tickled the backs of his fingers, and she smelled fantastic. Iain desperately wanted another taste of her lips, her smooth cheek, her hot throat, but he wanted to know what her pussy tasted like most of all. He imagined she would be tantalizingly sweet, like a ripe, juicy plum.

"I have to go," she said.

"You should stay. Kick the Russian out, and I'll spend the rest of the night making you come."

Her eyes grew huge. She was tempted, he could tell.

"No, I'm having dinner with my sisters. If I'm a no-show, I'll never live it down." She backed away from him, but Iain pulled her closer. He lowered his head and put every ounce of expertise into one last kiss. His tongue stroked hers and he gently sucked on her lower lip. Brynn responded immediately. Wrapping her arms around his waist, she kissed him back.

When Iain's cock was so hard he could barely tolerate it, he raised his head. He either needed to shag her or let her go. "Stay," he whispered. He'd been so wrapped up in business this afternoon, he hadn't gotten the chance to talk to her. Really talk. He wanted to fix that right now. Tonight. Iain wanted to hear all the details of her life and get to know her properly. He'd never felt like this about a woman in his entire bloody life, but everything about Brynn Campbell fascinated him.

"I can't." Brynn shoved at his chest, and Iain dropped his hands, disappointed. He was used to having his way. Being turned down by Brynn was a bit of a blow to his ego.

Before she got into the car, she gave him one last look. "How did you know my address? I'm not listed, so you must have checked up on me."

Iain stopped breathing. Too right he had, and if Brynn knew the extent of just how thoroughly, she'd probably get in her car and run him down. Brynn was a private person and he'd invaded every part of her life. Iain could justify it to himself, but he was starting to feel guilty about deceiving her. Yet what was the alternative?

"I have my ways. Good night, Brynn."

Chapter 7

THE NEXT MORNING, BRYNN STUMBLED INTO THE office grasping a large cup of black coffee. Sisters Night Out had been less of a meal and more of an interrogation. After busting Brynn's chops for being late, then handing her a margarita the size of a fish bowl, Allie had tilted her head to one side and stared Brynn down. Her oldest sister had known immediately something was off and began blasting Brynn with a million questions. She did her best to deflect them, all the while thinking about Iain—his handsome face, his gorgeous body, and *that orgasm*. But soon Monica joined in, alternately quizzing Brynn about her love life and nagging her to ask for a raise. Eventually they grew tired of her evasions. When Allie asked Monica if she was pregnant or just bloated, they started going after each other, leaving Brynn to stew in her margarita and thoughts of Iain.

When she'd finally gotten home and entered her bedroom, she took one look at the wrinkled comforter and grew hot all over again. Was it any wonder she couldn't sleep a wink? At one point, she'd flipped on her bedside light and grabbed her sketch pad. Her pencil flew across the page as she drew Iain, all of the expressions she'd seen cross his beautiful features—anger, amusement, sexual dominance. Then she drew his body from memory, thinking about how he felt, how he smelled and tasted. When her hand became sore, she finally put the pad away, but she still couldn't sleep.

As she got ready for work, she became determined to find a way to get through to Cass. Brynn couldn't be Iain's trainer—and not just for personal reasons. She was terrible at it and he wasn't learning anything. Brynn just wanted to put this whole incident behind her, get back to business as usual, and forget all about Iain Chapman. Yeah okay, that was unlikely, but she needed to try. He wasn't right for her. *Sure as hell felt right though, didn't he, jellyfish?*

Paige caught up to Brynn as she passed the break room. "I'm still bitter that my breakfast of choice, a.k.a., a Snickers bar, is now verboten. This"—she waved a KitKat—"is not the same." She ripped into it and gave Brynn a once over. "Wow, rough night? Were you working late again? You look exhausted."

"Yeah. Thanks again for covering for me yesterday."

"So are we on for sushi this afternoon?"

"Sure."

Paige placed her hand on Brynn's arm, pulling her to a stop. "What is wrong with you?"

"Nothing."

"Uh-huh. What did Cass do now? And how long are you going to put up with it?"

That was a familiar refrain. Seemed like Brynn had a consensus on her hands. Everyone agreed she needed to stand up to her boss. Yet if it were that easy, Brynn would have done it already. Life didn't work like that. Developing new character traits wasn't a quick-fix proposition. Brynn had taken enough training to know that. But she did need to get firm with Cassandra. Somehow.

As they rounded the corner, Brynn spotted Cass standing outside her office, arms folded. "Brynn. I need to speak to you."

"Well, here's your chance to make a stand. You can do it, Brynn." Paige toasted her with the candy bar.

Once in Cass's office, Brynn shut the door while her boss positioned herself behind the cluttered desk. Brown stains covered papers that hadn't been moved since Monday's coffee disaster. The binders were still haphazardly spread across the floor. What on earth did she do in here all day?

Cass's hair was loose, and static made the baby-fine curls shoot out from her head like filaments. White cat hair coated her black blouse, leaving it fuzzy. "I wanted to thank you for your kind words last night. I've been doing a lot of soul searching, and I realized something very important. I'm not perfect, Brynn."

Oh, Cass. "Glad I was there for you."

"But I'm a damned good woman," she continued, as if Brynn hadn't spoken. "I have a lot to offer some special man, one who can ejaculate in a timely fashion."

Brynn found herself nodding. "Of course you do." She began backing toward the door. "You hang in there, Cass. Your special man is out there."

"Wait, that's not the only reason I wanted to talk to you. I don't know what you did yesterday, and frankly, I don't care."

Yesterday? Brynn cast her mind back over the day's events. Iain. She'd nearly had sex with Iain. "I...I was working. Like always."

"You must have been. I didn't think you had it in you, kiddo, but kudos, Brynn. Kud. Ohs." Cass shoved aside a six-inch stack of papers, knocking over a pencil holder in the process.

Brynn stepped forward and, kneeling, picked up the pens and pencils. Keeping her eyes on the floor, her mind raced. What the hell had she done yesterday? Sent off a proposal to the savings and loan, finalized a cartoon for the dry cleaner, and conferenced in with the marketing people to run an ad in the paper. She shoved the pencil holder back on the desk.

Standing, Brynn settled her bag back on her shoulder. "Um, thanks?"

"Mr. Chapman was very impressed with you. Very. Impressed."

Iain. What was he up to now? "I'm not sure why. We didn't really get very far." Unless being held down while getting fingered counted. *Stop going there. Mind on something else.*

"Nevertheless, he wants his people to take a course in accountability and efficiency. He's given us carte blanche to create a specialized, intensive course for his core employees."

Panic raced through Brynn. He was clearly doing this in a bid to see her again. He was so freaking manipulative. "What does this mean for me, exactly?"

Cass threw her hands in the air. "You need to study his business firsthand. Talk to all of the employees and assess Mr. Chapman's needs."

Brynn already knew his needs. They actively involved his penis. "But that could take weeks."

Cass sat back, a smug smile on her bright orange lips. "It could take *months* if you do it right."

Iain Chapman didn't want training for his employees.

He thought her job was bullshit. He was pushing his way into her life once more. And Brynn, being Brynn, would let him. He was a control freak. A man determined to get his own way. It probably wasn't even personal with him—he just didn't like being thwarted.

After taking a breath so deep she became lightheaded, Brynn blurted out, "No, I won't do it. You'll have to find someone else."

Cass's mouth fell open. She stared at Brynn for a full minute. "I beg your pardon?"

Brynn realized what she'd just said—the dreaded word that always eluded her. Now she gathered all of her courage and repeated it. "No."

Cassandra rose. "Brynn, we're talking tens of thousands of dollars here. Months' worth of work."

Brynn opened and closed her fists, forcing her feet to remain in place when all she wanted to do was hightail it out of there and hide in her own office. "I know. But I'm too busy. I'm way behind on work as it is. I can't. I...I *won't*."

Scooting out from behind her desk and scuttling between stacks of folders, Cass moved toward her. "What's wrong with you?" she hissed. "I know you've got a lot on your plate, but you have to take this job."

Brynn needed to stick to her guns on this. Iain was a man hell-bent on seduction. But Brynn's libido was directly linked to her heart. She was afraid of falling so deep and so hard that she'd never dig herself out. "I'm sorry. I can't."

"TDTC needs all the income we can generate right now."

That sounded ominous. "Is the company in trouble?"

"Not exactly, but sort of." Cass placed two fingers against her temple. "Office rent is increasing, and we've already tapped out our existing clients. This is an important job. There is no one else, Brynn. Iain Chapman only wants you."

That summed it up. Iain wanted her. *You want him, too*. Yeah, but she had a stack of reasons why this wasn't a good idea. *And the mother of all orgasms that says otherwise*. She silenced that annoying voice that always told the truth whether Brynn wanted to hear it or not, and today—not.

Brynn gazed into Cass's eyes to try and gauge if the other woman was lying. The look of worry clouding her pale features was real. "Cass, I literally don't have time for this."

Cass's eyes hardened the way they sometimes did. "I'm not asking. I'm telling. You *will* do this for me, and you will get the rest of your work done. It's not up for discussion."

Brynn flinched.

Rubbing a hand across her stomach, she realized she was going to have to face Iain after all. She didn't have a choice in the matter. But that argument rang hollow, mainly because Brynn's heart was pounding like crazy at the thought of seeing him again. Of smelling that yummy cologne and staring up into his warm, brown eyes. Oh, this was bad. She was starting to develop real feelings for Iain Chapman.

Cass cleared her throat and forced a smile, flashing a smear of orange lipstick on her front tooth. Brynn let her bitchy side take the fore and didn't mention it. "Sorry. I'm just feeling stressed right now because of Michael.

Nef's not feeling any better either. Look, I don't want to argue. I just want you to do your job."

Brynn reined in thoughts of Iain and focused on Cass. "I hope you're serious about getting an assistant. I can't keep up this pace anymore."

"You do this for me, and we'll get you some help."

Brynn wanted to believe her, but she was skeptical. Last night, Monica had reminded Brynn how much Cass took advantage of her. Honestly, Brynn was tired of it, tired of being taken for granted, of being manipulated. She needed to fight for herself. Somehow, thinking of her sisters, of Iain, gave her the courage to start now. "I want a time frame, Cass. When are you going to place an ad for an assistant?"

"After this job is through. You create a customized curriculum for Blue Moon Corp., and I'll keep my end of the bargain. You are such a fabulous employee and a real friend. I'm glad you're here as my right-hand woman." She grabbed hold of Brynn's left hand and squeezed.

With a sigh Brynn felt all the way to her toes, she nodded. "Okay."

Cass brightened. "Great. Mr. Chapman wants to see you this morning. Off you go." She dropped Brynn's hand and waved her off with a shooing gesture. Brynn turned to go, but as she grabbed the door handle, she glanced back. "Cass. You've got lipstick on your teeth."

"Oh." She reached in her drawer for a compact. "Thanks for telling me. What would I do without you, Brynn?"

Walking out of the office, Brynn found Paige waiting

for her. "Well, what did she want?" she whispered. "I know you're not fired—you're too valuable."

Brynn headed across the room with Paige trailing behind. When Brynn caught a few questioning glances from the sales team, she lowered her eyes and slipped into her office. Paige crammed herself in the tiny space and shut the door.

"That guy who kept calling yesterday, he wants me to personally assess and train his employees." Brynn dropped into her chair, her shoulders slumping forward.

"What about all your other work?"

"I'll have to keep coming in on weekends until she hires an assistant."

Paige scoffed. "When will that be?"

"When I finish this job. If she doesn't follow through, I'm going to have to issue an ultimatum." *Confront Cass or get a pap smear?* Damn, that was a hard one.

Paige perched her butt on the edge of Brynn's desk. "Tell her to go fuck herself. You're too talented for this place, Brynn."

"I can't just leave her in the lurch, and this guy asked for me specifically."

"What's his hotness factor?"

"He goes to eleven."

"Good. At least you're getting some eye candy out of this situation. And you are *not* coming in on the weekends—I forbid it. Call me later. I'll take a rain check on the sushi." She pushed off the desk, and as she retreated from the office, she left the door open.

Ted poked his head into the room as Brynn gathered her things. "Hey, Brynn, I've been meaning to ask you something. Did you have time to put together a proposal for the savings and loan place?"

She glanced up. "Yeah, I sent it out yesterday."

He pointed his finger like a gun and winked. "Thanks, Brynn. You're the greatest."

No, she was the weakest of the herd. Easy pickings. The runt. Now, for more practical matters: How was she going to handle Iain? Maybe if she simply pretended like last night never happened, she might make it through the day. Brynn was really good at ignoring things she didn't want to face. It was one of her few real talents.

On her way out the door, Peanut Allergy Brandon parked in front of her. "Hey, Brynn, I've been meaning to ask you, could you send out an email blast for me? I just don't have the time. I can shoot you a list of my clients. Thanks." He tossed out a grin and walked off without waiting for an answer.

Taking a deep breath, Brynn called after him, "Brandon?"

He stopped and looked over his shoulder. "Yes?"

"I'd like to, but I'm really swamped right now."

"Me too." He took three steps toward her. "If I don't make my quota this month, I'm afraid Cass will give me the ax. I'm trying to hustle up a few new clients this week, and hopefully, I'll get a nibble. Plus, everyone's pissed off at me because of the peanut thing."

Brynn felt herself nod. "Yeah, okay. No problem."

Chapter 8

Iain tapped his fingers on the armrest. Why wasn't she here? Surely her boss wouldn't let Brynn back out, not with all the money he'd thrown at the Delaney woman. Given her free rein, he had. All he asked for in return was Brynn.

She's not a bargaining chip, you wanker. Maybe not, but she was a runner, and after what happened last night, Brynn would talk herself out of seeing him again. She liked avoiding uncomfortable situations. Well, too bad. Iain wasn't letting her off that easily. There was something between them, something he'd never felt before. Hunger, longing—yeah, of course, but Brynn stirred up emotions inside of him, a yearning for more than just another shag. Yes, the Trevor business was still forefront in his mind, but Iain's personal feelings for Brynn were becoming equally as important. That'd never happened before, and though he felt slightly disturbed by it, Brynn Campbell was a temptation Iain didn't want to resist.

He glanced at his phone screen again. He'd give her fifteen more minutes. If she wasn't here by then...he'd go fetch her.

When the office door opened, Iain automatically stood. But it was only Marc. Disappointment had him flopping into his seat once more. "Oh, it's you."

Marc walked farther into the room. "Ouch, mate.

That almost hurt my feelings. Sorry I wasn't here for our breakfast meeting. Melanie had me up half the night."

"Nice one."

Marc rolled his eyes. "I wish. She wanted to talk. All bloody night. Which is fine, but that's not what they mean is it? When women say they want to talk, what they mean is they want *you* to talk. But you never have the right answers."

"So what answers did you get wrong?"

"The future. Marriage. When? Where? How many kids?" Marc fell into the guest chair. "Who am I then, Mystic Meg? I'm not a bloody psychic."

"Seems rather simple to me," Iain said. "She wants to get married. All women do, at one point or another."

"But it's not simple at all, is it?" Marc dragged a hand through his long, untidy hair.

"It really is, mate."

"I'm not equipped to be a father, you know that." Marc's own dad took off while his mum was pregnant. She'd eventually popped out three more children by three different men, none of whom stuck around.

Iain removed the dice from his pocket and rotated them in his hand. "Just because you never had one doesn't mean you can't be one. Davy's dad was a good man."

"He was."

Iain glanced down at the red cubes. He'd worried the white pips off long ago and worn down the edges until they were smooth. "Seems fucked up, doesn't it, that Davy's not here and we are? Anyway, his dad was a good example to follow. Be like him, and you can't go wrong."

Marc pulled a blue poker chip from his own pocket and tossed it in the air. "I miss him."

"As do I." Davy had kept the dice and the poker chip in his pocket at all times—lucky tokens. Though they hadn't done him much good. "What a bloody tragedy." Thinking about his old mate threw a damper on Iain's mood.

"What about you?" Marc finally asked. "Think you'll have kids one day?"

"Don't know. Doesn't seem likely."

"You're good with Tyler," Marc said.

"Well, he's different, isn't he?" Amelia's boy was bright and engaging. Iain had become something of a Dutch uncle to the lad. "After kicking around the football a bit, I can send him home. Having one underfoot 24-7—don't know about that."

They sat in silence for a moment, then Marc roused himself. "Made any headway with Trevor Blake?"

"Not yet."

"Why don't you ask Brynn to set up a meeting? Shouldn't be difficult."

"But it's not simple at all, is it?" Iain repeated Marc's earlier words.

"Aw, shit." Marc shoved both hands through his hair and kept them there—he must have been truly overwhelmed. "You're fucking her, aren't you?"

Iain might have thought of it in those terms, but to hear Marc say it so bluntly struck him the wrong way. "It's not like that."

"Then what's it like?" Marc dropped his hands, leaving his hair in disarray. He stood and began prowling the room. "Please tell me you're not shagging her as part of some scheme. Please tell me you're not using that girl's feelings against her. Even you must have a shred of decency."

Iain stood as well. "Shut it. I'm not using her." But Iain heard the lie for what it was. Yeah, he was using her. In a way. That's why he'd hired her in the first place. Still, his feelings for Brynn were real. "I'm beginning to care about her."

With fists propped on his hips, Marc continued to walk the room. "But this isn't meant to be personal. It's business. You've always said never combine the two. It's one of your axioms."

"Rules were meant to be broken, eh? I can have both. I can use her connections and still have a relationship with her."

Marc stopped pacing. "A relationship? That's what you're calling it? And no, you Muppet, you can't have both. She's going to find out this was a setup from the beginning, and it's going to go tits up. She seems like a sweet girl. A smart girl. She's going to get hurt, Iain."

"Not if I have my way. You worry about your own problems, and let me worry about mine."

"Your problems are my problems," Marc said. "This affects us both, don't it?"

"Sorry to interrupt." Brynn stood in the doorway.

Iain shot out of his chair and tugged on the bottom of his steel-gray waistcoat. How much had she heard? He searched her face, looking for traces of hurt, of betrayal, but found none. Once he realized that Brynn was still oblivious, Iain sighed in relief and glanced over her once more.

Brynn grew lovelier each time he saw her. *Need.*

Desire. The words flashed through his mind as he stared at her.

Today she wore a white blouse and a gauzy orange skirt. The shirt's sleeves were short, showing off her trim, golden arms. His gaze trailed back up, over her slim hips, her small breasts, to the loose brown waves hanging freely around her shoulders. She was spectacularly unique in every respect.

"Not interrupting anything, is she, Marc?"

"Not at all. Good to see you again, Brynn."

"Would you like me to come back?" She directed her question to Marc. "Sounds like you were in the middle of something."

He smiled down at her. But not just any smile—no, the one he reserved for charming women out of their knickers. Tosser. "Please come in. Iain needs all the help he can get," he said in a loud whisper. Then he smoothly buttoned his jacket and headed out the door.

Now it was just the two of them. The only noise came from the ticking of an antique maritime clock. Some days its tick was reassuring, soothing even. Some days it drove him barmy. Today, it seemed overly loud as Brynn stood there, staring down at the Persian rug. She hadn't looked at him once. Well, that wouldn't do.

Iain adjusted the knot in his tie and stretched his neck. This was not the way he'd wanted to greet Brynn this morning. Having words with Marc had thrown Iain off his game. He'd had it all planned out. She'd come in irritated, flustered—naturally—but he'd quickly soothe her, maybe even kiss her into a better frame of mind. But noting her tense jaw, the tendon flexing as she ground her teeth together, made him realize it might take more than a smile and a few kisses to pull her out of it.

"Come in. Would you like some coffee?"

"I'm fine, thank you." She finally met his gaze, and her eyes flashed blue fire. Irritation might be downplaying it a bit. She seemed rather even tempered most of the time, but Iain was beginning to suspect he was a catalyst for her anger, the spark that stoked a fire inside of her. Interesting, that. At least she wasn't indifferent to him. "I'd like to get to work, if that's all right with you?"

Iain nearly fucking shivered at her tone. "Fine. Sit." He gestured toward the chair and took his own seat behind the desk.

Brynn remained standing. Heat must be licking up the sides of her neck, because it was turning red again. "My employer informed me that you require customized training for your employees. Can you give me some insight as to what you might need?"

Iain's eyes narrowed. He wasn't used to her acting so robotic, so cold. He wouldn't put up with it. Iain pressed the intercom button. "Amelia, two coffees. And bring those Danish things. My guest could use a dose of sugar. She's in a sour mood this morning."

Brynn's lips tightened, but she didn't say a word. Walking forward, she placed her bag on the floor and gracefully sank into the chair. Lowering her notebook, she opened it and clicked her pen. All without glancing in his direction. "Please describe the challenges your business is facing and goals you wish to achieve."

"No."

Her eyelashes fluttered, but still, she didn't take her gaze from the book in her lap. "What do you mean, no?"

"This is a pointless exercise. I don't intend on answering any of your little questions. You should observe the office and tell me what we need. Then we'll see if you and I are on the same page."

"*I* think—" She licked her lips and clutched the pen until her knuckles grew white. "I think you could use a lesson in common courtesy." She'd summoned up every ounce of gumption to tell him what he already knew. As she inhaled deeply, her chest rose, pushing those tiny, beautiful tits out farther. He'd feasted on them last night. Touched her long, plump nipples. His fingers involuntarily twitched around the dice as he ached to do it all over again.

"Courtesy is gobshite. Why not just be honest?"

"You want honesty? Fine. We both know I'm not here because of your business. You're manipulating my time in order to see me again. How's that for honest?"

"I figured you'd be too embarrassed about last night. But you weren't shy when I pinned you down or made you come. And you weren't bashful when I was sprawled out on top of you. In fact, you were every bit as keen as I was, until your annoying neighbor came barreling through the door. Then you retreated into your shell like a turtle. But you're not going to go running scared this time, Brynn. I won't allow it."

"You think I'm afraid of you?" She was breathing heavily now as she met his gaze.

"Oh yes, love, but more importantly, you're afraid of yourself." Her eyes widened and she recoiled. That's when Iain knew he'd struck a nerve. "Look at it this way—you can teach me how to value and nurture my employees, and I'll teach you to assert yourself. Seems like a fair trade."

"You don't want to help me. You want to..." She left the sentence unfinished.

"Fuck you? Course I do. You want to fuck me too. You'd admit that if you were honest rather than courteous."

Now her whole chest and face were infused in a deep, dark red. "I really dislike you right now," she muttered.

Iain grinned. "Good. I'd hate to settle for anything tepid. Did you think, after last night, I'd really let you walk away? Oh wait, you don't walk, you run."

"And Iain Chapman always gets what he wants." She sat back and crossed her legs and then her arms. Her tiny body bristled with indignation. This was the part Iain gloried in—her passionate nature. It went hand in hand with her caring, generous heart.

"That's right, pet. Always. Without fail."

"What about relationships?"

She cocked her head to one side and her eyes became less heated and more analytical. That calculating look made him wary. His natural defenses clicked into place. He liked her anger better—it was more predictable. "Interested in my love life, are you?"

"No, I'm interested in Marc."

Iain felt a pang of jealousy rise to the surface. He leaned forward, placing his elbows on either side of his laptop. "Marc is taken." Ice coated his words and anger boiled inside Iain's chest. He'd been sitting here, waiting for over a goddamned hour just to see her again, and now she was suddenly interested in Marc? "He's my best mate. He knows you're off-limits."

Brynn's lips pursed. "I'm not talking about Marc and me. I'm talking about the relationship between the two of you. How often do you argue?"

Relief flooded through him and Iain's shoulders dropped—he hadn't realized they'd been hitched up to his ears until that moment. He leaned back in his chair. "We argue sometimes. So what? Don't you ever argue with your sisters?"

"He looked very peeved when I entered the office a few minutes ago."

Iain fingered the dice once more. "It's not just me he's rowing with—it's his girlfriend, Melanie. Besides, he'll get over it. He always does."

"Avoiding conflict in the first place is better than apologizing later. Perhaps we could work on honing your interpersonal relationship skills." She marked something down in her book.

"Oh yes, let's. Though you and I got very personal last night, didn't we?"

Brynn jabbed her pen at him. "That is not—"

"Appropriate?" he finished for her.

She opened her mouth to say something else, something he'd probably find very amusing, when a knock sounded on the door and Ames wheeled in a cart. "Here we are. So nice to see you again, Brynn." She steered it toward the sitting area and poured out two cups of coffee. Amelia straightened. "Let me know if you need anything else. And you"—she jerked her chin toward Iain—"behave yourself."

"Bugger off."

"Don't let that grouchy exterior fool you, Brynn. Inside, he has a heart of gold."

Iain scoffed. "You've gone soft in the head, woman."

Amelia winked at Brynn and left the office, closing the door on her way out.

Brynn was staring at him again with that penetrating look, like she was trying to see inside his brain. He almost preferred it when she acted all shy and stared at her feet. Almost.

He pocketed the dice, then stood and strolled over to the couch. "Come over here and sit. I'll tell you what I've got on the agenda today. You're late, you know. I expected you to come hurtling through that door an hour ago."

Brynn wandered over to the corner seating area but didn't go near the sofa. She was wary of him, clever girl. She perched on the edge of the chair instead, trying to keep some distance between them. Like that would work. Iain planned on keeping her close by all day, every day, until he broke down the last of her barriers. Never give an opponent a chance to regroup. Brynn may not be his enemy, but the theory still applied.

"I don't hurtle," she said, in a prim, shirty sort of way.

"Of course you don't love." He offered her a cup of coffee. "You duck out while the shit hits the fan." He gestured at the pastries. "Which do you prefer, lemon or strawberry? They're both good."

"Neither, thank you." She half stood and accepted the coffee, giving Iain the tiniest glimpse of the valley between her breasts. Her bra was ivory, and he spotted a hint of lace. Taking a deep breath through his nose, Iain fought the urge to touch her again, lick her, arouse her until those puffy areolas deepened from powder pink to dark rose.

He slapped a napkin on the coffee table and set the pastry on top. "Eat it—you'll love it."

She met his gaze. "I'm not hungry, but thank you."

Oh, this was her way of telling him to fuck off, her little act of rebellion. It was a small thing, but he'd let her have it. With the morning sun falling across her dark hair and tanned skin, she looked bloody beautiful. There was a defiant gleam in her eyes. Iain might let her win these minor skirmishes, but he would win the war.

Brynn glanced at the napkin and stroked her thumb along the embroidered blue moon. "You named your company in honor of your favorite soccer team?"

He paused in surprise. "Football team. What else do you think you know about me?"

"There wasn't much to find."

Iain crossed his long legs and got comfortable. He paid talented people to keep it that way. Iain only released what information he wanted the public to know. The rest was personal, and no one else's fucking business. Not even Brynn Campbell's. Hypocritical, since he'd dug into every area of her life? Add that to his list of sins.

She was quiet for a moment as she stared into her cup. "Iain, I really don't think this working situation is conducive for either of us. You're undoubtedly busy. I have work to do. Real work. I'd like to find you someone who's adept at teaching in an unconventional environment. *I* feel that would be more beneficial."

"Sorry, love, not interested."

"I strenuously object."

Iain grinned at her phrasing. "Stop being so polite. I won't burst into tears if you tell me to fuck off. Say what you mean, Brynn. I always do. People may not like to hear it, but at least I'm honest. Come on, try it. You'll feel better." He took a bite of his pastry and calmly chewed.

She set her full cup on the table as her small, straight nose flared ever so slightly. Oh, she was well and truly brassed off. "I won't give you the satisfaction."

"It's not my satisfaction I'm worried about, darling. It's yours."

Her gaze slammed into his. Gripping the chair, she leaned forward, pressing her lips together, still holding back.

"Tell me to get stuffed, then. Go on."

She jumped to her feet. "You are...totally unbelievable."

A burst of laughter escaped him. He couldn't help it. She stood there, vibrating with rage, and all she could muster was a limp description of his outrageous behavior. He set the Danish down and brushed his hands together as he stood. "We both know that, love. Come up with something original. I know you can do it if you try."

"This is over. I'm out of here." She turned and stormed back toward the desk, picked up her bag, and slammed her notebook closed.

"Before you leave, there's something you should know."

"I'm not really interested in what you have to say right now, Iain."

"Oh, I think you will be. Your boss, Cassandra Delaney, has mismanaged what should be a successful business. She's nearly run the thing into the bloody ground."

Brynn slowly straightened and turned toward him. "What?"

"She's not embezzling, not as far as I can tell, but she's reckless with money. Her overhead is high, and she pays herself three times more than what she should be taking given the bottom line. The Delaney Training Center is sinking. Sooner rather than later. This influx of cash I'm providing, it could mean solvency."

Brynn blinked a few times. "So what you're saying is, if I don't stay on this job, she could lose everything?" Her face, so bright and red a few moments before, drained of color.

"That's it in a nutshell all right."

"She told me she could use the money, but I had no idea things were this bad." Brynn ran a finger over one brow. "I have more work than I can handle. The business should be on track."

"I imagine she gives you enough work for three people. And you do it all without complaint."

Brynn nodded.

Instinct demanded that Iain crush Cassandra Delaney and her business into a pile of dust. How dare she treat Brynn this way? Iain felt proprietary, like a dragon guarding what was his. *Brynn's not yours*. Not yet, but she would be. "I could buy the business if you'd like."

Her eyes flew to him. "Is that your answer for everything?"

"Most things."

"I don't need you sweeping in like some white knight to rescue me from my boss."

"Don't you?"

"No." She appeared startled at the sound of the word. "That's the second time I've said that today. *No*. No I don't want you to try and save me or ruin Cass or anything else that ridiculous."

"Pardon?" Iain Chapman was never ridiculous, not

even when he was wankered from drinking a pint too many. "Wanting to help you isn't ridiculous."

"You don't want to help me." She flung the words at him as she raised her voice. "You want to play with me. You want to fuck me." Brynn pressed a hand to her abdomen and shut her eyes, trying desperately, he supposed, to get a handle on that glorious fit of pique. When she opened them, she seemed calmer. "We need to stop making this personal. How did you get this information about Cass's business? For that matter, how did you know where I live?"

"I pay people for data. It wasn't difficult to find your address. A simple deed search did the trick, I believe. As for TDTC, it took a couple of days to get the records." He didn't like admitting that to her. Guilt twisted in his gut, sharp as a knife. After all, his file on Brynn was as thick as a bloody catalog. But the truly interesting bit was that she didn't doubt his word, didn't ask to see proof that Cassandra Delaney was near the end of her financial tether. On some level, Brynn trusted him—just as she'd trusted him last night. Iain held on to that, even though he didn't deserve it.

Brynn lowered her bag to the floor. "It seems I can't quit, unfortunately, so let's stop dawdling and get to work."

Now that was just offensive. Iain didn't dawdle. He was up by four every morning, exercising, reading the financials, and in the office by seven. He was neither ridiculous nor a dawdler. Time to set her straight about a few things.

With long strides, he moved toward her. Her eyes grew large as she took a step backward, her legs hitting the edge of the chair. When he came within reach, he leaned down until his face was close to hers.

"You seem very confused by who I am, pet. I'm not ridiculous or frivolous or fucking stupid. My time is sacred, and today, I'm giving it to you. So you'd best appreciate the sacrifice, yeah? And in the interest of total disclosure, I'm going to kiss you now." He cupped her shoulders and, keeping his eyes on hers, lowered his head, bit by bit.

But as Brynn watched him move closer, she grasped his sleeves, clutching at the expensive material. When he was mere centimeters away, she closed her eyes and tilted her head backward. Brynn Campbell wanted this, wanted him. But she was going to fight him every bloody step of the way.

When he didn't kiss her, her eyes fluttered open. "What? What's wrong?"

He released her and straightened. "I've changed my mind. I'm not going to kiss you now. I think I'll wait until you ask me. Nicely."

Brynn's arms fell to her sides. She angled her chin toward him and the tendons in her neck stood out. "You're a jerk, Iain Chapman."

That put a smile on his face, but he knew she could do better. *Time to dig deeper, Brynn.* "Am I, now? And yet, I had you naked in minutes last night. Doesn't say much for your judgment, does it?"

As her breathing became more labored, that gauzy shirt brushed against his suit jacket. He wondered if her nipples grew hard with the contact. Lord knew his cock had. She glared up into his mocking face. "You're awful and pushy and arrogant."

"Yes. I am. What else?" That ethereal quality mixed with her rage was fucking magnificent.

"And I hate you," she ground out. She must have immediately regretted the outburst, because her fingers flew to her mouth, as if to shove the words back inside.

Yes, he'd indeed burrowed right under Brynn's skin, and Iain didn't plan to let up. "And how did it feel, getting that off your chest?" The same chest where his eyes kept straying.

"I apologize, Iain." She tore her gaze from him and stared out the window at the wide blue expanse that blanketed the city. "There's no excuse for that kind of talk in the workplace."

"I think we've already established that this isn't a normal working relationship, Brynn."

"You like pushing my buttons."

"Yes, I do, but you're right. I should let you get to work." Iain's intuition told him to back off. He'd poked at her enough for now. Any more and Brynn might flit out of here for good, no matter how much her boss needed this contract. "Let's announce what you're doing here, and then I'll set you up in the conference room." He crossed to the door, assuming she'd follow. But when he glanced back, she hadn't moved.

"I need to assess your needs first. That's why Delaney was contracted in the first place. We should get your course out of the way. Start at the top and work our way down."

"We'll do this my way," he said.

"You've paid us for our expertise—why not utilize it?"

"Another bit of wisdom from a woman who's

never owned a business." He folded his arms across his chest. "Tell me, out of all of the people who teach these helpful seminars, how many of them have their own companies?"

Brynn nibbled her lips while she considered the question. "I don't know. I should do an analysis on that. But the fact remains that you still need to complete your leadership training."

"And I will. We'll start after lunch." He held open the door and waited for her to collect her things. Then, with a nod to Amelia, he led Brynn through the outer office.

After clapping his hands and snapping at everyone to gather round, the employees stood near the center of the room, waiting. Iain glanced at Brynn and she nodded encouragingly.

"Right, listen up. You all met Brynn the other day. She's here to sort out our training needs. Answer her questions and don't give her any trouble or you'll deal with me."

They continued to stare at him.

"Well, that's it. Get back to work." He turned to Brynn. "How was that?"

"You didn't swear, so we'll consider it progress."

Iain grinned and led her to the conference room. "I'll have Ames send everyone in, one by one. You can quiz them to your heart's desire."

Brynn took in the wall of heavy curtains. They hid the sun and gave the room a gloomy, depressed air. She set her book and purse down on the long, wooden table and moved to the bank of windows, parting the lined material. "This is an amazing view."

"Which is why I keep it covered. It's distracting for the worker bees when I'm in the middle of a presentation."

She turned to him. "Then why have a view in the first place?"

"It's all about location, innit? Open them if you'd like, and I'll meet you back here at noon." He turned to leave, but before he cleared the threshold, Iain looked over his shoulder. "And, Brynnie, pet, do be here. While I very much enjoy the hunt, I don't want to chase you down again today. I've got a full schedule, yeah?"

Chapter 9

Brynnie. Only her family called her that. When Iain said it, her heart flipped.

After he left, she felt keyed up—and for good reason. Forcing her into this situation, provoking her into saying hurtful things she couldn't take back—it was downright devious. Brynn wasn't given to outbursts, but Iain managed to bring out the worst in her. Since she had to take this assignment, to save not just her own job but her coworkers' as well, Brynn couldn't shake him if she tried. Iain was making himself a fixture in her life, and she resented the hell out of it.

Last night, he'd said they were inevitable, but Brynn didn't buy into fate. She preferred the idea of free will. She could choose to ignore this infatuation with Iain Chapman and not let his good looks cloud her judgment or her emotions to overrule her common sense. Besides, if everything that happened in life was a foregone conclusion, then what was the point? It would mean none of Brynn's choices mattered, that her mom's cancer had been predestined, and Trisha Campbell's five-year battle with the disease meant nothing. That was too depressing to even consider.

She shoved thoughts of her mom aside. It didn't change anything, and it only made Brynn sad for what she'd lost.

She whipped back the first heavy, green curtain,

then the next, until sunlight flooded the room. That was better.

Brynn situated herself in the middle of the glossy conference table. Taking the head would be a position of power, and she didn't want that, even if she could manage to pull it off. Brynn needed to gain the trust of Iain's employees. If she could get them talking, get them to contribute, she might be able to help this organization.

As she flipped on her laptop, Brynn's phone vibrated. Allie's face popped up on the screen. She probably wanted to make sure Brynn was all right. Allie was a worrier.

When their mom got sick, her big sister had dropped out of college, come home, and slipped into the role of surrogate mother. While Brynn appreciated everything Allie had done, Brynn was a full-fledged adult now. But Allie had a hard time recognizing that fact. Brynn didn't want to deal with it right now, so she ignored the call.

When a tentative knock sounded on the door, Brynn glanced up. A man in a long-sleeved, white shirt and black tie hovered in the doorway. She remembered him from the accounting department.

"Hi." Brynn stood. "Thanks for coming in." She waited until he took a chair before starting her spiel. "I'd like to ask you a few questions about Blue Moon, if that's all right? And your role in the company."

"Am I in trouble?"

"Not at all. I'm simply here to see if I can help your organization function more productively."

The man gazed out the windows. "You opened the curtains. That's sort of forbidden."

She gave what she hoped was a reassuring smile. "It's fine." Brynn sat in her own chair. "I'm sorry, I've forgotten your name."

"Dale Thomas. I handle invoices." His voice cracked. "I'm going to get fired, aren't I? He hates me."

"Who hates you?"

"Mr. Chapman. He has this look of disgust every time he walks into the accounting department." Sweat started beading across the man's wide forehead.

"You're not fired. I promise." Brynn said it with a certainty she didn't feel. Iain might very well decide to fire this man for any number of meaningless reasons. He instilled fear in his people—not loyalty, not trust, not any of those components vital to a healthy workplace.

As they talked, Brynn checked off the answers on her questionnaire and typed a few notes. Dale enjoyed his job, was on good terms with his coworkers, and liked Marc. But at the mere mention of Iain's name, he began to twitch. Twenty minutes later, when Dale left the room, his armpits were soaked and he looked a little green around the gills.

The next five people Brynn spoke with seemed just as nervous, if not as sweaty. Their eyes shifted around the room, and anxiety poured off them. They all repeated similar phrases:

"I love working here. It's very satisfactory."

"Mr. Chapman is an excellent boss. I love working here."

"I love my job. It's a satisfactory work environment. Mr. Chapman is really wonderful."

They'd rehearsed. It took Brynn time and patience to try and break through the rote answers, and even then she wasn't entirely successful. It was obvious they were all concerned about their jobs. Working for Iain might be more stressful than working for Cassandra Delaney but without the crazy sex stories.

Brynn had a steep hill to climb. No matter how specialized the curriculum, she couldn't change a fearful climate. It started with Iain. If he didn't make some adjustments in his behavior, no amount of advice or training would help.

Finally, after two hours, Marc sauntered into the room. He was the most laid-back person she'd encountered throughout the morning. But his smile didn't reach his pale blue eyes. He dropped into the chair across from her.

"How's it going, Brynn?"

She closed her laptop and folded her hands on the table. "I'm okay. How are you?"

He appeared startled by her question. Or maybe by the sincerity in which it was offered. "Fine. Good."

"Are you sure? It looked like you and Iain were having an argument this morning. I don't want to pry, but maybe I can help." What a load of crap. Brynn totally wanted to pry.

"I don't think so, but I appreciate the offer."

"Iain said you two have known each other your entire lives."

Marc's brows raised a fraction. "Did he, now? What else did he tell you?"

"Not much. He likes to share his opinions about everyone else, but he isn't as forthcoming with his own personal information."

"Yeah, Iain drives most people 'round the bend

within an hour of meeting him. You've still got your composure. You must be made of stern stuff."

Brynn had never been accused of that before. "What's he like as a business partner?"

"Depends on the day."

"He often ignores your advice. Doesn't that bother you?"

Marc's lazy gaze drifted to the window behind her. "I like it in here with the curtains open. Brightens the place up." He glanced back at her. "Listen, love, if Iain's high-handed attitude bothered me, I wouldn't be friends with him. He's a right pain in the ass most of the time, but he's my best mate going on thirty-some-odd years. He doesn't always go about things the right way, but he's not a bad lad. He might come across as a twat, but that's mostly on the surface. Don't tell him I said this, but he's something of a genius."

Amelia had said pretty much the same thing. What did Iain Chapman do to deserve this kind of loyalty? There must be a secret side to him, a decency he only showed to a select group of people. Brynn wished he'd show some of it to her.

Damn. She was letting her soft heart get the better of her yet again. *Time to knock it off, jellyfish, and get back to business*. "May I be frank with you, Marc?"

"By all means."

"Your employees are… apprehensive. I think Iain's fostered an environment of distrust and fear."

"You're very kind to put it like that. Truth is, Iain scares the shit out of everyone. 'Business comes first, everyone's expendable'—those are words he's lived by for years. I don't know how he's going to change that. It's who he is."

Iain didn't have a problem cutting people, letting them go without a moment's hesitation. Just like the hostess from yesterday. Brynn's greatest fear was that Iain would be so fantastic in bed—and out of it—that as soon as she lowered all her defenses, he'd drop *her* like a bad habit. Then where would she be?

When Marc glanced at his watch, Brynn realized she'd been sitting there, not saying a word for the last couple of minutes. "Sorry, I lost my train of thought. Iain didn't provide me with files on anyone. I'd like to see some stats if that's all right—performance records, exit interviews."

"There are plenty of those. Just tell Amelia. She'll get you everything you need." Before he left, he dragged his gaze over her face. "You know, I think you might be good for him if you can stick it out." Before she could comment, he was gone.

What did that mean? Had Iain told Marc about last night? Surely not. Brynn pondered it for a while, then, forcing her thoughts from Iain, finished typing up her notes—although it was a pointless exercise. Iain didn't think there was anything wrong with the way he treated people.

Brynn could half-ass her way through this entire assignment and charge through the nose. But that wasn't her style. She was either all in or all out. Whether Iain knew it or not, he needed help. He probably wouldn't take it, but that wasn't her problem.

"That's a mighty fierce look."

Brynn jumped at the sound of Iain's voice. He stood in the doorway, watching her, his eyes moving restlessly over her face, her neck, down to her breasts. He sure seemed to like them enough last night. *Stop that*. She had to quit thinking about last night. About seeing him naked.

Rising, Brynn closed her book. "Congratulations. Your employees are afraid you're going to fire them at a moment's notice. I talked to six of them this morning and they all looked like they were reading a prepared statement from a hostage video."

His shrug was casual, unconcerned. "I've told you, I don't give a fuck what anyone thinks. If they don't like working here, there's the door."

"How many people have you fired in the last year?"

"Couldn't tell you."

"How many quit?"

He squinted his eyes in thought. "Several. You'd have to ask HR if you want hard data." His face smoothed out. "Now come on with you. Let's grab some lunch. We'll try the bistro again."

Brynn began fiddling with her pen. "I should stay and get some work done. You and I need to continue your training today. Though when I say 'continue,' I actually mean *start*."

He walked into the room, hands in his pockets, his posture relaxed. "You started yesterday. In the car, remember?"

"Yesterday, you had several phone calls. While I understand you're a very busy man, I believe that if we work together, we can complete your training with a minimum of disruption for both our sakes."

"God, I love it when you talk like a corporate drone. So sexy." He wore a mocking grin—one she'd come to expect. And Brynn was getting pretty freaking tired of it.

She searched for the appropriate words, a way to

get her point across without sounding accusatory. "*I* don't like it when you make fun of me. You may not value what I do, but *I* believe I'm entitled to a modicum of respect."

Iain dropped the smirk as his expression turned serious. "I never meant to disrespect you, love. Truly." He paused a moment, as if carefully considering his next words. "I *am* sorry, and I'll try to pay attention today."

Brynn was stunned. She rewound the words in her mind. He'd been alternately mocking her and putting the moves on her since she'd met him. But the word *respect* had triggered a change. It dawned on her then that Iain Chapman was a man who placed a high price on respect. He demanded it from others. Maybe that's why he didn't give a damn if his employees feared him. As long as they respected him, it was all good.

Brynn nodded. "Thank you, Iain."

The smile returned but without the sarcastic hint. "Again."

"What?"

"My name. Say it."

She was helpless to do anything but comply. "Iain." He was different when he was like this. Not softer. There wasn't anything soft about him, but he seemed more... relatable. Attainable. *Don't even go there, Brynn. He's not attainable.*

Iain was drop-dead sexy, headstrong, and smart. Sarcastic and blunt, too. Brynn felt utterly drawn to him. She was so attracted that when he looked at her this way—with equal parts passion and complete absorption—fire consumed her body. Not from embarrassment this time, but from desire. Everything about this man, the good and the infuriating, provoked a response.

Iain reached out, beckoning. Brynn felt herself moving toward him, and before she knew it, she stood in front of him and placed her hand in his. This was exactly how she felt last night: entranced, under that crazy spell that Iain wove with the sound of his voice and his confident presence.

He slid his thumb over the back of her wrist. His touch was gentle, but his eyes were full of promise.

Lust. That's all it was. The body's automatic response to stimuli. Then why did it feel more powerful? Every time she touched him, kissed him, Brynn felt energized and muddled at the same time.

"You feel it too," he said, as if reading her thoughts. He brought her hand to his mouth, and instead of offering a chaste kiss, he turned her palm upward and stroked his tongue across the center. Sparks of heat zipped straight to Brynn's nipples. Her breasts ached for his touch. She'd never had a man do that before. Iain wasn't just rough around the edges—he was uncivilized, despite all the elegant trappings and expensive suits. And Brynn wanted more of it. She wanted Iain unleashed, in full-on barbarian mode.

When he released her, Brynn spun around and closed her eyes for a moment, tightening her hand into a fist. He was hers for the taking. She could have him, all of that passion, the hot, elemental sex. But after he was through with her, could she go back to a life of celibacy? Or even worse, go back to dating boring, normal men who played it safe in bed when she needed so much more? Iain had a calm yet powerful approach that made her feel safe enough to let herself go completely. To let him take full control of her. Last night, she'd trusted him. That was huge for her, and so unusual, it was almost frightening.

Brynn opened her eyes and focused on putting one foot in front of the other as she made her way back to the table. She grabbed her phone, stuffed it in the bag, and schooled her expression before facing him.

"Ready?" he asked. Was she? Even though she didn't believe in destiny, it seemed like Brynn had been on a collision course with Iain Chapman from the moment they'd met.

Was she ready to let down her walls and be vulnerable? Maybe not. But she was getting there.

In the car, Iain was ready to give Brynn his attention. And his hands. And his tongue. He could see she was as dazed by this strange attraction as he was. She'd nearly buckled when he licked her palm. Iain had done it like he did everything in life—on instinct.

But as soon as they settled into the car, Brynn's phone started ringing off the hook. Fucking annoying, it was. When she took the call rather than devoting herself to Iain, he didn't like getting a taste of his own medicine.

Even as frustration had him fondling the pair of dice, he watched her closely. As she fielded questions, offered advice, and took on more work than she should, she did so with a confidence that he hadn't seen in her before. She knew exactly what needed to be done.

She'd had the right of it earlier, in the conference room. In mocking her, Iain hadn't respected Brynn at all. He still didn't put any weight in this training bullshit, but she did. When Iain realized he'd hurt her feelings, he'd felt like a right knob. He vowed to do better.

Once the car parked at the entrance of the hotel, Brynn finally tucked the phone in her bag. "I apologize. Being out of the office two days running has sent everyone into panic mode."

"No doubt." Exiting from the car, Iain waited for Brynn and ushered her inside.

She peered up at him. "Promise me one thing."

He moved across the lobby, nodding. "If I can."

"Don't fire anyone today."

He sighed dramatically. "You're determined to ruin my fun, aren't you?" When they walked into the restaurant, the hostess he'd sent packing yesterday was ensconced behind the podium. When she saw him, her chin quivered.

"Mr. Chapman. Thank you so much for hiring me back. I can't tell you what this job means. I'm working my way through school—"

He held up his hand. "Do stop. And don't give me any more grief, yeah?" Then taking Brynn's elbow, he guided her through the dining room to the same booth they'd shared before. After scooting across the leather bench, she simply stared at him.

"Wha'?"

"You hired her back."

"You have a real talent for stating the obvious, love."

"Why?"

"You know why."

"Because it was the right thing to do?" she asked. A hopeful note caused her voice to rise in pitch.

"Hardly." Perhaps that played some part.

A little smile graced her generous mouth. "You did it for me?"

"No need to look all smug. I'm just trying to get into your knickers."

"Thank you, Iain."

He did like it when she thanked him in that sweet, soft American accent. *Fuck me, I'll be writing sonnets next, trying to find words that rhyme with Brynn.* Win. Spin. Twin. *Twins.*

The same waiter stopped by their table. Iain shot him a look full of loathing. He wanted five fucking minutes alone with her and his patience, what little he had left, was running out. "Same as before. Do hurry." The waiter couldn't get away fast enough. When Iain caught the look of disappointment in Brynn's eyes, he sighed. "You're not going to give me another lecture, are you?"

"Since that's technically why I'm here, yes. Let's brainstorm and come up with a solution to your grouch factor."

"Grouch factor?"

She nodded. "Yeah, you're very grouchy. Do you have low blood sugar?"

"No, I have a rock-hard tallywacker. If you did something about that, I'd be in a much better mood, I assure you."

She pursed her lips, all huffy and disapproving. He even liked that side of her. Brynn might not have come out and said what she was really thinking, but she got her point across. And goddamn if he didn't want to please her.

"How about we come up with a motto for you?" she asked.

"A motto?" Oh, bloody hell. "Fine, then. What did you have in mind?"

"*Be nice?*"

"Ah, that's just fucking sad."

She drummed her nails on the wood. "Okay, normally I wouldn't say this. It's not at all geared toward professional decorum, but I have a feeling it might resonate with you. You're my Eliza Doolittle, Iain Chapman."

He couldn't help but laugh at the comparison. "Let's hear it," he said once he sobered.

"*Don't be a dickhead*. When you're about to snap at someone or fire them for no reason whatsoever, just think to yourself, 'Is this something a dickhead would do?' and if it is, think about your choices."

Iain slanted his jaw to one side. "*Don't be a dickhead*. I like it. It's catchy. Back home, we'd say 'don't be a knobhead.'"

"I know. Both of my sisters married Brits."

"Did they, now?" He already knew that, of course. And Iain didn't want to talk about her in-laws. Made him feel guilty. Iain hated feeling guilty—bloody waste of time and emotion. Yet, that's why she was here.

Brynn smiled. "You remind me a little bit of Allie's husband, Trevor. The two of you would probably get along. You're both very sarcastic."

Yeah, that was definitely guilt he was experiencing. But now was his chance—the perfect time to ask for an introduction with Trevor. Still, Iain said nothing. The silence dragged on.

Soon, the waiter was back with appetizers and the

sommelier poured the wine. The moment had passed, and he couldn't bring it up now, not without sounding odd. What the bloody hell was wrong with him? Iain had gone to all this trouble to meet Trevor Blake, and he'd just sat here like a twat, saying nothing.

When the sommelier looked at them expectantly, Iain glared.

"I'm sure the wine's fine," Brynn said. "Thank you." Then she kicked his shin. "Iain?"

He gritted his teeth. "Yes, thank you. Thank you for doing your job. For opening a bottle and pouring out wine. Well done, you."

Brynn kicked him again, a little harder this time.

As the man slunk away, Iain frowned. He wasn't upset with that bloke. He was angry with himself. A golden opportunity had presented itself, and Iain had let it slip through his fingers. Because of his feelings for Brynn. "If you left a mark on my trousers—"

"I see I'm going to have to get tough with you."

Iain would have laughed out loud if she hadn't been so earnest. She couldn't get tough if her life depended on it.

"You were being a dickhead. A simple 'thank you' goes a very long way."

"I pay that prat. And I'll leave him a big, fat tip. Isn't that thank-you enough?"

She sighed and shook her head. He'd disappointed her again. He hated that it bothered him, but there it was. Iain never cared what anyone thought, but he desperately wanted Brynn's approval. Why was she so different?

"No, it's not enough. Not everything's about money, Iain."

"It's all about money, especially in this town. That's what I like about it."

"If you don't treat people with dignity and kindness, it doesn't matter how much you pay them."

"Bullshit."

She rubbed her lips together. "If you gain a person's trust, they'll respect you. Who taught you that fear is the same thing as respect?"

Memories, like snapshots, flashed through his mind. His drunk father, smacking his mum about, yelling at the top of his lungs, cursing, using intimidation to get his way. Iain never respected that old man. Hated him, more like.

But Iain was nothing like his dad. The only thing they had in common was DNA. Iain may not pat people on the hand and tell them how bloody wonderful they were, but he didn't mistreat them. He didn't abuse them. *Then what would you call it, mate?* Treating employees like bloody fucking grown-ups, that's what.

The waiter returned, setting plates of pecan-encrusted chicken in front of them. Iain nodded. That was all the thanks the bloke would get. Iain was bored with discussing this particular subject with Brynn, and he was tired of her tedious lectures.

"After lunch," he said, "I'll take you to the property I'm going to buy. Right now, it's a boarded-up building, but I want to turn it into luxury apartments. You can stick with me for the rest of the afternoon, offer me a few leadership tips or what have you." Though it was rubbish, all of it. Brynn was wasting her talents on this nonsense, but after she made a point of telling him how disrespected she felt, he couldn't say a word.

He and Brynn sat in silence for a few minutes. Iain longed to drag his phone from his pocket and complete a few tasks. Yet out of consideration for Brynn, he refrained.

It never ceased to amaze Iain what a man would do for a bird. He was putting his business on hold in order to impress her. Iain used to make fun of Marc. When his mate met Melanie two years ago, she'd had him by the short hairs from the start. Look at the poor sod now—Marc was twisted in knots. Was Iain heading down the same path? God, he hoped not. And yet here he was, *not being a dickhead*. He hoped Brynn appreciated the effort.

She glanced up and caught him staring. "What?"

"You're fucking gorgeous. You know that?"

She looked down at her plate, uncomfortable with his blunt speech. Well, she needed to grow accustomed, because Iain might modify his habits around her, but he wasn't changing. Not for her, not for anyone. Coming from less than nothing, Iain had done all right for himself. He didn't need to change.

Brynn laid down her fork. "What you said earlier, about my boss—is the business really going under?" Her mouth tilted downward as she chewed on her bottom lip.

"She's ass deep in debt. Has taken out two mortgages on her house. She's months behind in office rent. She's a disaster."

"Cassandra is very disorganized. I've been asking about an assistant for the last year. She has enough work coming in. I don't get it."

"Some people are just bad with money. Look at where you live, pet. Vegas is filled with people who've crapped out. Busted and broke, they keep going back for more. You know that."

"Yeah, but this isn't just about Cass. What about my friend, Paige? She just bought a house. Or Brandon and his peanut allergy? Burly Ted and Lori the receptionist? What are they supposed to do if Cass tanks the company?"

"Being honest, it's probably not a case of if but when." He threw his napkin on the table. "My offer still stands. I'll buy it, you can run it. Or better yet, I'll find someone else to head it up, and you can come work for me."

Brynn's left brow lifted slightly. "As what, the office concubine?"

"If you were a concubine, you'd be mine. And make no mistake, Brynnie, no one touches what's mine."

Her eyes darkened to a deep, troubled blue—the same color as the sea, right before a storm. Davy's parents had taken them all to Colwyn Bay on a caravan holiday. Iain never forgot how gusts of wind had churned up the water as the waves had crashed toward the pier. That's what Brynn's eyes reminded him of right now.

"In case you're not aware, that was a dickhead thing to say." She was becoming bolder with him. Iain rather liked it.

"Too right. I'm only getting the hang of this, love. I've been a twat me whole life. I freely admit it. Don't expect that to change in five minutes."

That appeared to appease her. She took a deep, steady breath and inclined her head. "You're right. Change doesn't happen overnight."

"You know," he said, dropping his voice, "I'm still thinking about shoving everything off my desk, hiking up that long skirt of yours, and shagging you silly. You could head my HR department during the day and play concubine in our off hours."

Brynn swiped her pink tongue across her upper lip while she fidgeted in her seat. She liked that idea. Brynn had thoroughly enjoyed that wee bit of domination last night. At first, Iain had wondered if he'd pushed her too far, but he'd quickly discovered the truth. Brynn liked to be taken in hand and controlled.

"Don't you already have one of those?" She closed her eyes for a second. "An HR person, I mean."

"I'd find him another position. A lateral move."

"People aren't pawns, Iain. And anyway, I can't leave Cass. Her cat's been sick and her boyfriend...the whole retarded ejaculation situation, changing his relationship status without telling her—she's a hot mess. If the business went under, Cass would lose everything. More importantly, if TDTC folds, everyone in that office is going to suffer."

"What the fuck is a retarded ejaculation?"

"He can't, you know, *come*." She mouthed the last word.

Iain's brows slammed together. "So what, he just keeps pumping, but the well is dry?"

"Sort of. I mean, he gets there eventually. Sometimes. That's not the point. The business can't fail. Too many people's livelihoods are at stake. Besides, Cass would never sell. It's her baby. It's the reason she gets up in the morning. She loves TDTC. She's just not very good at running it."

Iain stared at her, gobsmacked. "Your boss is

telling you about her partner's cock, and you call *me* inappropriate?"

"Out of everything I said, that was your takeaway? And you *are* inappropriate. That's not even up for debate. The fact that Cass tells me these things is a burden I don't want. Nevertheless, I know every disgusting detail."

"So the next time she starts spouting off, tell her you don't want to hear it."

She wagged her finger at him. "That's really easy for someone like you."

"What do you mean, someone like me?"

"You don't care who you hurt. I do. I care very much about hurting people's feelings. I'm still feeling terrible about insulting you this morning."

"When?"

"In your office, Iain." She threw up her hands. "I said some very unkind things to you."

He thought back. "When you said you hated me?"

She grabbed the napkin and buried her face in it, nodding.

Iain reached out and forced her hands down. "That was nothing. That was foreplay, right? I kind of liked seeing you get all cheeky. Turned me on a bit, I've got to admit."

"Does anything offend you?"

Of course—disrespect, disloyalty, betrayal to name a few. "Not much, pet. But back to your business problems. What can you possibly do to help these people in your office? You've a soft heart, Brynnie, and it does you credit. But you can't help everyone. In fact, you can't even help yourself, love."

Chapter 10

OUCH. IAIN'S WORDS STUNG. HE WAS CORRECT, BUT Brynn still felt the wound. And no, she couldn't go around saving everyone, but she had to try.

"I've hurt your feelings, haven't I?" he asked.

"I'm just too sensitive."

"You are. But it's a quality I quite like in you."

"You see me as soft and weak. You don't admire that. You're all brass balls and grabbing life by the throat."

Iain pushed his plate to one side, leaned his forearms on the table, and angled his upper body toward her. "I grew up hard. I'm not ashamed of it. Yeah, you could toughen up a bit. Wouldn't hurt you none." As his accent became heavier, his consonants slurred. "But you're a kind woman. Delicate. Tenderhearted." He reached out and stroked her bare pinkie fingernail. "You've got quality, Brynn."

She smiled. "I come from nothing. I grew up in a dilapidated house in North Vegas. There's nothing quality about me. The only thing of value I've ever had was my family."

His face became serious and a shimmer of tension threaded through his body, sending shock waves from his finger into hers. "Don't you ever let me hear you say that again. You're goddamned regal." Suddenly, as if he remembered where he was, who he was talking to, the arrogant grin whipped back in place, along with that deep-creviced dimple. "If anyone tells you otherwise, send him my way." Iain let go of her hand and pulled out his wallet. He dropped five one hundred dollar bills on the table. Then he stood. "Let's go, yeah?"

Brynn exited the booth and, standing next to him, placed her hand on his lapel. She felt the steady pump of his heart. Her hand rose and fell with each breath he took. "Thank you, Iain."

"For what? Telling you a few home truths?"

"Yes. And for lunch. And for rehiring that hostess."

"You know my motives. I'm just trying to impress you."

"Whatever you have to tell yourself. But I think you're quality, too, Iain Chapman." She walked toward the entrance of the restaurant. When she glanced back, he was still standing there, a harsh expression molded over his features. "Are you coming?"

Without another word, he caught up to her and placed his hand at the small of her back. His reassuring, warm touch ignited a fire inside Brynn's belly that was growing into a steady flame. While her sensible brain yelled for her to beat feet to the nearest exit, Brynn's heart fluttered and skipped every single time he grazed her skin.

As they waited in the front of the casino for his car to arrive, Brynn squinted at the bright sun. The warm wind picked up her curls and she held them back from her face.

"How come you don't drive?" she asked when the car pulled up.

"A service is more efficient. Driving is a waste of time when I could be working."

She climbed in, and he took his spot next to her, pressing his leg against Brynn's thigh. She should have moved away, but instead, she stayed put. Being this close—smelling him, touching him, even through layers of clothes—was heady.

"You know what they say about all work?" she asked.

"Yeah." He gave her a side-eyed glance. "Makes you fucking successful."

"What does being successful mean? To you, personally?"

He was quiet for a moment before speaking. "Having 'fuck you' money," he finally said. "Rich enough so that I can tell any wanker to sod off and not have it bounce back on me."

"That's it? Boatloads of money?"

He took her fingers and placed them on his leg. Clamping down on her wrist, he slowly dragged her hand from his knee, up his leg. Toward his crotch.

Brynn's breath caught in her throat. What was he doing? She glanced at the closed partition between the seats, then to Iain's face. The brown flecks in his eyes grew darker as he moved her hand closer to his dick. Of her own volition, Brynn splayed her fingers across his fly and spanned his erection.

He guided her palm, easing it up and down his long, thick shaft. "Success is getting what I want. When I want it. Right now, Brynn Campbell, I want you so fucking much, I hurt."

Brynn's brain sputtered out. Somewhere, in the recesses of her mind, she heard the word she uttered so often: *inappropriate*. But since it sounded weak and distant, it was easy to ignore. Staring up into his face, taking in his shadowed jaw, his intense gaze, Brynn continued to slide her hand over his cock. With long, steady strokes, she applied pressure toward the head and eased up as she neared his scrotum.

Iain let go of her hand and closed his eyes as a look of pleasure crossed his face. That was Brynn's undoing. Nothing short of a six-car pileup would have kept her from continuing.

"Unzip my pants," he said, his voice ragged. "Now."

He used that bossy tone that Brynn loved. She shifted slightly in the seat, leaning her body toward him, and eased the zipper downward. She took her time, felt the click of each metallic tooth pull apart as she lowered the tab.

"Brynn." It was torture for him. The lines at the corners of his eyes deepened. His lips compressed into a thin line, and his jaw became rigid.

He was *allowing* her to set the pace, she had no doubts about that. Yet if he ground out another order, she'd follow it without hesitation. Brynn was learning a few things about herself in this little adventure. It excited the hell out of her when he was forceful, but Brynn liked knowing that she wielded a sensual power over him, too.

When the zipper reached its end and his fly gaped open, Brynn shifted her hand inside and stroked through his silky boxers. She glanced down, saw that they were navy this time. Her hand slicked right over them and down his cock.

This was outrageous, fondling a man in the backseat during midday traffic. It was insane. It was wonderful. Excitement and nervousness caused her hand to shake. She could deny it all day long, but she *loved* this side of him. Loved that he could produce this level of arousal in her. For other people, groping in a car was probably tame stuff, but Brynn felt wild and out of control as her hand rested against his thick shaft.

Iain sucked in a breath between his clenched teeth. "Stroke me again. Slowly."

Brynn complied, then slid her finger upward, through the slit in the boxers, skin on skin. She was touching him for real now, gliding her finger over that deliciously hard dick.

Though Iain was calling the shots, for the first time, Brynn felt sexually confident. Touching someone, making love—it wasn't something to fear. It was something to celebrate. The fact that Iain wanted her so badly boosted her self-esteem. This beautiful, biting, intelligent man wanted *Brynn*.

Tilting her head, she dragged her finger over the head and behind the shaft so that she could pop it out of his shorts and have another good, long look. It was as impressive as she remembered. Two thick veins pulsed upward toward the glans, and there was a dewy bead of precome dotting the tip.

Heart hammering against her ribs, Brynn peeked up at Iain's face once more. Through tight, slitted eyes he peered down at her. His hands were clamped into fists on either side of his thighs. Brynn's shy touch excited him. God, that was...humbling. Even as she watched his chest heave, her own breathing became stilted. Her pussy grew damp by touching him, by observing his uninhibited response. Knowing how much he wanted her, seeing the evidence of it, filled her with longing. This lust growing between them fed on itself. Pleasing him rebounded and amped her up, made her pulse flutter and her breasts tingle. She was every bit as aroused right now as she had been last night, when Iain had been stroking her.

The driver continued to start and stop, but Brynn barely noticed. The Strip was crowded with tourists, the street flooded with other cars, and she didn't care. She was too caught up in this. Right now, every bit of her attention was focused on him, on his reactions.

His jaw muscle ticked and he opened his eyes. They were darker now, that deep, warm brown shade, and so expressive. Heat shimmered in their depths, making her stomach flip-flop. "Suck me, Brynn. As deep as you can manage. Lick me like I'm your favorite treat." His thick, broad accent was harsh, causing trembles to ripple through her body. Brynn's heart was beating so fast, so loud, she was certain it was audible.

Was she ready to do this? Go this far and take him in her mouth in semipublic? *Yes, she was*. Just thinking about it made her light-headed. She wanted this as much as he did, maybe more.

Lightly, she flicked her short nail down the length of him and then tried to jerk her skirt from beneath his heavy thigh.

Iain raised his leg slightly, releasing her. The second he did, Brynn slid to the floor of the car and maneuvered her way between his thighs. She gazed up at him, seeking guidance.

"Slowly, yeah?" he said. "Start by tasting me. Use your tongue." She'd never wanted anything as badly as she wanted to lick Iain Chapman.

If anyone in the past had asked her to do this, she would have thought the act so humiliating that she would have hurled herself out of the car. But Iain didn't make her feel that way. He made her feel safe and sexy at the same time. On her knees, her hands cradling his muscular legs, being commanded to lick him, suck him—she was so turned on, it was delicious torture, this heightened level of desire. Did he feel it, too?

Glancing up into his face, Brynn could see he did. Frustration and hunger coated his features. His cheeks turned ruddy, and stress lines framed his mouth. His entire body was as taut as a wire. Anticipation flowed off him.

Or maybe that was her.

She was anticipating this, too. She'd gotten a quick taste of him last night, but now she wanted to take her time and enjoy this.

Lowering her head, Brynn inhaled deeply and kept her eyes trained on his face. She watched his reaction, tracked every response as her tongue darted out and swept over the length of him. She swirled it around the little dot of moisture, savoring his taste.

When Iain let out a low, guttural growl, Brynn lifted her head. "Fucking hell. Do that again."

Brynn obeyed, using the tip of her tongue to trace one of the veins from the base of his dick to where it ended, then flicked across the tip. She stopped and waited.

"Again," he said, his teeth clenched as tightly as his fists.

With a secret smile, Brynn finally stopped watching his face and took a good look at his penis instead. There was no way she'd be able to take him deep. He was simply too long.

Brynn was no blow job aficionado. She'd only given head a handful of times and never found the experience that pleasant. But everything was different with Iain Chapman. He flipped her switch in ways she couldn't rationalize. And she wanted this—wanted all of him.

Wrapping her hand around his girth, she squeezed lightly. Judging by the moaning, he liked it. Brynn very gently cupped his balls with her other hand, squeezing just a bit. Then she bent down and engulfed the head of his cock between her lips, fluttering her tongue across the top of it—salty, sweet. He began panting and she delighted in it. She was doing this to him, causing his breath to quicken, his heart to race. She stayed there, nursing the tip while she gripped his base more firmly, moving her hand up and down his shaft, jerking him off.

To get her bearings, she slowly began moving over him. After experimenting with pressure and listening to his groans, she started sucking harder. By opening her mouth wider, Brynn found she was able to take more of him. His hitched breath and the way he whispered her name told her how much he liked it.

Up and down, using her hands in tandem, she worked him. Enjoying herself, Brynn inched her way downward, enveloping him as deeply as she could. She only managed to take half of him, but when he fisted a hand into her hair and groaned again, she grew bolder and lapped at his slit.

He didn't try and set the pace or force her head down farther. He ceded control but held on to her, petting the back of her neck with one hand while he kept a firm hold on her hair with the other.

Brynn began moving faster. Closing her eyes, she concentrated on keeping a steady rhythm. His skin was so smooth, so hot. She pulled her cheeks inward each time she raised her head. Just as she was starting to get the hang of it, Iain's hand stopped stroking her neck and, instead, gripped it roughly.

"Fuck it, Brynnie, don't stop what you're doing. I'm going to come, love." *Oh God. Yes, please*. She wanted this. His cock jerked against her lips. Warm spurts hit the back of her throat.

Brynn hummed in pleasure. Tasting Iain, swallowing his come, was the most carnal thing she'd ever done. The most intimate. She continued to bob her head, keeping up the pace as another jet shot across her tongue. His dick twitched once more.

"Brynn. Goddamn." He bucked his hips and sent one last short burst into her mouth.

Even when his hips stopped moving, he continued to pant. Still, Brynn didn't release him. Though he was semierect, she swirled her tongue around him, licking him clean. After a couple of minutes, she let go of his cock and dug her fingers into his thighs. Raising her head, she swiped her tongue across the corners of her lips where his salty taste still lingered.

He was staring at her with something like wonder. "That was the most fucking brilliant thing ever."

Her neck begin to heat up. "Good."

He sat there, legs wide apart, pants unzipped. He gave her a lazy, contented smile—possibly the sexiest thing she'd ever seen.

"Now it's your turn."

That's when reality hit. Brynn was in the *backseat of a car* in *broad daylight*, parked at a red light right in the middle of the Strip. True, the windows were tinted, the partition was in place, but it pulled Brynn back to her senses.

She rubbed a hand over her mouth. Her lips felt dry and she was parched. "Um, maybe another time? Thank you, though." That after-sex awkwardness began to penetrate the space between them. Now Brynn felt shy and strange and timid. She pushed off Iain's legs and swung back into the seat, farther away from him this time, practically hugging the door handle.

Iain's voice was soft as he tucked himself in and zipped up his fly. "Not happening, Brynn."

She stared out the window, at the flow of traffic and the pedestrians who watched the majestic fountains in front of one of the casinos. "What's not happening?"

"You're not going to shut me out now. I won't allow it. What you did—it was amazing."

That experience *had* been incredible. And if he meted out orders in that sexy voice of his, she'd do it again. He was magnetic, pulling her into his force field, making her lose all sense of propriety.

She let out a startled gasp when his arm snaked around her waist. He slid her along the seat to his side and gathered her skirt in his fist, raising it by inches. Brynn smacked at his hand. "What are you doing?"

He leaned down and whispered, "Spread your legs." When she hesitated, he bit down on the outer shell of her ear, gently, but she knew he meant business. Tingles sparked through her body. "Don't make me repeat myself." Iain wasn't through with her. That blow job had been a prelude.

What was he going to do to her? Finger her as he had last night? That had been fabulous. But she was in a car, zipping toward downtown, the driver a mere foot away. Common sense told her to stop, but somehow, knowing the risks made it even more tempting, which didn't make sense. Iain must have been some kind of sexual wizard, compelling her to do things she'd never dreamed of. Still, having already gone this far, Brynn couldn't help herself. She craved more. She was unfulfilled, and Iain was sitting right here, willing to take care of her. *So let him.*

With her pulse racing, Brynn complied, spreading her knees wide. In some ways, this was more dangerous than taking him in her mouth. Being on the receiving end, opening herself up, left her vulnerable—and so turned on that heat flooded her pussy.

Once again, Ian began lifting her skirt. She swallowed as the material climbed higher, exposing her calves, her knees, and finally her tanned thighs, all the way up to her waist. Yep, way more vulnerable.

"Take your knickers off."

"What?" She inclined her head and gazed up at him. He simply flicked his eyebrow, daring her to disobey. But the more imperious Iain became, the freer Brynn felt. When he took command, it liberated her, allowing her to be more courageous.

With only the briefest pause, she shifted her hips up and wiggled out of her panties, dropping them on the car floor. She thought she'd been exposed before. Nope. *This* was exposed. The cool air met her heated core, sending shivers all over her body.

Continuing to hold her skirt in his hand, Iain leaned closer and traced the tip of his nose along her cheek. "You're fucking lovely. Every bloody inch of you."

The way he looked at her, Brynn almost believed it. She was breathing so heavily, she couldn't catch her breath. She waited, her hands clenched into fists, anxious to see what he'd do next. Whatever it was, she was going to love it.

"Touch yourself. Glide a finger over your pussy."

She hadn't been expecting that. Why did he want her to do this? *Could* she do it? Touch herself in front of him? It was so intimate—more so than swallowing him.

Iain's mouth found her earlobe. When he sucked on it, she squirmed a bit and closed her eyes.

"Go on, pet. I want to watch." That accent struck something inside of her, made her melt like chocolate. At the sound of his voice, she turned into a shameless, throbbing, sexual being. Her entire pussy ached, needing to be filled, and every time he uttered something in that deep, English accent, she pulsed a little more.

Yes, she could do this. Iain was in charge, so Brynn didn't have to be. She unclenched her right hand, and with tentative movements, slid a finger down her slick folds. She tilted her head back as she brushed over her clit. It was swollen, pounding in time with her heart. A moan escaped her.

"Open your eyes, Brynnie. Look at me."

Her lids flickered open, and her eyes met his. He focused on her completely. His gaze darted over her face, then down to her hand. "Finger yourself. Make yourself come." *If only she could*. "But don't take your eyes off me."

He was so stunning, she never wanted to look at anyone else. That masculine beauty was the stuff of fantasies—Brynn's fantasies. It was incredibly erotic, sitting here, stroking herself per Iain's instructions while he looked on. So…naughty. As she continued to stare at him, she slipped her middle finger inside her.

Iain watched it glide into her pussy, his attention rapt. Parting his lips, he palmed Brynn's bare thigh. His skin was hot, and when he absentmindedly rubbed his hand across her leg, the sensations were almost too much. His eyes, his touch, her own finger—sensory overload.

"Now add another one." His breath was choppy, his words barely a whisper.

A second finger joined the first. She worked them in and out, remembering how Iain's fingers had touched her there. Maybe she'd be able to come this time. With Iain, anything was possible, and she desperately needed the release. Brynn arched her back as her fingers dove in deeper. She felt a small storm brewing inside her, but she'd gotten this close before with few results.

"Bloody hell, Brynn. You're making me hard all over again. Don't stop. Keep going."

Oh, that voice. Her movements grew frantic. That illusive rush started to build, just a little bit. But before Brynn could grasp hold of it and climb higher, the car drew to a stop. Just like that, the storm ended abruptly, snapping Brynn out of an erotic trance. Now she was wide-awake and utterly self-conscious. Her hand slowed.

What if the driver lowered the window? What if he hopped out and opened the door to find her naked from the waist down? Shit. Any hopes of having an orgasm came to a screeching halt. As usual.

"Don't stop," he said.

This time, Brynn didn't listen. She withdrew her

hand, hastily grabbed her panties, and wiggled into them. Yanking her skirt from his hand, she jerked the gauzy orange material over her legs, more embarrassed than she'd ever been in her life.

You loved every moment of that. Yes, all right, she had. But it was so…unlike her. Brynn didn't do crazy sexual things in broad daylight. Hell, she didn't do crazy sexual things in the dark. Since meeting Iain Chapman, her world had spun out of control.

"Why did you stop when I told you not to?" he asked. "You know I'm going to have to punish you later."

That should have been a threat, yet to Brynn, it sounded like a delightful promise. What would he do, spank her? Tie her up and have his wicked way with her? *That would do for starters*. God, what was wrong with her?

She held her body stiffly against his, then tried to scoot away, seeking some physical distance. When he was touching her, it was hard to think straight. But his arm tightened around her middle, keeping her by his side.

"This was a mistake. I was unprofessional. Let's go see your building, Iain, and then I need to get back to the office. Now that I know what kind of trouble TDTC is in, I need to burn through as many jobs as I can."

He surprised her again when he reached out, took her chin in his hand, and swiveled her head in his direction. "That's not what this is about. Stop using work as an excuse. What we did was *not* a mistake. You enjoyed it, whether you want to admit it or not. So what's the problem, Brynn? We're not getting out of this car until you tell me what's really going on."

She searched his eyes. He was serious. He wouldn't let her out of this car until she told him the truth. Yanking her chin from his hand, she twisted against his arm. "I don't want to tell you. It's embarrassing."

"What could it possibly be, love? You can tell me anything. I won't laugh. I won't judge."

She shook her head, refusing to look anywhere in his direction. But his strong arm gently squeezed her torso, weakening her resolve. *Way to stay strong, jellyfish.* "I have issues."

"What issues? Health issues?"

Brynn elbowed him in the ribs. "No. Doofus."

"I'm not sure what the hell that means, but it didn't sound like an endearment. Come on, tell me. I'm dying of suspense here."

"I'd really rather not."

When Iain's lips landed on that tender spot beneath her ear, Brynn sighed and closed her eyes. "That's so not fair."

"I never play fair," he murmured against her neck. "I play to win."

Lifting her hand, she threaded her fingers through his short hair. He smelled good enough to eat. Oh wait, she'd already done that.

"Tell me, love. What's troubling you, eh?"

Might as well spill. He was too tenacious to let it go. "I have orgasm trouble. They're difficult to achieve. All right? Satisfied?" This was it. Her moment of utter and complete humiliation. Iain Chapman, the sexiest and toughest man she'd ever met knew her secret. Brynn wished she could turn invisible. Or at least make a mad dash for freedom, but she was stuck in the car with Iain's arm latched around her. And he kept kissing an erogenous area that made her dizzy with desire.

Eventually, Iain raised his lips from her ear. His warm breath fanned her skin, sending quivers skidding across her nape. "So last night was your first? That's what you're telling me?"

"No. Well, my first with a partner." He was silent so long, she chanced a peek at him. His brow was furrowed.

"It was because I pinned you down. You need that bit of dominance."

Brynn slowly nodded. "How did you know?"

"I was paying attention. There's nothing wrong with a little bondage, love."

Brynn flinched. "I don't like to think of it as bondage. That's too hard-core."

"Right. Just a few commands, then. Holding you down a bit. Keeping you still while I ravage you senseless?"

"That sums it up." *Oh God. Let me die now. Right this minute, so that I don't have to continue this mortifying conversation*. She waited a moment, but her heart kept right on beating. A little unsteady, but given the topic, that seemed reasonable.

"There's nothing wrong with that, love. I like being in charge, and you like it when I take control. And you came. Where's the problem?"

Although she was still mortified, Brynn felt a small amount of relief, too. Iain understood. They got off on the same thing. "Apparently for me, it's not a fun, trendy thing to try. I *need* it. It just seems weird. Like I'm not normal."

"No one's normal, pet, and if they are, God, how

boring that must be. So what about when you wank off? Do you have an orgasm then?"

And the hits just kept coming. Brynn covered her face with both hands. "Occasionally but usually not."

"Vibrators?" he asked.

"I've tried several. Nothing worked."

"Hand?" He tugged on Brynn's wrists until she capitulated and uncovered her heated cheeks.

"That's gotten the best results. But only a few times."

"Have you concentrated on your clit?"

Brynn bowed her head, letting the veil of curls hide her face. "Yes, Iain."

"G-spot?"

Gazing up, she shook her hair back. "I don't believe in it. It's like a sexual Santa Claus—it doesn't exist."

He narrowed his eyes and nodded. What was he doing, making a mental catalog?

"But you've never come with a partner. Not even with oral?"

"Iain. I don't want to talk about my history with you. Okay?"

He paused a moment. "So, oral?"

"No. I've never come with a partner. Not oral, not fingers, not tongues. Dicks. Vibrators. Dildos. Just on my own, by myself."

"Until me." He sounded so smug. "And how many dicks are we talking about?"

"Trust a man to focus on that." She tried to pull away from him but his arm became a solid band across her waist. She slapped at his hands, but it had no effect on him at all.

"How many?"

"I've had two boyfriends. Now, can we go inside?"

"And neither one could get the job done." There was a hint of pride in his tone. "I told you we were inevitable. I'm the right man for this, Brynnie."

Brynn stopped breathing. The "right man" implied all sorts of things to her: marriage, kids, a life together. Iain Chapman was not the right man for any of those jobs. But every time they were together, he felt more than right. He felt perfect.

"Come on. Let's get to work." He pressed his lips to hers, branding her with a hard, unyielding kiss. Then he opened the door and stepped out of the car. He glanced up and down the street, his eyes watchful as he waited for Brynn to hop out.

When she exited, Brynn studied the neighboring buildings. Downtown had been in decline for years, but money had been pouring into Fremont Street, just a couple blocks away—bars, restaurants, taverns. However, this area was still lagging behind.

"What's your plan?" she asked.

"I've bought several lots. Fremont is saturated with bars, but not apartments or condos. I want to tap into that market." He led her inside the defunct office building.

In the lobby, a short man with a florid complexion waited for them.

"Brynn, this is Pete Anderson, my foreman. Let's show Brynn the lay of the land."

As Pete reached forward to shake her hand, the buttons marching down his protruding belly threatened to revolt and pop off his shirt. "Nice to meet you," he said. "Iain, this place needs a ton of work. I'm talking at least thirty million for the high-end buyers you want to attract. At least. And that's just the inside. I haven't even looked at the other two sites yet."

Iain nodded. "One at a time, yeah?"

Brynn's brows shot skyward. "That's a lot of money."

"Which is why I'm looking for investment partners."

He walked past Pete, farther into the darkened interior. From the outside, Brynn could tell the building had seen its heyday sometime in the late sixties or early seventies, though the wallpaper and carpeting had been upgraded in the eighties, as evidenced by the shades of mauve. The entire place smelled funky—smoke, stale air, and mustiness.

Iain turned to her. "Ready?"

She avoided eye contact. He acted so normal, as if she hadn't just been on her knees a few moments ago or told him her deepest secret. Iain concentrated entirely on business. How he could compartmentalize like that baffled her.

Since the electricity in the building had been turned off, the elevator was out of commission. Pete handed them each flashlights, and Iain led the way up the stairs. Brynn followed him, with Pete bringing up the rear. On the second floor, Iain carefully picked his way through the construction detritus. This entire floor had been gutted, the walls knocked down to studs and the floor stripped to concrete. Iain kicked a couple of five-gallon buckets out of his path and tossed a trowel into one corner.

He walked a wide circle around the room, his light moving over the massive space. Brynn could tell he was assessing, calculating, forming ideas. "What do you see, Brynn?"

"An ancient building in need of a massive cash infusion."

"True." He stopped near the window and set down the flashlight before removing plywood from the frame. A small amount of light punctured the darkness. "Come here." He crooked his index finger. As she stood even with him, he cupped her shoulders. The glass had been broken, and Brynn was careful not to stand close to the jagged shards still in place. "Now what do you see?"

Across the street was another old—by Vegas standards anyway—medical building. Next to it was a string of small businesses, including an auto body shop. "You tell me," she said.

"That building is going to be a gallery. See up the street? That's going to be a cinema. And over there, a row of boutiques. This place won't look the same in five years. In ten, it will be an established neighborhood."

"How can you be so sure? Just because the city is pouring money into planting a few trees and making a bike path doesn't mean it will be a success."

"Oh, it will be. I have no doubts on that score."

"You're a visionary."

His brows lifted a fraction as he gazed down at her. "I'm practical. Doesn't take a genius to see this is the next wave of development. Fremont is just the beginning."

"What if you can't draw people to the downtown area? What if they want to party here, but not actually live so close to the bars?"

"That's a valid concern, Mr. Chapman." Pete's knees creaked as he bent down to pick up a petrified paintbrush.

"Oi. You're giving your opinion freely—why?"

Iain cut people off, demanded respect, but offered

little in return. How could she trust a man like this? Short answer: Brynn wasn't sure she could.

She placed her body between Iain and his foreman, letting her inner mediator take over. Having grown up with Allie and Monica, it was second nature. "I'm sure Pete is voicing his concern because he cares about you and your business."

"That and I want to get paid," Pete said.

Iain scoffed and thawed a bit. "We all want to get paid, mate. I understand your concerns, and for what it's worth, Marc shares them. I'll meet you downstairs in a few, yeah?"

Pete tipped his head to Brynn, untucked his hand from the pocket of his baggy jeans, and left.

"I think you've forgotten your motto already." Brynn turned back to the window. "So why does Marc think this is a bad idea?"

"Like Pete said, it's going to be expensive. This is the first renovation of many. It's definitely risky. If we can't get outside funding, we'll have most of our capital tied up for years to come, which will make it difficult to invest in other business opportunities."

"But you said you had investors lined up."

He rolled his lips inward. "I said I'm looking for investors. I don't have them lined up. Yet." He abruptly bent to grab his light, then strode to the middle of the room. "But look at this place. This area is ripe for the picking. We can put our stamp here."

"Marc is your brake pedal."

"Pardon?"

Brynn kind of liked confusing him. It was a delightful change of pace, keeping him on his toes instead of the other way around. "He's your devil's advocate guy."

"Brake pedal. I quite like that. That's exactly what he is."

"Marc thinks this building is a money pit, right?"

Iain dipped his head in acknowledgment.

"You see the future in it."

Again, he nodded.

"Who's right?"

"I am. Or rather, I will be, eventually. We went over this yesterday. Marc is a clever bloke. I don't always take his advice, but I value it."

"And yet you're equal partners?"

"Yeah."

"Then why do *you* get the final say? Shouldn't Marc's opinion carry as much weight?"

"He trusts me. He gives me the control, just like you did last night."

Brynn fought her brain's need to rewind back to that highly erotic event. It was difficult, but she managed—barely. "Maybe Marc is your anti-Iain."

"Blimey fucking hell," he mumbled. "What does that mean?"

"He points out all the negatives and that gives you a place to put any doubts you might be feeling. He's the yin to your yang."

"He's just bloody good at his job and loyal to boot. Besides, he does the day-to-day bit with the office workers. If I had to be in charge of all that, it would do me head in. He and I each have our strengths."

"But do you value his opinion?"

"Of course I do. I just don't always agree with it."

Brynn smiled. "You don't always agree with him, but you give him the courtesy of hearing him out. You value him because he's an important member of your team."

"Oh God, here we go."

"I think your office could use a morale boost. Your employees need to get comfortable with you, Iain. They need to see that you care about them. Appoint employee liaisons. Representatives who come to you with their concerns." When he opened his mouth to speak, Brynn walked toward him and placed a hand on his arm. "If you take an interest, it will give them pride and ownership over their work."

He stroked the back of her hand, curling his long fingers around her wrist. "I don't care if they feel ownership, pet. I care if they do their jobs."

Brynn fought the urge to smack her forehead. This circular argument was going nowhere. She wrested her hand away. "I'm done trying to explain it. You need to at least *pretend* like you give a crap about other people's feelings. I hate to be blunt, but your office morale sucks."

"Will this idea of yours fix it?"

"It's a start. You need office lunches, the occasional party, maybe a dinner where their families can come and you foot the bill."

"Sounds like being trapped in hell. Anything else?"

Brynn reached up and patted his shoulder. His hard, firm shoulder. "Nope. I think I may have broken you already."

The look he gave her was one of such supreme arrogance, she immediately became intimidated. "Oh, you haven't broken me, love. I'm harder than these steel girders, I am. Nothing shakes me."

"I'll keep that in mind. Now tell me what you plan to do with this place."

Iain replaced the plywood and led her back down the stairs. Then for the next hour, he laid out his plans, showing her various configurations, blueprints, and artists' renderings. Pete gave his opinion on costs and the time frame.

As Iain laid out his ideas for the apartments—salvaged, stripped wood; industrial kitchens; an open-floor concept—his enthusiasm was infectious. Iain Chapman had a gift.

"What do you think, Brynnie?"

"I think you're either brilliant or a dreamer."

He negligently shrugged one shoulder. "I like to think I'm a little of both."

Now that surprised her. To Brynn, there was nothing but an earthy, gritty realism to this man.

Brynn turned to Pete. "Can you give us a second?"

Pete glanced at Iain, who nodded. "You can go for today. Write me up a cost projection. I'm meeting with the architect in a few weeks. I'll have Amelia call you."

"Great." Pete nodded to Brynn. "Good to meet you." When he left, the metal door banged closed behind him.

"Couldn't wait to get me alone, eh?"

"Kind of. But only to talk about work."

He puffed his cheeks and blew out a gusty sigh. "I'll relent on your liaison idea. What more do you bloody want?"

Brynn nearly felt sorry for him. "If *I* recall, this method was your idea. You could take the course online. It would only take two or three days. You wanted to do this your way. So we're doing it your way."

"What now?"

"Tomorrow, let's start thinking about how your team sees you."

"Team, huh? Call them what they are, Brynn—workers, employees. I've had quite enough of this PC language bullshit for one day."

Brynn pulled in a long, steady breath. Iain was starting to frustrate the hell out of her. "What do you want to get out of this process?"

He twisted his mouth to one side and studied her. His eyes moved over her, landing on her breasts and lingering there. "You know what I want. I thought I'd made that perfectly clear, but obviously, it needs repeating. I. Want. You."

Hearing the words heated Brynn's blood and stirred her ire at the same time. Was it exciting that he wanted her? Yeah, that part was pretty hot, but he was wasting her time and she resented the hell out of it. Brynn was weary of wrangling with him. The man was tireless in his resistance. And she'd finally had enough. "If you want me, then act like a normal person and ask me out on a date. Woo me. Win me. But stop arguing over every suggestion I make, because it's starting to piss me off."

A grin spread over Iain's face. "I do like to get the best of your temper, love."

Without another word, Brynn spun on her heel and stormed toward the door. Back at the office, she had real clients with real problems. She needed to figure out what to do about Cass and the sinking ship that was the Delaney Training Center. Brynn needed a little time away from Iain, too. When he was around, she couldn't think about anything other than him, gauging his response, watching his expressions, listening for changes in his accent.

It was time for Brynn to get back to her life. She wasn't a twitterpated fourteen-year-old girl.

Outside, Brynn waited for Iain to emerge. She didn't say anything on the drive back to his office. He ignored her as well, spending his time talking business on the phone and texting.

When the car slowed at the front of Iain's building, Brynn wanted to turn on her heel and leave him standing there, but his words about running away taunted her. Instead, she stood next to him on the sidewalk, waiting until he hung up from his latest call.

"I'm headed back to my office, Iain. Think about what I said, and I'll see you tomorrow."

He dipped his head for a swift kiss, but she ducked out of reach. If he kissed her again, all bets were off. He'd have her upstairs and naked on the conference room table. Her resistance to him was less than zero. She walked backward, keeping him in her line of sight.

He simply stood there, looking very annoyed.

"Remember your new motto. Don't be a dickhead."

Chapter 11

IAIN STOOD NEAR THE ENTRANCE OF THE BUILDING and watched Brynn disappear. Somewhere along the line, he'd fucked up, because she'd barely looked at him on the ride back to the office.

Sure, Iain may have quibbled about her ideas, parties and the like. Hardly the worst sin he'd ever committed. He didn't give a toss about employees' opinions either. If they had any good suggestions, they'd be running their own show and not working for him.

Still, if Iain's plan was to impress Brynn, he'd missed it by a mile. And maybe she had a point. Perhaps he could be more pleasant. Wouldn't kill him, would it?

When Iain replayed his time with Brynn, he could admit the truth. He'd acted like a bit of a knobhead. And he may have gone about things the wrong way. Woo her, she'd said. Win her. In order to do that, Iain was going to have to be...sociable. *You can do it for business, so why not for Brynn? You learned to play golf, you wanker.* Bloody hell. Iain needed to stop whinging and simply comply with her wishes. Wasn't difficult, was it? He was just being hardheaded. It would all be worth it if he could have Brynn.

She wasn't his usual type of woman. Actually, she was so much better—sensitive, kind, sweet, gentle. He'd had her naked twice now, and he wanted more. She was lovely inside and out.

He'd been chuffed when she'd finally been honest and admitted to her sexual kinks. She liked it when Iain took control. When he'd told her to suck him off, he could clearly see how excited she'd become. Her lids had grown heavy, her mouth had parted, her breath had quickened. Brynn, his beautiful, delicate Brynn, had gotten on her knees and taken him in her mouth. She didn't do that type of thing lightly. Yet she'd swallowed him. Every drop. It was the most delicious, erotic memory he had. And last night, he'd given her an orgasm. Those other two blokes hadn't been able to do that. Filled him with bloody pride, that did. He wanted to do it again.

But right now, Iain needed to head up to his office and—oh God—make small talk. Try and form a connection with these people, somehow. He should probably start with the accounting department, as they seemed the most timid of the bunch.

He took the elevator up to the office, but instead of heading straight to his suite, Iain cut a left. At his presence, every bean counter turned to stare, then dropped their eyes. Brynn did that too, sometimes. Was he really that much of a blighter that people couldn't look him in the bloody face?

Tom, head of the department, stood and approached him. "Something I can do for you, Mr. Chapman?"

"No, just wanted to see how everyone was doing. Think I'll make the rounds." Iain walked to the nearest employee, a slight man who sweated profusely.

Iain thrust his hands in his pockets, fumbled with the dice, and searched for something to say. Anything. When his mind came up blank, Iain decided to do it the

English way and talk about the weather. "Getting hot outside, innit?"

The man swallowed audibly and stared at his computer screen. "Yes. Very hot, sir."

"Tell me what you're doing."

"Invoices to all of our...your...building tenants."

Iain and Marc had started with strip malls and moved up to office buildings. Doctors sometimes paid late, lawyers were dead on time, but dentists were the worst. "Everybody up-to-date?"

"A few are delinquent. But they always pay the late fee."

What was he supposed to say now? Bloody hell. "Well done."

The man gazed up at Iain with a surprised expression. "Thank you, sir."

Iain moved to the next cubicle. He couldn't use the weather gambit with everyone. Small talk was a waste of time, so Iain just got right to it, asking each person what they were doing, if they thought the current system was efficient. One woman, Brittney, if he remembered correctly, thought their software should be updated. A man called Ronnie had a newborn and showed him pictures.

By the time Iain made it back to his office, he'd clocked in fifteen minutes of face time. He hadn't enjoyed it, but it hadn't been as dreadful as he'd assumed it would be. Brynn would be proud of him. He couldn't wait to see her again so he could tell her.

Iain stopped walking. Earlier in the day, he'd realized that he wanted to impress her, but there was more to it than that. She actually mattered to him. A great deal.

Well, shit. He'd…think about that later.

Iain continued on and stopped in front of Amelia's desk. "How was your morning?" she asked. "Is Brynn coming back this afternoon?"

"No, but I want you to carve out some time tomorrow so we can sit down with her and discuss morale. Marc too. If I have to suffer, so does he."

Her hand paused on the keyboard. "Morale?"

"Brynn thinks I can lighten the atmosphere around here."

Amelia grinned. "I think that's a terrific idea."

"Well, I don't." He pulled the dice from his pocket. "But I'm doing it anyway."

"Okay, I'll set it up. Would you like me to have coffee and bagels? Maybe some of those Danishes you love."

"Whatever, just do it." He walked into his office and slammed the dice on his desk. This whole business was bloody tedious. Seemed he and Brynn were both stepping out of their comfort zones.

Brynn didn't bother to sneak into her office that day—she was too wound up. Irritated and aroused with Iain on one hand, worried about TDTC's future on the other.

Taking the elevator, Brynn got off on her floor and walked past Brandon, assuring him she'd see to his email blasts. When Cass tried to intercept Brynn and corral her for an impromptu meeting, Brynn shook her head. "Now's not a good time. I'll send you a summary of my progress." Then she kept veering toward her tiny office.

Paige overheard and her eyebrows shot upward, but

Brynn ignored her as well. She needed to figure a few things out.

True, TDTC wasn't her business, she had no ownership in the place, and yet she bore a certain amount of responsibility for these people. But Brynn couldn't force Cass to pull herself together any more than she could coerce Iain into treating his employees like human beings.

Some days, people were nothing but a freaking frustration.

Brynn had booted up her computer and settled down to work when her phone rang. She glanced at the screen. Allie again. Speaking of frustrating.

"Hey."

"How are you?" Al asked.

"Fine, just really busy right now."

Allie hesitated. "Brynnie, I can tell something's bothering you."

She closed her eyes, counted to six, and let her breath out in a whoosh. "I don't like it when you and Monica gang up on me. I'm an adult." She kept her tone calm and thought about what she needed to say next. "I don't come running to you with every problem anymore, Allie, because I don't need to. You did a great job of raising me, and I'm grateful. I love you, but I don't want to be smothered anymore." Normally, she bit her tongue and kept all that buried deep inside. Or just ignored Allie's phone call. This afternoon, she'd been honest with Iain, and now she was speaking her mind with Allie. It felt empowering.

Allie said nothing for a moment. In the silence, Brynn heard her sister stifle what sounded suspiciously like a sob. Immediately, Brynn felt guilt and pain constrict her chest. Then Allie spoke. "I didn't raise you, Brynnie. I just helped. Thank you for that, though. It means a lot." She sniffled a couple of times and cleared her throat. "You're right, I do tend to smother you, and I apologize. I want you to be happy, and I don't think you are. Honey, you haven't dated anyone in ages. You work constantly. I worry."

Brynn wondered if she should say anything about Iain. It was so tenuous, and Allie would only nag her about it—she honestly couldn't help herself. Still, if Brynn wanted to be treated like an adult, she needed to start forcing Allie to see her as one. That meant being truthful. "Okay, if I tell you something, you can't ask questions and you can't bring it up again until I'm ready to talk about it."

"Promise."

"I like someone."

Allie gasped. "I knew it. I knew something was different last night. You should invite him to our house for dinner, introduce him to the family."

Nice try, but Brynn wasn't fooled. "Introduce him to the family" meant "interrogation over Cornish game hens." "I appreciate the offer, but no. Besides, I don't know how serious this thing is between Iain and me." It felt serious. Brynn had done things with Iain she'd never done with another man. And she'd been honest about her sexual needs. Another first.

"Just think about it. No extended family. Just Trevor, Cal, Monica, and me. We'll see you on Sunday. Seven o'clock." Then she hung up.

Like hell. Why would Iain want to subject himself

to a family dinner? He probably only viewed Brynn as a temporary fling anyway. And while Brynn adored Trevor, he'd act all superior and snotty toward Iain. Cal would ask him about cars, and since Iain didn't drive, he'd fail that test, too. Iain's pride would get bruised. Words and insults were bound to ensue. Posh versus working class—a clash of the expat titans. No thanks. Besides, Brynn wasn't actually dating Iain Chapman. What happened in the backseat—every time she thought about *that*, heat flooded her cheeks—didn't matter in the long run. While it was a hot, sexy memory that made her clench her legs together out of piercing need, they weren't *dating* dating.

Brynn tried to put Iain, this afternoon's sexcapades, and her sisters from her mind. She spent the next two hours editing a cartoon film about hand washing when her phone rang. Monica this time. Brynn ignored it. She'd had about all the confrontation she could handle for one day. Telling the truth was exhausting.

Two minutes later, when her phone rang again, Brynn sighed and gave in. "Busy now."

"Me too." *Iain*. "And yet, I can't stop thinking about the way you swallowed my cock. It was the highlight of my day."

Brynn was speechless for a second. "I thought you were my sister."

"Has a cock, does she? Which sister? I don't want to make a gaffe."

"I don't want to talk about this afternoon. It was very"—Brynn stopped and licked her dry lips—"irregular of me."

"Irregular. There's a word. Not a good one, though."

Why didn't Brynn ever have a witty comeback ready? "Was there something you wanted?" She winced at her choice of words.

"I thought we'd already settled that, love. Also, I rang to make sure you got to work safely and to take you to task for not letting me kiss you good-bye. Bad form, that."

"Yeah, well, none of us are perfect."

"Some of us come close," he said.

"Really? You think *you're* close to perfect?" The arrogance of this man was astounding.

"Not me, love. You."

Brynn's breath caught in her throat. "That's not true. I've got a ton of faults."

"It is true. I already told you, I say what I mean. You're as close to perfection as I'll ever get, Brynn Campbell. Now, should I pick you up at the office or at your home?"

Brynn was still reeling from the compliment, too shocked to say anything.

Iain filled the conversational void. "You said to woo you. Win you. I plan on doing just that, starting tonight."

Brynn pressed her hand to her warm neck. "What did you have in mind?"

"None of your business, nosy parker. By the way, I called a meeting tomorrow with Marc and Ames. To discuss our morale situation."

Compliments? Compliance with her suggestions? A plan to woo her? Brynn couldn't process any of it. "Who are you? The Iain I left two hours ago was fighting me every step of the way."

"You'll have to see for yourself. I'll pick you up at

seven, yeah? At your office. And, Brynn, my darling, lovely girl, if you're not there, I'll be quite cross."

"I've never seen you anything but cross."

"Not true. I wasn't cross in the car this afternoon. Seven. Be there."

Brynn could keep fighting it, this heat between them, but it was a losing game. She was hooked. "Yes. I'll be here."

When she hung up, Brynn crossed her arms behind her head and grinned. Somehow, she'd become smit by a Brit. She'd probably end up a brokenhearted basket case, but for right now, this minute, Brynn had never felt more alive.

After half an hour of daydreaming, reliving each kiss Iain had given her and her display in the car, Brynn finally roused herself and got back to work, plowing steadily through her list. She called clients, checked copy for a newsletter, and sent Brandon's email. She was just about to proof a new online ad when her office door opened.

Cassandra stole inside and leaned against it. "What's going on? Why aren't you speaking to me?"

Should she confront Cass about the business? No, Brynn needed more preparation for that conversation.

"Just talk to me again, Brynn. Please. You're angry that I sent you back to Blue Moon, aren't you?" Cass appeared paler than normal, and the orange lipstick clashed with her coloring.

Brynn spun in her chair and faced her boss. She understood why Cass was so anxious to get her hands on Iain's money, but Brynn hated being played. She'd have to broach the subject eventually, but it didn't have to be today. "I'm just really busy, Cass. Since I'm now working as an educator, I'm having a hard time playing catch up."

Cass took two steps into the room. Any farther and she'd plow her face into the far wall. "How did today go? How was Mr. Chapman? What's he like, anyway? He sounds very brusque on the phone."

"That's one way to describe him."

"I had to take Nef back to the vet during my lunch break. She's on medication, but she's not any better. And Michael called to officially break things off—as if I don't check his social media at least ten times a day. He's coming by the house to pick up his stuff." Cass crossed her arms as her face crumpled in a mask of despair. "I put up with so much of his shit—the sexual dysfunction, his mother issues…I even got Nef declawed for him. But he never bought me a ring, did he?" Large tears filled her eyes. "My life is a steaming pile, Brynn. I'm so lucky to have you. You're a really good friend."

No, she wasn't. Brynn had been an unwilling sidekick in Cass's life drama. While she felt sympathy for her boss, Brynn just wanted to get back to work. All of these personal revelations were too much. She straightened her shoulders. Time to find that backbone and say something, once and for all. "Cass, I'm really sorry about Michael, but—"

"I know, I know. I deserve better. But I'm forty-two, Brynn. When is my Prince Charming going to show up?" Then the tears started falling.

When Brynn stood and held out her arms, Cassandra moved into them and rested her head on Brynn's shoulder. Now wasn't the time to be assertive. Not when Cass had been kicked in the proverbial balls.

Brynn patted her shoulder. "You're a wonderful person. Very loving." Cass was loving to her cat, and that counted, right?

"All…I…have"—Cass was crying so hard that her words fell out in short bursts—"is this…business… and Nef, who pisses…everywhere. What happened… to my life?"

She cried until Brynn's shoulder was damp, then the sobs finally tapered off. When Cassandra pulled away, she wiped at her red nose. "We're just alike, you and I. Two single girls making our way in Vegas. All alone in the world. No man in sight."

"Um, okay." That hit a little too close to home for Brynn. She didn't have much of a life, hadn't dated since college. Brynn worked late every night and most weekends. She suddenly realized her world was very small. And very depressing.

"What do you say we get shitfaced after work and trash-talk my ex?" Cass said. "My treat."

Brynn couldn't think of a worse way to spend an evening. For once, she was going to be selfish and do what was right for her. She wasn't about to break her date with Iain. And she sure as hell didn't want to watch her boss get wasted on tequila shots or listen to any more sex stories. "That sounds nice, but unfortunately I have plans. You understand."

Cass looked ready to argue for a moment.

"Plus," Brynn added, "I have all this work to do. Unless you want to help, because that would be great. I could offload six or seven of these projects."

Dabbing at her eyes, Cass shook her head. "No that's okay. I'm feeling better." She glanced around. "I'll leave you to carry on." Without waiting for an answer, Cassandra walked through the door and left Brynn standing in the middle of her tiny office.

Typical Cass. She claimed to have dedicated her life to this business, but it all fell on Brynn's shoulders. Well not tonight. Tonight, Brynnie was going to have hot sex with Iain Chapman.

Iain showed up at Brynn's office twenty minutes early. It wasn't as if he didn't have work to do. Or emails to answer. Or phone calls to return. But he didn't want to do any of those things. Instead, he sat in the back of the car and rolled the dice in his palm. Back and forth, they made a dull clack as he shifted them with his fingers.

It took all of his willpower not to get out of the car, slam into that building, and find Brynn. Iain wanted to see her. Now.

But that would have been the act of a desperate man.

Growing up, desperation had been his constant companion. It clawed at his insides and left him hollowed out, empty, with nothing to fill the void but anger. It would have consumed him entirely if it hadn't been for Davy's parents. They were so wonderfully normal. They'd provided a safe haven for Iain more times than he could count.

When Iain was a very young lad, he had been scared to death of his father. Never one for steady work, James Chapman had spent his days at the pub, pissing away what little money he had. When he'd staggered home in the wee hours, he'd been full of ale and impotent rage. By the time Iain was ten, he'd spent enough time around Davy's father to know how a man should act. One night, instead of pulling the covers over his head to drown out the sound of his father's screaming and his mum's tears, Iain shot out of bed and ran to the kitchen. He still remembered the scene as if it were yesterday—his father, hand raised, holding his mum up by the throat. She was pleading with him, begging him not to hit her. Without thinking, Iain pushed her out of the way and tackled the old man to the floor. His scrawny body was no match for the bastard.

Iain took a walloping that night, had a black eye and a bruised jaw, but he wasn't afraid anymore. He knew exactly who his dad was—a weak little cunt who wasn't smart enough or brave enough to go after what he wanted. Iain was smart—even his harassed teachers told him so. And he was ambitious, determined to be different from his father in every way.

He'd decided from that moment that he'd become a man in charge of his life. He wouldn't wait for things to happen. Iain would make them happen.

But he also knew what boundaries were. He ignored them when it suited him, but sometimes, they were important. So while he wanted to see Brynn, he could wait twenty fucking minutes for her to come out of the building. Though he was entranced with her, he wouldn't resort to desperate measures.

When his phone rang, it jarred Iain out of his memories. He didn't spend a lot of time thinking about his youth. Tried not to think about it at all, truth be told.

He glanced at his screen. Brynn. Iain wasn't sure why

Brynn Campbell ticked all of his boxes. Maybe it was her sweetness or her concern for others—or it could be that when she kissed him, it made Iain's blood sizzle in his veins. She wasn't even aware that she had an advantage over him. Probably for the best, that.

He hit the talk button. "You're not thinking of canceling, are you, love?"

"No." Her voice was light, teasing. "Text when you're here and I'll come out."

"I just pulled up. I'll meet you at the front door." Iain kept himself from leaping out of the car. He hadn't been this eager and excited about a woman in…ever.

Calmly, he walked toward the front door of the aging office building. Security in this place was nil. As he entered, he noted the lobby could have used a refresh about fifteen years ago.

Iain tucked the dice away and leaned against the wall. He flicked his finger along the peeling seam in the wallpaper. Brynn's boss, Cassandra Delany, was seriously behind in her rent. He knew for certain this place didn't cost much. Her personal creditors were hounding her as well. Not good news for Brynn and her friends. But he wouldn't think about that now. Tonight, he was all about wooing.

When the lift bell rang, Iain straightened. Brynn stepped off the carriage, and dear God, she was a sight. He was always struck anew by her loveliness, by the intelligence and honesty in her eyes. Brynn was one of those rare creatures who believed the world was a good place, full of good people. She was wrong, of course, but he appreciated her optimism.

She smiled shyly and advanced toward him. "Hey."

"Hey, yourself."

They simply stood there, like a couple of idiots, saying nothing but wearing big, wide grins. Finally, Iain took the heavy bag from her shoulder.

"What's in here? Gold bricks?"

"Work."

He said nothing. No reason to. The only thing Brynn would be working on tonight involved her orgasm. Poor Brynnie, she must have been frustrated as hell over the years. Iain was glad he could help her out. Provided a valuable service, he did.

He held the door open and followed her to the car. "How was the rest of your day?" he asked. Sliding into the backseat next to her, he dropped the bag on the floor and worked his way closer to Brynn.

"I have a question. Will the money from the Blue Moon account fix all of Cass's financial problems?"

He flicked her a glance. "Could do temporarily, if she handles it carefully. But she won't."

Brynn sighed and placed a hand on her stomach. "You must have had Cass checked out pretty thoroughly to know all about her finances. Do you conduct a background search on everyone you do business with?"

Iain suddenly felt as if he were treading on a frozen lake. One wrong step and he could wind up in frigid waters. "Occasionally. She sounds like a real character, your boss."

"She could definitely benefit from a life coach. And a business manager. And possibly a team of mental health professionals."

Iain felt a rush of relief. He'd successfully changed the subject. With two fingers, he stroked one of her long, brown waves, sorting through the strands. "What could you benefit from, Brynnie?"

She leaned her head back against the seat. "A weekend off."

Iain propped his forehead against her temple. "Then you should take one."

"Not likely. I need to work double time now." She pulled away to glance up at him. "I think I'm going to have to confront Cass."

"That's why you run, to avoid it." Not a question. Merely an observation.

"Ridiculous, right? You'd think after all the seminars I've taken, I'd be a pro at conflict resolution."

Iain wisely refrained from telling her what he thought of those seminars. Why start the night with an argument? He patted himself on the back for not being a dickhead.

"So how was your day?" she asked.

Not productive. He'd been too busy thinking about Brynn and their little tryst. "Fine. You are going to help me with this morale rubbi…idea, aren't you?"

"Of course." Brynn patted his leg. "And good catch. You almost said rubbish, but you stopped yourself. I applaud your restraint." When she eased herself against him, Iain's entire body relaxed. She felt good here, cradled against his arm. He continued to stroke the top of her head as she rested it against his shoulder.

"This is weird."

"What, love?"

"That I'm talking to you this way. I barely know you."

"You know enough. My grandparents barely knew each other. Met on a Monday and were hitched five days later."

She lifted her head. "Really? What were they like?"

With a gentle nudge, he eased her back toward him. "Never met them. Mum told me that story. She thought it terribly romantic."

"It is romantic."

Iain blew out a little laugh. "Granddad probably just wanted into her knickers and the only way to get there was through the vicar."

"That's a very cynical attitude."

"I'm a very cynical man, Brynn," he whispered against her hair. It smelled good, fresh and delicious. Just like the rest of her.

"I don't believe that. I think underneath that shell of sarcasm beats the heart of an optimist."

Brynn was all fluffy clouds and good intentions. Bless her. Iain's heart had been hardened by the time he could walk, but he wasn't about to dissuade her. If she wanted to think the best of him, well and good.

The car drove along the Strip. As the sun became a low orange ball in the distance, it colored the sky with streaks of purple and pink. Neon lights and moving billboards became brighter, beckoning tourists.

"Where are we going anyway?" she asked.

"I'm taking you to bed."

Chapter 12

Her body tensed against him. "I thought you said we were going to dinner."

"We're having dinner at mine." When her shoulders stiffened slightly, he added, "Brynn, you don't have to do anything you don't want to do."

"That's the problem." Her voice was so low, he had to strain to hear it. "I want to do everything."

"Why is that a problem, pet? We're two consenting adults."

"I'm just a little nervous about, you know, if it will happen again. It may not, Iain. Last night might have been the first and last time I have an orgasm with you. Just promise me, no heroic measures."

"I have no bloody clue what that means, but I think I know what will help you. Been putting my massive mind to it most of the afternoon."

"What?"

"Not telling, am I? I'm going to leave you hanging in suspense."

Looking away from him, Brynn remained silent, but Iain smiled. Now her brain was working overtime.

The car stopped at his apartment building along the Boulevard. Iain had bought the place as an investment during the bust a few years back. Now it was worth twice what he'd paid for it.

Upon exiting the backseat, Iain scooped up her

workbag—the one she wouldn't be opening tonight—and helped her out. Brynn tilted her head back and gazed up.

"Let me guess, top floor?"

"Of course." He guided her in, past the concierge, and through the lobby. Whipping out his key card, Iain waited at the lift and watched her in the polished doors. She was nervous, his Brynn. With her teeth, she worried her upper lip and sucked on it. Her apprehension was thick and tinged with sexual curiosity. He could feel it dancing around her as she shifted from one foot to the other. Occasionally her gaze washed over him. She was worried about wanting him, about his plans. She needn't have been. Iain had nothing but her pleasure in mind.

They stepped into the lift and rode upward in silence. Occasionally other occupants came and went. Iain recognized a few faces, nodded, but said nothing.

By the time they reached their destination, Brynn's eyes had grown huge and her arms were tightly crossed over her chest.

When Iain stepped out, Brynn didn't move.

He glanced back at her. "It's going to be all right, yeah?" Slinging her bag onto his shoulder, he held out his hand.

Brynn looked at it with suspicion, but slowly, she dropped her arms. Then taking one step forward, she reached out. Another step and her fingers brushed his. When she placed her cold palm on top of his hand, Iain felt a little victorious. It was a small step, but an important one. He needed her to trust him. *You haven't earned her trust, mate*. Iain had met her under dubious circumstances, but he would strive to win her, be worthy of her. She deserved that and more.

He unlocked his door, letting Brynn enter first. Stopping at the alarm, he punched in his code as Brynn wandered into the formal sitting room.

Turning in a circle, her sharp eyes took in the hardwood floor, the ivory walls, the gray-toned artwork. "Why did you come here, anyway?"

He strode forward. "Describe *here*. This apartment? Vegas? America?"

She lowered her eyes from the modern, chrome chandelier down to his face. "Yes."

"This apartment was an investment. Vegas is a city that thrives on money, not your background or your lineage—only money. And America—it's the land of opportunity, yeah?" That wasn't all of it, of course. Davy was the reason Iain and Marc had come to Vegas, but he didn't want to talk about that. In fact, he didn't want to talk at all.

As he walked toward her, Brynn stumbled backward. "What about your family?"

Iain froze for a moment. "What about them?"

"Don't they miss you?"

He stalked forward once more. "Doubtful." Now wasn't the time to talk about his deceased parents, either.

"But—"

"Let me show you the place." He curved an arm around her waist and led her into the dining room. The view was spectacular. High above the Boulevard, lights blazed in the night sky.

Brynn glanced around the room. "Very modern."

"Mmm."

She eyed the dining room table, a long stretch of teakwood and glass, which he'd never used. "Do you host large dinner parties?"

He peered down at her. "Never. You don't like it?"

Brynn's tongue flicked out, moistening her lips. "It's very chic."

"And that's a bad thing?"

Spinning out of his embrace, she glanced up at him. "Your office is traditional—Chesterfield sofas and Chippendale chairs. But this place is the exact opposite. So which one is you?"

He shrugged. "Neither. Both. Does it matter?"

"I'm just trying to figure you out."

"You're not going to do it by examining my furniture, love."

Brynn's eyes drifted over his face. "So how do I get to know the real you?"

He stepped forward, settling his hands on her hips. "I'll leave that to you to figure out." Lowering his head, he dropped a soft kiss on her lips.

Bringing her hands to his face, she cradled his cheeks and kissed him back.

Lust, hot and strong, flooded his system. He longed to throw her over his shoulder and drag her off to his bed. His ache for her had been constant since she'd left him standing on the sidewalk that afternoon. He'd been consumed with thoughts of her all day. Yet when her tongue darted out and brushed the tip of his, he held himself back and kissed her tenderly. Iain needed to draw this moment out, make it last. This was their first real time together, so he couldn't rush it, even though his cock told him otherwise. Brynn Campbell was a wonder he wanted to explore. She made him feel things he'd never thought possible. Affection and desire became intertwined. Though he hadn't known her long, what he felt for Brynn went deep. He'd never experienced this before, and if Iain were being honest, it alarmed him. Brynn had him wrapped around her finger.

When she pulled away, Iain's heart pounded against his rib cage. "Brynn."

"Show me the kitchen?"

The bloody kitchen? "Sure you don't want to see the bedroom?"

"Eventually."

Removing his hands from her, he took two paces backward. She was killing him. Slowly. Torturously. But for now, he'd let her continue to take the lead. She needed to relax a bit and get comfortable.

Iain pivoted and walked past a smaller sitting room and on to the kitchen. He flipped the switch and the space flooded with light. Silver pendant fixtures reflected off the black quartz countertop.

Brynn stepped in behind him. "Wow. You've got top-of-the-line everything. Do you ever cook?"

"No." He crossed to the refrigerator and opened it. "Are you hungry? I had the food delivered an hour ago." But Brynn stood in the doorway on the tips of her toes, as if poised for flight.

"Brynnie," he said softly.

That seemed to calm her. She lowered her heels to the floor and took a deep breath. "I'm really nervous."

"You had me fooled. Look as cool as a cucumber, you do."

That brought a smile to her lips. "Do you at least have

dishes?" She crossed the threshold. Her sandaled feet made soft clicks across the tiled floor.

"Have a look around. I know you're dying to."

"I kind of am. That's a Viking stove, dude." She crossed to it and trailed her fingers along the top of it, over the burners, and across the control buttons.

Iain shrugged out of his jacket and tossed it on the counter. "I assume that's a good thing."

"If you cook, it is." She opened the cabinets.

He had the odd pan or two. Amelia had set it up for him, told him if the apocalypse ever came, he'd be up shit creek because he couldn't boil water.

Brynn moved on, opening each sleek black door to see what he was hiding. "How do you live? You have no food, two pans, and"—she opened a drawer—"flatware for four."

Iain pointed behind him. "I have a coffeemaker. And if you pay enough, even the best restaurants deliver. Besides, I'm rarely home."

"A workaholic, huh?"

He quirked a brow. "I prefer driven. Working hard is not a disease."

"So what do you do when you're not working?" Brynn hopped up on the island and swung her legs back and forth. The orange-colored skirt was so long, he could only manage to get a glimpse of her toes—varnished peach today.

Standing in front of her, Iain grasped her ankles and slid his hands under the soft, flowing cotton, up her bare calves. "I watch football, but you knew that."

"Soccer?"

"Football."

He gently parted her legs and stepped between the draped fabric. Brynn looked into his eyes and placed her hands on his chest. "Americans play football."

"Americans play bastardized rugby." Keeping one hand on her leg, he used the other to cup her jaw and, with his thumb, traced the line of her wide, lush lips. They parted, so he teased the tip of it inside her mouth, scraping the pad of his thumb across her bottom teeth. Her pupils grew wide as she clutched at his shoulders. While her pulse fluttered at the side of her neck, Brynn's eyes darkened, and her breathing grew rapid. Nervous or not, she wanted him. That Iain could produce this kind of reaction was positively intoxicating. *He* gave Brynn pleasure. No one else ever had. And if he had his way, no one else ever would.

He eased his hand from her mouth and caressed the silky skin of Brynn's jawline. Although square, it was delicate and feminine, just like the rest of her. He traced the line of her throat, so graceful, so supple. Brynn Campbell captivated him completely. Everything about her, from her voice to her tanned, petite body, to her long fingers fisting his Italian wool waistcoat—it all appealed. No, more than that. Brynn brought him to his knees. Humbled him. Dazzled him. He craved her in a way he didn't begin to comprehend.

Iain continued to glide his hand downward and flattened his palm over her chest. He cupped her breast, giving it a light squeeze. Then tugging her leg with his other hand, he pulled her closer to the edge of the counter, closer to him.

Eyes drifting shut, Brynn wrapped her legs around

his waist, anchoring her feet behind his back. His cock throbbed, and he pressed it against the juncture of her legs.

"Open your eyes."

Brynn obeyed him instantly and blinked twice before meeting his gaze.

"You want this."

The heightened desire in her navy eyes had him spellbound. "Yes, I want this, Iain."

"You *need* me to fuck you."

She answered with a dip of her chin.

Taking his time, Iain lowered his head and kissed her. Her lips were lush, yielding beneath his own. He groaned as her hands started roaming over his chest. Then Brynn grabbed onto his arms, digging her short nails into him. He gloried in it. Brynn Campbell may have been timid on the outside, but underneath all the flowing garments and bashful ways was a woman of passion. He could feel it, restrained and caged, ready to be set free again. He wanted to do that for her.

As he stroked his hand along her back, Iain thrust his tongue against hers. When Brynn boldly met it with her own, it surprised him. Encouraged him. He kissed her harder, and Brynn kissed him back. Iain moved his hand to her breast again. This time when he squeezed, he used a little more force, eliciting a moan from her. That felt like a bleeding triumph, it did.

He ran his thumbnail over her nipple, and she pulled back slightly. He opened his eyes, noted that hers were still closed.

"Iain." She murmured his name like a plea.

That was all he needed to hear. In a swift move, he

removed her hands from his shoulders and worked his fingers beneath the filmy blouse. Tugging it over her head, he nearly ripped it off in his haste to get her naked. With a flick of his fingers, he had her bra unsnapped before whipping the straps down her shoulders.

When he stepped back, Brynn brought her hands up to cover herself, keeping the ivory lace in place. "No hiding," he said. Without pause, she dropped her hands and the cups fell from her upturned breasts.

She was stunning. With careful movements, he peeled it off her, past her elbows, down to her wrists, and over her braided, colorful bracelets. Then Iain let the bra fall to the floor.

"You're a beauty, you are." He placed her hands back on his shoulders as he took her in. Those meringue-pink tits made his mouth water. Iain licked his lips, hungry for another taste.

"Thank you." Uneven red streaks colored her neck.

"Look at me, pet." She swallowed but kept her eyes on his Adam's apple. "I ache for you, Brynnie."

With her chin tilted upward, she bit her lip and slowly lifted her gaze. Taking a shaky breath, she looked him in the eye. "Me too."

"Unbutton my waistcoat."

Brynn twisted her wrists from his grip and began to fumble with the buttons. He didn't help her, even though impatience had him clenching his hands.

She slid the garment over his shoulders, and Iain shook his arms a bit until it hit the floor. She reached for his black tie with a look of utter concentration and started loosening the knot. This was taking for-bloody-ever.

"Brynnie."

Her hands stalled and she gazed up at him. "What? Am I doing something wrong?"

Iain's heart thawed a little more upon hearing those words, the uncertainty behind them. He sought to reassure her by grasping her hand. "You're brilliant, love. Just terribly, painstakingly slow."

A knowing smile graced her lips. "Oh, you want me to hurry."

He kissed her hand. "Yes. Just tear the bloody rags off me."

Rather than hasten her actions, she took her own sweet time, exaggerating her movements. Brynn shot him a teasing glance as she worked each button from its hole.

"Now you're just being cruel."

Bending her head, she placed a kiss in the center of his chest. "I'm heightening your anticipation."

"You're making me mental." And yet, her strategy was working. Iain was fired up, raring to go. Need bit at him, slicing through him until he was almost shaking with it. He'd never wanted anything the way he wanted Brynn Campbell. Not money, not a business deal. Nothing compared to her.

Suppressing a restless sigh, he fixed his eyes on her breasts as she freed another button. She was only halfway done. Bloody hell. Still, he let her set the pace, though he did help her along by jerking his shirt free from his trousers. Finally, after she sprang the final button loose, she spread the edges of his shirt wide to reveal his chest.

"I think you're gorgeous," she whispered, her gaze roaming over him. That sweet compliment, shyly uttered, nearly sent him over the edge. Nearly. But Iain managed to hang on to his ragged self-control.

"Who are you, Brynn Campbell?" She'd enchanted him. Her giving nature, her kind heart, her tender ways—her sensuous body. She was far too good for the likes of him, but Iain was too much of a selfish bastard to walk away.

She peeked up at him through her long lashes. "I'm just a normal girl. Nothing special about me."

"You're a marvel. Everything about you is special."

Color filled her cheeks as she peeled the shirt over his shoulders and down his arms. Iain ripped at his cufflinks and shrugged it off.

For an instant, they were both motionless, staring at each other's bare torsos. And then, as if by some unspoken mutual agreement, they lunged for one another. Iain bumped his chin against her forehead, and Brynn smacked her nose on his sternum.

She laughed then. Dear God, he'd never heard a more beautiful sound. He grinned back at her. "Shall we try it again?"

"Can I go first?"

"Yes."

She stretched her hand out but didn't touch him right away. Instead, she looked at him as if she were trying to memorize every square inch of skin.

If she didn't make a move soon, he'd lose what little patience he had left. "Brynnie."

She gazed up at him. "My family calls me that."

He hadn't known. The report he received didn't contain nicknames or a childhood pet or her favorite color. "If you don't like it—"

She shook her head and a wayward curl danced against her cheek. "I do like it." Brynn placed her palms flat on his chest before squeezing his pecs.

God, yes. Finally, her hands were on him.

Brynn traced the curve of each muscle with her thumb and brushed her fingers over his nipples. He sucked in a breath. This was brutal, having her touch him like this and not touching her back. Still, he held himself in check. Letting her get used to him all over again. When she did, he'd take charge. They'd both enjoy that.

Brynn leaned forward and circled his nipple with the tip of her tongue. That felt like heaven. "Do that again." She did, and added a little bite for good measure.

Working her hands slowly downward, over his rib cage, she seemed particularly interested in his abs, and smoothed those nimble fingertips over each and every indentation. It felt amazing, made him harder than he'd thought possible. "I'd love you to sit for me," she said.

"Pardon?"

Brynn's hands wandered back up to his shoulders. "So I can draw you. I want to catch all the shadows and nuances of your body." *Nuances of his body*. That was the sexiest thing anyone had ever said to him.

"I'll be a willing model." He stopped her exploration by moving her hands to his hips. "Time's up. Now it's my turn."

He couldn't touch everything all at once, so he started with her enchanting face and brushed his finger across the arch of one eyebrow. She lowered her eyes once more. "Be brave," he whispered.

Lifting her head, her jaw tensed. "I'm not a brave person."

"Oh yes, you are. You're here with me, despite that voice in your head telling you to run. I've never met anyone like you."

She scanned his face then, probably searching to see if he was having her on.

He wasn't. "I don't lie, darling. I tell it like I see it."

"And what do you see in me?"

"Kindness. Goodness. A gentle heart."

"You don't value any of those things," she said.

He trailed a finger down her cheek, across her jawline. "I do when I see them in you, Brynn." With her pretty, upturned face and her bare chest, she was so vulnerable right then. Insecurity shone in her eyes. "I'm not playing with you, pet."

His expression was serious, his tone sincere. That teasing dimple was nowhere to be found. For some reason, Iain Chapman wanted her. From the moment they'd met, the attraction between them had been combustible. *Inevitable*.

Brynn had never felt this close to a man, had never let herself be this open and trusting. But she felt a connection with Iain. It was crazy. Beyond explanation. Everything about him was intimidating, and yet he stood there between her legs, stroking her face, telling her she was a marvel.

Keeping his eyes trained on hers, his warm hands caressed her cheeks, her jaw, down the sides of her neck, sending little tingles in his wake. The heat under her skin shot upward and she could feel the splotches and silently cursed them. Iain didn't seem to care. He wasn't looking at her splotches. He wasn't even staring at her tits now. He just kept eye contact as his hands moved lower, over her shoulders. Then, with breathtakingly light movements, he skimmed his fingers over her breasts.

Brynn had always been self-conscious about pretty much everything, but especially her breasts. But Iain called them perfect. He had a way of speaking so bluntly that she believed him.

He cupped each one in his hands. Then lifting them, he didn't pinch her nipples but rather squeezed her areolas. At first he was gentle, almost too gentle, but he gradually increased the pressure, causing a delicious ache.

Finally, Iain lowered his eyes and stared down at her chest. "You like that."

She nodded. Her breaths were becoming more rapid, her heart raced faster. "Yes," she whispered. She'd screwed her eyes shut. Every tug on Brynn's breast sent a corresponding pull straight to her clit. She was damp and needy. But it was more than that. She felt almost cherished when Iain touched her. What was it about this brash, hard man? Somehow, in spite of barely knowing him, she was starting to trust him—with her body, if not her heart.

When Iain took one breast completely in his mouth, her eyes popped open. He sucked and licked at the same time, knowing just the right amount of pressure to exert. Brynn basked in the contrasting sensations—his teeth gently biting her nipple while his rough stubble scratched along her rib cage. She ground her hips downward and squirmed in an effort to find some relief. "Iain."

His mouth eased off, and he gave her a last lick before raising his head. Brynn gazed down at her breast. A wet swath glistened on her puckered nipple. When Iain softly blew on it, Brynn shivered.

Then he pulled away and lifted his head. "Lie back, Brynn."

Dazed and desperate to ease the hot bolts of desire shooting through her, Brynn unhooked her feet from his waist and lowered herself to the counter. But the granite was cold, causing Brynn to arch her back, thrusting her breasts upward.

Iain slid one finger between them. "I can see the outline of your bathing suit. You like the sun."

"I have a pool," she panted.

"Have you had sex in it?" His voice had grown hoarse. The dark brown flecks in his eyes became more pronounced as he touched her, tracing along her tan line.

"No, never."

"We'll have to change that."

Brynn gasped in surprise when Iain grabbed handfuls of her skirt, jerking it downward. Brynn automatically lifted her hips so that Iain could tear it off. Once he did, he raised her knees, then placed her feet on the edge of the counter.

The only thing that stood between them was a wisp of silky panties. For a long, heated moment, Iain simply stared at her. As he did, all of her old doubts and fears rose to the surface. What if he couldn't make her come? What if last night had been a one-off, never to repeat itself?

Iain stroked her thighs. "What's wrong?"

"Nothing."

He shook his head. "Now, love, I know that's not true. You're worried about the orgasm bit, aren't you?"

Brynn rubbed her lips together. "I'm fine. Please continue."

He laughed at that. "I do love when you get all polite and demure." He slipped one finger over the elastic waistband of her panties. "But we're past that."

Then he ran his hand over her inner thighs, down to her calves. With a light touch, he caressed her ankles, then reversed his path until his thumbs rubbed the curve where her ass met her legs. But his gaze remained on her, giving Brynn a thread of calm. "Do you know what your problem is? You think too much."

"Says the man whose brain never stops working." The words came out in choppy gasps, as if she'd been sprinting.

"Sometimes, my mind dims a bit while my cock takes over. You're the one who blathers on about feelings, but when it comes to this"—one of his thumbs slipped beneath the elastic and skimmed over her slit—"your brain kicks into overdrive, yeah?"

"Yes." Closing her eyes, Brynn tried to relax. When he circled her clit, she nearly leaped off the counter. "That...that's really good."

Instead of continuing, Iain's thumb stopped working its magic as he removed it from her panties. Then he clamped his hands over her thighs.

"What?" she asked. "Why'd you stop?"

"From this moment forward, we're doing it my way." His accent was stronger now. His brusque tone sent a sharp thrill zipping through her. This was the part she liked the best, when he got bossy. A steel hand in a velvet glove.

Not knowing what Iain had in mind should have scared the hell out of her, but hearing him take charge had the opposite effect. "Yes."

She'd barely gotten the word out before he straightened, took her hand to help her sit, then scooped her off the counter. With his arm beneath her legs, the other wrapped around her back, Iain nuzzled her neck as he tromped through the living room and down the hall. His shoes echoed off the wooden floor with each step.

He walked so fast, Brynn felt a little dizzy as he took her into a dark bedroom. She was disoriented, couldn't see a thing except for the silhouette of Iain's face. He lowered her to the bed with great care, placing her on silky bedding that felt cool against her skin. He stood and moved away. She missed his body heat.

With a click, Iain turned on the bedside lamp. Brynn got an impression of dark, sleek furniture and chrome accents, but she didn't focus on any of that. She was too busy watching Iain unbuckle his belt. His body was more than impressive. It made her weak just looking at him. She'd never been that interested in muscular men, but that was before Iain had held her in his strong arms. As she continued to observe him, those thick slabs of muscle in his chest and abs bunched and contracted—beautiful, fluid movement.

While Brynn enjoyed the view, Iain watched her. "Lie down."

That pulled her out of her daze. She didn't know what he was planning, and anxiety fluttered in her belly once more. She sat up, pulling her knees to her chest. "Wait." Brynn needed some ground rules before they started. "I'm not sure how far I want to go with this. Maybe we should decide on a safe word." The thought of nipple clamps and paddles nearly made her break out in a nervous sweat. Light spankings, harsh commands—all good. Anything more would be too much. But what if Iain needed more?

His face softened, and he moved to the bed. Reaching out, he ran a hand through her hair. "We decided this afternoon, yeah? We're not hard-core. You don't need a safe word, love. Tell me to stop if you don't like what we're doing. Just make sure you mean it. Now lie down."

She took a deep breath. With his reassurance, the anxiety was replaced by a thrill of excitement, a rush of adrenaline. This time, without hesitating, Brynn did as he commanded. The tension weaving its way through her belly ratcheted up when Iain tugged on his leather belt. It slid around his waist, breaking free of each loop. He was going to use that belt on her. She knew it, could feel the purpose in his deliberate movements.

Was he going to tie her up? Turn her over and spank her ass? Brynn had no clue. Usually, the unknown was something to fear. Familiar tendrils of panic would wind their way around her chest. That little voice would whisper, *You can still make a run for it*. That had always been her MO—to run, to hide, to hover in the corner and stay invisible. Not this time. Brynn couldn't wait to see what Iain had planned. For once, she wasn't scared. She was titillated, breathlessly anticipating what he'd do next.

Iain had been wreaking havoc on her nerves all day. She'd been on the edge of arousal since he'd instructed her to touch herself. Damp and hot and empty. After what they'd done and how her body had responded, she could only imagine how amazing it would feel once Iain was finally inside her.

So because of all that, running wasn't even an option. Instead, she stayed put and did the opposite. Bending her legs in a seductive pose, she thrust her breasts upward. Her tits drew Iain's attention, and his face grew tight with lust. Brynn felt sexy and beguiling. It was intoxicating.

After kicking off his shoes and toeing off his socks, Iain unbuttoned his trousers, letting them fall in a puddle at his feet, but he kept the black leather belt tight in his fist. When he removed the silk boxers, she got another view of that hard, long dick. Had it only been this afternoon when she'd sucked it and taken it deep in her mouth? Brynn bit her lip. She wanted to taste him again. In fact, she wanted to sample all of him. Because the rest of Iain's body was every bit as compelling as his cock. His biceps were large. His thighs were well defined, too. Smooth skin, steely ropes of muscle, a delectable cock. In a word: lickable.

"Brynn." His voice was low, almost a growl. "You keep looking at me like that, love, and it'll be over too soon."

Yeah, his accent was definitely thicker now. More evidence of his arousal. As if the eight inches staring her right in the face weren't enough.

He took a step closer to the bed. "Stretch your arms above your head. I'm going to tie you up."

Chapter 13

Brynn's heart stuttered as she waited, struggling to breathe normally. This was what she'd always yearned for. To surrender completely to a man's will while still feeling safe. Protected. But not just any man. Only Iain.

As he looped the belt around her wrists and wrapped it tight, his cock was right there, next to her lips. Brynn needed another taste. With the tip of her tongue, she licked across the broad head, dipping into the crevice.

Iain drew an audible breath. "I didn't give you permission to do that, pet." He took a half step back, just out of reach.

Nibbling her upper lip, she tilted her head, staring up into that beautiful face. "I wanted to taste you again."

"Then ask for it."

For once, Brynn didn't feel embarrassed or shy. Even though she was submitting, she wasn't powerless in this situation. Just the opposite. "Can I *please* suck your cock, Iain?"

He held himself still as his hands ceased their movements. Then the belt slackened around her wrists. "Open your mouth wider."

He was permitting this, and he could take it away at any time. Her pussy pulsated almost to the point of pain. Her stomach muscles quivered as his gaze burned over her, so hot it was almost tangible. He may have been in control, but he wanted it as much as she did.

That afternoon's interlude in the car had been the most exciting thing that had ever happened to Brynn, but this…this was even better. She was about to have sex with Iain Chapman, and that was nothing short of miraculous.

She opened as wide as she could, and Iain gave a shallow thrust of his hips, guiding his cock between her eager lips. While he wasn't exactly gentle, he didn't shove himself down her throat either.

Instead, Iain cradled the back of her head and leisurely fucked her mouth. As he slid in and out, Brynn slicked her tongue over the head every time he moved forward. Closing her eyes, she relaxed her throat, willed him to go deeper, but he remained steady. Brynn could get addicted to this—tasting Iain, sucking him dry.

When she moaned, he jerked free from her. She opened her eyes and glanced up at him.

"Enough of that, Brynnie." He bent over her and readjusted the belt, wrapping it around her wrists before cinching it. His torso blocked out the bedside lamp. With his body cocooned around her, Brynn took a deep whiff of his chest. His arousal mixed with the heady aroma of his cologne. She wanted to wrap herself in that smell.

Before he straightened, Brynn swiped her tongue over his flat nipple. She gasped in surprise when he took a fistful of her hair and gave it a small tug. "Enough."

Experimentally, she tried to pry her wrists apart, but they were tightly bound together, restricting her movement.

Iain used her hair as leverage and forced her head

back. His eyes were dark in the muted light. "Trust me, love."

The words calmed her and Brynn's heart found its rhythm again.

"I'll be right back." He walked across the room to what she assumed was a closet. When he reemerged, he carried a blue-and-white striped tie in his hands. "I'm going to blindfold you."

Brynn didn't know what to think. Yes, she'd played these scenarios out in her fantasies, but this was the real deal.

"If you tell me to stop, I will," he reminded her.

"Okay." She lifted her head from the pillow and Iain placed the silk tie over her eyes and secured it behind her. Brynn flopped her head down and tried to adjust to the darkness. Her ears were now attuned to new noises—the click of the air-conditioning, Iain's quiet movements.

When he lowered himself to the bed, Brynn's breath became trapped in her throat. She flinched when Iain stroked his hand across her cheek, touched the corner of her lip, tapped his fingers over the hollow of her throat. Brynn swallowed that breath as his hand dipped lower—over her chest until finally, he cupped her breast.

"Stop," she blurted out.

True to his word, Iain lifted his hand so that he no longer touched her. But she could feel it hovering. Still. Waiting. Heat radiated off his palm and leeched into her skin.

When Brynn inhaled, her nipple grazed Iain's hand, but he didn't move. Not being able to see his expression or anticipate his reaction—it was both maddening and tantalizing at the same time.

Brynn took another deep breath. Again, her nipple brushed his skin and hardened on contact, yet Iain remained immobile. For a third time, she pulled air into her lungs and held it. When she let it out, bit by bit, her breast tightened and became heavy, tingling with sensation as it dragged against him.

Brynn craved his touch. She needed to feel it again. "Go."

As soon as the word left her mouth, Iain lowered his hand and captured her nipple, rolling it between his thumb and forefinger. "Who's in control, Brynn?"

Just hearing him say the words made her pussy clench. "You're in total control."

While toying with her breast, Iain leaned down and kissed her. Hard. His gentleness from earlier had dissipated, along with his patience. He wasn't holding back now. His mouth was bruising, letting her know just exactly how close to the edge he was.

And Brynn liked it. She started to kiss him back, but he pulled away. Brynn opened her mouth to protest, to chide him for being a tease, when Iain crawled farther onto the bed and settled between her legs.

He slipped his fingers into the waistband of her panties. "Lift your bum."

She hoisted her hips upward and Iain dragged the material down her ass, over her legs. Wrapping his hand around an ankle, he slid the silk off one foot, then the other. Now Brynn was completely naked. Constrained by Iain's belt, her hands were useless. Blindfolded, she was at his mercy. Brynn had never been more vulnerable. She'd never been so aroused.

Iain placed his hands on her knees and parted them. Prying her legs open, he rubbed his stubble against her inner thigh. "Look how pretty your pussy is. Plump and pink. So very lovely." He let go of one knee and using his fingers, spread her outer lips. "And wet."

Brynn felt so light-headed, she was afraid she might pass out and miss all the good parts.

"What do you think, Brynn, should I lick you or finger you again?"

"Um, both?"

"Greedy girl." Then he slid two fingers inside of her.

Brynn moaned as he pumped them in and out. With a torque of her hips, she met his next thrust, but as soon as she did, Iain withdrew his fingers.

"No moving, love. These are my rules."

Panting, Brynn tried to remain still, but she felt empty without him—empty and aching. Still, she clung to silence, obeying him.

After a long minute, he said, "You're going to hold still now."

Brynn clenched her hands into fists. "Yes."

"Good."

He flicked her clit and Brynn fought a squirm. She bit her lower lip and willed herself to remain motionless.

Then, instead of continuing where he'd left off, he grasped her waist and glided his hands up to her breasts, gently squeezing the undersides, leaving her starved-for-affection nipples alone. He continued to torture her. *Squeeze, then ease off*. He did it over and over. It was exasperating, and Brynn bit her bottom lip to keep from crying out.

Then, finally, Iain moved his hands up and pinched her nipples, pulling them, rolling them between his fingers.

Brynn let out a long moan. Yes, this was what she needed.

"You like that. Now, thank me nicely, Brynn."

"Thank you, Iain." The words were torn from her. She couldn't take an even breath. She was a quivering mass of desire.

Lowering his head, he lapped his tongue over one swollen nipple, replacing his fingers with his mouth. That was good. So freaking good. Every time he licked at her breast, her clit throbbed. It was swollen too. Achy and heavy, her pussy begged for mercy.

Brynn fought against the tidal wave of desire coursing through her. Her sensory nerves were on overload. Her skin felt too tight, too sensitive. She couldn't see a thing. Iain had instructed her not to move. Frustration filled every part of her.

She wanted to come again. Wanted his hand on her mound, his fingers buried deep inside of her. And it dawned on Brynn that he was in charge of her orgasm. Whether he penetrated her. Whether he left her like this—pent up, in sexual distress. But he wouldn't, and that's why she trusted him. All Brynn had to do was enjoy it.

In that moment, she stopped pulling against the belt and relaxed. She focused on the pleasure, the feel of his teeth scraping over her nipple. She became more vocal too, groaning loudly each time he suckled.

Time had no meaning. Brynn was lost to the mind-blowing, skin-tingling sensations. She didn't know how long Iain worked her tits. Occasionally, he'd switch, covering the other one with his mouth. He'd move his hands over her ribs and dig his fingers into her hips. He wasn't in a hurry. And Brynn couldn't have moved him along if she tried—because he had the power right then, and she was his willing captive.

By the time Iain lifted his head, Brynn was past frustration. Her brain had shut off some time ago, and her body was ragged, exhausted, needy.

"You've got amazing tits, Brynn." Using his tongue, Iain licked his way down the middle of her chest, over her stomach, over her mons. Brynn cried out as he swirled that talented tongue around her clit.

Carefully, he parted Brynn's folds. "Beautiful," he muttered. His warm breath danced along Brynn's slit, slick with moisture. Even that felt exotic.

But Iain didn't lick her, as she expected. Grasping her inner labia between his thumb and forefinger, he worried it, then tugged on it, as he had her nipple. She'd never felt anything like it. Pure pleasure.

Another loud groan escaped her. "Iain." Each move of his fingers wound her tighter, higher. The storm from that afternoon grew inside her and gathered momentum. Brynn clenched her stomach muscles and tried really hard not to move, but she couldn't help an involuntary jerk of her hips.

Iain didn't chastise her. Or punish her. Instead, he rewarded her by lapping her clitoris, then pulling it between his lips. That combination of rubbing and sucking sent her over the edge.

Brynn's orgasm rocked her hard, from the top of her spine down to her toes. "Iain." No waves of pleasure this time—her entire body seized up as she came. It slammed into her all at once with a violent force that didn't stop, didn't subside. She tried to pull her hands apart as her muscles tightened, but the belt kept them in place.

It seemed to go on forever and Iain never let up, never

gave her a breather, but continued at a steady pace. Brynn curled her fingers inward, digging her short nails into her palms as she rode it out.

Finally, with her clit continuing to twitch against his tongue, her muscles relaxed. She tried to catch her breath, but she was spent, still high but floating downward.

Iain gave her one more lick and released her labia. "I made you come again, Brynn Campbell."

"At the risk of inflating your ego, that was amazeballs."

He stretched his body over hers, his dick thick and heavy against her hip. "That's possibly the oddest thing I've ever heard." He kissed her lightly, his tongue following the seam of her lips.

Then Iain moved off the bed. With her eyes still covered, Brynn was tempted to doze off. Sated, her legs became limp and she briefly bent her elbows to relieve the stiffness in her arms. Her heart finally returned to its normal rhythm.

Brynn heard a drawer open, heard the crinkle of a foil wrapper. "Wait."

He ceased moving.

"Can I watch you?" Brynn had that dopey, giddy feeling, like she'd slammed one shot too many.

"Watch me do what, love?"

"Touch yourself."

"Don't know if I can hold out if I do that." He placed his hands on her face, then slipped the tie over her head.

Brynn blinked against the light and squinted her eyes. With her wrists still tied, she lowered her arms and sat up. "But you're in control." She smiled as she said it.

"You're trying to do me in, aren't you?"

"Please, Iain?" She hadn't known she could pull off a

seductive voice until that moment. Husky and pleading, that tone was all sex kitten. "Just a stroke or two?"

He looked as if he were about to say no, but then his eyes roamed over her face. "All right."

Iain stood and faced the bed. "Come here so you can have a good, long look."

Brynn rose to her knees and moved closer to the edge of the bed. "Will you show me how you do it? Tight grip or loose?"

Iain closed his eyes and tilted his head back. "Tight." He grasped his dick at the base and stroked up to the tip, then back down. The tendons in his neck distended, his abs bunched together, but he held on to his self-control. Up and down, with even movements, he jerked himself. The tip became redder, the veins along the shaft more pronounced. Occasionally, he'd clench his ass and thrust his hips forward. It was beyond erotic. She longed to touch him like that, take him to the brink with *her* hand.

When he abruptly stopped, he stared down at her. His expression hardened, his lips thinned. "Enough of this. I'm going to shag you now, Brynn." He rolled the condom over his stiff shaft. "Turn around, bend over, and keep your knees together."

With that, Brynn's sated state flew out the window and her body began to hum with sexual tension once more. Doing as Iain commanded, Brynn lay back, then rolled over onto her stomach.

"Up you go." Iain looped an arm around her torso and pulled Brynn to her knees. She stretched her forearms on the gray comforter. "God, you look amazing like this. But don't think I've forgotten about your punishment."

His words made her shiver. Brynn bit her lip,

anticipating a little tap on her ass. So when it came, she wasn't surprised. The second tap was a little harder and left her stinging. The third had her gasping. "Iain."

"That's for stopping this afternoon. I told you to keep going, to keep touching yourself. You disobeyed me, Brynn."

Her bottom was feverish, but he hadn't hurt her. He seemed to know just the right amount of stimulus to use. Brynn's body started throbbing all over again.

She glanced over her shoulder and took him in. He stood there, naked and proud. And so terribly handsome. She could spend a lifetime staring at Iain Chapman, and it wouldn't be enough. He was everything she'd ever wanted in a man—strong and self-assured. He put her pleasure before his own. He didn't judge her or make her feel weak. It wasn't just about the sex either. Being here with him, opening herself up to this—Brynn felt strong. She knew what she needed, what she wanted. He'd helped her accept this side of herself. "Iain."

He'd been rubbing her tender bottom, but when his gaze met hers, his hand froze. They stared at each other for a long moment. She saw the heat there, but there was something deeper in his eyes as he stared back. Brynn wasn't sure what it was, but it warmed her heart. Soon, his eyes grew glassy, unfocused.

As she watched, he gripped her hips and eased his cock inside of her. Brynn moaned as her pussy tried to accommodate him.

Everything had been leading up to this—the culmination of all the foreplay, all the oral. Now, at last, Iain was fucking her, and it felt so *right*. When he twisted his hips, exquisite shock waves vibrated through her. Heat seared along her nerve endings, delicious and powerful, igniting a fire inside her.

"Finally," he said. "I've been needing this since the moment I saw you, Brynnie."

He'd started slowly, letting the friction build, but that didn't last long. Soon, Iain's fingertips sank into her skin and he clung to her. Then he picked up the pace, ramming in and out of Brynn's pussy. Iain stretched her, filled her. It was heaven.

He continued to pump into her, each hot thrust bringing her closer to another release. When he let go of her right hip to grab her breast, Brynn lost it. She came so hard that when she closed her eyes, white stars burst against her eyelids. She cried out, long and loud, as her inner muscles squeezed his cock.

Iain came then, his hand clenching her hip as he bucked against her. "Bloody hell," he bit out. He spasmed inside her and, after one last push, became motionless. Then he leaned forward, resting his chest against her back.

As he lay against her, Brynn's arms trembled from the strain of holding herself up. Even so, she wasn't ready for him to leave her body. Not yet.

Eventually, Iain kissed her shoulder blade and pulled out. She rolled over then, curling herself into a fetal position. Once Iain got rid of the condom, he climbed back on the bed, sitting behind her. Leaning into her, he rubbed her hip. "You liked that."

Brynn let out a shaky laugh. "How could you tell?"

He reached across her and untied the belt. "I didn't get it too tight, did I, love?"

Brynn flexed her wrists. "Everything was perfect." She turned her head and gazed up at him. "Thank you."

"You're so welcome." Iain eased down and nestled her against him, draping an arm across her breasts. She was glad he held her afterward. She needed it, the comfort of it. They remained like that, silent but united, for a long while.

Then Brynn's stomach growled.

Iain burrowed his head in her hair and kissed her. "I guess I should feed you, eh?"

Brynn didn't want to move. She wanted this closeness to last a little while longer. "Not yet."

"We have all night."

She rolled over and faced him. Reaching up, she stroked his hair. "I should go home. It's getting late." Brynn didn't want to leave. She wanted to spend the night in Iain's arms and hear him speak with that sexy accent. She wanted him to touch her like he was now—with intimacy. But she didn't like to presume.

"Don't go." His lips brushed her forehead. "Stay with me."

Brynn smiled. "All right."

"And let's eat. I'm starving." He climbed off the bed and walked out of the room. Buck naked. He didn't possess a scrap of self-consciousness.

Brynn sat up and pulled her knees to her chest as she watched his perfect ass. When he realized she wasn't following, he stuck his head through the doorway. "Come on then, chop, chop."

"I'm not going to the kitchen naked."

With an exaggerated roll of his eyes, Iain sauntered to the bathroom and came back with a blue robe. He held it open for her and Brynn stood, shoving her arms into sleeves that were far too long. Iain spun her around and tied the sash. "There. Now you're properly covered. Time for dinner." He strolled out of the room, still naked.

She scuttled to catch up. This time, as she moved through the apartment, she took a more thorough look around. Modern, sophisticated furniture and artwork filled the space. Sleek. Contemporary. Sterile. Like a showroom more than a home.

"How long have you lived in this apartment?" she asked, rolling up the robe's sleeves as she trailed him into the kitchen.

"Five years."

Brynn stopped, her hand mid-roll. "Five years?"

Iain glanced back at her. "Yeah, why?"

"It's just…" She was going to say *soulless* but that sounded harsh. "It's very utilitarian."

He walked to the fridge and started tossing cardboard containers onto the counter. "Huh. Utilitarian. Say what you mean, Brynn."

His wide shoulders shifted and muscles played beneath his skin. Brynn's gaze followed the line of his back all the way down to his tapered waist and then over that juicy rear.

"Brynn? Be blunt, love. And do you want wine with the lasagna?"

"What else do you have?"

"Beer."

"I'll have one."

His brows shot up.

"What?" Brynn plucked at the sash of the robe. "I like beer."

He stuck a carton of food in the microwave and twisted the cap off a bottle. When he walked toward her, his cock swung freely. Brynn covered her eyes with her forearms. "Dude, get dressed. God." Then a small laugh escaped her. Iain Chapman was audacious in every way. He'd just done the most outrageous things to her, but Brynn was embarrassed. Go figure.

He yanked on her sleeves, exposing her face. "You're a conundrum, you are. It's only bits and bobs, love. Do get used to them." He handed her the beer. "And don't think you're going to get out of telling me how you really feel. What's wrong with this place? I paid a fucking fortune for it."

Brynn ran her finger around the rim of the bottle. "It's seems cold."

"You're not talking about the temperature, are you?"

"Your office—"

"My office is designed to impress. I bring punters in there, they see the Old World shit, and they know I'm a legit businessman, yeah?"

"Punter?" Brynn peered up at him.

"Moneymen. Some bloke comes in, I'm looking to entice investors or what have you, he sees that I've got high-end shit—the real deal, mind you, not knockoffs—and he figures I know me onions."

"As I've mentioned, both of my sisters married Brits, but half the time, I have no idea what you're talking about."

Iain took a swig from his own bottle. "That's because they're toffs. They don't speak like normal people."

"Yes they do." *Toffs*. She knew that term. It meant highborn. The upper of the upper class. "Anyway, how do you know they're toffs? They might be regular joes, just like you."

Iain's entire body went motionless. Then he took a deep breath, leaving Brynn to wonder what he'd been thinking just now.

"Nowt about me is regular, love." It took a minute for Brynn to understand him. "Nowt" stood for nothing. He was silent a moment and took another swig of beer. When he started speaking again, he'd toned down his accent. "And if they speak differently, that must mean they went to public school, had nannies, and all the rest of that rubbish. Am I right?"

"Sort of." Brynn took a seat at the counter. The steel chair wasn't only fugly, it was also damned uncomfortable. She hopped down just as quickly. "So let me get this straight, you have a fancy office so that people will take you seriously."

He tipped the bottle at her. "Spot-on."

"But you prefer this place?" She placed a hand on the back of the stool.

"No, I don't really give a toss. It's just a place to rest me bones, innit? You know, your place could do with a bit of sprucing, if you don't mind me saying. That furniture of yours is ancient."

Brynn, who'd been leaning against the counter, straightened. "You don't like my house?" She'd spent months on that place, picking every color, scouring flea markets and garage sales, looking for perfect midcentury, vintage pieces. "The wallpaper in the living room is an original Eames design. I can't believe I was lucky enough to find it. That house was built in 1963, right in the middle of nuclear testing. Did you know that Frank

Sinatra's mistress lived two blocks down the street? My house is decorated in the classic Rat Pack era."

Iain held up one hand. "All right. Simmer down. Didn't mean to get your hackles up. Seeing you get riled, Brynnie, is going to turn me on."

Brynn slammed her bottle on the counter. "For God's sake, I can't eat with your penis staring me in the face." She turned and walked to the bedroom, not slowing until she stepped into Iain's closet. Make that dressing room. Row after row of suits lined one wall. Button-down shirts in every color filled the other. One small section held business casual. Inside the brushed steel dresser, Brynn found ties, socks, and more silk boxers. She snatched a pair and looked at him, lounging in the doorway.

Brynn tossed the boxers at him. "I don't see any jeans or T-shirts."

"Don't own any." He pulled on the boxers and snapped the waist. "Clothes make the man and all that."

Brynn was finally starting to put it together. The office—it reflected a gentleman of refinement, of taste. The suits—they reflected a man who could afford the best. She reached out and brushed her hand along the sleeve of a light gray suit. The finest material. Iain put a lot of stock in his presentation, how he looked, how others perceived him.

She glanced back at him. "I thought you don't give a fuck what people think about you."

Even with his casual posture, he exuded arrogance—and was almost too handsome to be real. "I don't. But people set a store by all that shit. Most simply look at the shiny package and rarely see past it."

"I see past it," she said.

"You think you do. But you don't have a clue." His voice sounded rusty.

She understood more than he thought. Iain hadn't grown up with money, and that's why it was so important to him, why he worked so damned hard. The ritzy office, the antique furniture, the handmade suits—underneath it all was the boy from Manchester, trying to prove himself. Success, money, his business—it all boiled down to respect. From others and for himself. Iain was a proud man who demanded it.

As she stared at him, Iain stared right back. His arrogant veneer was locked down tight, making him appear just as formidable as if he were wearing his three-piece suit.

"So show me who you really are," she said, taking one step toward him.

Iain held her gaze for a moment more. Then he pushed off the doorjamb. "Let's eat."

Chapter 14

Iain was a heavy sleeper, always had been. But that night, with his body curved around Brynn's, his brain wouldn't shut off. Not just his brain, his bloody conscience. Her hand entwined with his, she slept deeply, while he lay awake and felt like the dickhead she'd accused him of being.

Over dinner, Brynn had poked at her lasagna, keeping her eyes lowered for so long Iain had known something was on her mind.

"What is it, love?"

At last, she'd gazed up at him. "It's not a big deal, and I don't want you to feel obligated."

"Now I'm intrigued."

"My sister Allie has invited us to dinner. Sunday night. Just my sisters and their husbands."

This was exactly what he'd wanted—to meet Trevor Blake, present him with the downtown expansion project, and let the chips fall where they may. Goal achieved. So why did Iain feel like goddamned Judas? The inner tug-of-war must have been visible on his face, because Brynn immediately began backpedaling.

"It's not a big deal. We don't have to go. I'll tell them you had other plans."

Iain forced his lips into a semblance of a smile. "No." He set his beer on the counter. "I want to meet your family. Even the highborn wankers."

"Really, Iain, it's too soon. Not that I'm assuming you'll ever want to meet them."

He threaded his fingers into her hair. "What time?"

"Dinner's at seven."

"Then it's a date."

And now he lay here, unable to sleep, feeling like a sad arse and wishing he'd told Brynn everything from the beginning. Brynn accused him of treating people like pawns and that's what he'd done to her. Iain was a manipulative, cunning bastard, but he wasn't sorry that he'd forced his way into Brynn's life. He couldn't be, not with her here in his arms, smelling so sweet.

God, what a fucking mess. She could never find out.

As carefully as he could, Iain let go of Brynn's hand, eased out of bed, and silently closed the door behind him. In an effort to get his mind off his bad behavior, he spent the next four hours in the office down the hall, working.

At six, he crept back into the bedroom. With dawn just breaking, the room was still dark and he could barely make her out. She lay on her side, hands tucked beneath her cheek. Like an angel. He woke her by kissing that spot below her ear.

Brynn rolled over, rubbing her eyes. "Hey. What time is it?"

"Six." He continued kissing his way down her neck. When he drew the sheet lower to uncover her breasts, he bent down and latched on to one. As he laved his tongue around her nipple, Brynn moaned, fisting her hands into his hair.

"Yes," she whispered. "This is much better than my alarm clock."

Iain lifted his head to smile up at her. "I should think so. Put your hands behind your head." He methodically worked his way down her body, his tongue flicking out, tasting her skin. He was gentle with her this morning, not as demanding but still in charge. His Brynnie needed that to get off. While Iain didn't *have* to call the shots, he liked doing so. Made it better for him, more intense. He liked testing his own self-control.

When his face was level with her pussy, Brynn slightly parted her legs in invitation. "Wider." She followed his instructions. Iain kissed her mound, then slid his tongue along her slit before licking inside of her.

Brynn nearly sprang off the bed. "Oh, Iain. Right there. Please." His Brynn—his quiet, shy Brynn—was telling him what she liked. He loved that.

When Iain's thumb grazed her clit, her hips rose off the bed. It wasn't long before an orgasm tore through her. Her muscles became taut, rigid. He'd done this to her. Iain made her writhe and twist against his mouth in pleasure.

"Iain. Oh God."

Hearing her groan his name never failed to stir him. His cock, hard and throbbing, needed its own release, but Iain continued to slide his tongue inside of her slick channel.

After one final cry, Brynn's body convulsed again, then went slack. As she lay panting, she peered down at him. "That was the best wakeup call I've ever had."

Iain pulled his head away from her and glanced up the length of her lovely body. "Then I'll be sure to do it often."

Eyes half-closed, she wore a dreamy smile. "Promise?"

"Promise. Grab a condom, would you, love?"

Brynn moved her arms from behind her head and reached over to the bedside table, knocking his dice on the floor in the process. "Sorry." She reached for them.

"I'll get them later." As he crawled up her body, he dropped light kisses on her skin.

Brynn grabbed a condom, but when she tried to hand Iain a foil packet, he rose to his knees, straddling her hips. "You do it."

She opened the package and gazed up at him before using two hands to roll it over his cock. "Tell me if I'm doing it wrong." Her tight grip felt fantastic. "Is that okay?"

Iain opened his eyes and stared down. "Better than. I'm going to take you hard now, Brynnie."

She nodded. "Yes."

Iain moved over her once more, resting his weight on his elbows, and kissed her temple before gently guiding himself inside her. Once he was balls deep, he pulled out and surged forward. Iain had never been with anyone like her—so trusting, so idealistic.

Brynn clung to his shoulders. "Harder? Please, Iain," she asked with that soft, lovely voice.

Iain complied. He slammed in and out of her. She was so tight, his Brynn. As he pumped his hips, he gazed down at her. The room was lighter now, giving him a view of her dark blue eyes. They'd glazed over and her cheeks were flushed. Bloody gorgeous.

Iain came, burying his face against the crook of her neck. A hint of vanilla tickled his senses. Brynn held him as he thrust into her again and again, until he was spent.

When it was over, Iain couldn't move. He needed

a minute or two to recover. Finally, he shoved himself off Brynn and onto his back. "Bloody hell, pet. Sorry I flattened you."

She laced her fingers with his. "I like it when you're on top of me. I like it when you're inside of me. I pretty much like everything you do to me, Iain Chapman."

"*I* believe we're in agreement. Your moans provide me with constructive feedback, so that I can enhance my performance, thus maximizing your pleasure. This arrangement is mutually beneficial, giving each of us the satisfactory outcome we desire."

Brynn lifted her head and looked at him with something akin to awe. "You're talking in corporate speak."

He grinned. "How do you *feel* about that?"

"I love it. Do it again."

He angled toward her, leaning on his forearm. "Effective strategy." He lowered his voice and drew out the words.

Brynn laughed when he licked the side of her neck. "More."

"Active." He kissed her chin. "Listening."

"Oh, baby. That's so good."

Now Iain laughed too. "Developmental strategizing."

"You read my manual," she accused.

"Maybe." He gave her cheek one last peck before he climbed off the bed, walked into the bathroom, and threw away the condom.

Brynn followed him and snuggled into his robe. "You did. You read my manual." She remained silent until he turned to face her.

"I may have glanced at it." In truth, he'd skimmed through all of it.

"You probably thought it was boring, useless."

Not completely. She made a few good points. Could have written it in plain English and it would have been half as long, but he wasn't going to tell her that. Sensitive, she was. "I liked that bit about respecting the people you work with. You were right—I need to do more of that."

She canted her head and stared up at him. "You don't believe that."

He grabbed her fingers. "I'm trying, love." He pulled her close and wrapped his arms around her shoulders.

"Could you call your concierge?" she asked against his chest. "I need a taxi."

"We're going to the same office. I'll grab a quick shower and shave, then we'll run by your house."

"I left my car at my office."

"I'll have my driver take you to work after our meeting." He planted one last kiss on the top of her head and let her go, but patted her ass before strolling toward the shower. He glanced over his shoulder. "Want to join me?"

Brynn shook her head. "I'll go make some coffee." He'd already wrung a loud, strong orgasm out of her. Brynn didn't want to be selfish. Or late.

Iain walked into the stall. "Okay. I'll be out in a few."

Brynn spun and raced for the kitchen. She didn't trust herself to be that close to Iain. Naked. Water flowing down his perfect body. Nope. She just didn't have the willpower not to jump him.

In the kitchen, Brynn made a strong pot of coffee

and went hunting for her clothes (still on the kitchen floor, but kicked to one corner) while it brewed. Once she was dressed and had poured them each a cup, Brynn walked barefoot through the apartment. She had a hard time picturing Iain there. Did he ever relax in the small sitting area, with its blocky chairs and shaggy, white throw rug? Or lounge on the stiff, gray sofa, watching a soccer game? Doubtful. Iain's work was his life.

Brynn could relate to a certain extent. She worked too many hours. But her home was her oasis. Brynn loved being in her all-pink kitchen, trying new recipes. She took naps on her peacock-blue sofa and ate breakfast at her '50s-style dinette. She'd only lived there about a year, but it was warm and comfortable. This… Brynn curled her lip at the sculptured side table.

Although she had to admit, the view from the wide picture window was spectacular.

Brynn took a sip of coffee and contemplated last night. It had been hot. This morning had been…loving. Brynn didn't know where she fit into Iain's life, if at all, but she was starting to really care about him. Did he feel the same way? Yes, he'd agreed to meet her family, but he hadn't looked happy about it. When she'd mentioned it, he'd gotten the strangest look on his face.

Before she could ponder it anymore, Iain stepped into the living room. Today he wore a black pinstripe suit with a sky-blue tie. He smelled of bergamot and shaving cream.

"Five minutes, yeah?" He stopped to stroke her cheek before moving to the kitchen. "You're an angel, you." He returned with a cup in his hands. "You poured me coffee."

"I'd have made breakfast, but you don't have actual food."

He regarded her for a moment. "I'll make sure the fridge is stocked next time." And when would that be? Brynn was dying to know, but she'd rather cut out her tongue than actually ask.

After Brynn slipped on her sandals, she rinsed out her mug and set it on a paper towel to dry. The man didn't even own a dish towel. This was like a hotel. Only less personable. Nothing said Iain Chapman lived here. Except for the dice. He hung on to them like a talisman.

"Ready to go?" He grabbed her bag—the one filled with too many jobs that required her attention—and side by side, they made the long elevator trek to the lobby.

Iain spent the ride from his apartment to her house on his phone. By the time they reached her home, Brynn had mentally run through her day. It was going to be a full one.

To her surprise, Iain didn't stay in the car, but followed her up the walkway to the front door. "You don't have to come in."

"Maybe I want to watch you get ready."

Brynn unlocked the door and turned to him. He squinted against the morning sun. "Not a good plan." She stepped into the house with Iain on her heels.

"And why not?"

"Because we'll be late for our meeting with Marc."

His arm shot around her waist. "He won't mind."

"I'll mind." As he lowered his head to kiss her, Brynn laughed and avoided him by averting her head. "Seriously. No more sex this morning."

He managed to nuzzle the side of her throat. "That's no fun. Where's your sense of adventure?"

Brynn swatted at the hand cupping her breast. "Do you remember who you're talking to? I'm not the adventurous type."

"Last night you were very adventurous."

"Good morning, Brynn. Englishman."

Iain raised his head and Brynn whirled around, with his arm still clamped around her waist.

"Tash." Her neighbor was clad in a pink-and-black leopard-print robe. Her hair was a fright, and without false eyelashes and heavy makeup, Natasha looked much younger. "Did you spend the night?"

"Yes. Zeke and I have huge fight." Moose and Squirrel danced around her feet. "I let dogs out to piss. Sorry I interrupt." Then she disappeared into the kitchen and Brynn heard the back door slide open.

She turned and gazed up at Iain. By his narrowed eyes and compressed lips, Brynn guessed he was annoyed. This wasn't the way she wanted to spend her morning either, but she couldn't just ignore Natasha. "Why don't you have a seat in the living room? I'll talk to her and get ready. Thirty minutes tops."

"I'll wait in the car. And if you're ready in thirty minutes, I'll eat my tie." He pivoted and strode out of the house.

Brynn wandered into the kitchen where she found Tash sitting at the pink table with tears in her eyes. Brynn had never seen her friend so distraught before. Angry, bitter, homesick, yes, but Tash was a tough cookie.

Brynn pulled a chair out and sank down. "What happened?"

"Zeke is dick. I want my mother and sister to come for visit. But he says no."

"Why not? You miss them like crazy."

Tash nodded, dislodging a few more tears. "He say if they come, they never leave. And we cannot afford plane tickets. I want to go home, Brynn. I thought coming here would be good thing, but I am unhappy. I may as well be unhappy with my own family."

Brynn patted her hand. "Listen, why don't you stay here for the day? Just relax and don't make any hasty decisions, okay?"

"Yes. Thank you, Brynn."

"You're welcome. I've got to get ready for work. You'll be all right here on your own?"

"Yes. I am fine. You go."

Brynn felt terrible leaving her here, but she had too much going on, especially since Cass's company was circling the drain. Brynn rose and left Tasha sitting alone in the kitchen.

After grabbing a hasty shower, she pulled her wet hair into a loose ponytail and threw on a long, blue dress, making it out the door in record time.

She climbed into the backseat next to Iain and adjusted her skirt around her legs. "Hey."

"So what's her sob story this time?"

"Iain, she's homesick. Her husband won't let her mother and sister come for a visit. It's sad. This was her dream, coming to America."

"Duping a stranger into marrying her."

Brynn whipped her head so fast, her ponytail went airborne. "That's a really cruel thing to say. And it's not true. They communicated for a year. Tash thought she knew everything about Zeke."

"You're telling me it was a love match, are you?"

"I'm not telling you anything. But your lack of compassion is disturbing. Natasha is hurting. Maybe *you* can look at someone who's in pain and turn them away, but I can't."

"You're too kindhearted for your own good. By letting her pop over every time she fights with her husband, you aren't doing her any favors. She should stay put and fix her own mess."

And there he was—the hard-assed businessman. Whenever Brynn thought she saw a glimmer of something more, the heartless side of him always reared its head. She stared out the window and ignored him for the rest of the drive.

When the car stopped in front of his office building, Iain placed a hand on her leg. "Brynnie. It's none of my business what you do, love. I just don't want to see you get taken advantage of."

She didn't look at him. "Caring about people isn't a flaw, Iain, but a lack of compassion is. I pity you." She grabbed her bag, slipped from beneath his touch, and out of the car.

Brynn didn't wait for him as she walked into the building or when she hopped into the elevator before the doors slid closed. No matter how fabulous the sex or how many orgasms he gave her, if Iain couldn't show even a modicum of human decency, then he wasn't the right man for her.

Brynn forced a smile on her face when she walked into the Blue Moon offices, said hello to a few people, and headed straight for Marc's office. She rapped on his door once and after hearing him mutter something, she opened it and peeked through the crack.

"Brynn, come on in." He looked more rumpled today. He hadn't shaved and his hair appeared a little unkempt. The overall affect was sexy and disheveled, but Brynn had a feeling that wasn't the look he was going for.

She walked toward his desk and set her bag in the guest chair. "I came to get you for our meeting." He had dark circles under his bloodshot eyes. "Are you all right? We can reschedule."

"No need for that. Just women troubles. The worst kind, eh?"

"And here I thought man troubles were bad."

Standing, Marc walked from behind his desk. "Iain giving you problems? He's good at that."

"But why is he so"—she made claws with her fingers—"urgh?"

"I knew it was only a matter of time before you'd want to strangle him. We've all felt that way a time or three." Marc walked to the door and held it open. "It's part of his charm."

That was an infuriating answer that told Brynn nothing. And Iain's hard-assed ways weren't the least bit charming. What made him so disconnected from other people? *Are you looking for a reason to excuse his behavior? There is no excuse, jellyfish*. Maybe not, but this was Brynn's Achilles' heel—her faith in people, her belief in their innate decency. What was Iain's tragic flaw? Everyone had at least one.

Probably his cold heart. Or the fact that he couldn't care less about anyone else's feelings. Yet he'd read her manual. Even found something nice to say about it. He could be funny and warm and generous. But he could also be an asshole. Those glimmers of humanity kept her hanging on. The rational part of her wanted to give up on him, but the *glass half-full* Brynn thought he deserved another chance. Still, after their argument in the car, she didn't want to face Iain alone. That's why she'd sought out Marc. He could act as a buffer.

Marc waited while Brynn warred with herself. She hadn't come to any conclusions. Iain was both kind and cruel. She couldn't separate the two. He was a total combo platter.

With a sigh, she grabbed her stuff and exited the room. Marc kept pace with her, and they walked toward Iain's office.

Amelia saw them and rolled her eyes. "He's in a mood. Coffee and breakfast are on the cart. Tell him I'll be there in a sec." Her blue gaze scanned Brynn's face. "Don't let him rattle you, sweetie."

Brynn's feet dragged her forward. Only Marc's solid presence at her back kept her from skedaddling out of here.

Entering the office, Brynn's gaze searched the room and found Iain sitting on the sofa, one leg crossed over the other, his face a mask of irritation. "About time you two showed up. Let's get on with this. Get Amelia in here to take notes."

Marc walked to the cart and poured himself a cup of coffee. "Keep your hair on. She'll be here in a mo." His glance slid between Brynn and Iain. "You two having a tiff or wha'?"

Iain's expression darkened. "Mind your own." His eyes cut sharply to Brynn. "Going to stand there or have a seat? Or maybe you'll just run. You're so very good at it."

Swallowing her discomfort, Brynn raised her chin in the air. This same man had tied her up last night. Had his tongue all over her, *in her*, just a couple of hours ago. If he ever wanted to do it again, he'd better shape up. She wasn't going to take this shit from him. "I'm not going anywhere. And if you can't put your personal grievances aside, perhaps we should table this meeting for another time when you aren't feeling so emotional." Shock flickered across his face as she strode forward, grabbed a napkin and a bagel, and dropped into a chair. From her bag, she dug out her notebook and a pen.

Iain leaned forward, elbows resting on his thighs. "I don't get emotional, pet. That's your department."

Marc watched them, his head swiveling back and forth as if he were watching a tennis match.

"And yet," she said calmly, "you're the one who seems bad tempered this morning."

"Can't imagine why."

Amelia walked into the room. "Iain, stop causing trouble." She sat on the opposite end of the couch, her tablet and stylus at the ready. "I believe we're discussing office morale?"

Her cool demeanor allowed Brynn to direct her energy toward the meeting. For the next thirty minutes, she threw out ideas, which Iain shot down, one by one. Exasperated but trying desperately to hide it, she placed her untouched bagel on the side table. "All right," she said, "what are your suggestions? We want your employees to feel valued. You don't like any of my ideas, so you must have a few of your own."

"Cash. Cold, hard, *unemotional* cash," he said. "If they make certain goals for the quarter, they get a bonus."

"We've already discussed this," Brynn said. "Several times, in fact. Money won't change the environment in this office. Your attitude will."

Marc sighed and rubbed his eyes. "For crying out loud. The two of you have obviously rowed, and frankly, I don't have the patience to sit through this nonsense today. Amelia, let's leave them to it."

"Agreed." She faced Brynn. "But I'm supposed to order lunch for the entire office?"

"Yes. They're going to pick their delegates."

Iain gazed out the window. "Bloody waste of time," he muttered.

"I'm sorry, I didn't hear that. Why don't you speak up so that we all can partake of your wisdom?" Brynn wasn't sure where this snarky mood was coming from, and she was too ticked off to care.

Iain glared at her from the corner of his eye. "I said, what a fucking waste of time."

Marc stood and placed his cup back on the cart. "I'm out. Just shag you two, and get it over with. You're driving me mental."

Amelia stood as well, cutting a chic figure in her green dress. She placed her hand on Brynn's shoulder as she passed.

Once they left, Brynn closed her book. "I'll finish talking to your employees so that I can make more useless suggestions that you won't follow. You're right. This is a waste of time." She rose but stiffened when Iain popped out of his seat.

"I don't need your pity."

"What?"

He skirted the coffee table as he moved toward her.

"You pity me? What a laugh. You're going to continue to live a pathetic little life where you blend into the background and try not to offend anyone. *I* feel sorry for *you*."

Anger had her trembling. She raised a shaky finger and pointed it in his face. "I've told you what I want, but you're too stubborn and rude to hear anything but your own yapping. My life may seem pathetic to you, but at least I have people who care about me. You're going to die old and alone, having alienated every person who gives a damn about you." She swung around and stormed out of the room, slamming the door behind her. Tears filled Brynn's eyes as she hurried past desks and left the office.

Damn it, she hated everyone seeing her like this, hated being the center of attention—it was embarrassing. On top of that, she couldn't just speed out of here. Because she'd left her car at work, Brynn was going to have to catch a taxi, and she'd rather walk than use Iain's driver.

Iain Chapman can seriously blow me. What a dickhead.

As soon as she huffed out the door, Iain knew he'd made a howler. Amelia was in his office three seconds later to confirm it.

"What the hell is wrong with you?"

Hands on his hips, Iain stared down and watched the traffic. "If I knew the answer to that, I could avoid these delightful conversations."

"First Marc, now you. Neither one of you know how to treat a woman. Didn't I teach you anything?"

"If this morning's fiasco was anything to go by, apparently not."

"I was going to ask you to speak to Tyler, but you're clearly not yourself."

Iain turned. "What's wrong with him?" At twelve, Tyler was smart and athletic, but he could be a bit rambunctious. "Getting into trouble at school, is he?"

"Yes. His grades have been slipping. Now, what's going on with you and Brynn?"

"None of your business." He walked forward and slammed the dice down on his desk. "She's exasperating and wonderful, and I'm a dickhead."

"So go apologize."

Fuck that. He didn't want to apologize. Brynn should be apologizing to him. Iain was successful—a self-made man. He had money and prestige. He didn't need some wisp of a woman trying to change him. "I so appreciate the concern, I can't even tell you. Why don't you go help Marc now? He could use some of your sage advice."

"Save the sarcasm. I'll stay out of it. But if you lose that girl, you're going to regret it. I see the way you look at her. The way she looks at you. Just think about swallowing your pride. For once." She banged out of the office the same way Brynn had.

After several minutes, Iain forced himself to sit down and get to work. He had plans and bids and inspections to deal with. The row with Brynn would have to go on the back burner.

The problem was, every time he started to study the numbers, her words came back to him. *You're going to die old and alone, having alienated every person who gives a damn about you*. He didn't have anyone in his life except for Marc and Ames. *You could have had Brynn.*

Pushing back from his desk, he stood, tugged on his waistcoat, and walked out of his office. "Is she in the conference room?"

"Nope." Ames didn't look up from her computer screen. "She's gone."

Panic shot through him. "Gone?" She'd run out on him *again*. Well, this was the last time. Iain'd had enough. "I'll be out for a few. What time is Tyler coming?"

"Not until five. He has a soccer game after school."

"Text me the address. I'll be there." He walked out and swept past the HR department. But before he made it to the door, Iain turned back. "James, what's going on?"

The tall, blond man stood. "Sir?"

"What's going on in the office? Surely you have the pulse on the employees and their concerns. What's happening that I should know about?"

James's eyes slid away. "I'm not sure what you're asking, Mr. Chapman."

"Is everyone content?"

"Um..."

"For fuck's sake man, are there any problems? Complaints? Is anyone unhappy and is there anything I can do about it?"

"Well, Gina in sales is going on maternity leave in two weeks. I know that parties are frowned upon."

"No, no. Have a party or whatever the hell you people do to celebrate a baby. I'll start a fund, yeah?"

James's head bobbed. "Also, Charles's wife is in the hospital. She broke her leg."

This was how it started. Show concern for one of them, and it never stopped. People were so bloody needy. Iain sighed. "Which one is Charles?"

"Glasses. He's in PR."

"Tell Amelia to send flowers." This liaison idea was a good one. He needed other people to tend to this type of thing. He was busy. Amelia was busy. She shouldn't be required to take care of all these details. "And tell everyone to select two groups. Liaisons and a team to take care of this type of thing—flowers and parties and whatnot."

"Yes, sir."

Iain walked out without looking back this time. He didn't want to get mired in any more minutiae today.

When he reached the lobby, Iain signaled to his driver. "Get the car."

The man jumped out of the chair where he'd been chatting with the building's security guards. "Yes, Mr. Chapman."

Iain stood on the hot sidewalk, letting the sun wash over him while he waited. Brynn Campbell was going to regret walking out on him. It was the bloody final straw.

Chapter 15

When Iain walked into the TDTC office, he took a good look around. Shabby. The carpet had been worn thin in places. Pieces of the vertical blinds had snapped off, giving them the appearance of a gap-toothed smile. Even the droopy, fake plant in the corner seemed ready to call it a day.

He walked up to a dark-haired woman. "I'm here to see Brynn Campbell."

She stood, pointing at him with her chocolate bar. "You're that Blue Moon guy who kept calling the other day."

"Right."

"I'll see if she's busy."

"She will be. But point out her office anyway."

She considered a moment. "She said you went to eleven. I can see that. She's over there." The woman indicated a narrow door on her right.

"Thank you." See—he could do polite. It just took up so much damned time.

Iain stared down two men sitting in the center of the room. At his unflinching glare, they lowered their eyes. Damn, he was doing it again. Dominance just came naturally to him. All this friendly, open business felt disingenuous.

Iain didn't bother with knocking. He walked into the boxlike room. Felt as though the walls were closing in on him, it did. How could Brynn stand to lock herself away in this tiny hellhole? He shut the door and leaned against it.

Brynn's eyes grew huge when she saw him. "What are you doing here?"

"I've heard the coffee is outstanding. What do you think?" With one step, he stood directly in front of her, his suit jacket brushing the front of her dress. "The question is, why are you here? You're meant to be in my office, questioning my employees."

"I'm not doing it anymore. According to you, Delaney is limping toward failure. I have other clients, real clients, who need me, and you don't."

"I do need you." Iain barely recognized his own voice. He'd come here to vent his frustration, his anger, but it had all dissolved the second he'd walked into this shithole of an office. Brynn reduced him to a schoolboy, made him forget his goals, his commitments. She'd become more important than any of it. "I need you, Brynnie. I'm an ass. I can be cold and uncaring. Unfeeling. Wrapped up in meself and blind to anyone else's problems." He paused. "You can stop me at any time, you know."

"Keep going. You're on a roll." She crossed her arms.

"You're not going to make this easy, are you?"

"Why should I?"

"What happened to the sweet little Brynnie who wouldn't say boo to a goose?"

"Maybe she's finally learning to stick up for herself."

Iain couldn't help but admire that. It wasn't easy for her—he could see it in her eyes, the way she had to force herself to meet his gaze head on.

"I'm sorry for the cruel things I said, love."

Her arms fell. "Me too. I feel terrible. I'm sorry I ran away. It's my fallback. I hope you'll forgive me."

How could he not? "Course I will. I'd forgive you of just about anything." He leaned down and kissed her cheek.

"Thank you, Iain. And just for the record, Tash isn't taking advantage of me. She misses her family. I know what that's like. When my mom got sick, my world turned upside down. That's what's happened to Tash—everything she knows is gone. I'm not going to abandon or give up on the people I care about."

He tucked a curl behind her ear. "Does that include me?" Iain swallowed and impatiently awaited her answer. He wanted to matter to Brynn. This wasn't a fling—it wasn't temporary. Not for him.

"I do care about you. More than I should."

"I care about you too, Brynnie. It's bloody inconvenient, isn't it?"

She laughed and drew her finger down the length of his tie. "Very. I don't want to like you, but I can't seem to help it." Her navy eyes were full of humor, and her smile made Iain sigh in relief.

"Can we put this behind us?" He placed his hands on her shoulders and used his thumbs to rub the soft skin at the base of her throat.

"Yeah."

He gave her a heated kiss, and when she wrapped her arms around his waist, Iain's world shifted back into its proper order. Reluctantly, he lifted his mouth from hers. "I'll let you get back to it. And I'll follow your suggestions about morale. I already talked to James in HR."

She smoothed her hand down his chest. "Give it six months. If it doesn't work, you can go back to scowling at everyone."

"Deal. Can I see you tonight?"

"I don't know. I need to check on Tasha."

Iain bit his tongue. "I can bring dinner over for the three of us—if I have to."

She smiled. "I'll call you, let you know."

He opened the door.

"Hey," she said.

Iain glanced back.

"It took a lot for you to come here and apologize. Thank you."

"You're most welcome."

Iain had a lunch meeting with his investment group. These meetings always went on too long. The Pecan Grove was doing a steady business, but no profit yet. One of their busiest nightclubs routinely came up short of money at the end of the night. It had been going on for three weeks now. So the group voted on an audit and an in-house investigation.

After the meeting, Iain smiled, lingered for a bit, chatted up his partners. While he never doubted that getting in with this group had been a good move, Iain liked having a more hands-on approach with his projects, which was why he needed someone like Trevor Blake as an investor.

Iain left the meeting with a renewed sense of purpose. He wasn't going to let this apartment project flounder. The time to move was now. If Trevor didn't want to invest, he'd surely have other contacts. Sunday dinner with Brynn's family was the perfect time to meet Trevor, feel him out, and see if he'd be receptive to a deal.

Before heading back to the office, Iain stopped by Tyler's school to watch his football game. He cast an eye over the parents in lawn chairs, screaming instructions and encouragement in equal parts. Iain noted there were as many dads as there were mums. These parents took time out of their busy day to come and watch their kids play. He had a hard time wrapping his head around that. According to Iain's mum, his father hadn't even shown up at the hospital when Iain was born. Too busy getting plastered. The old bastard had his priorities after all.

Tyler was a bit shorter than most of the other boys on the team. Iain wondered if he was self-conscious about it. But the lad could kick. When he scored a goal, Iain felt a smile tug at his mouth. Found himself clapping and shouting with the other parents.

It was a close game, 6–7, with Tyler's team taking a hit. As the lad ran toward him, Iain greeted him with a smile and a pat on the back. "Nice goal."

Tyler's ginger hair, drenched with sweat, clung to his forehead. He had Amelia's blue eyes. "Thanks. What are you doing here?"

"Came to watch you play."

Tyler took a long pull on his sports bottle. "Mom sent you here to lecture me, didn't she?"

Iain didn't know the first thing about parenting, but he knew this kid, had since Tyler was in nappies. "Yeah, she did. She's worried about you. Come on, we'll stop and get something to eat on the way to the office."

"I usually get a ride with Todd's mom."

"Not today, mate." Iain placed his hand on Tyler's damp back and directed him to the car. "So how often does your mum come and see these games?"

"Only on Saturdays. It's cool. She has to work."

Iain instructed his driver to take them to a burger place. Tyler ordered enough food for his entire team and then proceeded to gobble down every bite. Reminded Iain of himself at that age. All arms and legs. Davy's mum would fix a huge tea, knowing that he and Marc would invariably show up and eat her out of house and home. Fish fingers—that's what Mrs. Franklin usually served. The melancholy ache that always accompanied memories of Davy wasn't as sharp today.

Iain set aside the past and fixed his gaze on Tyler. "Why are your grades on the decline, mate?"

Tyler shrugged and lowered his head.

"Oh, that moody bullshit might work with your mother, but it ain't going to work on me. Answer the question."

Tyler stared out the window. "Some of the guys have started making fun of me, for being so small. It's like, embarrassing. They say stuff online and it pisses me off."

"As it should. Are these knobs on your football team?"

Tyler faced him. "You're in America. It's time to call it soccer."

"Never."

"No, the guys on my team are fine. It's some of the other guys in my class."

"How is this affecting your game with the ladies?"

Tyler rolled his eyes. "What ladies? Girls don't even notice me. I have red hair and freckles, and I'm short."

"So naturally you should fail your classes to prove that you're brainless as well, eh?"

"It just doesn't seem to matter." He shrugged again.

"You like your footb…soccer?"

"Yeah. It's the best part of the day."

Iain whipped out his phone and pulled up a picture of Wayne Rooney. "Take a good look at this bloke." He showed Tyler the screen. "Not exactly George Clooney, is he? But he's brill on the field. Focus on what you're good at. And if you want your mum off your back, get the grades up."

"It's easy for you. You're tall and girls like you. But for me, life sucks."

"It sucks for everyone, mate. But if it's all too bloody difficult, then give up. Fail your classes, forget that fancy school I'm paying for, and get kicked off the football team. It's your life, innit? Never pictured you as a quitter, but I've been wrong a time or two." He swiped the screen and checked his email.

"You're terrible at this."

Iain's brow rose. "At what?"

"Pep talks."

"What are most pep talks like?"

"You're supposed to tell me I'm smart. That I shouldn't listen to the dicks who tease me. That I'll grow up and all this will be behind me."

"Is that what your mum tells you?"

"Yeah."

"Has it worked?"

He flopped his sweaty head against the back of the seat. "No."

"They're not physically beating you, are they?"

"No. They just call me a leprechaun. They post gnomes on my wall."

"Then I'm going to tell you straight, yeah? This doesn't just apply to school, it applies to your life. You can let the fuckers have power over you, or you can have power over yourself. But you can't do both. So you need to decide. Simple as that."

Tyler remained silent for the rest of the drive. When they reached the office building, Iain climbed out first, handed the driver a couple of bills for the mess in the backseat, and waited for Tyler to emerge with all his gear.

Iain followed the boy inside. Once they stepped on the lift, Iain nudged Tyler's arm. "You're really quite good as a forward, but you leave yourself open. Need to look up every once in a while and watch for your teammates."

They stepped off and walked down the hall to the Blue Moon offices. As Iain reached for the door, Tyler glanced up at him. "I want the power."

"Yeah. So what are you going to do about it?" Iain asked.

"Ignore the haters."

"That's a start. And here's what I've learned in business. Everyone is self-conscious about something. Study your opponent. Really watch him. Find his weakness. Then use it against him."

Tyler nodded. "Got it."

The rest of the day passed quickly, but Iain made sure he spoke with Ames before she left. "You need to hire yourself an assistant."

"What?"

"Hire someone, train them, then you can cut out early when you need to. No reason for you to stay till after six each night."

Amelia's lips pursed. "What are you trying to say, Iain? That I can't handle my job? Because I assure you, I'm on top of my game, mister."

Iain briefly closed his eyes, then stood. "This is what I get for trying to be considerate. I don't think you're falling down on the job, Ames. I just think Tyler would like it if you showed up at his football matches. If you were home a little earlier, you could spend more time with him. He needs you right now. He'd rather eat his own tongue than admit it, but it's true."

"What's gotten into you?" Amelia whispered. "First you're talking to employees, and now you're concerned about Tyler's soccer matches? This is Brynn's doing isn't it? I'm going to have to send her a thank-you note."

"Oh, come off it. You know I'm crazy about Tyler, but I never thought of it until now. And just because I'm mucking about with that lot out there"—he pointed at the office door—"doesn't mean I've lost my edge."

"No one's accusing you of that, Iain. It's just you're… acting like a person instead of a dictator. Everyone's noticed. They like the change."

He rolled his eyes. "I haven't changed. I'm just giving Brynn's ideas a try. They're going to fail in the end. It's all tosh." But maybe Brynn was right about a couple of things. He could behave like more of a human being and less of an asshole. People did respond to friendly patter. Iain still didn't see the need for it, but others did. Made them feel appreciated. Perhaps it wasn't complete rubbish.

"Anyway, go home, Ames. Enjoy your weekend. And bring that little twat into the office after school if you want. He can do his homework at an empty desk. Might pick up a thing or two about business."

"There's the Iain I know and love, calling my twelve-year-old son a twat. Warms a mother's heart." She smiled and left the room.

Brynn called Iain and let him know that Natasha was back in her own home. But before he could suggest that she go over to his place, she invited him to hers. Brynn liked her comfy little home much better than Iain's expensive, sterile apartment.

He offered to bring dinner and wine. Brynn promised dessert.

Since she had cookies to bake, Brynn decided to leave a little earlier than normal. But as soon as she emerged from her office, Cass pounced, as though she'd been lying in wait.

"Brynn, my office."

The two remaining salesmen shot her looks of sympathy. She didn't need sympathy. She just needed a brain break. In the last few days, Brynn had been working furiously to catch up on her assignments. She'd made some real headway, but there was always more to do.

Cass sat behind her desk. As far as Brynn could tell, not a thing had been disturbed since her last visit.

Folders still rose toward the ceiling, the binders she'd toppled were exactly as she'd left them, and boxes of promotional products were stacked in the same corner.

"Iain Chapman was here this afternoon?"

"Yeah, he dropped by." Iain took time away from business to see her. Just when Brynn was ready to give up on him, he'd do something unexpected. Thoughtful. She may never figure out all the inner workings of Iain Chapman, but he kept her on her toes.

"What did he want?"

Brynn pulled her head out of the clouds. "Um, I left his office early today to cover a few things here."

Cass tapped her fingers nervously on her desk. "We can't afford to alienate him, Brynn. He's too big of a client. What the *hell* were you thinking?"

That talk she needed to have with Cassandra about the business was long overdue. She couldn't procrastinate anymore. "I know you're having financial troubles. The business is teetering on the brink of failure, Cass."

Cass sucked in air as her blue eyes flashed with anger. "Who told you that?"

"It didn't take a genius to figure out." Only a millionaire with access to her boss's personal information. It dawned on Brynn that maybe Iain'd had her checked out, too. But she had no secrets, nothing to hide. Until recently, Brynn's life had been a very short, boring book.

"You can't tell anyone else, Brynn. I don't want to panic the others."

"What are you going to do to get back on track? Iain must be paying you a fortune. Is it enough to turn things around?"

Cass, the boss who'd described her last period in

excruciating detail, suddenly became affronted. "That's absolutely none of your business. I can handle my own financial matters, thank you very much. You work on finishing your inbox and we'll be fine."

Cass was bluffing, and her tell was the way she swiped the curls back from her forehead.

Brynn overlooked Cass's snappy attitude. Every time she got backed into a corner, Cass came out hissing. "I know some financial people. My brother-in-law, for instance. He could hook you up with someone. The two of you could go over the books, make a plan for solvency."

"I said I'll handle it." *Swipe, swipe*. "You're coming in this weekend. Right?"

Other than Paige, Brynn wouldn't call the people she worked with friends exactly, but she'd hate to see them unemployed. Still, Brynn desperately needed some downtime. She wanted to head out to the desert with her camera. She wanted to lie in bed all day with Iain. She wanted to bake and take her nephews to the movies and hit the flea market. Brynn was tired of working seven days a week. "I'll come in on Saturday, but not Sunday."

Cass's eyes bulged. "I'm going to have to insist that you do." *Swipe, swipe*.

"If you're really concerned about the business, you'll either start taking some of the load off me or at least hire a temp to help out. Good night, Cass."

Brynn left her sputtering boss and the office with a bounce in her step. She'd done it. Brynn had stood up for herself, and it felt liberating. Why did it feel so good to stand up to Cass, but barking at Iain this morning had left Brynn wracked with guilt? He'd never admit it, but her words had wounded him; she'd seen it in his eyes. She had the power to hurt him, and she took that seriously.

Brynn hopped in her car and sped through traffic, zipping between lanes. As soon as she made it home, she hit the shower, chose a short sundress for a change, and whipped up some chocolate chip cookies. She was taking the last batch out of the oven when the doorbell rang.

Iain stood on her porch with a pizza box in one hand and a bottle of wine in the other. He looked her up and down. "That dress is bloody brilliant. I can see your legs for a change."

She stepped aside to let him in. "You've seen my legs before."

"Oh, yes I have."

"Let's go into the kitchen."

"Smells like a bakery." When he got to the doorway, Iain drew to a standstill. "Fuck me. It's pink."

Brynn took the pizza out of his hand and laid it on the table. "You don't like it?"

"Who the fuck has a pink fridge? And stove?"

"A fifties housewife. I have pink appliances, too. You should see my toaster."

He slipped his jacket off and looked around. "It's just so…bloody pink."

Brynn laughed and grabbed a couple of wineglasses. "You never cook anyway. Your kitchen could be purple and it wouldn't bother you."

"Trust me, if my kitchen were purple—no, you're right. I still wouldn't care." He sat down at the table and Brynn placed a plate and a cloth napkin in front of him.

"Thanks again for stopping by my office today."

He grabbed her by the waist and pulled her onto his

lap. “You’re welcome. But you’ll come back to Blue Moon next week, right?”

“Iain, do you really need me?”

His brows lowered and the lines across his forehead deepened. “Yes. We’re doing that liaison thing. Also, I told James to pick some kind of planning committee for flowers and parties and all the rest of that bullshit.”

Brynn leaned back and studied him. “That was a really great idea.”

He stuck his finger in the neckline of her peach-colored dress and peered down at her bare breasts. “I’m full of good ideas. I’ve got one right now.”

Laughing, Brynn smacked his hand away. “After dinner.” She angled her head and gave him a teasing kiss, not too deep, with just a hint of tongue. Then she bounded off his lap and took a seat next to him.

“You’re playing with fire.”

Brynn smiled. “How was the rest of your day?” She slid a piece of pepperoni pizza onto his plate.

“What do you know about twelve-year-old boys?”

“Not much more than when I was a twelve-year-old girl. Why?”

“Amelia’s lad, he’s going through it. He’s smaller than the other kids. Ginger. Freckly. Cute as hell, but of course the girls haven’t noticed that yet.”

Brynn wiped her hands on a napkin and stared at him. “Tyler, is that his name?”

“Yeah. The other kids are making fun of him. I don’t know if the advice I gave helped or hurt. Giving advice, that’s your specialty.”

Brynn poured the wine and acted like what Iain had

told her was no big deal. In reality, her heart melted toward him even more. *Okay, shape up, jellyfish. He's not a saint*. No, but he cared about someone other than himself. Really cared. Enough to ask her opinion.

"So what did you tell him?"

"I told him not to give his power away and to use his opponent's weakness to gain the upper hand."

Brynn took a sip of wine. "Okay. I might have gone a different direction, but Tyler looks up to you and you gave him solid advice—minus the revenge factor."

"Revenge is always a factor." Iain ripped the crust from his pizza and ate it first.

"Remind me never to get on your bad side."

"Don't think that's possible, love."

Now her heart was completely melted, like a Bomb Pop in the middle of July.

"And Marc is still rowing with Melanie. Bad business that. She wants to get married."

"How long have they been together?"

"Two years."

"He loves her, but he's not willing to make a commitment? I don't understand men."

"Sadly, love, we're not that complicated."

"Not true. If Marc loves Melanie, why doesn't he want to get married?"

"He's afraid he'll muck it up, right? What if it all ends badly?"

Brynn shook her head. "It *is* going to end badly, by the sound of it. If he doesn't step up to the plate, he's going to lose her now."

Iain poured her another glass of wine. "It's like this—men have to be mentally ready to commit. And if he's not ready, he'll always feel trapped. How is it for women?"

Brynn shrugged. "According to my sisters, they just knew. They fell in love and they knew. My brothers-in-law were slower on the uptake."

"We men often are. So how was the rest of your day, love? Get enough oxygen in that miniature room of yours?"

"Barely. I confronted Cass about the business."

He set his glass down. "Well done. How did it feel?"

Brynn knew her grin was goofy, but she didn't care. "It felt really good. It didn't solve anything, of course. Cass is still Cass and she's going to run the business her own way. But I told her I wasn't going to work all weekend. I'm taking Sunday off."

His eyes turned to that molasses color, warm and hot. "Excellent. Then we have a date—lazy Sunday sex."

"Followed by dinner at my sister's house. Which we can still decline."

He blinked and his eyes went back to their normal shade. Iain took a long swallow of wine before responding. "I say we get it over with. Awkward handshakes, boring small talk, and all the rest that goes with meeting a girl's family for the first time."

"Okay."

They finished off the pizza, and when Brynn gave Iain a couple of cookies, he bit into one and nearly swooned. "Bloody hell, woman, these are delicious. You could start your own bakery."

"Iain, it's the recipe from the back of the chocolate chip package."

"Don't care. You're brilliant." He reached toward her

and swept his thumb across her bottom lip, then stuck it in his mouth. "Had a bit of chocolate."

His eyes held hers for a long moment. Then the doorbell buzzed.

Damn. "It's probably Tasha."

Iain stood and grabbed his jacket.

"You don't have to go," Brynn said.

"I'll leave you two alone. Besides, after spending the afternoon at Tyler's football game, I still have work to do."

Brynn stopped, her hand on the doorknob. "You actually went to his game?"

"I don't know why you keep looking at me like I've grown two heads. Let the Russian in so she can give that doorbell a rest, yeah?"

Brynn shook her head and opened the door. With a dog under each arm, Tasha pushed past Brynn. "He goes too far this time. I am done." Her feet slowed upon seeing Iain. "You are back. How thrilling."

"Good to see you too." He rubbed one of the dog's heads before kissing Brynn good-bye. "I'll call you tomorrow."

"Thanks for dinner." Brynn watched as Iain strode away while fixing the collar of his jacket. Before he got into the car, he glanced back, gave her a smile, and waved.

"You like the Englishman," Tasha said.

Brynn lifted her brow at Moose attempting to hump her throw pillow. "Natasha, dogs. Sofa. Now."

With a heavy sigh, the other woman placed them at her feet. "He is rubbing off on you, the Englishman."

Was that such a bad thing? Brynn had become fearless when it came to sex. Maybe that attitude was spilling over into the rest of her life. "I think he is."

"It is time. You good person, Brynn. The Englishman is good for you."

Brynn shut the door. "Hungry?"

"Starving. Since Zeke will not let my family visit, I am on strike. I do not wash his clothes. I do not cook. I have not been to grocery store for a week. And forget about the sex."

"And what's his response to this?"

"He withhold allowance. Like I am child. I am so tired, Brynn. I want to go home." Then brave, matter-of-fact, brash Tasha burst into tears.

Chapter 16

IAIN SPENT SATURDAY NIGHT AND ALL OF SUNDAY naked. Partly to shock Brynn—he loved getting a rise out of her, then slowly overcoming her objections, one stroke at a time—but mostly because he couldn't get enough of her. Clothes only hampered the process. They made love in his sitting room with Brynn leaning over the couch—what a glorious sight that had been. The bright sun shone through the windows, casting a beam of light across her sweet little bum, pink from a recent spanking. They'd christened the dining room table, where Iain had propped her in the middle of the tabletop, then devoured her, lick by lick, until her body trembled, desperate for release. They fucked twice on the white shag rug. Seeing Brynn spread eagle, her skin golden against the ivory carpet, hair fanned out behind her—bloody beautiful.

They'd finally worked their way back around to the bed, where they spent most of Sunday afternoon. As they lay facing each other, she asked about the dice he always carried. Instead of brushing off her question, Iain answered honestly.

"My dad was a right bastard and Marc's dad did a runner before he was born. But we had a friend called Davy. He was a good lad. Funny. Clever. Marc and I stayed at his house as often as we could. His parents knew what our home lives were like. They practically adopted us. The three of us were closer than brothers."

Iain had never opened himself up like this before, not like he did with Brynn. While it felt strange and a bit terrifying, he rather liked it. Which sounded like a load of rubbish, but it was the truth. He wanted her to know about him. Not everything, naturally, but the important bits.

"Davy had two dreams—going to university and coming to Vegas. He had a pair of dice and a poker chip he'd found in the arcade. Said once he graduated, we'd all come to Vegas, get pissed, and win a fortune. We were all so poor, none of us had even been to London. Vegas was an impossible idea." He stroked her arm as he talked. It was so soft, like satin.

"I wound up quitting school early. Marc never took his GCSEs, but Davy, he was the bright one. Got into the University of Manchester. We wound him up a bit, like mates do, but we were proud of him. Then one night, as he was walking home from the liquor store, he got hit by a car. My best mate died by the side of the road. It's a good thing they never found the person who did it or I'd probably still be in the nick for killing 'em. Davy was one of the good ones. He didn't deserve to die like a dog in the street."

Brynn stroked his face. He found her touch tender, reassuring. "I'm so sorry."

Iain took a deep breath. "That's the way it goes, innit?" He turned his lips into her palm. "Anyway, Marc and I knew there was nothing for us back home. So we decided to honor his memory and come to Vegas. We started our first business and it stuck."

"Does Marc have the poker chip?"

Iain played with her fingers, kissing each one in turn. "Yeah."

"Poor Davy. His parents must have been devastated."

"Still are. Tried to get them to move here, but they wouldn't have it. They live in Majorca now. They're happy there."

Brynn took her hand back and sat up. The way she stared at him, with such compassion in her eyes, nearly did him in. "You and Marc take care of them, don't you? Financially, I mean."

For some reason, being caught in a good deed embarrassed him. He couldn't look at her, not without feeling terribly uncomfortable, so Iain rolled out of bed. "We'd better get ready for dinner. I'm going to have to put on clothes whether I like it or not."

"Iain." Her hair hung in a wild tangle about her shoulders. Rising to her knees, she was completely naked and didn't try to cover herself from his gaze. Her navy eyes were big, bright, and full of some emotion he couldn't name. "You're a good man."

Only Brynn would think so. He wished it were true, that he was upright and decent, but she saw things in him that weren't really there. Iain should dissuade her, tell her he was nothing but an opportunist, but he basked in her good opinion. Made him want to live up to her ideal. He rather liked seeing himself through Brynn's eyes—even if it was a lie.

Though Iain had been to Trevor's house on the night of the garden party, where he first saw his lovely Brynn, he hadn't been inside the house itself. Guests had been rerouted to the garden. Made sense. Iain wouldn't want hundreds of people tramping through his home either.

But as he followed Brynn through the mansion, every room he passed reminded him of a bloody museum. Walls were lined with swords and daggers and framed bits of ancient tapestry. Clear glass cases held antiques of all sorts.

The night of the gala, the garden had been dark, illuminated by strings of lights. But now he stood on the terrace in the waning light. As he glanced around at the bright flowers, Iain was struck speechless. Perhaps a first for him. The garden rivaled the queen's. Lavish, it was. In the middle of a bloody desert. Now *this* was fuck-off money.

The sun quickly faded behind the mountains while the garden lights twinkled to life. Brynn stood next to him, holding herself as stiff as a rod, full of visible tension. He placed his hand on her back, hoping his touch lent her a sense of calm, but she didn't relax. Instead, she remained like a soldier standing at attention.

For the first time in a very long time, Iain was out to make a good impression. Not only did he want Trevor's approval—and his money—but he also didn't want to shame Brynn with his usual brusque behavior.

Iain was odd man out tonight, here to be inspected, and though he may have worn the best suits and looked rather swish, he wasn't in the same class as Trevor and Cal. Had to mind his manners for once. He wouldn't ask for money outright or talk about his plans for the downtown properties—at least not overtly. That would be bad form with this set. No, tonight was about sowing the seeds, downplaying his accomplishments, and most importantly, convincing them he wasn't a tosser who shouldn't be allowed anywhere near Brynn. That last bit was absolutely true, but her family didn't need to know it.

He shook hands with Trevor and Cal in the British way—by not using a firm grip.

Trevor seemed a cold fish. His icy, gray eyes dissected Iain. Didn't miss a trick, that one. Allie was lovely, with long, silver-blond hair, though she bore little resemblance to Brynn.

"So glad to meet you, Iain," she said. "Welcome."

"Thank you for having me." He handed her a bottle of wine. Not too expensive—he didn't want to appear to be trying too hard—but not plonk, so they wouldn't think him cheap.

"That's so nice of you." Allie glanced pointedly at her husband.

But Trevor wasn't impressed. He raised a brow and lifted his snooty nose in the air. "Lovely. Would you care for a drink—Iain, is it?" Wanker knew his name. He'd probably done a background check on Iain that was every bit as detailed as the one Iain had commissioned on him.

"Whiskey, if you have it."

"Of course." Trevor moved away to the drinks cart and poured him a couple fingers' worth.

Iain took the glass. "Cheers."

No shrinking violet, Brynn's sister, Monica, wore a skintight scarlet dress. Her hair hit the middle of her back, a mass of untamed curls. Her hard-as-nails glare said she suspected he might make off with the silver… or her sister. Charming. "Iain, tell us about yourself."

"I'm from Manchester. Came to Vegas over a decade ago. I very much like it here."

Monica's husband, Calum Hughes, looked on with a bored air. He was a bit of a puzzle. He had a pedigree but restored old cars. A toff with working-class sensibilities, he wasn't afraid to get his hands dirty. His brown mop of hair was untidy. He wore faded jeans with a tailored suit jacket and spoke with a plummy accent.

"Like cars, do you?" he asked and took a sip of his drink.

"Not really, no," Iain answered.

Both Cal and Trevor managed to look affronted.

"Sorry?" Cal asked, shaking his head, confused by Iain's answer.

"Not everyone's a gearhead." Monica patted her husband's shoulder, as if to soften the blow.

Trevor handed Brynn a pink cocktail. She took it with trembling fingers. Poor girl was a nervous wreck. Iain didn't understand why, unless she was embarrassed to have him here. After all, she'd tried to talk him out of this dinner more than once, but Iain wasn't having it. This was his chance to make contact with Trevor. He wasn't about to pass that up.

"Thanks," she whispered. All the progress she'd made over the last weekend—opening herself up to him, allowing herself to be honest and vulnerable, bit by bit—had vanished in the last five minutes. Brynn was back to the shy wallflower who refused to ask for what she wanted. And if Iain knew anything, he knew Brynnie wanted to get the hell out of here—the faster the better.

He stroked his hand along her back and turned to Trevor. "Your garden is lovely. Do you tend the flowers yourself?"

"No," Trevor said. He didn't elaborate and he barely glanced in Iain's direction. This was going to be a bloody long night.

"Maybe Brynn could show you around." Allie to the rescue. "The roses are blooming like crazy."

Iain almost fell to his knees in gratitude.

"That's a good idea." Brynn took Iain's hand and all but dragged him down the terrace steps and along the lighted pathway, deep into the fragrant blooms.

"What in God's name is wrong with you?" he whispered. "You're ashamed of me, aren't you? You don't think I'm good enough to meet your family. I know I'm a Manc, a social pariah. If you want me to leave, have the courage to say so." Iain had never felt like this before—inferior. He found he didn't like it.

In the past several years, Iain had surrounded himself with wealthy, influential people, some of Vegas's elite, and he'd never batted an eye. Tonight, doubt nipped at his heels. Seeing Brynn crawl back into her shell, knowing that he wasn't good enough for her—it made him rethink his plan for the hundredth time today.

"Of course I'm not ashamed of you," she whispered, placing her free hand on his arm. "It's just that my sisters drive me crazy. They're going to start asking you a bunch of personal questions and it's going to get awkward. Besides, you're not exactly acting like yourself and that's making me even more nervous."

"Wha'? I'm acting like meself."

"No you're not. Normally you're rude and cocky and arrogant. Tonight you've been downright polite."

Now Iain was utterly confused. "I thought that's what you wanted."

"I'm not making any sense."

"No, you're not. But I can swagger back and tell them all to fuck off. Would that make you happy?"

Brynn actually laughed, and some of her stiffness fell away. "No. Maybe. I'd love to see Trevor's face if you said that. He'd probably tell you to go fuck yourself twice as hard."

He palmed her jaw, stroking her cheek. "I'll avoid answering questions about the two of us. If they start getting personal, I'll handle it. But you need to stop acting like you're about to make a run for it, eh?"

Brynn grabbed his tie and pulled him toward her. "Deal." She stood on her toes and kissed him hard, then stepped away. "Okay, let's go."

Iain watched her walk toward the house. The gentle sway of her hips in the long black-and-white patterned skirt had his heart beating double time. But he couldn't let his feelings get in the way of his goal. Somehow, Iain had to make himself likable, so that Trevor wouldn't hate his guts. Had his work cut out for him, he did.

Dinner was a long affair, peppered with questions and served with duck.

Monica: "What do you do for a living? Do you have any sisters of your own? No? Then you don't know how protective they can be, do you?"

Allie: "What exactly are your intentions regarding Brynn? My husband calls me the ballbuster—did Brynn happen to mention that? She's a very gentle soul, you realize that, right?"

Cal: "What do you mean you don't drive? Have you ever been behind the wheel of an Aston Martin, mate? It'll change your life."

Iain successfully evaded personal questions, smiled politely, and watched as Brynn, who sat across from him, quietly got pissed. She barely spoke and hardly touched her food, but she managed to down the Sauvignon Blanc like it was bottled water. He was the only one who seemed to notice. Her sisters were too busy being intrusive.

Trevor watched him closely and added little to the discussion. After pudding was served, he stood up from the table. "Come along, gentlemen, let's sit out on the terrace and have a cigar. Chapman, you can fill us in on your business interests."

Like a bloody gift from above. Now was his chance. Iain could casually drop a hint about downtown and the lack of living space, suss out Trevor about his thoughts on the city's proposal to beautify the area. Maybe Trevor would like to stop by and see his latest building.

But after taking one glance at Brynn with her drooping eyelids, all of his plans withered. He couldn't leave her like this. His poor girl was well and truly sozzled.

Iain stood, as well. "Perhaps another time. Brynn's had one glass too many."

She waved him off. "I'm fine. Sober as a judge."

Iain felt the chance of a lifetime slip through his fingers. Nevertheless, he didn't have a choice, not really. Brynn was more important. He moved to the other side of the table, wrapped his arm around her waist, and helped her stand.

"How much did you have?" Allie asked.

"Don't remember," Brynn said, blinking up at Iain.

"She had four glasses and little food," Iain said, lifting her to her feet.

"She's always been a lightweight," Monica said. Not a terribly helpful observation.

Allie stood to one side, her brow furrowed. "She should spend the night here."

Iain lifted her in his arms. "She has work in the morning. I'll take her home, tuck her in."

"Will you now?" Trevor asked.

"Keep your shirt on, mate. Her neighbor's been staying in the guest room. I'll leave her in good hands, yeah?"

Brynn looked up at him, a sloppy smile on her face. "You weren't a dickhead tonight."

"I tried my best, pet."

Allie led the way to the foyer. Outside, Iain's driver waited, and when he saw them emerge, he immediately flew out of the car and opened the back door.

Iain climbed in with Brynn on his lap. As he settled in the seat, she flopped against him like a rag doll.

Allie and Monica leaned their heads inside the car.

"Take care of her," Allie said.

"Call me tomorrow, Sis. Damn." Monica withdrew. "We should have gotten pics. I've never seen her this drunk before."

The driver closed the door and Iain stroked Brynn's hair. "It's all right, love. We'll get you home."

"I don't usually get hammered."

"No, you don't say."

"It's true. I love my sisters, but they're annoying, you know?" She slurred her words together until it sounded like one jumbled sentence. "I couldn't run off and leave you because they'd eat you alive. You were really nice tonight." She reached up and tapped his cheek. "Good job." Then she snuggled against his shoulder and fell asleep.

Once they arrived at her house, Iain couldn't rouse her. If he wasn't mistaken, she may have drooled on his pocket square. Picking her up, he trotted up to the front porch and kicked on the door until Tasha opened it.

"What is problem?" she asked, then saw Brynn. "What did you do? I warn you, Englishman, if you hurt her—"

"Stuff it, would you? She's drunk. Let us in." As soon as Tasha moved out of the way, Iain carried Brynn into the house and down the hall.

In Brynn's bedroom, Tasha flipped on the overhead light and hovered in the doorway. "I will check on her tonight. You can go home."

"Come and remove the duvet, would you?"

With a melodramatic sigh, Tasha pulled back the covers. Iain laid Brynn on the bed and stared down at her. He was reluctant to leave her. What if she awoke in the middle of the night and needed something? Besides, he'd gotten used to sleeping next to her. Kneeling, he removed her sandals, then covered her with the blanket.

"She will be fine," Tasha said.

He knew that. Of course she would. Everyone went on a bender now and again. Most people anyway. However, Brynn had done it to escape the dinner with her family. She kept running from her problems, in one way or another. Her sisters ran roughshod over her, gave her hell, and Brynn allowed it. *The way she allowed you to blaze into her life. Into her bed.*

God, how Iain hated this now-familiar guilt. And he was choking on a big dose of it tonight.

One of Tasha's little dogs started yapping for attention, until she picked it up and cuddled it in her arms. "Fine, Englishman. Stay. I grow weary of arguing with you." She turned and walked away with the second dog trailing after her.

Iain turned on the table lamp, shut the door, and flicked off the main light. He'd already fucked up his meeting with Trevor Blake. May as well stay and make sure Brynn was taken care of. Honestly, there was nowhere else he'd rather be.

The next day, Brynn awoke with a vicious hangover. Her mouth was dry, her eyes felt swollen, and Iain didn't say a word about it as he set a mug of coffee on her bedside table. She watched him dress, knotting his tie as he stared into the mirror on her chipped white dresser.

"About last night—"

He turned and slung on his vest. "Let it rest, pet. Take your time getting to the office." Grabbing his jacket, he shoved his arms into the sleeves and walked over to the bed, dropping a kiss on top of her head. "I'll see you later, yeah?"

He was disappointed in her. He didn't need to say it—she could read it in his face, in the tight line of his shoulders. *What do you expect, jellyfish? Of course he's disappointed. You let him down.* He turned and disappeared, shutting the door softly behind him.

As Brynn watched him go, she felt like shit—both physically and emotionally. She'd left Iain stranded last night, at the mercy of her sisters and their husbands and all those prying, personal questions. She was nothing but a coward. Brynn should have taken Allie and Monica to task, told them her relationship with Iain was no one's damned business. But instead, she'd hung him out to dry and downed glass after glass of wine.

Iain was a good man. He wasn't always the nicest person, but he had his own kind of integrity. He deserved her support. She'd fucked up, and somehow, she was going to have to make it up to him.

When she heard the front door shut, Brynn picked up her coffee and sipped it slowly. Yeah, that was the stuff. Made her feel almost human again. Didn't soothe her conscious, though.

She had settled back against the headboard, praying her temples would stop pounding, when Tash walked into the bedroom without knocking. She wore short shorts and a rhinestone-encrusted T-shirt. When she settled Moose and Squirrel on the bed, Brynn didn't offer a protest. She was in too much pain to care. She set her mug aside as Tash flopped onto the mattress.

"Your Englishman carry you to bed last night. He is not total asshole."

"I got drunk. I never get drunk."

"Well, you get drunk last night. Why?"

Good question. Brynn could put the blame on her sisters. They were a pain in the ass sometimes, no matter how much she loved them. But it wasn't their fault. It wasn't Iain's fault either. He'd thought she was ashamed of him. Not even. What woman wouldn't be proud to have a brilliant, beautiful Iain on her arm? No, Brynn was ashamed of herself.

She hadn't wanted to face the personal questions and her family's larger-than-life personalities. Allie was always overprotective and a little suffocating. She meant well, but Brynn felt burdened by the weight of all that energy. Monica's in-your-face persona was aggressive—and exhausting. Trevor remained coldly silent, always judging. And Cal…well, Cal was the most easygoing one in the group, but even he hadn't been very welcoming toward Iain. So instead of handling things like a competent person, Brynn had checked out.

Breathing out a sigh, she reclaimed her mug and took a sip. "I get overwhelmed sometimes. Allie and Monica are so…loud. They pick at me and then start badgering each other."

"What is this badger?" Tash asked, rubbing Moose's belly.

"Quarreling."

Tash nodded. "Yes, it is same with my sister. She is bitch. Yet I miss her. Some days, I hate her. And yet, I would kill anyone who dared to harm her. That is the way of family."

"You're right. But I always feel like it's two against one."

"When they…*badger* you, tell them to eat shit. Simple as that, yes?"

It probably *was* that simple. But Brynn had always struggled to be heard in her family. She'd always been the quiet one. When her mom got sick, Brynn withdrew even further. It was the way she coped with Allie's bossiness and Monica's bitchiness. Yet she wasn't that little girl anymore. She was a grown woman who wasn't taking care of business. That seriously needed to change.

She finished her coffee while the two dogs softly snored and Tasha complained about Zeke.

Brynn let her friend run out of steam. If she was going to start tackling things head-on, she may as well start with Tasha. She loved this woman, had nothing but sympathy for her. Brynn liked that she could provide comfort and solace when Tash needed it. But she also knew Tash would stay for two weeks if Brynn let her. She'd done it before.

The problem was, Natasha and her pups weren't great roommates. Tash used up all the hot water, never cleaned up after herself, and allowed the dogs to poop on Brynn's back porch. Plus, Brynn would feel obligated to spend time with Tash, when she'd rather spend her nights with Iain. She needed to send Tash home, but damn, why did it have to be so hard?

"Tash." The other woman glanced up. Brynn took a deep breath. "You know I'm your friend. That I care about you. I'm glad that when you're in crisis, you know you can always come here. But *I* really believe if you go home and talk to Zeke, you can work things out. Communication, that's the key." Did Brynn feel like a fraud for giving Tash advice she herself didn't take? Um, yep. But it was past time to start setting some boundaries in her life.

Tasha sniffed and looked away. "I have talked until my face is blue. He is cruel man. I never go back to him."

"He's not cruel. He's just set in his ways. And you're not always the most flexible person in the world."

"I flexible. See." She bent one leg behind her head in some bizarre yoga pose. Since she wasn't wearing underwear, Brynn put up a hand to block out the sight of Tasha's well-waxed hoo-ha.

"Okay, please stop doing that."

Tasha resumed her normal position, lounging at the foot of the bed.

"It's time to fix things with your man. I think you guys should see a therapist, someone who will help you come to a compromise."

Tash pursed her lips. "So you are kicking me to curb."

Brynn felt the slightest twinge of guilt. This thing with Iain was new, and Brynn wanted to nurture it. To do that, she needed her nights free. Plus, Brynn wanted her home back. "I'm not kicking you out. I'm sending you home."

"Fine. I go." Tash grabbed the dogs and stomped off to the guest room. A few minutes later, she wheeled her Louis Vuitton luggage past Brynn's bedroom door. She poked her head inside. "You take luggage, I get dogs."

"Deal." Brynn was still wearing her dress from the night before. She stood and made a vain attempt to smooth her hand over the wrinkled skirt. As she passed the mirror, she saw her mascara had migrated south, rimming her eyes and leaving streaks along her cheek. Iain had seen her looking like this. Wonderful.

She grabbed Tasha's bags, walked her across the street, and gave her a big hug. "It'll be okay. I'll help you find a therapist if you want."

Tash sniffed in her ear. "I want."

Brynn added that to her mental list of things to do, then ran back home and quickly got ready for work. Her headache had settled into a mild pounding, which was manageable.

Speeding off to Blue Moon Corp., she hoped to see Iain, maybe apologize and take him to lunch. However, when she ducked into his suite, Amelia informed her that

Iain was gone. In fact, he'd be out for most of the day. Disappointment settled in her chest as she walked into the conference room to continue interviewing employees.

After a solitary lunch, she headed back to her own office, tried her best to avoid Cass, and started chipping away at her pile of work.

When Iain finally called her at five, relief flooded her. He was still talking to her after last night. She'd thought maybe she'd screwed it up for good.

"Dinner at mine, yeah? Make sure you bring clothes for tomorrow. I want you to stay the night. I'll pick you up at your house in an hour." In his typical bossy fashion, he didn't ask, he just expected her to fall in line. It gave Brynn a secret little thrill. When anyone else bossed her around, she felt like a doormat. When Iain did it, she got turned on.

The rest of the week passed quickly. Brynn worked like a fiend every day and went home to Iain every night. They spent most of their time at his place. Though twice they stayed at Brynn's. She liked that best, being at home, surrounded by her own things. She'd cook a simple dinner, and Iain would help her with the dishes. That surprised her—seeing him roll up his sleeves and pitch in.

She made space in her closet for a few of his suits, and he shifted some clothes around in his dressing room so that she had a whole rack to herself. After knowing each other only two weeks, they were practically living together. Normally, Brynn would have been plagued by a million doubts. Things were moving so fast, it left her spinning, but with Iain, she didn't even question it. She was happier than she'd ever been. There was only one little thing niggling the back of her brain: Allie's dinner party.

When Brynn tried to apologize again, Iain cut her off. "Everyone's gotten drunk a time or two. No harm in it. Drop it, Brynnie."

So she did. But the shame stayed with her, haunted her. Brynn silently vowed to do better.

Throughout the week, Brynn had tried several times to bring up TDTC business with Cass. Unfortunately, her boss didn't want to discuss her floundering company and stubbornly refused to get outside help. Instead, she overshared about her new boyfriend who had two cats of his own, and neither of them got along with Nef. The sex, however, was spectacular. Same old, same old.

Brynn started working until five every night. She couldn't care more about the company than Cass did. Even if Brynn worked 24-7, she wouldn't be able to save the businesses, not if Cass continued to bury her head in the sand. Brynn grappled with fessing up to her coworkers, especially Paige. They deserved to know the truth about TDTC's dire circumstances. She wrestled with her own decision, too. Leave a sinking ship or ride it out to the end? Despite asking herself the same questions over and over again, she never came up with any answers.

On Friday, she finished her evaluation of Blue Moon. Brynn would no longer spend her days in Iain's office, and she was going to miss it. She'd gotten to know the staff pretty well along with Amelia's boy, Tyler, who'd started hanging out in the conference room a couple of times a week. He loved telling her about his latest video game obsessions. And Tyler spoke about Iain as though he were a superhero. "Iain lets me sit in on his meetings, and even though I don't understand half of what's going on, it's so cool the way all the other dudes listen to him. He's awesome." Brynn agreed. Iain *was* awesome.

Brynn was also pleasantly surprised, and not a little jealous, when Amelia mentioned she was getting her own assistant. "It was Iain's idea. He wants to free up my afternoons so that I can spend more time with Tyler."

It only confirmed what Brynn already knew—Iain could definitely be one of the good guys. He may have tried to hide it, but his heart was in the right place—if only he'd let that side show more often.

While her work life might be in transition, Brynn's personal life was bliss. Iain was opening up to her, telling her personal things about himself—his struggle to build a business, his turbulent childhood. Brynn felt closer to Iain than anyone else, including her family.

And the sex left her legs wobbly. Iain was completely uninhibited, and he had Brynn embracing a sexual side of herself she had never known existed. While she enjoyed being dominated and having Iain command her, he could also be tender. In those sweet moments, she wondered if forever might be in the cards.

Brynn wasn't sure when she'd fallen in love with him, but it dawned on her Saturday morning as they were both getting ready for work. Brynn watched as he fastidiously knotted his tie, then grabbed Davy's dice off the bedside table and shoved them in his pocket. She realized in that moment that she loved him and had for a while. Possibly since she walked into his office for the first time and saw him standing behind his desk. The feeling was unexpected and scary. Brynn kept it to herself and carried on as if she didn't have this burning secret deep inside of her. There were reasons enough to be wary.

Although he opened up to her, he didn't tell Brynn everything. Something was bothering Iain, keeping him from sleeping each night. She usually awoke in the wee hours, reaching for him, only to find Iain's side of the bed was cold. One night, she went looking for him. Tossing on her kimono, Brynn walked down the hall and peeked into his office, but it was empty. Instead, she found him in the sitting room. He stood completely naked at the window, staring down at the Boulevard. He was eating ice cream from a carton.

She wrapped her arms around him from behind. "Couldn't sleep again?"

"No." He offered her a spoonful of chocolate-cherry swirl.

"Where have you been hiding this? The only two things in your freezer are ice and vodka."

"Called the concierge and had him bring it to me."

It caught her off guard, seeing Iain Chapman stress eating in the middle of the night. Something heavy must have been weighing on his mind. "Want to tell me what's wrong?"

He remained silent and his body froze like a statue. Then he turned in her arms. "No. Stand with your back to the window."

She hesitated for a moment. He was using sex to keep her from asking questions. She realized it for the deflection that it was. It *was* very distracting. For both of them.

Brynn walked two feet to the floor-to-ceiling window and turned around, waiting. If nothing else, Iain's sexual imagination always surprised her.

"Undo your robe. Take it off."

Brynn peeked over her shoulder. It wasn't dark outside, not with all the neon flashing up and down the Boulevard. No one could see through the tinted windows, though. Probably. Biting her lip, Brynn held back a shudder.

"Brynnie. Don't make me repeat myself."

That voice. She whipped her head around and, with nervous hands, unbelted her robe, letting it slide off her body. She stood before him naked and breathless. She could be shameless like this without feeling self-conscious. A first for her. Iain thought she was beautiful, telling her so often. And when he looked at her like she was tastier than that ice cream in his hand, she felt like it.

"Hands above your head. Keep them there."

The window was cold against her back, but she did as he requested. Raising her arms, she thrust her breasts out and was rewarded when Iain's gaze darted to them. He licked his lips and stepped closer. Just a few inches away. His body heat rose off him in delicious waves, bringing with it the smell of chocolate and his own intoxicating scent.

Brynn had become addicted to this—his demands, his touch, his spontaneity. And Iain was caught up in this rising tide of desire as much as she was. His cock was rock hard and his breath sounded unsteady. He never remained unaffected by these games they played.

Dipping his finger into the carton, he scooped out a dollop of ice cream and held it up to her mouth. "Lick."

Brynn decided to tease him a bit. She knew he'd punish her if she did, but she liked that, too. Pushing his buttons was a thrilling ride. She never knew exactly what retribution he'd mete out. So instead of taking his finger in her mouth, as she knew he wanted, she barely lapped at the frozen treat. "Done."

"Oh, who's being naughty?" he asked, his voice raspy. Leaning down, his kiss was ruthless. Relentless. He thrust his tongue roughly into her mouth, pulling back only to bite her lower lip just hard enough to sting. Yeah, that was most definitely addictive. "Now do behave. Lick it properly. Like you would my cock."

Brynn's heart kicked up. Every time with Iain was new and electric. He aroused her so easily, with merely a glance or a touch. Low-gasm Brynn was history.

Tilting her head forward, Brynn kept her eyes trained on Iain's as she took his finger into her mouth and sucked it gently.

Iain groaned so deeply, Brynn's nipples ached at the sound. "That's it, love. Deeper."

She obeyed, wanting him to experience the same pleasure he was giving her. She took him farther into her mouth, making sure she licked the length of his finger and every last bit of chocolate-cherry flavor. Best ice cream she'd ever tasted.

When she lifted her head, Brynn's tongue swept over her lower lip. Slowly. Seductively.

Iain's narrowed eyes trailed it. Once more, he swooped down to kiss her. He was gentle this time, stroking his tongue along her lip, sucking it afterward. This was her reward for following his instructions. The way Brynn looked at it, whether he punished her or rewarded her, it was a win-win proposition.

Iain stuck his finger back into the carton. When he brought it out, he held it to Brynn's throat and drew a line down her sternum. The cold made her shiver. So did his creativity. As Iain painted her, his hand was the slightest bit shaky.

A bolt of heat shot through Brynn when Iain bent down and followed it with his tongue. Her arms were still raised above her head. Obedient. Helpless. But she liked it that way.

Once more, he scooped a bit of the ice cream onto his finger, this time using it to circle her nipple. First one, then the other. He used his mouth to suck it off her skin.

Brynn's legs trembled. This was a luscious game of torture. The ice cream numbed her breasts, but Iain's tongue sent warmth radiating through her system.

When he finally raised his head, he gazed down at her, his expression inscrutable. "Put your arms down. Keep them pinned to your sides."

She lowered her arms, impatient to see what body part he'd paint next. Her pussy was aching by now, desperate to feel him—his tongue, his fingers, his cock. She didn't care which.

Iain threaded his sticky fingers through her hair and grabbed hold. He tilted her head back, sucking and nibbling his way from her neck down to her breasts. Brynn longed to touch him, feel the ripple of muscles against his back, sift her fingers through his short hair. But she did as he'd ordered and kept her hands at her sides. She bunched them into fists, her body so sensitive right then, she trembled.

"You're good at obeying, aren't you, darling?"

She merely nodded, not trusting her voice at this

point. Because if she opened her mouth, she'd beg him to fuck her. And she'd learned the hard way that Iain was unpredictable. Sometimes he would give in and take her so hard she couldn't remember her own name. Other times he would hold out, keep her waiting, delay her orgasm until she nearly sobbed for relief. Begging was too much of a gamble.

Only one thing about their lovemaking remained constant. Iain was always in control. Of her. Of his own reactions. He never lost himself in it the way Brynn did.

Now Iain knelt before her and rubbed ice cream over her ribs and around her belly button. Brynn gasped at the blast of cold and sucked in her stomach. By the time he'd licked her clean, she was about to collapse on the floor.

But Iain set the carton aside and lightly bit her inner thigh. Brynn's head fell back as she moaned. God, she wanted him. Needed him. He wound her up, time after time, until she was a basket case. In those moments, fulfillment became her sole reason for existing.

"Spread your legs apart, Brynnie." She did so immediately, but her knee almost buckled. Iain caught her and propped his hands on her waist, literally holding her up. Then he parted her folds and lapped her. His tongue slipped inside her, and he flicked it wildly while his thumb found her clit.

Brynn instantly fell apart. She couldn't hold back anymore. Her hands shot out and found his head, holding it right where she wanted. If Iain hadn't been supporting her, she would have collapsed onto the floor. Delicious tingles of pleasure radiated throughout her body.

Each orgasm Iain gave her was different. Some were mellow, some were all-consuming. By varying his technique, he could elicit a different response. But no matter what route he chose, he *always* made her come.

Once the tremors subsided, Iain still didn't let up. His thumb continued to flutter over her swollen clit. His tongue still swirled inside her. Brynn felt that now-familiar sensation start to ramp up again. Where before she could barely have one orgasm, now Iain played her body like a well-tuned instrument.

Passion built on itself, working its way through her system once more. Soon, another surge of pleasure, twice as intense as the first, blew through her like a fire, consuming her. Brynn gasped for every breath she took.

Her body was still shaking when he lifted his head and gazed up at her. "I thought I told you to keep your hands at your sides."

"I've been a bad girl, Iain. I'll totally let you spank me, but first, I need a minute to calm down. That last one was a doozy."

"No." He rose, walked to the side table, and shoved his hand into the orange hand-blown glass bowl. Since last weekend, he'd started keeping condoms strategically stashed throughout the apartment and her house as well. "No minutes. No resting. And tomorrow, when you can't walk because I've fucked you so hard, you'll thank me."

Arrogant Brit. God, how she loved it.

He rolled the condom on as he walked toward her. Brynn watched him in the semidarkness, her eyes playing over his hard muscles. She needed to draw him like this, with bright pops of neon flashing over him.

Iain drew to a stop in front of her and, without a word, placed his hands on her ass and lifted her up. She wrapped her rubbery legs around his waist while he drove into her and kissed her at the same time, swallowing her cry.

This was exactly what Brynn needed. To be possessed by Iain. He didn't hold back as he slammed into her over and over. That was okay. Brynn liked it when he got rough. She held on, clinging to his shoulders, lost in the pleasure. And the emotion. When Iain was deep inside of her, she felt the bond between them strengthen. It wrapped around her heart, tight and unshakable, drawing her closer to him. He was a part of her now.

He gazed down at her, wearing a fierce frown, gritting his teeth as he sought to stave off his own orgasm. "Brynnie. God, you feel good."

He felt good too. When he finally let himself go, his cock jerked inside her and his hips bucked. She gazed up at him, past his corded neck and his raised chin. She loved him so much.

Iain looked down at her, never breaking eye contact as he continued to shudder. "*Brynn*."

Afterward, he held her. She rested her head against his chest, heard the unsteady thump of his heart. She wanted this to last forever—this closeness, this feeling of being cosseted by Iain Chapman.

He brushed his lips over the top of her head. "I've never met anyone like you, Brynn."

"Is that a good thing?"

"Oh yes, pet. Very good."

She lifted her head and gazed up at him. "Why couldn't you sleep?"

He paused. "Work. Just…thinking about a particular problem I have."

"Can I help?"

He was quiet for a long moment. "No, I don't think so. We should probably get a shower, wash off the stickiness."

This was frustratingly familiar. Iain could open up to her, share things about his past or his relationship with Marc, but when she brought up his business, for some reason, he shut Brynn down. Maybe he was afraid she'd lecture him again.

He carried her to the bathroom, still buried inside her. She wanted him to trust her, the way she'd come to trust him. "You can tell me anything, you know. I promise I won't quote from a manual."

He didn't laugh, as she'd intended. "Don't want to talk about it. It's something I have to figure out meself."

Feeling chastised and dismissed, Brynn said nothing when he finally slid out of her. Instead, she turned her back on him and flipped on the shower. She reminded herself again that even though she was crazy about him, they hardly knew each other. Not really. And his business was his own.

Still, she felt hurt. Rejected. Brynn had lost her heart to Iain. She only hoped he'd handle it with care.

Chapter 17

Brynn was having the worst Monday imaginable. It had started out well enough, with Iain kissing her breasts, sucking them, laving his tongue across her nipples until she woke up writhing, the dark gray sheets in a tangle around her legs.

Wet and ready, she'd reached for him. They didn't play games in the mornings, and he didn't waste time, either. Entering her in one slick motion, Iain thrust his hips forward, withdrew, then did it again—over and over with dizzying effect. Brynn's loud moans filled the silence as she wedged a hand between their bodies and, using one finger, circled her clit. She came in minutes. Iain had opened that door for her. Brynn didn't know if it was simple biology or if the love she felt for Iain mixed with her body's response.

After her gasps subsided, Iain increased his speed. He stroked faster and faster, shuddering and hoarsely moaning in her ear. Afterward, they lay together, their bodies cooling as dawn broke out over Vegas and long shadows fell across the room.

Brynn didn't want to go to work. She'd rather stay there with him, wrapped in his warmth, sated and drowsy, until he was ready for another round. But since having sex for the rest of the morning wouldn't pay the mortgage, Brynn kissed his shoulder and crawled out of bed. She glanced out the window, catching a glimpse of the Strip on her way to the bathroom. The city, so lively and chaotic every night, looked a little tawdry at dawn. Litter lined the street and the bright neon lights began to dim as the sun rose. This was her town, and even at its shabbiest, Brynn loved it.

After a quick shower, she threw on a purple peasant skirt and a lavender blouse. She and Iain moved around each other in a badly choreographed dance. She'd bumped into him twice, once at the bathroom sink and once at the coffeepot. She'd nearly spilled her travel mug all over the floor. She managed to pull her hair into a fishtail braid and grab her things before finally heading for the door.

Iain stood in the living room, a bemused expression on his handsome face. "You're forgetting something, pet."

Brynn stopped in her tracks. She had her bag, a bagel secured between her front teeth, a full mug, and her keys. "What?" she mumbled.

Fixing his cufflink, he stared at her with raised brows. "I need a kiss good-bye, don't I?" He moved forward and bussed both of her cheeks and her forehead, then brushed her neck with his chin. "You're meeting me for lunch at the bistro, yeah?"

"Uh-huh." Then she flew out the door and made the long elevator journey to the lobby. The concierge now knew her by name. Brynn nodded and smiled. It should have been weird, staying there most nights, nodding at Iain's neighbors every morning, but though it wasn't home, being with Iain was worth it. Despite the ugly furniture.

She navigated rush-hour traffic and got to the office by eight. But the minute she entered, Brynn's day turned from stressful to shit. Her computer was dead. No noise from the hard drive, no blinking cursor, just a horrible, blank screen. Brynn turned it off and tried again. And again. Oh no. This was bad. This was worse than bad—this was catastrophic.

Whipping out her phone, she called the off-site IT guy and, in a panic, explained what happened.

"Sounds like a complete hardware failure," he said. "Tough to know until I can see it. I'll be by sometime this afternoon."

Anxiety had Brynn grasping her braid. "No, I need you now."

"Brynn, babe, I've got five people ahead of you."

"So escalate the ticket. Bump me to the front of the queue."

After some begging and an offer of two hundred in cash, he promised he'd make an appearance that morning. Her computer was old, the software obsolete. She'd inherited it from the last poor sap who'd constructed curriculum.

Working the kinks out of her neck, Brynn slogged to Cass's office and knocked on the door.

"Enter." Cass stood with her back to the window, staring at three cocktail dresses draped over the desk. "Oh good, Brynn, you can help. I need to decide on one and return the other two." She grabbed the black satin with a ruched shoulder. "What do you think?"

"Cass, my computer's dead. I can't access any of my work. The IT guy is coming to pick it up soon, but in the meantime, I have nothing. The animation for the Pampered Pooch franchise, the manual on how to close a sale, my notes on the car dealership—all of it's gone."

Cass placed the dress back on the desk. "Didn't you back everything up?"

"Yes, of course. I back up my data every Friday afternoon. But since my computer's fried, it doesn't matter. Even if the IT guy can revive it, I don't know how long that will take. What are we going to do?"

Cass fell into her chair. "See if you can use Paige's or Lori's computer."

"They don't have the software I need. If you authorize me to get a new computer, I'll have to get new software too. What I've been using is too ancient for a new system. All of the due dates are going to have to be pushed way back. This could take weeks."

Cass sat staring at her desk. She didn't speak. She didn't blink. After several minutes passed, she placed her head on the orange satin dress and began weeping.

Brynn snatched it off the desk and flung it at the chair. Cass couldn't return a dress covered in mascara stains. "Oh God, Brynn." She lifted her head and tears poured from her eyes. "I thought I could handle it all, but I'm up to my neck in debt. I barely make payroll every week. The vet's threatened to stop treating Nef if I don't pay my bill. What am I going to do?"

Things were as bad as Brynn had feared. She walked the narrow path to her boss's desk, careful not to step on anything or accidentally knock over a stack of folders. She halfheartedly patted Cass's shoulder. "You *have* to get some kind of financial person in here to straighten it out. Today."

"Who? I can't afford to pay anyone."

"My brother-in-law might know someone."

Cass pulled back, shaking her head so hard, the baby

fine curls sprang around her head. "No. Word will get out. Everyone will know. I'll be a laughingstock in the industry. I'll find a way, you just have to be patient. We'll get a computer next week."

Reality and her boss didn't always see eye to eye. This was one of those times. Brynn bent down and patted Cass's knee. "Of course everyone is going to find out. There's no way around it. But this can't go on. You're barely solvent. If you don't call someone today, I'm going to have to quit. I can't continue to support your bad choices." For once, Brynn stood her ground and didn't feel bad about it. Cass needed a dose of tough love.

She gazed at Brynn with watery eyes. "You don't mean that."

"I do." Brynn had been a fool to trust Cass for as long as she had. She'd made excuses for her boss, put up with her manipulations, and worked her ass off for nothing. If Cass didn't change, they wouldn't last another week. "You need someone to look over all the financials, put you on a budget, and get this company back on track. If you're not willing to do that, I'm out." Brynn had clients who liked working with her. She could go freelance, and she'd be fine. It was Paige and the rest of the team she was worried about.

Cass dabbed her fingers beneath her eyes and nodded. "I guess I have to. Call your brother-in-law. After all this is over, we're doing tequila shots."

Brynn rose and retraced her path to the door.

"Have you ever thought about having a roommate, Brynn?"

"Not a chance." It flew out of Brynn's mouth before

she had time to craft a more diplomatic answer. With her hand on the knob, she glanced back. "I mean, I like my space." *Having Cass and her cat as roommates or living in my tiny office for a month—no showers?* The hovel won.

"Right. I guess I should cancel my date tonight. A new one. He sounded like a winner. He owns a Corvette and only has one ex-wife." She started sobbing again as Brynn quietly left.

Paige waited outside the door and followed Brynn into her office. "What's going on? And don't say 'nothing.'"

Though she hated delivering bad news, it was time for Brynn to be honest. Paige deserved to know the truth. "Cass is in deep financial trouble. She said she could fix it with the big contract from Blue Moon."

"How much trouble?" Paige's face turned chalky.

"Get-your-résumé-in-order kind of trouble."

Paige stumbled backward. "How long have you known?"

Brynn hesitated. "A couple weeks."

"Weeks? You've known for *weeks*, and you didn't tell me?"

"I'm so sorry." Brynn rubbed her aching forehead. This day was getting out of control faster than a loser on a winning streak.

"I thought we were friends, Brynn. I have bills and rent and school loans to pay off. You should have told me."

"Cass promised me she'd get back on track."

"Huh, and when was the last time she kept her promise?" Paige made a show of peeking under the desk and looking behind the bookcase. "I don't see that assistant she's been promising you. You're a sap, Brynn. And a bad friend."

A bad friend? Brynn had never been accused of that before. "Listen to me, please. I'm going to talk to my brother-in-law and see if he can recommend a financial advisor. We have clients. The sales team has leads. Let's not give up."

Paige thrust her jaw out and crossed her arms. Brynn didn't need to consult her *Body Language and You* manual to know her friend was right at the edge of mutiny.

"Please?"

"What choice do I have? If I quit without having another job lined up, I'd be an idiot. At least if Cass lets us go, I can collect unemployment until something else comes along. But that doesn't make things okay between us, Brynn. That was a shitty move you pulled, not telling me sooner."

"I'm so sor—"

She didn't get to finish, because Paige had already slammed out of her office.

Brynn fell onto her chair and, snatching up her phone, dialed Trevor.

"What is it?" he answered. Surly. If she had to use one word to describe Allie's husband, that would be it. He wasn't that way with Al and the boys, but with the rest of the world, he was full of surl.

"Hey, Trev. How've you been?"

"As ever." His dialect was the opposite of Iain's. Cold, crisp, and supremely snooty, his accent alone would make any commoner feel inferior. And Brynn was about as common as it got. "What do you need?"

"A financial guru at rock-bottom prices."

"Explain."

"My boss is in over her head and we're all about to

get canned if someone doesn't come in here and whip her into shape. Like right this minute."

"Mmm. Sounds like you'd be better off finding another job. Like right this minute." His words were clipped, his tone mocking.

"Well, you know me. I'm loyal to the end."

"Indeed, I do know you. You care too much for other people when you should be worried about yourself. I rather hoped you'd have outgrown that annoying trait by now."

"The people in this office have families and bills and all that crap. They need their jobs."

"Yes, quite. I'll send someone along this afternoon. Good enough?"

Trevor had never denied her anything. He cared about Brynn and her family, in his own snotty way, and she loved him for it. "Thank you. This means a lot to me."

"You might very well end up unemployed despite your best efforts." He paused. "How's that working-class Manc you've been seeing?"

Brynn smiled. "Full of awesome."

Trevor sighed, long and deep. "Good God, you've fallen for him, haven't you? You can do better, you know."

"I don't think so. He has a good soul."

"I wish you could hear yourself right now. You sound bloody ridiculous. If he hurts you in any way, I'll crush him. Do tell him that for me." Then he hung up.

Over the next hour, the IT guy arrived and examined her computer. "It's not looking good. I think you're going to have to kiss this baby good-bye, but I'll see what I can do." Brynn had a sinking feeling he was right. It would cost Cass thousands to upgrade the programs she had stored on that old laptop. Programs she needed to do her job.

As she sat contemplating her next move, her phone rang. Iain.

"Hey," she said.

"I'm sitting here in the restaurant. Where are you?"

"My computer died, taking all of my work with it. Cass can't afford another one. She's been living in some kind of dream world where cats rule the universe and financial woes magically disappear. Paige isn't talking to me. All in all, this day has sucked." Brynn placed one hand against her warm neck.

Iain was quiet a moment, then, "Started out well enough."

"Right? I knew I shouldn't have gotten out of bed this morning. I called Trevor and he's sending over a financial guy to get Cass's shit together. So there's hope."

"Why'd you go to Trevor instead of calling me?" He actually sounded pissed.

"Because I didn't want to burden you with my problems, Iain. You'd just tell me to come work for you, which is not a solution I'm willing to entertain."

"Not a solution you're willing to entertain. I like that phrase. Might steal it for future use. I'm sorry you're having such a hard day, pet. I've had a pretty shitty day myself. My building didn't pass code and it's going to take a fuckload of money to get it there."

"Is this the downtown apartment building? The one that needs investors?"

"Yeah."

"Maybe you could ask Trevor for help. For being a hermit, he knows a lot of people." He was silent for so long, Brynn glanced at the screen. "Are you still there?"

"Yeah. Do you think Trevor would be willing to lend support?"

"Maybe. It wouldn't hurt to ask. Why don't we stay at my place tonight? I'll cook."

"You don't need to ask me twice, love. You're a bloody brilliant cook. Even if you do it in that horrendous pink kitchen."

"It's pretty and I like it. So bite me."

"Gladly. I'll bring the ice cream."

Brynn smiled at the memory. "Deal."

"So what are you going to do without a computer?"

"I don't know. But I'm worried. Cass is hanging on by a thread."

"And you're still not ready to throw in the towel?"

"Not yet."

"There is such a thing as a lost cause, Brynnie."

"Not in my world."

Iain threw down a few bills and left the restaurant. As he walked out into the afternoon heat, he rubbed his jaw. Brynn had offered up Trevor's services. He'd be an absolute fool not to take her up on it. This was what he wanted, what he'd planned. He couldn't watch all of his dreams crumble around him, not when Brynn had handed him this perfect opportunity. It would be idiotic to have come all this way and not ask for the man's opinion. Still, that guilt sat right in the middle of his chest and refused to budge.

Iain climbed into the backseat of the car and

slammed the door. "Back to the office," he said, then raised the partition.

Retrieving the dice from his pocket, Iain tossed them in the air before catching them. Why was he on the fence about this? He and Marc could make a bloody mint off this project. Trevor stood to make a pretty packet as well. Brynn would call it a winning outcome. So what held him back?

Brynn. It started and stopped with her. Going to Trevor seemed like a betrayal of Brynn, and made him the worst sort of bounder imaginable. But it wasn't *really* a betrayal, was it? Brynn was personal. This was business. He'd always kept them separate in the past. No reason for him not to continue that tradition.

When Iain got back to the office, he didn't go to his own suite, but headed straight for Marc. He needed another opinion, someone to tell him he wasn't an asshole for exploiting the resources available.

As he marched forward, a woman stepped in his path. Her huge belly told him this was…God, what was her name? Gina, that was it.

"Mr. Chapman, I wanted to thank you personally for the baby shower. I'm so glad you were there."

"You're welcome. Gina."

She smiled at the use of her name. "I wanted to show you this." She held up a black rectangle.

"Look at that," he said, having no idea what he was meant to be staring at.

She pointed. "Here's his nose."

"Oh, that's the baby."

"Of course, what did you think it was?"

A Rorschach test? "You're having a boy, then?"

"Yeah. We're decorating his room in sky blue and white, in honor of Manchester City. My husband's turned into a real soccer fan over the last year."

Iain was strangely touched. "That's very good of you. Congratulations again." As he walked on, a few employees smiled, a couple dipped their heads, and Paul from data collection called out, "Hey, Chap." It was all rather odd.

When he entered Marc's office, Iain found his mate staring out the window. "Have you noticed a change around here? Everyone's acting very friendly."

Marc didn't turn around. "Yeah, people aren't terrified of you anymore. What's up?"

"Brynn suggested that I speak to Trevor Blake about our downtown plans. This is it—the perfect opportunity."

"Perfect," Marc echoed, his voice flat and unemotional. "You're getting exactly what you wanted."

"What *we* wanted, mate."

Marc finally turned to face him. "No, *I* wanted to sell it."

Iain scoffed. "You always advise caution, but we decided to proceed with the plans. And what's wrong with you?" Iain asked. "You've got a face like fizz, you do."

"Melanie is threatening to leave me. She's been unhappy for the last couple of months. She's quiet and distant, and when we are talking, we row like two alley cats. I don't know where it went wrong."

Iain hadn't gone to Marc to offer condolence. He needed advice for himself. "What would make her happy? Getting hitched?"

"I thought so, but now she refuses to even talk about it." He flipped the poker chip in the air and caught it in his right hand. "So, this is good news, eh? This Trevor Blake business. If he decides to invest, we'll make more money, and the world spins 'round."

Marc wasn't himself. This Melanie situation had done him in. He didn't need any more worries. Iain could handle this one on his own. "Yeah, exactly. Why don't you and Mel have a holiday? I'll hold things down here. It would do you good to get away."

"Maybe." He thrust his hands into his hair. "I'll talk to her about it."

Iain left Marc to brood and went back to his suite. Amelia had had a second desk moved into the outer office and was talking to a young woman who hopped to her feet at the sight of him.

Ames gave him a pointed glare but continued to smile. "Iain, this is my new assistant, Katie."

He shook her hand and nodded. "Welcome."

"Thank you, Mr. Chapman. I'm so excited to be here. Amelia's been great." In her early twenties, she was all shiny and eager. God, how exhausting.

"Super." He moved to the door. "Oh"—he turned back—"if Brynn Campbell ever calls or pops 'round, she has permanent access, yeah?"

"Yes, Mr. Chap—" Iain shut the door on her chirruping. Brynn would lay into him for not being respectful. But he was feeling like a right tosser at the moment. This thing with Trevor Blake had Iain second-guessing all his plans. Iain never questioned himself. Never. Made him feel more cross than usual.

He spent several frustrating hours talking with architects, foundation experts, and the environmental consultant. Frustrating wankers, from the first to the last. But in the back of his mind, Iain thought about Brynn. In another three or four hours, he'd get to hold her. Kiss her. Shag her until she made those throaty moans that drove him mad.

And she was cooking for him. She actually enjoyed doing things like that, taking care of people. Of him.

The last person who'd cooked for Iain had been his mum. Bangers and mash. Terrible, it was. Greasy and tasteless. But he still remembered that dish fondly. One time, when Iain was about six, his father had been out on an extended bender—they hadn't seen the old man in days. Things in the shabby little flat had been peaceful for a change. For tea one evening, instead of wringing her hands and snapping at him, his mum had stood in the kitchen, humming. He'd never heard her do that before. She'd ruffled his hair and given him a quick hug. The two of them had sat at the scarred kitchen table, eating those horrible bangers in comfortable silence. That was one of the strongest memories he had of his mum. God rest her soul.

Suddenly, he couldn't wait three more hours to see Brynn. He nabbed his jacket, nodded to Amelia and the new girl, then headed out. On the way to Brynn's house, Iain stopped at a flower shop. Was he buying her flowers to ease his guilt? Yeah, most likely. But Iain had run through every financial avenue available. Every sensible road led back to Trevor Blake and his multimillions. What other choice did Iain have?

He picked a massive bouquet of colorful blooms including something the clerk called frangipani. Whatever the hell they were, they smelled sweet and fragrant. Their dusky petals reminded him of the color of Brynn's pink-tipped breasts. Brynnie. The one person who truly believed in him.

Are you going to screw her over? Betray her trust? For the thousandth time, Iain told himself that Brynn had nothing to do with his business. The two were independent of one another. After all, he'd been attracted to Brynn from the second he'd clapped eyes on her in the garden that night. Now that he had her in his life, he felt savagely protective of her—needed her in a way he'd never needed anyone. But business had always been Iain's salvation.

Back home, he would have ended up in the nick for petty crime, at a dead-end job, or on the dole, like his old man. There had been no future for him back in England. By taking over Davy's dream, coming to Vegas, Iain had reinvented himself. Carved out a new life. He couldn't throw all that away. Not even for Brynn.

Yet he'd pulled her into his business *and* his life when he hired her. He'd made a cunning, calculated move to meet Trevor. Iain had it all figured out. Now, he wasn't sure about anything.

Goddamn it. He didn't know what to do. Iain was never at a loss about what path to take. He visualized an outcome and went about getting it, step by step. Nothing stood in his way. No one. *Everyone's expendable*. Except Brynn wasn't expendable, was she?

On the drive to Brynn's house, Iain sat in the backseat, balancing the flowers on his thigh. He tugged at his tie, finding it difficult to breathe properly. His heart beat erratically. The truth of his situation finally hit him. He was ass over teakettle for Brynn Campbell. He'd fallen hard and fast. He was in love with her.

In love. Un-fucking-believable. Out of nowhere, Iain felt—amazing. *Hopeful*.

Then and there, he knew what he had to do. His loyalty was to Brynn. He wouldn't be asking Trevor Blake for anything, not even the fucking time of day. Iain had to make a choice, and he chose Brynn.

A serene calmness stole over him. This was the right decision, come what may. Iain had never put anything before business. Making money had been the only thing that mattered. But Brynn was his salvation.

Even so, that didn't mean Iain had lost his edge. Far from it. Not asking Trevor Blake to invest in his project didn't mean he was going soft. *Right, mate. You're sacrificing your dreams for her*. Not true. He would make the downtown development happen without Trevor. Somehow. He'd find another way. He was Iain Chapman, Kicker of Asses, Buster of Bollocks. This wouldn't break him. Iain would tackle this problem the way he tackled everything else—with single-minded determination. There must be some idea he hadn't thought of. Simple as that.

When the car pulled up to Brynn's house, Iain told the driver to leave and stepped out. Clutching the bouquet, he strode up Brynn's walkway and knocked on the door.

When he heard her yell something, he tried the handle. "Brynn," he called, stepping into the entryway.

She poked her head out of the kitchen. "Hey, you." Then her eyes lighted on the flowers. "Are those for me?"

He felt a stupid grin take over his face. "No, they're for your neighbor. Thought I'd make a good first impression."

She pointed at him. "Funny." She stepped out of the kitchen, and Iain's blood pressure spiked as his grin faded. Her long, golden legs were bare. Completely and utterly bare. She wore a frilly, pink half apron tied at the waist and her blouse revealed her shoulders. It was white and sheer and he could see those puffy pink areolas right through the material. Was she even wearing knickers? With her hair tied up in a messy knot, long tendrils curled around her face and along the sleek column of her neck. His gaze tripped over her once more, all the way down to her feet. She wore no shoes, but her toenails were painted a light, shimmery pink.

"Iain? Why are you frowning like that?"

Was he frowning? He didn't know. Couldn't think about anything other than finding out what was under that apron. "Do you have something in the kitchen that needs your immediate attention?"

"No. I just set the timer for forty-five minutes."

That was the smell. Savory and spicy—he didn't know what she was making, but it smelled delicious. However, food didn't hold his attention for long. "That might be enough time."

Iain tossed the bouquet on the sofa, took three long steps toward Brynn, and grabbed her by the hips, pulling her onto him. "Wrap your legs around me."

She jumped onto him and linked her arms behind his neck. "What are you doing?"

"You can't dress like that and think I'm not going to fuck you this instant."

"Iain," she said, half shocked, half laughing.

He strode to the bedroom and walked to the bed. "Stand on the mattress, yeah?"

Brynn untangled her legs and stood. He lifted up the apron and saw that she wore an indecent pair of cutoff shorts. Sexy as hell.

"Turn around." He raised his index finger and circled it. "Turn."

She spun and the shorts made his cock stand at attention. Her curvy bum was on full display below the frayed edges of denim, and those luscious cheeks were just begging for his attention.

Brynn glanced over her shoulder. "They're Daisy Dukes."

"They're fucking perfection." He finally stopped ogling her ass and glanced up at her. "I'm going to fuck you from behind, Brynn. If you're good, I may slap your ass a time or two."

She spun to face him and stroked the hollow of her throat with one finger. "Promise?"

"No." Iain quickly shucked his jacket, waistcoat, tie, and shirt. Why did he always wear so many goddamned clothes? A right encumbrance. When Brynn started to remove her blouse, Iain placed a hand on her arm to stop her. "My job."

She watched as he shed the rest of his clothes with haste. Now he stood before her, naked, hard, ready.

"Iain."

"I love to hear you say my name, Brynnie."

She grinned as he approached the bed. "Iain Chapman."

"Who's going to fuck you?"

Her eyes changed to that stormy color that he adored. "You are, Iain."

He grabbed her shirt by the stretchy shoulders and tugged, freeing both breasts. He was mouth level with her nipples. How very convenient.

Pinning her arms behind her back, he feasted on one—sucking hard and nibbling softly—then he'd go to work on the other. Brynn swayed toward him, her balance shaky on the mattress. With his free hand, he untied the apron, then went to work on the button and zipper of those tiny shorts. They were nearly obscene, and yet Brynn managed to look innocent no matter what she wore.

Still keeping her wrists penned, he yanked down her shorts and brushed aside her tiny little thong—pink with a bow right over her mound. Bloody adorable. He leaned down to kiss the little satin bow, then removed her knickers with his teeth.

Laughing, Brynn leaned her torso against him while he worked them off of her. When she stepped out of her shorts and knickers, she kicked them off the bed.

Iain stared up at her, awestruck. He'd never encountered anyone like her. She was a one-off, and so lovely it made his heart ache. For some stupid reason, she liked him. Of course he couldn't betray her. He was a twat for thinking he could go through with it.

As he continued to gaze at her, the apples of Brynn's cheeks turned a charming shade of pink. She pushed against him and straightened. Iain finally let go of her hands, grabbed her blouse, and slid it down her body. She was a fucking dream, standing there with her hair falling out of the topknot. "Turn around." A tiny smile played on her lips as she obeyed. They seemed to be made for each other. A perfect fit. "Spread your legs wide." Iain held on to her hips to keep her stable. Placing his hands on both of her ass cheeks, he kneaded them. "That apron really did it for me."

She laughed, then yelped when he nipped her bum. "I'll wear it more often."

"See that you do, love." He gave her ass a sharp tap. "Now, bend over. Palms on the bed."

Brynn tipped over and spied him from the narrow opening between her legs. She was a stunner. Stepping closer to the bed, he splayed his hands across her ass. He leaned forward, gave her a long, slow lick. Her breath audibly hitched, and he smiled.

With Brynn, Iain felt vital, alive—like he'd been living in some kind of bleak, gray world for years and now the clouds had lifted. He knew that sounded idiotic, even as it popped into his mind. He'd never admit it out loud, but Brynn made him look up from his life and realize that everything around him was made of colors and textures.

God, he loved this woman.

He slid his hand down her outer thigh. She rewarded him with a moan. She was so trusting, his Brynn. She knew he'd never hurt her, would only bring her pleasure. It was humbling, that trust, and he'd violated it before they'd even met. Iain closed his eyes and pushed the thought away. He wanted to be in this moment, right now, rubbing Brynn's tight, naked ass.

With one finger, he traced the bumps of her lower spine, over the curves of her bum, all the way down to her lovely slim legs. Then he reversed himself and swatted her pussy lightly. She hissed, letting him know how much she liked it.

"Spread your knees farther apart, Brynnie."

She did, opening herself up to him. What a sight. Brynn, bare to him. Willing to take whatever he gave her. Iain wanted to bring her nothing but satisfaction.

He placed his hands on either side of her ass and parted her. Her inner lips glistened. Wet. Swollen. Hungry. But he wasn't ready to touch her there, not yet.

He concentrated on her pussy, spanking just hard enough to sting. "You love that." It wasn't a question. It never was. Iain simply stated facts. He knew what she liked, how she liked it. By now, he was as familiar with her body as he was his own.

"Yes." She sounded breathless. "Harder? Please?"

Iain tapped her ass again, firmer this time, until his hand stung. Then he slapped her pussy once more. The sounds of his palm against her flesh made his cock ache. He alternated, never staying in one place for long and switched up light, soft raps with sharper smacks. Brynn's ass was now pink in some places, redder in others, and she was wetter than before.

He reached around and cupped her breasts. Brynn's breath quickened as he played with her nipples. Those gorgeous, plump nipples.

"Iain." She pressed her bottom against his chest. "Please make me come."

"Oh, I plan to, love. Say the words. Let me hear them."

"Fuck me, Iain." She groaned his name, pleading.

How he loved seeing her like this—unashamed, bold, ready to take him. His bashful girl liked getting spanked and was using dirty words to tell him what she wanted. "You want my cock. All of it. Hard and fast." Iain slid his hands to her stomach. She was a little ticklish, so he lightly trailed his fingers over her ribs, causing her to squirm a bit. Then he returned once again to her sweet bottom, changing up the pressure with each tap, careful not to be too rough. Her toned muscles clenched and her moans grew louder. "I'll give it to you, then. When I'm ready." He finally stopped and let her rest for a moment. "You're a wild one when you want to be."

She glanced at him from over her shoulder. "You make me that way."

"You were never meant to sit on the sidelines, Brynnie. You're too special for that."

Brynn hung her head downward, not speaking for several seconds. "Please, Iain?" Her vocal cords sounded shredded.

She was on the edge. He'd barely need to touch her before she fell apart. Iain glided his hand up her thigh before sliding two fingers into her sweet, plump cunt. Brynn was so ready for him—hot and tight and wet. He worked those fingers in and out of her pussy. When he felt she was ready, Iain slipped in a third finger.

She hunched her back. "God, that feels good."

With his other hand, Iain caressed the globe of her ass. Her skin was hot to the touch. Lightly, he slid that hand around her hip, until it rested on top of her mound. He worked his hands in tandem, his fingers pumping while his other hand pressed downward, applying pressure. In seconds, Brynn came, flexing her shoulders and rolling her hips.

"Iain."

"I'm right here, darling." He kept at it until her orgasm burst through her. He felt her spasms all the way up to his wrist. It was a strong one. He so enjoyed playing with her, seeing what made her come hard and what made her orgasm less intense.

When Brynn's body stopped moving, her pussy still contracted, yet Iain didn't stop fingering her. He wanted her to come again. He was the only man who could do this for her.

He leaned forward and bit her ass. The moment he did, another round of shudders wracked her body, causing goose bumps to break out over her skin. He didn't let up, not until her inner walls stopped clasping at his fingers like a fist.

When she was finally still, inside and out, he removed his hands from her body. Brynn fell to her knees, recuperating, sucking in lungfuls of air as she tried to catch her breath.

"It gets better every time. How is that possible?" She rolled to her side, knees bent.

Iain picked her up, kissed her temple, then dropped her so that she lay horizontally. She let out a squeal of surprise and stared up at him.

"It's going to keep getting better." He opened the bedside table, grabbed a condom, and rolled it on. Then he climbed on top of her, settling between her legs and propping himself on his forearms. He stared down at her, unable to look away from that gorgeous face. The golden skin. Those big, blue eyes. His cock prodded her hip. He was so bloody hard, he hurt, but he made no move to do anything other than hold her. He wanted her badly—not just right now. Not for tonight. For always.

The thought shocked him. Iain had never given a toss about forever or commitment. But Brynn had him rethinking everything.

"Iain?" She blinked at him, her brow furrowed. Reaching up, she cupped his jaw. "You're looking at me funny."

"Am I?"

She scrunched her nose. "Yeah. Are you okay?"

Iain was better than okay. He was in love. Madly, deeply, unabashedly in love. "We're getting married." Again, not a question. The words came tumbling out of his mouth before they were even a fully formed thought, but it felt right. *Permanent. Lasting.*

Brynn's mouth popped open as she pushed at his chest. He didn't budge. "What...what are you talking about?" Her words were breathy, but she hadn't said no, so Iain took that as a victory. "We barely know each other."

"What's that got to do with anything?" He leaned down and brushed her nose with his own before kissing her. A whisper-soft kiss that barely touched her lips. "I'm marrying you, Brynn Campbell. End of. And I'm going to devote my life to making you happy."

Her eyes shimmered with emotion. Perhaps there was a little disbelief mixed in as well. "Why?"

A smile tugged at the corners of his mouth. "Well, I don't want to make your life misery, do I?"

She slapped his shoulder. "Not that part. Marriage."

"Because I love you, of course." She opened her mouth to speak, but Iain beat her to the punch. "You may not love me back. Not yet. I know that. But you will." He lowered his head and kissed her harder this time and lowered himself slightly, enjoying the feel of her soft body. "I swear to you," he said against her lips, "I'll make you proud. I'll strive to be worthy of you every day."

A sob broke from her, and he captured it, slanting his mouth over hers once more. He gave her a long, hot kiss. Deep. Slow—every bit as intimate and intense as when they made love. He tried to show her how he felt in that kiss. Gave all of himself, held nothing back.

Brynn must have felt it. She wrapped her arms around his neck and kissed him, her fervor matching his own.

When Iain pulled away and opened his eyes, Brynn stared up at him, dazed. Then a grin crept over her generous mouth. "I love you too, Iain Chapman. I will absolutely marry you."

He hadn't realized his muscles were tightly coiled until that moment. He let out his breath in a rush of air. "You love me."

She nodded shyly, her gaze fastened on his chin.

His tongue darted out, licking a hot trail across her neck, circling her pulse. He felt it increase its pace. Brynn was his—to love, to protect, and all the rest of it. She was *his*.

Something primitive seized hold of him. He bit down and nipped her skin, claiming her. Iain prided himself on his rigid control, but right then, he could barely think. Could only feel. *Possessive. Uncivilized.*

Iain kissed her again. It was bruising, filled with every emotion coursing through him. There was nothing practiced or prim about it. Carnal. Ruthless.

When Iain entered Brynn, he did it with one hard thrust. Her body was wet and willing. As he pounded into her, he sucked her bottom lip and bit down, probably too hard, but Brynn moaned into his mouth. He couldn't have stopped himself if he'd tried.

Hot passion rose within him. There was nothing gentle in the way he fucked Brynn.

Her hips met his, and she looped her calves around his waist. All the while, Iain continued to kiss her, thrusting his tongue into her mouth the way he plunged his cock inside her pussy—unyielding and relentless.

Iain pulled his mouth from hers, shoved his hand into Brynn's hair, gripping it at the scalp. Bucking his hips, Iain slammed into her as he stared into her glazed eyes. This was a claiming in every way. *Mine. Mine. Mine.* The word ran through his mind over and over again.

He didn't know how long he fucked her. She raked her nails down his back and tightened her muscles around his cock. The feeling started at the base of his spine. When he clenched his ass, it moved to his balls. He was so close. So goddamned close.

Iain's groan was primal as he came. He squeezed his eyes shut and pounded at her. He lost all sense of himself, where he was. He only knew Brynn—her scent, the feel of her skin, her little moans. On and on, it shot through him as he continued to thrust into her. If he hadn't known better, Iain thought he might have blacked out there for a minute.

When he opened his eyes, he'd stopped moving. He lay on top of her, panting. Stunned.

Ashamed.

He'd sought his own pleasure without giving a thought to Brynn's. After a few minutes, when he could think clearly again, he rolled off her. Grabbing a tissue from her bedside table, he removed the condom. "Don't know what happened just then. You all right, love?"

When he glanced back at her, she wore a tired smile. "Iain. That was unbelievable. Wow." She breathed a little sigh. "That was great. Like, I-can-hardly-remember-what-day-it-is great."

He threw the tissue away and lay on his back. Brynn scooted closer and flung her arm around his chest.

Despite her reassurance, Iain was embarrassed. He'd just exposed a part of himself he usually kept hidden—that harsh, baser side. By having his armor locked in place, Iain'd always kept a rein on that untamed part of himself. Yet he'd abandoned it with Brynn. Sweet, delicate Brynn.

Iain prided himself on his control. For a long time, that sense of pride had literally been all he had. No money, no prospects, no education. Only pride. But with Brynn, his rigid self-discipline didn't just slip, he'd cast it aside—willingly. Now he felt weak, like his old man—savage and unpredictable. Iain had re-created himself in a way that would've made Davy proud. The complete opposite of his drunken sod of a father. Or so he'd assumed. Perhaps he and the old man had more in common than he'd thought.

His glance grazed over her, took in the swollen bottom lip. He'd bit down too hard. She'd liked it, but what if he'd gotten *too* rough? What if he had accidentally hurt her? Iain would never be able to forgive himself. He couldn't allow himself to slip up like that again. She was his to protect.

"You okay?" Brynn leaned up and placed a chaste kiss on his Adam's apple. Her hair was a mess. Her cheeks were flushed a rosy pink. A hint of worry slid behind her eyes. "Are you regretting your proposal? Because we can pretend it didn't happen."

He cut that line of thinking off at the pass. "It wasn't a proposal, love. It was a fact. We're getting married. Let's do it tomorrow." He didn't want to give her too much time to think. She might just run away again.

Brynn sat up, gliding her hand over his stomach. "That's crazy. I can't plan a wedding in one day."

"This is Vegas, pet. Of course you can. And do you really want to go through months of planning and preparation? With Allie and Monica hounding you about every detail?" *Find your opponent's weakness...*

She shuddered. "God, no. That would be awful."

"If you decide you want something more formal down the line, well and good, but let's do this our way. Privately. Just you and me." Iain was surprising the bloody hell out of himself tonight. That's exactly what he wanted—just the two of them reciting vows, exchanging rings. "It's the perfect time. We could take three days for ourselves. Cass agreed to let Trevor's financial people come in and help her. If I know accountants, they'll want to go through everything with a fine-tooth comb. Until then, you don't even have a computer to work with." He sat up and leaned against the headboard.

"When was the last time you took three days off?" Her nails made lazy circles across his thigh.

Iain narrowed his eyes and remained quiet for a full minute. "I'm thinking."

"Yeah, that's what I thought. But if we do this, I want to go full-on Vegas."

"What does that entail?" He grasped her hand and brought it to his mouth for a kiss. He glanced down at her naked finger. After tomorrow, she'd wear his ring. Which reminded him—he needed to get a bloody ring. "Should we have Elvis marry us? Or use a chapel drive-through?"

Brynn rolled her eyes. "Think outside the box. *Everyone* uses Elvis. We're better than that. Since this was your idea, I expect you to come up with something spectacular."

Iain let out a laugh. "Are you serious?" He looked at her eager expression.

A mischievous smile played on her lips and she nodded eagerly. "Yep. Vegas at its tackiest. Just you and me."

Iain had never been able to resist a challenge. He grabbed the back of her neck and drew her forward, resting his forehead against hers. "Darling, I'm going to give you the tackiest fucking wedding this town has ever seen."

She palmed his jaw and kissed his cheek. "Thank you, Iain."

Chapter 18

Brynn's head was spinning. Who knew Iain had a romantic streak? When he'd said he was going to marry her, Brynn could see that he was as taken aback by the words as she was. But then he'd said those sweet things about making her happy and wanting to be worthy of her. She could hear the honesty in his voice, could see it in his light brown eyes. He'd come into her life like a whirlwind, leaving her gasping for breath. She'd tried to guard her heart at first, but he'd owned it from the start.

A warmth spread over her, starting in the center of her chest and working through the rest of her body. Iain Chapman, the most complicated, formidable man she'd ever met, loved her.

"Oh my God. We're getting *married*." She grinned up at him.

He held her gaze and smiled back. "I know."

When a buzzer sounded, Brynn didn't know what it was. Then she remembered. "Dinner's ready."

With lazy movements, Iain leaned down and reached for his boxers. "Why don't you get a shower? Surely I'm capable of taking food out of the oven." Then he pulled on his shorts and turned to look at her. "It is called an oven, correct?"

"Cute. There's a salad in the fridge." She hopped out of bed and gathered her discarded clothes on the way to the bathroom. "I'll be out in a few."

She shut the door and stared at herself in the mirror above the sink. "You're marrying the man of your dreams tomorrow, jellyfish. How did you manage that?" Happiness, like champagne bubbles, fizzed through her.

She hopped in the shower and washed quickly, thinking about Iain's proposal. And the way he made love to her. He'd been in a frenzy. She'd never seen him like that, and while it shocked her, it excited her, too. Even during sex, Iain had always remained in charge, never lowering his defenses. But tonight, there'd been something wild in his eyes. He'd let himself go completely—because he loved her. He seemed a little shell-shocked by it. Well, now he knew how she felt every time he got through with her—dazed, shaken, and extremely satisfied.

She toweled herself off, secured her messy hair back in its bun, and threw on a strapless baby-doll dress. Then she raced to the kitchen.

Iain had uncovered the casserole dish and plated the salad. "Smells delicious."

He stood at the sink, arms crossed, hair ruffled. He'd dressed but hadn't bothered to button his shirt. Brynn's gaze danced over him. With the five o'clock shadow covering his jaw, he looked casually sexy—all the way down to his bare feet.

"Keep looking at me like that, pet, and we'll wind up back in bed. And while I wouldn't mind, I still have a wedding to plan, don't forget."

She grinned at that and distracted herself by opening a bottle of wine. "Okay, dinner. My mother used to make these awesome sausage rolls around the holidays. It's an old family recipe. I thought you might like it."

She'd already set the table, using her favorite vintage linen—a flea market find with hand-embroidered pink flowers along the hem. When she glanced up, Iain was staring at her with a strange look in his eyes.

"What was she like, your mum?"

It still hurt to talk about it, even after all these years. Brynn wasn't sure the pain would ever go away. "She was funny and smart, always helped me with my math homework because she was a whiz with numbers. She worked as my dad's accountant for years. Before she got sick." Brynn removed the cork and glanced up. "You know when you said I shouldn't sit on the sidelines? She said almost the exact same thing to me before she died. She told me that I only had one chance to get in the game." Tears pricked her eyes, and Brynn blinked them away. "I miss her, you know? I was only ten when she was diagnosed with cancer. After that, everything changed. We all fell apart."

Iain walked forward and tucked his arms around her waist, pulling her closer. "How?"

Brynn hugged him back, placing her cheek against his bare chest. "Her health became our sole focus. The chemo and radiation left her exhausted. She didn't have the energy to do all the mom things she used to do."

"Must have been hard on all of you."

"It was. Toward the end, my dad just kind of gave up. Monica became the wild child, and Allie tried to hold us all together. I don't know how she managed."

"What about you?"

Brynn listened to the steady, calm beat of his heart. It comforted her, softened the memories a bit. "I hid in my room, kept to the shadows. Allie and Monica fought constantly. I just tried to smooth things over or stay out of the way." As her mother's cancer progressed, Brynn's family had imploded. When it became clear that her mom was dying, Brynn had desperately wanted to get away from the heavy sadness that permeated the house. It had been a stressful, depressing time. Things were better between Allie and Monica now, but sometimes, Brynn still felt like that scared child, trying so hard to keep the peace. Her mom's illness altered Brynn forever. She never felt safe after that, not really. Not until Iain. She could let down her walls with him in a way she'd never done with anyone else.

Brynn eased away from him. He'd told her that his mom died of a heart attack a few years ago and his dad had drunk himself to death. Iain hadn't been close to either of them. "Do you miss your parents at all? What if they'd changed? Your dad might have stopped drinking and your mom could have found herself."

He huffed. "Life doesn't work like that. You can't go around wishing things were different, can you? You have to accept your past and move on." His face was as placid as a calm lake, but deep emotions rippled through him, causing his shoulders to stiffen. He spoke of his childhood memories with Marc and Davy, happy times, times when they'd fought like brothers. He'd even detailed Davy's death, the funeral, the way he felt afterward. But Iain's parents were a sore spot. While Brynn didn't want to push, she longed for details. What had Iain been like as a little boy? Probably just as determined and headstrong as he was now. She bit back the questions. He'd tell her when he was ready.

"Brynnie." His eyes were serious, and she sensed a

sadness in him. "Right here, right now, this is all that matters. Not the past."

"I don't think so." The past molded them. Her mother's death had shaped Brynn into the woman she was today. For better or worse. Even though Iain denied it, he was the same way. His past had driven him to become a success. He'd had to fight for everything, and Brynn respected that.

He leaned down and kissed the tip of her nose. "We can't go back and change anything, love. So what's the point in dwelling on it?"

She shrugged. "Let's eat before it gets cold."

He let her go, but she felt his gaze on her as she moved back to the stove. She dished up two plates and brought them to the table.

Iain held out a chair for her and kissed her bare shoulder before taking his own seat. When he bit into the sausage roll, he actually moaned. "Woman, this is brilliant."

Brynn laughed. "I'm glad you like it."

"My mum was a dreadful cook. It took me years to realize food wasn't meant to be black on the bottom and raw in the middle." He poured them each a glass of wine. "She made bland, tasteless food. God love her, she tried."

Again, Brynn refrained from asking any questions, but when he offered up little stories about his family, she soaked up each tidbit. "I learned my culinary skills from Mrs. Hubert."

"Who is Mrs. Hubert?" he asked.

"Trevor's cook. She's a genius. I'm not even in her league."

He set down his fork and played with the stem of his wineglass. "Are you close to him? Trevor?"

"I am. He comes off as aloof and remote, which he is, but he loves Monica and me. He bought my dad and his wife a coastal home in Texas. Trevor can be very caring. You just have to get to know him."

"He probably won't like a working-class wanker in his ranks."

"It's a good thing you're not marrying *him* then. And he'll come around."

Iain gave her a confident smirk. "I doubt it. But I'll carry on. Somehow."

"I don't have a wedding dress, you know."

He set down his glass. "Brynnie. Love. Everything you wear is flowing and covered in lace. Nothing more bridal than that. Besides, you could show up starkers and look beautiful."

Her stomach fluttered at the compliment. "We don't have a song. We don't have rings. Or flowers, or a photographer."

He placed his hand on her arm. "Stop worrying, you. I'll have it covered."

Brynn believed him. When Iain put his mind to something, he got it done.

Once they finished eating, Brynn began to clear the table. As usual, Iain filled the sink with hot water, rolled up his sleeves, and started scraping the plates.

"I'm going to like having a husband who does the dishes." Brynn patted his butt as she walked by.

He grinned down at her. "Be honest, love. You'd like me even if I didn't do dishes."

"You're so cocky."

"Yeah, well, you like that too."

Before she could answer, the doorbell rang. Brynn set down a bottle of salad dressing and hustled to the door. Looking out the peephole, she saw Tasha standing on her front porch with a dog under each arm. *Oh boy.*

With a deep sigh, Brynn twisted the handle. "Hey, Tash. Are you and Zeke fighting again?"

"That is it. I am done with him. I go back to Belarus as soon as possible." She shoved the dogs at Brynn and instead of pulling in one suitcase, Tash tossed three into the foyer. The smallest one knocked into her wall and chipped the paint. "I am up to here." Tash waved a hand over her head.

"What happened this time?" Brynn asked.

Iain stood in the kitchen doorway. He still hadn't buttoned his starched, white shirt. He looked hot and handsome. Despite the fact that he was wiping his hands on a pink floral dish towel, he didn't look the least bit domesticated.

"You again, Englishman?" Tasha asked.

"I could say the same for you, Ruskie." Iain didn't head back to the kitchen. Instead, he leaned against the wall and slung the towel over his shoulder. "What's the trouble this time?"

"It is not your business," Tasha said.

"It is my business, because it involves Brynn."

Brynn thrust the dogs back at Tasha. "Let's not argue. Let's dialogue. Tasha, tell me what happened."

"My mother and sister get time off work to come to Las Vegas. Zeke forbid it. He say we can no afford. He say I spend too much money on my hair and nails and clothes. Now he want to make babies. I have babies."

She jostled the dogs. "If we cannot afford my family to visit, how we can afford children?" She walked to the sofa and plopped down, setting a dog on each side of her.

Brynn automatically moved to the sofa, scooping the dogs up and relocating them to the floor. Then she parked herself on the coffee table and patted Tasha's knee. "I'm sorry. What are you going to do?"

"She's going to go home and work it out with her husband," Iain said. "Coming here won't solve the problem, will it?"

Tash curled her lip. "Why is he talking about my life? What does he know?"

Brynn shot Iain a warning glare. "Do you want something to eat?"

"No," Tasha said with a sniff. "If you want, I go to hotel."

"Don't be silly. I'll go get you a cup of tea, all right?"

"Make it vodka."

Brynn stood. She moved past Iain on her way to the kitchen. "You're not being helpful," she whispered.

"Not trying to be, am I?" He followed her. "Her problems shouldn't affect you."

Brynn just looked at him. "I just feel bad that she's so unhappy."

Iain heaved a sigh. He yanked the dish towel off his shoulder and tossed it on the counter. "From what I can tell, she's always like this. And this won't do when we're married, will it?"

She patted his bare chest. "I'll talk to her again. Just for tonight, okay? I'll explain that this is the last time." She grabbed a shot glass from the cupboard.

"Brynn, pet, you don't owe her anything. She takes advantage, coming over here all the bloody time. You're not helping her either, eh?"

She stopped and peered up at him. "What are you talking about?"

"Do you think this is fixing her marriage, her running away every time they have an argument?"

That sounded a little too close to home. Maybe Tash *did* need to stay and work things out with her husband. He wasn't a horrible guy. He and Tasha simply had different expectations of marriage. They'd only known each other from chatting online. They hadn't spent any real world time together—otherwise they might have discovered they were completely incompatible. Which, *hello*, was almost the exact same situation Brynn found herself in.

"Are we rushing into this, Iain? This marriage thing?"

He took the glass from her and set it on the counter. Then, bracing his hands on her shoulders, he leaned toward her. "Brynn, I've never been surer about anything in my life. I want to marry you. I want to spend the rest of my life with you. But I want you to promise me right now that you won't run when things get tough. You'll stick it out. You'll talk to me instead of hying off."

She wanted that. Brynn wanted a marriage like her parents'd had. Even as her mother's health deteriorated, her dad had been right there by her mom's side, every single day. It wasn't until after they'd found out the experimental treatments hadn't worked that he'd fallen apart.

Brynn took a fortifying breath. "I promise I won't

run. But for tonight, I'm going to stay here. I'll remind Tash that things need to change."

Iain raised his brows.

"I'll make sure she understands this time."

"See that you do." He kissed her hard, as if he were sealing the deal. When he raised his head, he looked into her eyes. "I've texted my driver—he should be here in a few. I'll pick you up in the morning, eight thirty. We'll get a license and get married. Totally Vegas. Just you and me."

Both frightened and elated, Brynn nodded. "Okay."

He kissed her one more time, then turned and left the kitchen. Brynn's fingers drifted up to her lips. She was getting married.

After staying up past midnight listening to Tasha's marital woes, Brynn spent the night tossing and turning, wondering what kind of wedding Iain would come up with. She hadn't told Tash about their plans, but Brynn had made it perfectly clear that Tash couldn't drop in unannounced anymore. Nor could she spend the night—unless she absolutely needed to. But Brynn tried her best to be firm. Tash took it marginally better than Brynn had expected, then started listing her grievances against Zeke all over again. Brynn tried to listen, but her mind kept wandering back to Iain's proposal. Well, more of a demand, really. So typical of him, and so perfect for her. They had nothing in common, their personalities were at opposite ends of the spectrum, and yet they were a good pair.

Trying not to wake Tash the next morning, Brynn got

ready as quietly as possible. She only had the slightest twinge about leaving Allie and Monica in the dark. She loved her sisters, and while they wouldn't mean to take over her wedding, they would. This was supposed to be *her* day. The idea of doing this privately with Iain appealed to her romantic side. Like he said, they could always have a ceremony with the family later.

Besides, Allie and Trevor had eloped, so it wasn't like Allie could throw stones. Of course, her family knew Trevor pretty well by that time. Brynn's sisters didn't know Iain at all, and that was Brynn's fault. Next time, she'd make sure they got better acquainted in a safe, mutually respectful atmosphere—i.e., not Allie's house—and Brynn would guide the conversation. She was turning over a new leaf, taking charge of her life, developing boundaries. She didn't want her tombstone to read: *Here lies Brynn Campbell Chapman, a jellyfish of a human being*. She was finding her voice more and more every day. It wasn't always easy for her, but it was worth the effort.

Now, Brynn stood before her mirror and appraised herself with critical eyes. She'd fixed her curls into a loose style and tucked one of the freesias from Iain's bouquet behind her ear. The off-the-shoulder ivory dress was semi-bridal. Her mother's inexpensive charm bracelet dangled from her wrist.

Brynn shook with nerves and she paced the living room, waiting for Iain to arrive. At eight thirty on the dot, she heard a car pull up out front. Grabbing her small purse, Brynn had the door open before Iain hit the porch. She glanced past his shoulder to the Hummer limo parked along the curb.

"Wow." She gazed back at him. "It's Barbie pink."

Iain said nothing about the car. He'd stopped midstride and simply stared at her. The morning light slid over him, making his brown eyes look amber. His hair was so dark, certain strands appeared almost blue-black. Wearing a dove-gray suit and silver tie, he was so handsome, she had to stop and catch her breath.

"You're a princess, you are." His long legs ate up the distance between them. Brynn shut the door quietly behind her. "How did I get so lucky, eh?"

She placed her hand on his chest. He covered it with his own. "I have something old"—she gestured to the bracelet—"the flower is new. My toenails are blue. Do you have anything I can borrow? You know, just to keep with tradition."

Iain pulled Davy's dice from his pocket. "Hang on to these."

She was touched that he shared them with her. "I won't lose them."

He dipped his head and kissed her lips lightly, solemnly. "Are you ready?"

She nodded, not trusting herself to speak further. This was her wedding day. The only person she wished were there was her mother. Maybe Trisha Campbell was watching over Brynn. She liked to think so anyway.

Iain tucked Brynn's hand into the crook of his arm and escorted her to the most hideous car she'd ever seen. Inside, resting on the hot-pink pleather seat, she found a lovely bouquet of peach-tipped roses.

"I hope they're all right?" Iain said, climbing in beside her. "I know we said tacky—"

"They're beautiful." She stuck the dice in her bag and

took his hand, intertwining their fingers. His skin was warm, solid. Iain Chapman made her feel safe and cared for. She hoped he felt the same way.

The chauffeur shut the door, leaving them shrouded in darkness. Except for the hot-pink neon strips of light rimming the floor.

Brynn gazed around. "This is so awesomely bad."

"Worst I could find." He already had a glass of champagne waiting for her.

Brynn began laughing when they clinked glasses. "I never went to my prom, but this is what I imagined it would be like."

Iain slid his arm along the back of the seat. His fingers brushed her bare shoulder, gliding over her skin. She shivered at his touch. "Why didn't you go to the prom?"

"The boy I liked, Rob Baker, didn't ask me. I wouldn't settle for second best." She sipped from her flute and eased back, snuggling next to him.

"Whoever this Rob bloke was, he was a right idiot. Passing up a chance to go to prom with Brynnie Campbell. He should have his head examined."

"You're being very sweet, doing all this. You look incredibly handsome by the way."

He shrugged. "I do my best."

Brynn enjoyed the ride—every minute of rush-hour traffic. Not only because she was cuddled next to Iain, but because sitting in the pink monster was kitschy fun.

Applying for a license only took fifteen minutes. Next, they headed down the Strip, and Brynn glanced out the window, wondering what Iain had planned for the ceremony.

When he handed her another glass of champagne, she

gazed at him through narrowed eyes. "Are you trying to get me buzzed? It's nine thirty. I'm usually on my third cup of coffee by now."

"Wait until you see what I have in store. You're going to need that drink, trust me."

"Give me a hint."

"No. No hints of any kind."

The limo slowly made its way toward the end of the Boulevard, to the smallest chapel in Vegas. There were no other cars in the lot. Good thing too, because the Hummer took up a lot of room.

Iain escorted Brynn inside and to her utter delight, while the building appeared humble and ordinary on the outside, inside, the walls were covered in faded flocked wallpaper and chipped gold scrollwork. The threadbare zebra-print carpet had seen its best days decades ago.

A photographer met them at the door and began taking candid shots. He probably caught Brynn gasping.

"I made sure we'd have the place to ourselves," Iain said. "What do you think?"

She gazed up at her future husband. "It's awful. I *love* it."

He raised one brow. "Thank God. I was worried it might be over the top."

"Oh, it's over the top." She rose up on her tiptoes and kissed him. "You're amazing."

"We're not through."

"There's more?"

Iain led her through a set of double doors, and there, waiting at the end of the aisle, stood a Cher impersonator holding a rhinestone-encrusted microphone. With huge hair, a black beaded gown, a feathered headdress, and six-inch heels, if Brynn squinted and tilted her head to the side, she could definitely see a resemblance to the real thing.

The wedding of her Vegas dreams.

"Oh, Iain."

Brynn clung to his arm as he escorted her down the aisle. Faux Cher licked her lips and vamped it up as she talked about the sanctity of marriage.

However, when Iain placed an antique band of diamonds on her finger, it suddenly got very real. Her eyes met his and she held her breath. This wasn't a fantasy. It wasn't a lark. She was *marrying* Iain Chapman, pledging herself to him. Forever.

Something in her heart shifted then. Brynn had never thought she'd find someone like him. Allie and Monica were settled and in love. She'd always wanted that for herself, but Brynn never believed it would happen. She didn't even allow herself to hope. But in two short weeks, Iain had changed her life.

She gazed down at the ring, tears blurring her vision. "It's gorgeous."

"I wanted to buy the biggest bloody diamond they had," he whispered. "But I thought this would suit you better. If you don't like it—"

"I'm never taking it off." It fit perfectly, and she tilted her hand to view it from every angle.

When it came time for Iain's ring, he'd thought of that, too. He produced a thick gold band from his pocket and handed it to her. Her fingers trembled as she recited her vows and attempted to shove the ring on his finger. It took a couple of tries.

"Buck up, Brynnie. We're almost done."

That settled her nerves a bit. When it came time for the kiss, Iain framed her face with both of his hands. "I do love you, darling." Then he kissed her so tenderly, her knees nearly gave out.

After the ceremony, they were treated to Cher lip-synching "Believe." It was cheesetastic, every bit of it. Brynn couldn't stop smiling. To her amazement, Iain couldn't either.

"If you ever get tired of buying buildings, you can become a wedding planner."

He grabbed her hand and spun her around. "Not in a million years, Mrs. Chapman."

The whole thing took less than an hour. The photographer acted as a witness and took a million pictures.

When they left the building, Brynn found herself standing outside on the pavement in the hot morning sunshine. She glanced down at the ring again. She was a married woman.

Iain hustled her into the Hummer. Once they merged into traffic, he picked up her hand. "Feel any different?"

"Not yet. You?"

He nodded. "Everything's different."

She didn't know where they were going, didn't much care. Brynn was in a romantic haze and she never wanted to sober up.

The chauffeur dropped them off at Iain's apartment complex, where the concierge offered his congratulations. Brynn and Iain rode the elevator side by side in silence. Iain hooked his arm around her waist. He hadn't stopped touching her since they left the chapel.

Once they reached the top floor, Iain hurried to unlock the door. His long, quick strides had Brynn almost jogging to keep pace with him. He was in a hurry. But so was she. She wanted her husband—her freaking *husband*—naked and inside of her.

As soon as they stepped into the apartment, Iain spun around and pressed Brynn up against the door. He began kissing her, stroking his hand from her neck to her breast with a sure, sensual touch. But Brynn twisted her head to the side and dropped her purse and the bouquet to the floor. "I want you naked."

"Ask nicely."

Surprising him, she tugged on his tie. "Really, Iain. I want you naked first. Please?"

He rested his hands over Brynn's, stilling her movements. He looked down at her, his gaze skimming her face. Lowering his head, he paused before kissing her. In the past, he'd been rough with her, emotional, tender, and soothing. But this kiss…this was a promise. She felt it as his lips moved over hers with purpose. When he straightened, he looked her square in the eye. "I'd do anything for you. You know that."

She nodded, not trusting herself to speak.

"All right then." He divested himself of his jacket. "I'll go first." Together they worked the buttons on his vest and shirt. Brynn ripped at his clothes until his chest was bare.

As Iain tugged on the low shoulders of her dress, Brynn grabbed his hands. "I want to touch first. Just this once."

"Touch later."

"This is my wedding day." She leveled her hands on his chest. "And I want to grope my husband." Brynn slid her fingers up to the notch in the cap of Iain's shoulders and gave his left pectoral an open-mouthed kiss.

Bracing his hands against the door on either side of her head, Iain closed his eyes and sucked in a deep breath. His stomach contracted, causing his muscles to flex. "Brynn. No, pet."

For once, she ignored him and, very lightly, slipped her hands down his warm, solid flesh. Her nails gently raked over his flat nipples, turning them hard. She spread her hands wide over his ribs and felt along his sides, down to his narrow waist. His dick strained the fly of his slacks and let her know just how much her touch affected him.

When he opened his eyes, his gaze fixed on her lips. "Fine. Unzip my trousers." As usual, he demanded.

"Not this time." She smiled as his eyes grew wide. Frustration caused his lips to flatten. "I'm not done."

"You are if I say you are," he ground out.

"Nope." She reached around and grabbed his taut ass, squeezing as he tightened his cheeks.

Using one finger, she followed the back seam of his slacks, over his ass, moving downward. Then she massaged her way up to his waistband, and guided her palms along his belt until she reached the buckle, but she left it alone. Instead, she used butterfly touches to caress his abs.

"Why are you provoking me? You know I'm going to have to punish you." At her rebellion, Iain's arms shook as he strained against the door. What would it take to make him lose control again?

Brynn rose to her toes and, angling her head, swiped her tongue across his throat, tasting his salty skin. Then she sucked him there, gently, careful not to leave a bruise.

That was the final straw. Brynn found her mouth wrenched away from his neck. Iain's hands gripped her shoulders. "I'm close to the edge today, Brynn. Now take off your dress."

She shook her head. His domination was her trigger. That's how she got off. Today wasn't about that. She wanted *him* to let go. So far he was holding on to that rigid self-control, but today, *this* day, Brynn wanted to see it snap. She wanted Iain wild and reckless, as he'd been last night. She liked that untamed side of him. He always sent her crashing—with his words and his hands and his mouth. She wanted to do that for him.

"I want you, Iain. So much." Her palm rubbed against his cock.

Without warning, he grabbed her hand and his lips slammed over hers. His tongue invaded her mouth. All the skill he'd shown in the past was absent. His teeth bumped against hers. His hands cupped her breasts and roughly kneaded them.

Brynn's nipples hardened as her bra's scratchy lace abraded her breasts. She tried to kiss him back, but Iain was too aggressive. And she loved it. She loved every forceful bit of it. This was how he made her feel—aching with desire—every single time.

When Iain ground his hips against her lower belly, Brynn groaned into his mouth. She reveled in Iain's brutish treatment. Each harsh thrust of his tongue made her clit throb. She matched his fierceness with her own and nipped his lip.

He pulled back then, panting. "Do you know what you're doing?"

"Fuck me right now, Iain. Here against the door." She wanted him to take her, claim her—and lose himself in the process.

He was on her again in a flash. As he continued to kiss her, he unzipped his pants and removed his cock. Pulling away, he whipped out a condom. He rolled it on in seconds, then his lips covered hers once more. He shoved the dress up over Brynn's hips. Grasping her ass, he lifted her, never breaking contact with her mouth.

Iain reached between her legs and tugged at her panties. She heard a brief tear, then a longer one as he tore them off and threw them to the ground. Then he was inside of her, filling her up, stretching her.

There was nothing easy or civilized about him right then. Even when he tied her up or pinned her arms to her sides, Iain was always very aware of what he was doing. She was the one who broke, never Iain. But right now, his need overrode everything else, and Brynn was right there with him.

As he pounded into her, her body absorbed each hard thrust and wanted more. Digging her nails into his shoulders, she buried her face in the crook of his neck. His skin was slick with sweat and he smelled so damned good, she just held on and breathed him in.

In minutes, Iain tightened his hold on her hips and came. As he shuddered, he bit down on her shoulder. It stung, but it felt good, too.

The muscles in his back bulged as he drove into her one final time. His body stilled and Brynn continued to cling to him, soothing her hands across his back and nape. She didn't come, but she wasn't sorry. She'd sent her new husband right over the edge. It was amazing, this primitive side of him.

Then it was over. She felt the emotional distance immediately. When Iain pulled out of her, the muscle in his jaw ticked. He set her down and walked away. Turning his back on her, he removed the condom, his shoulders tense, his movements jerky.

Brynn tugged at her dress and stepped in front of him, waiting for him to say something—how amazing it had been or how much he loved her. But he wouldn't even look her in the eye.

"What's wrong?" She tried to stroke his cheek, but he flinched and pulled away.

He zipped his fly and bent to retrieve his discarded clothes. When he got to her panties, he paused, then snatched them up. He raised his head but still wouldn't look at her. "Sorry about that, Brynn. It won't happen again, love."

A frisson of alarm slid up her spine. Why was he acting so weird? Something was wrong. "What are you talking about? I wanted that."

His startled gaze fluttered to her eyes. "Not possible. I know you like it rough, but that was… I took you like a bloody animal," he bit out.

She closed the distance between them and, standing on her toes, took his face between her hands. "You really hate being out of control, huh? I pushed you there, Iain. On purpose. I wanted you like that, and I'll want it again. Not every time, but you know, anniversaries, birthdays, maybe Christmas."

He pursed his lips together and wrenched his face from her hold. "I was brutal. I treated you like—"

"Like a whore?"

"Yes," he spit out. "Like a bloody whore. I just whipped my cock out and had at you."

Brynn wrapped her arms around his waist and hugged him tight. "Whatever we do together, it's okay. I didn't tell you to stop, and I could have. I wanted that, Iain. I don't know how to make it any plainer."

His arms remained stiff at his sides, but Brynn hugged him a little harder. After a long moment, he dropped the clothes and embraced her.

"I never want to hurt you, Brynn."

"You didn't," she whispered. "You couldn't. You love me."

"Yes, I do. More than anything." He kissed the top of her head, then rested his cheek on her crown. "This wasn't the way I planned our post-wedding sex."

She reared back and looked up at him. His eyes were still troubled, but the regret and shame that had blanketed his features were gone. His earlier expression ripped at her heart. He really thought they'd done something wrong. What a role reversal.

She gave him a little smile. "You thought about our first boink as man and wife? You're such a sweetie."

"You just used the words *boink* and *sweetie* in the same sentence. Think about that. And go have a gander in the bedroom while you're at it." His eyes cleared and any lingering tension between them dissolved.

Now she was fascinated to find out what he'd been plotting. Stepping out of his arms, she walked to the bedroom and stopped at the door. Brynn's hand flew to her mouth.

The room was filled with flowers. Vases and vases

of flowers in every color imaginable. They sat on the bedside tables, the dresser, and petals littered the floor like confetti. Their fragrance reminded her of Allie and Trevor's garden. An ice bucket filled with champagne stood to one side of the bed. And there was a jeweler's box sitting in the middle of the gray duvet.

Iain stepped behind her and placed his hands on her hips. "*This* is what I had planned."

Chapter 19

She turned in his arms. Guilt now engulfed her. "I ruined it for you, didn't I?"

He shook his head. "I ruined it for you."

"Iain, you didn't. It gets me *crazy* when you go all caveman like that."

A shadow of doubt clouded his eyes before he masked it. His gaze scanned her face. "Were you really all right with my…behavior?"

Brynn nodded. "I seriously loved it."

He breathed out a light sigh. "Go on, then." He tipped his head toward the bed. "Open it."

"When did you have the time to do all this, anyway?"

"It's amazing what you can accomplish with enough money."

She walked to the bed, picked up the box, and opened it. Inside was a drop necklace with one large diamond encased in an art deco setting. It was obviously old.

Brynn glanced up at Iain. "This is beautiful." She removed it from the box and held it out to him.

"It's vintage," he said. "Which, you know, is another term for *used*."

"Stop. I love it." She gave him her back so that he could fasten it.

Iain draped the cool metal around her throat. After he attached the clasp, he kissed her nape. "Let me see."

She spun around. "Well?"

"Lovely." Using one finger, he followed the chain down to the middle of Brynn's chest. "Now I want to fuck you properly."

"Shall I close my eyes and think of England?"

He huffed out a laugh. "Oh, you're a real comedian, you are." Then he tugged the dress off her shoulders. Brynn wiggled out of it, revealing her body. She wore only a strapless bra, since Iain had ripped off her panties.

Brynn bent her arms behind her and unhooked it. Just two weeks ago, she could barely talk to him. Now they were married and she was comfortable being naked in front of him. She felt so sexy and brave with Iain—free, as if she'd broken out of a cage of her own making. She liked being sassy and playful.

She stood in just her sandals and threw back her shoulders "How does it look now?"

Iain grasped her chin. "I don't deserve you." Then he kissed her roughly. Brynn's toes curled in her sandals and she kicked them off. "Now lay on the bed. Arch your back again. Thrust your tits out."

She hopped onto the bed, bouncing once, and fell back. With her back arched, her breasts on display, she posed for her wonderful, arrogant husband.

"You've suddenly become very brazen. I rather like this Brynn." He grinned and unhooked his belt. His pants and boxers went flying before he sprawled out next to her.

"I think it's the ring." She wiggled her finger at him.

Iain leaned over her. Slowly, almost reverently, he covered her face in kisses, starting with her forehead, then her cheeks, her nose, her chin. She was already breathless, and he hadn't even gotten to the good parts yet.

When he removed the freesia from her hair, he bent his head over the bloom and inhaled deeply. "I'm glad you wore this for me."

Iain had so many facets to his personality—high-handed, thoughtful, and passionate. He was protective toward Marc and Amelia, and he still took care of Davy's parents. Just when Brynn thought she had a handle on him, he flipped the script. One thing she was certain of—he loved her. She felt it all the way to her soul.

Iain trailed the waxy bloom down the length of her cheek and over her lips. The sweet smell surrounded her, along with the scent of the other flowers in the room. He'd done all this for her. But he didn't need to do any of it. "You make me happy. You know that, right? Just you."

"I'm glad." There was something unfathomable behind his brown eyes. He seemed…unsettled.

Iain lowered his gaze and continued trailing the flower over her chest and then circled the freesia around her breast. He barely touched her with it, but her nipple budded tightly and was more sensitive with each pass. He lightly dragged it across her areola. There was something erotic about watching Iain clutch the delicate flower in his large hand, caressing her, arousing her.

"Iain. Please." She reached out to grab his shoulder.

"Not yet." He tossed the flower aside and used his hands, covering her small breasts and tugging her nipples between his fingers. He wasn't gentle, but he wasn't out of control either. The pain grew sharper, more exquisite as he pinched a little harder.

Rubbing her hands along his forearms, she wanted him again. Inside of her. Now.

Iain let go of her breasts and skimmed his fingertips along her stomach. Hands spanning her waist, he brushed his thumbs over her hip bones and moved inward. He rained scorching kisses and used tiny flicks of his tongue across her torso, along her belly, all the way to her thighs.

"Put your feet on my shoulders, Brynnie."

Looking down at him, Brynn smiled. "How did I get so lucky?" she asked, repeating his earlier words back to him.

Iain didn't smile back. His expression grew dark and somber. Then he lowered his head and licked across her inner folds. Quickly, with featherlight strokes, his tongue danced over Brynn's slit. When he thrust his fingers inside of her, it was almost her undoing. Pressure coiled deep in her stomach and spread outward. She was so close.

Brynn's hands flew to her breasts, circling her nipples as Iain continued to sweep over that swollen bundle of nerves, using just enough pressure to make her lose her mind.

As her orgasm cut through her, Brynn closed her eyes, letting the sensations roll over her. Her muscles tightened and her pussy contracted as she came. She fisted Iain's hair, holding him in place.

He didn't stop. While he continued to use the tip of his tongue, Iain wiggled another finger inside of her, until a second jolt of pleasure scored through her. Brynn bowed her back. As she clutched at the duvet, she grasped handfuls of velvety flower petals. The smell of them flooded her senses. Iain's tongue and fingers continued to move on her, in her. She convulsed one last time before her body stopped twitching.

When she finally came down, Iain's hands stopped moving, and he removed his mouth from her tender clit. Brynn's eyelids fluttered open.

"How was that, Mrs. Chapman?"

She grinned down at him. "Can't. Talk." She let her head flop back on the bed.

"You don't have to talk." He removed his fingers and crawled to his knees, pulling her legs with him. He reached for another condom, then draped her calves over his shoulders before slowly, carefully gliding inside of her.

Brynn lay sprawled across the bed, while Iain lay next to her, sleeping. Brynn needed hydration. Quietly, she climbed off the bed and walked into the dressing room. She donned one of Iain's many dress shirts—one with red stripes and a white collar. As she slipped the buttons through the holes, she tiptoed back through the bedroom and paused to watch him.

Iain's face was softer than she'd ever seen it. The lines across his forehead were barely visible. He'd captured her heart, taught her about sex, and gave her the courage to be bold. Brynn adored him so much, it almost scared her a little bit, this depth of feeling.

Reluctantly, she stepped away from the bed and walked through the apartment. In the entryway, she picked up her purse, where she'd dropped it by the front door. From inside, she retrieved Iain's dice and turned them over in her hand. The white pips had worn off and the edges were blunted. He'd kept hold of them all these years, to remind him of the friend he'd lost. Brynn was beginning to understand Iain's level of loyalty. He was steadfast, her husband.

Brynn laid the dice on the entry table and picked up the pile of clothes strewn there, including the tattered remains of her panties. She remembered the look on Iain's face after they'd had raw, hot sex. *Shame*. Brynn never wanted him to be ashamed for relinquishing control, not with her. There was a story there, but he may never reveal it. There were parts of Iain he still kept hidden. While she didn't like it, she understood.

Brynn walked through the living room. The afternoon sunlight bounced off the windows across the street and caused her to shield her eyes as she made her way to the kitchen. This apartment wasn't any more inviting in the daytime. It dawned on Brynn that Iain might not want to live in her house. Her midcentury, Vegas dream home. And she didn't want to live here. It left her cold just thinking about it. There were a lot of details they hadn't thought through. What about kids? Brynn wanted at least a couple. Did Iain even like kids? One of many things she didn't really know about him.

Brynn grabbed a bottle of water from the fridge and glanced down at the ring he'd placed on her finger that morning. Iain made her happy. Period. What could be more important than that? They'd figure out the rest in time.

Iain awoke to find Brynn sitting next to him. With her knees pulled up to her chin and wearing his shirt that was far too large for her, she looked pretty and vulnerable. But then she smiled and held up a bottle of water. "Thought you might need this."

Sitting up, he took it, and as he drank, he studied her. He was still upset over what had happened earlier. Losing control like that—it was totally out of character for him. Brynn claimed she liked it. Iain didn't. Hated it, in fact. He'd promised himself last night that it wouldn't happen again, yet he'd taken his bride without the slightest thought for her pleasure. He'd been an animal.

Brynn reached out, caressed his face with the back of her hand. "We should talk about it."

"No."

"Yes. Iain, I love you. I love all of you. If you'd been hurting me, I'd have asked you to stop. And you would have."

He gazed into her eyes. They were full of compassion. "I'd rather cut off me own right arm than harm you. God's truth."

"I know." Her fingers drifted to his hair, and he leaned into her touch.

How could Iain make her understand? He hadn't talked much about his parents. There wasn't a hell of a lot to say—none of it pleasant. He couldn't give her part of it without telling her everything. Iain hated rehashing the past. Brynn thought the past defined them. He'd always claimed otherwise, but maybe she was right.

"My dad was a skive," he said. Brynn stopped toying with his hair and grabbed his hand. "Never worked a goddamned day in his life. The council flats looked like a prison—gray concrete and shabby as hell. My mother was haggard, looking at least ten years older than she really was. We had ugly, third-hand furniture covered in cigarette burns. Barely enough food to scrape by. The old man spent all of his time and money at the pub.

"Every night, without fail, he'd come home drunk and one of three things would happen: he'd pass out—which is what my mother prayed for—or he'd slap her around over something stupid." Iain closed his eyes as the memories flooded back. That horrible flat that reeked of fear and smoke. God, how he'd hated that place. Brynn talked about her little rundown house, her mother's illness, and while it gutted him to hear her story, at least she'd had a family.

"What was the third thing?" Brynn asked, lacing her fingers with his and squeezing tight.

Iain said nothing. He didn't want to utter the words out loud. Shame coated him, made him feel dirty.

"What did he do, Iain?"

"He'd drag me mum off to the bedroom and have at her. I could hear him, grunting like a fucking pig. Afterward, he'd start snoring and she'd come into the lounge and turn on the telly like nothing had happened."

Brynn lowered her knees, let go of his hand, and crawled into his lap. "You're nothing like that. What we did today, it was mutual, Iain. *I* provoked *you*, remember?" She placed her hand on his cheek. "I wanted you. It excites me when you let yourself go. But that doesn't mean you're like your father."

He clenched his jaw and remained quiet.

"You're a decent, honest person."

That wasn't true at all. If she knew just how dishonest he was, Brynn never would have married him. He couldn't bear this. She was singing his praises, thinking he was an honorable man when the opposite was true. He captured her hand and pulled it from his face. "No, I'm not, love. Never confuse me with someone decent. But I promise you one thing, Brynn Chapman—I'll always be good to you."

She kissed his chin. "You are good. And one day, you're going to realize it." She leaned her head against his shoulder and they sat in silence for a long time. Finally Brynn glanced up at him. "I'm going to have to tell my sisters about us."

"We don't have to tell them anything." He smoothed a hand along her thigh, until his fingers dove under the hem of the shirt. Latching on to her bare hip, he stroked her silky skin. "Plan a family wedding, and we'll do it all over again. The first wedding will be our secret. Let Allie and Monica fight over the details. We'll know the truth."

"I couldn't lie to them like that."

Iain's hand stilled. "Not sharing all the details isn't the same as lying, is it?"

"Yes it is. I'd be letting them think it was our first time. Lies of omission are still lies."

Fuck. Iain had never planned on telling Brynn the truth. Even if he had been tempted, after hearing her pronouncement, he'd have changed his mind. And it would always be between them, this secret. He hated carrying it around, along with the guilt. But he had no choice.

"I'll see if we can have a family dinner or something," she said. "I'll have to call my dad and tell him, too."

"What's he like, your father?"

"Nice. Normal."

"Are you close?"

"I talk to my dad and his wife, Karen, every couple of weeks. He used to fix refrigerators, but now he gets to fish every day, so he's happy."

"If you tell your sisters, they're going to give you hell, you know."

"I do know. I've had a lifetime of it. But it was worth it. Our wedding was perfect, Iain. You totally outdid yourself."

"Tacky enough for you, then?"

"Romantic too."

When she gazed up at him with a wistful smile gracing her lips and a hopeful gleam in her eyes, Iain vowed to become the man she believed him to be. Good. Decent.

But you'll never be an honest man, mate. You've already fucked that up for good.

On Friday morning, Iain did something unusual—he grinned. On the ride to work. On the way into the office building. At every person he passed.

He may have even whistled. Iain Chapman was one lucky tosser.

Although hesitant to leave Brynn's arms, Iain had been up by four, looking at the financial news. He'd wanted nothing more than to stay in bed with her, but they'd had three days of fucking, sucking, and spooning. No one told him marriage could be so bloody wonderful. After he told her about his father, they didn't speak of it again. She didn't push him either. Instead, they fell back into their pattern. Iain took control and Brynn followed his lead. Things were on an even keel, and Iain felt…peaceful.

At six thirty, he'd brought her a cup of coffee and kissed her awake. No time for a lazy round of sex—they both needed to get back to work. But she was incredibly tempting, lying there with her hair spread over the pillow, her lips swollen from his kisses.

After Brynn woke, she shadowed him into the bathroom and, sitting cross-legged on the counter, sipped her coffee as she watched him shave. It was distracting.

"What have you got on for today?" he asked.

"Hopefully, Cass has talked to Trevor's financial people. I'll get my new computer and all of the software I need."

She set down her mug and swiveled to look at him, except her eyes were fixated on his earlobe. A sure sign that she was working herself up to say something she thought he wouldn't want to hear. "Maybe tonight, we can discuss our living arrangements."

"Meaning?"

"Meaning that we have two homes. I know you're comfortable here. But I'm comfortable in my own house. If we work together, we can find a compromise that will satisfy us both."

He took one last swipe at his cheek, dropped the razor, and picked up a towel. "You're parsing your words again. You don't have to do that with me, pet. You hate it here, but your house comes with a crazed Russian and no office. What do you suggest?"

"Maybe we can find a home that suits us both."

Iain stepped in front of her and, bracing her jaw, kissed her. "Sounds like a plan. In the meantime, if you can stand it, I'd like to stay here during the week, yeah? That way, I can work in the early hours.

Weekends, we'll continue to stay at yours. How's that for a compromise?"

"It'll do for now." She raked her hand down his bare chest. "You know, I think I have just enough time for a quickie." She wiggled her eyebrows at him. "How about you?"

He didn't, not really. He'd made time anyway. How could he have possibly refused his wife's request?

Now, as Iain walked into his office, he was forty minutes late, but he didn't give a monkey's. The quickie had turned into a longer session, and he wasn't a bit sorry.

He strode into his suite. "Morning, Ames. Everything's still standing, I see."

Amelia's red lipsticked mouth formed an *O* and then quickly turned into a frown. "What the hell happened to you?"

"What do you mean?"

"I get one lousy text saying you're taking three days off. You never take time off, and when I called, you didn't answer. I was about to send out a search party."

"No need for dramatics. I was a little tied up." Actually Brynn had been tied up. He'd bound her to one of the decorative columns that separated the living and dining room, and then he'd taken her from behind. It had been a lovely afternoon.

He realized Ames had spoken. "What was that?"

She sighed. "Marc hasn't come in either. Melanie's gone. She packed up and left Tuesday night, and I haven't heard from him since. Neither one of you could bother to pick up your damned phone."

Iain rubbed his forehead. "Shit." While he'd been in a sexual marathon with Brynn, Marc had been having a rough time of it. Made him feel guilty as hell. And fuck all, Iain hated that feeling. "I'd better go check on him."

Amelia stood and grabbed her purse from the bottom drawer. "I'm coming with you."

"No," Iain said. "Stay here. Hold it down."

As he left the office, he hadn't realized he'd taken the dice from his pocket, but now, as he stared into his palm, there they were. He rubbed them together like worry beads and hoped Marc was all right. Anxiety ate at him, forcing him to hasten his steps. If Marc wasn't answering his phone or showing up for work, he could be in serious trouble.

Brynn strode into her office and expected the worst. Tuesday morning, she'd texted Cass, saying she was taking three days' personal time, but offered no other explanation. Of course, Cass had called—several times—but Brynn hadn't even bothered to answer, letting everything go to voice mail. Now, she had to face the music.

Friday mornings were reserved for sales staff meetings, so she wanted to catch Cassandra before it started but was running a little late. The quickie with Iain had taken longer than she'd anticipated.

During the last three days, Brynn and Iain had done nothing but eat, sleep, and oh yeah, fuck like rabbits. Lots of scorching hot, raunchy sex. It was the best time of Brynn's life.

She felt buoyed by it. By love. By being around Iain and his no-nonsense ways, which were rubbing off on her. When Brynn had awoken that morning, she had known she'd have to tackle the Cassandra situation head-on. Hopefully Cass would use the life preserver Trevor had provided, but if not, Brynn was going to need to look at all of her options—including making good on her threat to quit. At that terrifying thought, her steps faltered right before she opened the office door.

When Paige spotted Brynn, she hopped out of her seat and grabbed Brynn's arm, dragging her into the alcove. "Where the hell have you been? Cass has been going insane—more so than usual. Strangers took over her office on Tuesday and she's been spazzing ever since."

"Good. Not good that she's freaking out, but good that somebody's taking control of this place. If she follows their advice, the business might just make it."

"What if she doesn't?" Paige's blue eyes filled with worry.

"Then we may have to leave Cass and find better jobs."

"What the hell is going on with you, Brynn Campbell? You're all…decisive."

Brynn held up her left hand. "It's Brynn Chapman, and I think I might have grown a spine."

Paige snatched Brynn's hand and inspected the ring. "Oh my God. You got *married*? To the Blue Moon dude?"

"Iain. He's…awesome."

"You thought he was a jerk. You didn't even want to work with him."

"He's reformed. Sort of. And he makes me smile."

Paige's eyes traveled over Brynn. "You've got it bad, girl, and while I'm still pissed that you didn't tell me about how much trouble the business is in, I'm happy for you." She pulled Brynn into a hug. "Congratulations."

"Thanks, and again, I'm really sorry for not telling you sooner. Now, I'd better go see how Cass is doing." Brynn stepped away from the alcove and headed for Cassandra's office. But the woman herself emerged from her office. Her pale hair resembled fuzzy dandelion seeds. Purple, puffy half-moons circling her eyes contrasted with her pale skin.

"Brynn, grab Paige and get in here. Right now." Then she sailed into the conference room and slammed the door.

The entire sales team eyed Brynn with varying degrees of curiosity.

Paige crept up behind her. "This is bad. What do you think she wants?"

"Let's go find out." Brynn wove through the desks. Easing open the door, she slipped inside with Paige on her heels.

Cass paced back and forth in front of the windows. With one hand on her hip and the other clutching her head, she mumbled to herself.

"Cass," Brynn said, "are you all right?"

She stopped talking and drew to a halt. "No! Of course I'm not all right," she snapped. "There are people pawing through my files, snooping into my finances. It's all very invasive. And where were you, Brynn? If you didn't show up today, I was going to call the FBI. It's your fault they're here in the first place."

Brynn exchanged a glance with Paige. Cass was in full meltdown mode. "I texted and said I was taking a few days off. Besides, I didn't have a computer, so I couldn't do my job anyway."

Paige raised her hand. "Um, on that note, the IT guy

called. The computer is shot. He wasn't able to get it up and running. He said unless you hire the manufacturer to retrieve the bits off the hard drive, it's gone. That's a really expensive procedure, by the way, and it may not work."

Just as Brynn had feared. Months' worth of work—vanished. "Since the old software won't be compatible with a new PC, I'll have to redo everything, dating back weeks. There's no possible way I can do that alone."

Cassandra shoved her hands into her curls and fell into a chair. "I know that, Brynn, but what do you want me to do about it? My life is shit, girls. The financial guy says I need to take a seventy-five percent pay cut, consolidate all the business loans, possibly declare personal bankruptcy, and fire half the sales team. I can't *live* like this."

Brynn approached her slowly. "Cass. What else can you do? I hate that you have to get rid of half the sales team, but if you don't, we're all out in the cold."

Cass's head snapped up. "Did you not hear me, Brynn? I may have to declare bankruptcy. That means I'm going to lose my house, probably my car. Where are Nef and I going to stay? We'll be homeless." She broke down on the last word and began sobbing.

Brynn patted her shoulder, and Paige sighed before walking toward them. "I'll help you find an apartment."

Cass sniffed. "They need to allow pets." She pulled a Kleenex from her bra.

"We'll figure it out," Brynn said. "We'll put our heads together and come up with a plan—scale back, get rid of the office. The important thing is that you follow the financial guys' advice. This is a setback. Not a life sentence."

Cass said nothing. She stared out the window and sniffed.

"Cass?" Brynn asked. "Are you on board?"

Still, she remained silent.

Paige took a deep breath. "I can take over the day-to-day operations. I'll help you get organized."

"I'll help too," Brynn said. "But before we go any further, I need a computer and updated software. That has to be the priority."

Cass leaped from the chair. "Your computer, Brynn? What about my *life*?" She began pacing once more.

When Brynn glanced at Paige, she saw her own frustration reflected in the other woman's eyes. As usual, they weren't getting through to Cass, who dramatically thumped her fist on her chest. "I worked for years to make this business a success, and now those bastards come in here and start ordering me around. I had to sell my soul to the devil. If I didn't agree to give them veto power over every dime the business spends, they wouldn't help me. So now I have to get their approval for everything. If you want a computer, you'll have to ask your new bosses. That's not my prerogative anymore." Fat tears rolled down her cheeks. "I have no say over my own damned company."

Brynn stepped forward, standing in front of Cass, blocking her path. "But the business isn't a success. It's a failure. That's the hard, cold truth." Brynn hated confrontation, but sometimes it was necessary. She didn't like being so blunt with Cass. Her boss was very fragile right now. But she was also eye deep in denial. "And if you don't do what they tell you, you're not going to have a business at all."

Like a child, Cass's face crumpled. "This isn't fair. My life wasn't supposed to be this way." She began crying in earnest. Though Brynn was sympathetic, she wasn't going to comfort Cass with a hug and reassurances. Not this time.

"Listen to me. You need to get yourself together because everybody in this office is looking to you, Cassandra. You need to lead by example, and if you can't handle it, then tell us now. Let us go and shut down the company."

Paige and Cass both ogled her. Brynn had never sounded so forceful—Iain's influence at work once again.

Paige nodded. "I agree. And for God's sake, enough with the waterworks."

Cass sniffed. "Why are both of you being so mean to me?" Did Cass even care that every member of the team was about to lose their job? She was still making it all about *her*.

Brynn felt as though she were having some strange out-of-body experience—as if she was seeing things come into focus for the first time. Cassandra wasn't going to change. Her boss was a mess, personally and professionally. She'd gotten herself into this trouble, and along the way, she'd manipulated Brynn into working seventy-hour weeks. Brynn had stupidly allowed herself to be used because she'd been too weak to stand up for herself. Never again. She was tired of being a doormat. It finally clicked. Brynn could still care about Cass—she wasn't a bad person after all, just flawed—while putting herself first for once. It wasn't about being selfish. It was about survival. Iain had taught her that as well. "I quit," she blurted out. With her heart pounding, she wondered if she should take the words back. No. No, they felt right. Brynn was quitting. It was time.

Cass's mouth dropped open. After a moment, she drew an unsteady breath. "You can't quit, Brynn. I need you. We have clients. You have a responsibility to this office. I'll make sure you get a computer."

"It's your business, Cassandra. You had a responsibility to this office too. Yet here we are." Brynn turned to Paige. "I'm sorry, I have to go. I can't do this anymore." Brynn didn't know where this rush of courage was coming from. In ten minutes, she'd probably be shaking like a gambling addict with his last chip, but right then, at that minute, Brynn felt good. Strong.

She walked out of the conference room. The sales team looked up, their faces questioning, worried. They should have been. For that matter, Brynn should have been scared witless. But she wasn't.

Pausing briefly at her office door, she kept right on walking. There was nothing in the hovel that she needed.

When Brynn heard footsteps behind her, she assumed it was Cass.

"Wait for me." Brynn turned to see Paige following her. "You're the real talent in this place. I'm coming with you."

"But I don't know what I'm doing," Brynn whispered.

"I do. You're starting a new company. And you're going to need a partner. The clients love you, and I have faith in you."

Okay, now the terror started to set in. Brynn would be okay if she was only responsible for herself, but if she had Paige's future in her hands…

"Hey," Paige said, "we'll figure it out together. No pressure. I know I'm taking a gamble."

That alleviated some of Brynn's worry. But not much. She nodded and moved to the door. She took one last peek over her shoulder. Every eye in the office was riveted on her, even Cassandra's. Brynn Campbell Chapman was the center of attention, and for once, she didn't care.

Chapter 20

IAIN SLAMMED OUT OF THE CAR AND QUICKLY walked to Marc's front door. When he and Melanie moved in together, Marc had bought this house—a fucking Mediterranean mini-mansion. Five bedrooms, six baths, a gated community. It even had a wine cellar, and Mel was the only one who drank the stuff. Iain couldn't blame her for getting irritated with Marc's foot-dragging. Everything about this house, this neighborhood, screamed marriage and family. Kids. Commitment. What was the poor woman meant to think?

When Marc didn't answer, Iain walked to the window and, cupping his eyes, peered inside. Hopefully, his mate was just pissed off his ass and hadn't done anything stupid. Marc had done many arsed up things in his life, but he wouldn't off himself. However, he could have got so plastered that he'd taken a tumble down the stairs. Shit.

Iain lifted his leg and kicked above the door handle. *Fuck, that hurt*. The shock of it registered all the way up his leg. He stepped back to take another run at it when Marc opened the door. Starkers. Not a stitch on him.

"What the bloody hell are you doing?" Marc slurred the words and swayed a bit.

"What am I doing?" Iain asked. "What are you doing, answering the door with your willy hanging out?"

"Fuck off." Then he turned and shambled back into

the house, leaving Iain to follow. Even in the foyer, the place smelled like a bloody brewery. Iain shut the front door and when he turned around, Marc had disappeared. The drunken twat couldn't climb the stairs that quickly, so Iain wandered down the hall and found Marc in a spare bedroom, spread eagle on the bed, showing his naked bum. The room reeked of beer and stale sweat. Empty bottles covered the bedside table and floor.

Iain paused, his heart in his throat. They'd been through everything together—tough childhoods, losing Davy, starting over here in Vegas—with nothing but their will and the desire for a better life. Iain was the happiest he'd ever been, and Marc was at the end of his tether. Life was a fucking bitch sometimes.

Iain grabbed a bottle, walked into the adjoining bog, and filled it with cold water. He stepped back in the bedroom, where Marc lay snoring. God, what a sight. Iain poured the water down Marc's crack and onto his bollocks.

Marc rolled over and screamed like a tiny girl. "What the bloody hell?" He leaped up and staggered, holding on to the wall for support. "What the fuck are you doing, Iain?"

"I'll go put on some coffee. You"—he pointed at Marc's cock—"put that thing away, before you hurt someone. And take a shower while you're at it. You're rank, mate."

Marc's red-rimmed eyes moved around the room, then landed on Iain. "Get out."

"I know Mel left you, and I'm sorry. But I'm not leaving."

Marc shoved both hands through his hair. "She says I

care more about you and the business than I do for her. It's not true, is it?"

"No, it's not." Marc was hurting, broken. Iain couldn't imagine what the poor bloke was going through. Until Iain met Brynn, he hadn't been able to imagine what it meant to love another person more than yourself. To care about her welfare above your own. If he ever lost Brynn—no, he couldn't even fathom it. Not having her in his life—it was unthinkable.

Iain left the room and wandered to the kitchen. After hunting in the cabinets, he found the coffee and brewed a strong pot. When he heard the shower turn on, he felt a bit of relief. At least Marc was up and moving around.

After half an hour, his mate ambled into the kitchen. He was still unshaven and his breath smelled like death, but he was dressed.

Iain poured him a cup of coffee. While Marc slumped onto a stool, Iain grabbed a rubbish bag, went back to the bedroom, and cleaned up all the bottles. When he returned to the kitchen, Marc had finished the cup.

"Tasted like ashes, it did."

"I made it strong on purpose. Now tell me what happened."

"You already know. Mel's gone. Said I didn't truly love her, and she was tired of playing second fiddle."

"You offered to marry her, yeah?"

"Yeah." Marc dragged a hand through his wet hair. "Grudgingly. I don't know what's wrong with me. I love her. I do. I'm gutted that she left. But I couldn't pull the trigger, could I?" Marc's life had been falling apart for months, and Iain had barely even noticed. He had been too caught up in his own agenda—the downtown buildings, meeting Trevor Blake, pining over Brynn.

Iain pulled out the stool next to him and placed his hands on the granite island. "So what are you going to do about it?"

"Don't know." They were quiet for a few. "Do you ever think that we're living Davy's life? The life he was meant to have. That it's all one big cosmic mixup? You and me, mate, we were meant for the nick or worse."

It was true. If Vegas hadn't been Davy's dream, neither Iain nor Marc would have even thought of it. "Not fair, is it?"

"No." Marc glanced over and noticed Iain's wedding ring. "Oh my God. You married her, didn't you?" He sounded shocked, his voice faint as his gaze moved to Iain's face. "You bloody, arrogant wanker. You married that girl."

"I love her." Iain did. With every cell in his body.

"The hell you do. You want everything that comes with her. Trevor Blake, with all of his money and reputation. You don't give a toss about that girl."

Iain's mouth settled into a grim line. "Just because your life has turned to shit, don't take it out on the rest of us. I'm going to spend the rest of my life making Brynn happy."

Marc threw his head back and laughed. It sounded strained and bitter. "Oh that's rich. You, devoting your life to something other than yourself. How long will that last, eh? Until you get tired of fucking her?"

"Shut the hell up."

"You're going to hurt her, Iain. You'll leave her. You and I both know that."

The fuck he would. Rage, stronger and more powerful than he'd ever known, knifed through him, making his vision blur, his ears ring. Turning, Iain lashed out and punched the wall behind him. Then he punched it again. Dry wall dust coated his knuckles. He'd come damned close to smashing Marc's stupid face in but managed to rein himself in at the last minute.

Marc barely glanced at the fist-sized hole. "Hit a nerve, did I?"

"Shut your gob, mate. I'm serious. You are not going to talk about me wife that way."

Marc shifted his jaw from side to side. "Your wife. You're not worthy of her any more than I was worthy of Mel."

Iain knocked the stool to the tiled floor. His foot still hurt from trying to kick in the bleeding door, and now his knuckles ached like a bitch. "I know that, right? I'm nothing but a conniving sod, but I love her."

"You poor bastard." Marc shook his head. "You still think you've got a happy ending coming, don't you? I've fucked it all up, good and proper, Iain, and you will too."

No, he wouldn't. Iain had a will of iron, and he was determined not to muck things up with Brynn. His marriage would be a success. He'd settle for nothing less. But he wasn't going to fight about it with Marc. His mate was hurting. Saying things he didn't mean. What he needed was a swift kick in the arse, and Iain was the man to give it to him.

"So that's it, then? Are you telling me that you're going to roll over like some castrated dog? Mel walked out and you're just going to drink yourself stupid? That's your solution?"

In a move that was almost too quick for Iain to follow, Marc stood, picked up his cup, and chucked it at Iain's head. It clipped the corner of his ear before smashing into the wall behind him.

"Fuck me, that hurt."

"Good. Now get out before I really do some damage. I feel sorry for Brynn. I really do. She's going to find out the truth about how you set her up."

Iain's hands clenched into fists. "Is that a threat?" Fear grabbed hold of his gut and squeezed hard.

"Nah, mate. I'm not like you, hurting people to get ahead. But she will find out that you manipulated the entire situation. How's she going to feel about you then, Iain?"

"She'll never know. I decided I'm not taking a dime from Blake. Don't worry, we'll find another way to develop the properties."

"*You're* not taking a dime? *You* decided? Fuck you. We were never partners, not really. You make the decisions and expect me to back them. Well, I'm through. I don't care what you do with that property. Shove it up your ass. Give it away. I just want out."

Iain felt like he'd been kicked in the teeth. Marc, quitting the business? It was ridiculous. "You're still drunk, mate. You don't know what you're saying. Of course we're partners. You and me. We're in it together."

"No we're not. Haven't been for some time. Everyone's expendable, isn't that what you always say?"

Iain's head was starting to pound. What the hell was going on? "I wasn't talking about you."

"Weren't you? Brynn will become expendable too. Just you wait. When she's delivered Trevor Blake, you'll get bored."

Even as the anger burned through his veins like acid, he knew Marc was right about one thing—Iain had treated his old mate as if he were a stick of furniture.

"Just get out of here, Iain." With his back to the refrigerator, Marc slid to the floor. Elbows resting on his knees, he cradled his head in his hands.

Iain had never seen him like this. Despondent. Hopeless. Not even after Davy died. Marc and Iain were alike, fighters the both of them.

"I'm going to forget we ever had this conversation, yeah? It's not doing either of us any good. I'll talk to you later."

"No," Marc said. "I'm done. It's over."

Iain didn't know how to respond to Marc's accusations. Because they were all correct. Iain worked his ass off to get what he wanted, and he mowed down anyone who dared get in his way. It had worked for him all these years.

And it'd cost him his best mate.

Shuffling, Iain left the house, feeling weary clear to his bones. How could a day turn to shit so quickly? Iain wanted Brynn right then—her comfort, her kindness. He wanted to smell her hair and hold her, feel her body against his.

She said he was a good man, but Iain had more in common with his father than he ever dared admit. His old man had been a mean bastard who'd never cared what people thought of him. Never had a kind word to say about anyone. Wasn't Iain exactly the same? Before Brynn came into his life, he hadn't even known his employees' names. Iain used people, just as he'd been ready to use Brynn.

God, he was a miserable fuck. What did Brynn see in him? She was a starry-eyed optimist who didn't believe in lost causes. And for once, instead of pitying her, he was glad for it.

As he climbed into the backseat of the car, his phone alarm reminded him he had a meeting with a building manager in twenty minutes. On the ride through downtown, he stared out the window deep in thought. Iain needed to make things right with Marc, but he didn't know how.

Brynn will know. She'd have a manual on how to apologize for being an ass, some words of wisdom. That's what she did, his Brynn. She helped people in trouble, and Iain was in the middle of a full-blown personal crisis.

Brynn parted ways with Paige. They made plans to meet up later and start plotting business strategies. Right now, though, Brynn needed a few hours with her husband. He was going to be proud of her for taking a stand. She couldn't have done it without him. He'd helped her tap into her confidence both in and out of the bedroom.

She parked in the garage across the street and jogged to Iain's building. Once she hit the office, Brynn noticed the change in atmosphere. People were smiling, chatting with each other. The vibe was open and friendly. A few people waved, a couple called her name.

Brynn smiled and stopped to talk. This was like walking into a completely different office. Iain had done this. With her help, yes, but he'd fostered a respectful, welcoming environment. That man deserved lunch. And maybe, if he was lucky, some oral sex.

Strolling into Iain's suite, Amelia looked up and gave her a tired smile. "Hey, what are you doing here?"

"I thought I'd surprise him."

Ames shook her head. "He's away. Back-to-back meetings this afternoon. By the way, this is Katie, my new assistant."

Katie smiled. "So nice to meet you. Mr. Chapman said you're welcome anytime."

"Great. Thank you." Brynn turned back to Amelia. If she knew Iain, he'd have his phone glued to his ear for the rest of the day. Anyway, she wanted to tell him the news about quitting in person. Maybe she could scribble him a sexy note instead, teasing him with all the things she wanted him to do to her. "Can I go in and leave him a message?"

Amelia waved her toward the door. "Sure. Make yourself at home."

Brynn walked into Iain's office, closing the door behind her. It seemed strangely empty without his larger-than-life presence, but it smelled of bergamot mixed with his clean aftershave, leather chairs, and strong coffee. She inhaled deeply.

Brynn crossed to his desk, pulled back his chair, and sat down. The tufted leather was slick but cushy. Easing her hands along the padded armrests, she took in the furniture—the maritime clock, his enormous antique desk. None of this represented the tough but loving man she'd come to know. Too stuffy. His apartment wasn't a reflection of him, either. Brynn wanted to make a home where they'd both be comfortable, where Iain could relax a little bit. In jeans. As hot as he looked in a suit, dude needed to go cazh every once in a while.

His desk held a computer, an expensive pen with gold accents, and a small pad of notepaper with the Blue Moon logo. She needed an envelope for privacy. She planned to use quite a few dirty words in this lust note.

Smiling, Brynn opened the shallow middle drawer. But what she saw there stole the breath from her lungs. Reaching inside, Brynn pulled out a stack of photos. All of her. Candid shots along with old school photos and her driver's license. *What the hell?*

As she shuffled through the pictures, her heart pounded so hard it hurt. Some of the pictures went back months.

Brynn felt like she'd been punched in the stomach. What was Iain doing with these? Where did he get them?

Dropping them on the desk, she began rifling through every drawer but found nothing else. There had to be something there, some clue as to why he had photos of her. She turned on his computer and tried a few different options for passwords but came up empty.

Tucking the photos back where she'd found them, Brynn stood and rubbed her shaking, clammy hands along her skirt. Schooling her features, she opened the office door and poked her head out. "Hey, Amelia, I need to check my email and my phone's about out of juice. Can I use Iain's computer?" The smile she wore was fake, forced. Surely Amelia could see right through her. But Ames simply smiled.

"Of course, honey." She hopped up and hustled past Brynn to the desk. She typed in a code and patted Brynn's shoulder on her way out. It was that easy.

Moving with slow steps, Brynn walked to the desk and fell onto the chair. She searched through his files, and it didn't take long to find what she was looking for.

With trembling fingers, Brynn clicked on the file bearing her name and wished to God she hadn't. Not just pictures this time—documents. Financial statements going back years, copies of her college records, her credit card bills, a detailed account of her daily activities. Brynn looked through everything again, starting with the first page and painstakingly read every dry fact of her life, from her mother's illness to her father's remarriage. Then there was Trevor. There was a lot of information on him—his investments, his net worth.

When Brynn got to the last page, she read the summary, dated four months before she'd met Iain. Brynn had been singled out as Trevor's only single relative. Then it all fell into place.

Trevor. All roads led back to her brother-in-law.

All the times Iain had subtly asked about her family, her sisters, her hobbies, he had already known the answers before they ever met. He only needed money for his downtown properties. It was all part of his master plan—to get to Trevor through Brynn, the weak link, the single female. It had all been a setup from the start.

Pain lanced straight through her. Iain didn't love her. He'd never loved her.

All the things she'd done with him, giving him control over her body. Her heart. That dickhead had made her fall in love with him. Tears burned her eyes at the humiliation. At the pain.

God, how he must have congratulated himself. She'd been so easy. Pathetic little Brynn, the jellyfish, desperate for attention. Heat barbed her cheeks and neck.

Her head pounded. Her stomach roiled. She was going to be sick. Swallowing convulsively and taking deep breaths helped keep the nausea at bay.

Brynn took a few minutes to get herself under control. She didn't want Amelia to know anything was wrong or she'd call Iain. Brynn had to get out of here now, before she lost it.

Plastering a fake smile on her face, Brynn exited the office, trying to act normal. Huh. Normal. Her entire world had flipped upside down—nothing would ever be normal again. Swallowing the hysteria that threatened to overtake her, Brynn hustled to the door. "See you, Ames." Her voice sounded a little squeaky, so she cleared her throat.

"Hey, are you all right, hon? You look pale."

Brynn nodded. "No, fine, just hungry. Take care." She didn't make eye contact with any of the employees as she walked swiftly out the door and onto the elevator, where a wave of nausea hit her again. How Iain must have been laughing his ass off.

By the time she reached the lobby, Brynn was practically running to the exit. Stumbling out into the bright sun, she sprinted across the street to the parking garage. She numbly climbed into her car. She could hardly feel her own body, but the pain and grief inside her swelled, threatening to overwhelm her.

She wasn't sure how long she sat in there in the heat, not moving. Hardly breathing. It was a sauna. Trickles of sweat rolled down her cheeks. Or were those tears?

When she started feeling light-headed, Brynn finally fumbled with the keys and started the engine.

Holding a hand over her mouth, she breathed deeply. *He used you. He used you.* It played over in her mind like a bad song. Iain didn't care about her. It was all bullshit.

Never confuse me with someone decent. He'd told her he wasn't a good person. She had thought he was being too hard on himself, but he was just being honest for once.

All those people who sought Brynn out only because they needed a favor—Iain was one of them. A user. A liar. He'd betrayed her in the most hurtful way possible, making her fall for him in order to get what he wanted. Sick, disgusting bastard.

Brynn glanced down at her wedding ring, and with a scream of rage, ripped it off and threw it at the passenger window. It made a high-pitched clink against the glass before falling out of sight.

She scrubbed her hands down her face and tried to think. *Run away, jellyfish. That's what you do best.*

She could. Just start driving. No destination in mind.

But she wasn't going to do that. Not this time. Iain had been right about one thing: it was time for Brynn to stop running away from her problems.

It didn't matter where she went anyway. She could never outrun this heartache.

Chapter 21

Brynn went home and sat on her blue sofa, clutching a pillow, thinking about all the times Iain'd said he loved her—each one a lie. Every touch, every kiss, every hot, sexy moment. Lies.

What if Monica had been single? Would Iain have gone after her instead? *Of course he would have. She's the sexy, adventurous one, not you.* He probably wouldn't have given Brynn a second glance.

That penetrated and burrowed deep into Brynn's fractured heart—past the pain, past the shock. Iain Chapman was nothing but a fucking liar. The hurt and humiliation she felt were still there, but rage was stronger now, and she welcomed it.

When her phone rang, she glanced at the screen. It was after five o'clock. She'd been sitting there for hours. "Hello, Iain," she answered.

"Where are you, love? I came straight home, didn't even bother to stop by the office, but you're not here."

"I'm at my house." She hung up without saying anything else.

She finally roused herself, turned on the orange vintage lamps and waited. He called twice more, but she refused to answer.

Iain must have had told his driver to step on it, because he landed on her porch in twenty minutes. Brynn answered the door and stared at him through new eyes. Iain stood there, looking beautiful and masculine, wearing a concerned expression. Brynn's dumb, traitorous heart skipped a beat.

"You sounded strange on the phone." His gaze darted over her face. "What's wrong, love?"

Why did she want to throw herself into his arms? He was a dickhead. Nevertheless, her body still responded to him, even though her brain knew better. Brynn needed to hold on to that feeling of misery and anger, let it protect her from making another stupid mistake.

Turning, she walked back to the living room with Iain on her heels. As he reached out and brushed her shoulder, Brynn shrugged him off. "Don't touch me." She quickly darted around the sofa, using it as a shield between them. She gripped the back of it until her hands ached.

Iain's eyes grew wary. "Brynn. Darling, you're scaring me. Tell me what's wrong."

"You're wrong. Everything about you is wrong and twisted."

"What are you talking about?" His brows dipped as he took a step toward her.

"Stop!"

He froze and his expression changed. He knew. She could see it in his eyes. He knew she'd found out the truth. She could practically hear his gears turning, wondering how he could talk his way out of this one. More declarations of love? More sexy commands? *Not this time, asshole*. Brynn had finally wised up. No matter how much her body might have wanted him, she'd never let him near her again.

"Did you laugh?" she demanded.

"Wha'?"

"When you found out how easy it was going to be, when you realized what a pushover I was, did you laugh? Or did you feel sorry for me? Poor Brynn with her orgasm troubles." Her voice cracked and she took a shuddering breath to steady herself.

"Brynn." He shook his head almost imperceptibly and licked his lips. "It's not like that, love."

"Did you laugh?" she bit out.

"No." His warm eyes met hers, and she felt her resolve starting to slip. "I'd never laugh at you, love. Never." His voice was hoarse. She hardly noticed. It didn't matter anyway. He could have said the sky was blue, and she wouldn't have believed him. "I've wanted you from the start Brynn. From the first time I saw you in the garden."

Brynn frowned, confused. "What are you talking about?"

"I went to that gala thing for your foundation. I saw you there, in Trevor's garden. I wanted you then, but when I walked toward you, you ran."

Oh God. This was more fucked up than she imagined. He'd been playing a long game all this time. "So you had me followed? You went through my financial records because you *wanted* me? You know what middle school I attended because you were attracted to me?" Each word came out louder than the last. "Bullshit, Iain. The only thing you wanted was Trevor's money. Was fucking me a bonus or a chore? Maybe one of my sisters would have been more to your liking, but you got stuck with me." All of her insecurities surfaced, each one tempting her to crawl back into her shell and stay there.

"Don't you ever say that. Do you hear me?" He growled

the words. "Yes, I wanted an introduction to Trevor, I won't deny it. But I fell in love with *you*, Brynnie."

"Don't call me that."

He took another step forward. And another. Brynn clung to that sofa and didn't let go, even though she wanted to back away. She would hold her ground if it killed her. She needed to do this, to confront him and not allow herself to be intimidated. But it hurt, seeing him for what he really was. She'd have liked to live in that contented little bubble a while longer—which made her even more pathetic.

She shook her head, trying to clear it of memories—of all the times Iain had made her feel safe and loved and desired. Because none of it was real. "You planned this from the beginning. You told me so, that first day in your office. You said we'd be lovers. But I thought it was because"—her voice hitched—"because you wanted *me*." Pain tore at her insides, shredded her heart. She blinked as tears burned the backs of her eyes.

"I went about this all wrong. I wanted you *and* I wanted to meet Trevor. I hedged my bets, getting all that info on you. I didn't want to leave anything to chance."

"Because you're ruthless when it comes to business. And that's all this was. That's all I was—a means to a business transaction. I guess I should charge you a finder's fee. I've earned it, haven't I?"

He flinched. She'd hurt him with that one. Oh, wait. Nothing hurt him, because none of this was real.

"If I'd pursued you, asked you out, I'd have scared you silly."

He was absolutely correct. That didn't make him right.

He moved toward her again. Another two steps.

She was within arm's reach now. Tilting her chin, she remained rooted in place. Her gaze swept over his face. Just this morning, he'd made love to her with such tenderness. *He fucked you, jellyfish. Love didn't have anything to do with it*. Brynn briefly closed her eyes and almost doubled over from the heartache and loss. *You can't lose what you never had*.

When she opened her eyes, Iain's gaze bore into hers. "Brynnie. I fucked up. I admit it. I'm so sorry, love. I'll make it up to you. Please, let's just go home."

"I am home, and if you want to make this right, give me a divorce and stay out of my life."

"Wha'?" At first he looked stricken, and then his eyes hardened. "No. Uh-uh. You're stuck with me until the end. We made vows, Brynn. That wedding may have been ridiculous, but it was binding. I'm not giving you up. Ever."

Brynn wasn't a violent person, but right then she wanted to hit him. She wanted to strike that fierce expression from his stupid, handsome face. Still, she was determined to retain a sliver of self-control, even though tears blurred her vision. "You're disgusting. Any vow I made was to a man who doesn't really exist. I don't even know who you are. You've been lying to me from the start." When she blinked, a lone drop trickled down her cheek. "Get out," she said through clenched teeth.

Iain flexed his jaw. "You know exactly who I am. I've shown you parts of me no one's seen. Not even Marc. If anyone's a liar here, Brynn, it's you. You promised me you wouldn't run away when things got tough. Yet here you are." He grabbed her left hand, his grip just this side of painful. "You said you'd never take my ring from your finger, yet it's bare. I never lied to you."

Brynn jerked her hand from his. "You seduced me to get your hands on Trevor's money. You stalked me for months. You weren't honest. That's the same thing as lying."

He took that final step, closing the space between them. With his chest pressed to hers, Iain scowled down at her. Heat rose off his body, bringing with it that familiar scent. God, how she hated him.

"I hired you so that I could gain an introduction to Trevor, yes, but I didn't go through with it."

Then something niggled at Brynn. Iain had *hired* her. That first day, Cass said she didn't have any facilitators on hand. That's why Brynn had to go to Blue Moon herself. But that was a setup, too. "Did Cass know?" Brynn asked. "Was she in on the game?"

"There was no game, love."

"Did. She. Know."

Iain took a shaky breath. "Yeah. I paid her extra to have you instruct me personally. But I never meant to hurt you. Brynn, please, listen to me."

The pain was almost unbearable. Her heart literally ached in her chest. In a matter of minutes, her world had fallen apart. Yet even now, Brynn *wanted* to believe him. She wanted to believe every word coming out of his mouth. And that made her an idiot.

"What can I do to convince you?" There was a note in Iain's voice she couldn't identify. Almost mournful.

"You married me to make sure you'd have an investor. That's all I ever was to you—a means to an end. Little Brynn Campbell, so weak and trusting.

Give her an orgasm or two and she'll follow your orders like a puppy."

"No, it wasn't like that. I've never taken your trust for granted." Iain shook his head. "I seduced you because I ached for you. Still do. I fell in love with you because I couldn't help meself." His accent was stronger now, his voice deeper.

Brynn pressed a hand to her stomach. She wouldn't soften toward him. *He used you, jellyfish. He said he loved you, and you bought it.* "You made a fool out of me. I'll never forgive you, Iain."

His body stiffened. "We can work this out, Brynn. Just come home with me. I love you."

Brynn hardened herself. "Every time you say it, it makes me sick to my stomach. But I guess I should thank you for one thing—I'll never let anyone take advantage of me again. You taught me to believe in lost causes. Now seriously, get out."

As Iain's posture grew more rigid, he rolled his shoulders. "I'm leaving right now. If you don't stop me, we're through. And you know I mean what I say."

Brynn raised her brow and upped the ante. "Go fuck yourself."

His eyes widened slightly. She didn't know if it was her choice of words or the cool steel underlying them that convinced him, but after nodding once, Iain pivoted and walked out the door, closing it with a quiet click.

Iain was livid. Gutted. But he pushed the devastating pain aside and concentrated on his anger. He let it consume him and he stoked it by blaming Brynn. She had thrown him out like he was nothing. How dare she stand there and accuse him of lying when she'd broken every promise she ever made? She'd said she wouldn't run, that she'd stick with him, no matter what. *You never deserved her, you twat. Living on borrowed time, you were.*

Didn't matter, did it? She'd agreed to marry him, to merge their lives, and now she was reneging on her promise. Iain wasn't a saint in all this, but she'd betrayed him.

It was over. Completely, utterly over. Iain had lost the love of his life, the woman who made him see people instead of drones. Who made him laugh. Iain had rarely laughed before Brynn. She made him want to be a better man—a futile attempt on his part. Now he could go back to being himself once again. His boorish, rude, hateful self. Making everyone in his life bloody miserable.

On the drive back to his apartment, Iain replayed her words. He disgusted her, did he? Well, she'd never have to see him again. Never have to hear his declarations of love. Didn't mean the feelings weren't still there. Goddamn feelings. He hadn't had many of those either until she'd shown up, with her *I* feel this and *I* believe that nonsense.

Closing his eyes against the flash of neon and wandering tourists, Iain remembered that tear falling down her cheek. Iain had made Brynnie cry. He shoved that feeling of concern down.

She had also told him to go fuck himself. She'd been hard then. Controlled. Huh, Iain had taught her well. That wasn't the Brynn he was used to. Flashes of her smiling, sleepy and satisfied after they'd made love, flooded his mind—as did the times when she'd cushion her words, or when she wore that little apron, or when she curled up in his arms every night.

Grabbing the dice from his pocket, Iain tried to take a deep breath. It was damned difficult. His chest was constricted. If he had a heart attack and died, he hoped Brynn would feel guilty for the rest of her long, sad life.

You're the one who made her sad.

Iain tried to drown out that voice by going over the litany of Brynn's sins. Problem was, she didn't have many. She felt used by him, and rightly so. Iain would have felt the same in her position.

Fuck. He couldn't hang on to the anger. It was a mist that evaporated, leaving him with nothing—nothing but crushing, excruciating pain. What was he meant to do now? He couldn't go back to the apartment. He'd see her clothes, smell traces of her warm vanilla scent. There was only one place he could go, really. One person who understood.

When Iain left, Brynn stood alone. She was in a daze. The silence was deafening. She couldn't stand it another minute. She needed her sister. Allie may have driven Brynn crazy sometimes, but when the chips were down, she always had Brynn's back.

Brynn drove to Henderson on autopilot and replayed the conversation with Iain. He'd kept saying he loved her. Why? Did he really think she was stupid enough to believe him? After she'd learned the truth? Probably. He'd played her from the beginning, and she'd been so freaking gullible. He probably thought that if he looked sincere, used that wounded voice, she'd fall for it a second time. Not likely.

When Brynn reached Allie's house, Arnold, the butler, opened the door with a smile. "Miss Brynn, so good to see you." But after taking one look at her, his smile slipped. "Oh, dear. Come along." He wrapped his arm around her shoulder and guided her to the conservatory.

Allie, Trevor, and the twins sat at the little table near the fountain. They looked so happy. They were a family. A real one. Brynn would never have that with Iain. All her dreams, her hopes for the future, crashed and burned. She was an idiot for having them in the first place. Brynn Campbell was a wallflower. This was what she got for stepping away from the sidelines—nothing but pain.

Arnold cleared his throat. "Miss Brynn has arrived. I'll make tea."

When the twins saw her, they leaped up and ran to hug her legs. "Aunt Brynn," Zach said.

"Did you come to swim with us?" Thomas asked.

Allie's eyes scanned Brynn's face, and she paled. Standing, she tortured her napkin, wringing it with both hands. "What happened, Brynnie? What's wrong?"

Brynn couldn't bring herself to speak. She was empty inside, as if she'd lost a piece of herself.

Trevor's cool gray gaze traveled over her. "Boys, grab your football and go out back. I'll be right there." They ran out of the room with stomping feet. "Are you unwell, Brynn?" he asked.

Allie let go of the napkin and rushed to her side. When she held open her arms, Brynn fell onto her sister and began crying. Reeling from the agony of Iain's deception, a mental fog settled over her brain. She half remembered Allie leading her upstairs to a guest room where Brynn fell onto the bed, sobs wracking her body. Allie threw one arm around her shoulder, letting Brynn get it all out. Finally, the tears slowed. Her eyes were left swollen and gritty.

"It's okay," Allie said. "Whatever's wrong, we'll fix it."

Iain had shattered Brynn's heart into tiny fragments. That was an unfixable offense.

Brynn moved away from her sister and curled up in a ball. *He used you*. It hurt to breathe. She squeezed her eyes shut.

Allie lay down next to her, petted her hair. "It's okay, Brynnie," she kept saying, as though if she repeated it often enough, it would be true.

In her mind, Brynn rewound time, back to the first moment she had seen Iain standing behind his desk. He'd made her so nervous, she couldn't even look him in the eye. And the whole time he'd planned on fucking her to get what he wanted.

Brynn didn't know how long she and Allie had been lying there in complete silence. Still she said nothing, but at some point, the door opened and light dispelled the darkness.

"What the hell is going on?" Monica had arrived. Just perfect.

Brynn sat up, narrowing her eyes against the harsh glare. "Iain and I broke up."

Allie rolled onto her back and patted Brynn's leg. "I'm sorry, honey."

"You only knew him for a couple of weeks." Monica

parked herself at the end of the bed and kicked off her heels.

Brynn was going to have to tell them everything. There was no way to avoid it. "Actually, we got married."

Allie scrambled up, her brows furrowed. "You did what?"

"On Tuesday." Then she explained the rest—Iain's betrayal, the file she'd found, their heated argument. By the time she finished, she was crying all over again. "I hate him so much."

Monica's eyes slid to Allie and they exchanged a glance. "Sounds to me like you love him," Allie said.

Monica adjusted her miniskirt and swung her hair over one shoulder. "Let me get this straight. You got married and broke up in the span of three days? That's something I would have pulled, Brynnie. Are you trying to take over my title for being the family fuckup?"

Allie glowered at Monica. "Is that your idea of being supportive?" she whispered, as if Brynn weren't sitting six inches away. "If so, it could use some work."

"Excuse the hell out of me. Trevor called and said Brynn was having a breakdown. I'm just trying to wrap my head around all this. Cut me some slack."

"You cut Brynn some slack," Allie said. Then she turned to Brynn. "And you. I can't believe you got married and didn't tell me."

"You'd have tried to talk me out of it."

Monica sighed. "I wonder why."

Allie set her sights on Mon. "You've made your share of mistakes."

"And you'll never let me live them down," Monica said sweetly—with a sneer.

Brynn rubbed her pounding forehead. "Would both of you shut up? I love you, but I'm tired of listening to you argue. It was old ten years ago, and now it's obnoxious. This is why I don't tell you guys anything." Neither of her sisters said a word for a full minute. It was a nice reprieve.

Then Monica reached out and patted her leg. "I'm sorry, Brynnie. You know Allie and I fight, and it doesn't mean anything. And hey, things might work out between you and Iain. I mean, look at Cal and me. We had a split, but now we're good. Maybe you guys will fix your problems and find your happy ending."

Brynn stared at Monica with swollen eyes. "Did Cal lie to you?"

"No."

"Did he fuck you, marry you, and make you believe that he was madly in love with you in a devious, underhanded plan to get his own way?"

"Um, no."

"Then I repeat, shut up."

Monica's brows lifted almost to her hairline before she shrugged. "Yeah, that's fair."

Iain rang the bell for a good five minutes before Marc answered—wearing trousers this time.

"Go away." He tried to shut the door, but Iain wedged his foot in the gap to prevent it from closing.

"I've heard that one too many times tonight, so sod off." He shouldered his way past Marc and into the house. It smelled worse than before, if that was possible.

Feeling hot and unable to take a deep breath, Iain

ripped off his jacket, jerked at his tie, removed his cufflinks, and threw them on the floor.

"If you're here to give me a lap dance, no thanks."

Iain rolled up his sleeves. "She found out."

"Brynn?" Marc barely uttered her name. He was so drunk he could hardly stand on his own. "Told you," he slurred, then shuffled toward the living room at the back of the house. There were a few empty beer bottles scattered about the place, but Marc had started on the hard stuff. He handed Iain a bottle of Jack.

"You can afford better." Iain took a swig and handed it back.

"No, that's you, mate. Always wanting the best. Wanting to make a name for yourself." Marc tried to sit on the sofa, but his ass missed the cushion, and he landed on the floor. "How'd she find out?"

Iain removed his waistcoat and tossed it on the coffee table. "Evidently, she went to my office. She must have seen the file, because she knows everything."

"Fucking hell." He took another drink. "Do you ever wonder how we got here, mate?"

Iain sat on the floor next to him. "What do you mean?"

"We have everything, don't we? But nothing lasting. Nothing important. No women. No kids. No fucking dogs."

Iain thought about his buildings, his goals, his plans for downtown. "No, nothing important. She hates me. Called me a liar. Said I was disgusting."

"Yeah, they do that."

Iain snagged the bottle and took a long swallow. "She lied to me, too. Said she wouldn't run away."

"So she's supposed to keep quiet and just get on

with it? Of course she left you. Didn't have a choice, did she?"

"Said she wants a divorce."

"Are you gonna give her one?"

A divorce? The mere idea made Iain start to sweat. Let Brynn go? Let another man touch her, love her—no. Never. Despite what he'd told her, they weren't through. Not by a long chalk.

Marc had said something earlier today, about living Davy's life. The reality was, Iain had hijacked his dead mate's dream. He'd been working his ass off all these years to prove he deserved it. He'd even dated women Davy would have been attracted to—hard women who were looking for a good time and a payout. When Iain had seen Brynn, he'd wanted her for himself. Someone that could be his alone. Just as he'd become hers, body and soul. He couldn't let her go. She'd ripped his fucking heart out tonight. How could he spend the rest of his life without her? "I'm going to get her back," he said, sounding far more confident than he felt.

"How you going to do that?" Marc's eyes were starting to drift shut. His words were punctuated by long pauses.

Iain took the bottle and gently tipped Marc over. Once he was lying on the floor, Iain grabbed a tan throw from the sofa and covered his mate.

Iain had no idea how to win Brynn back. Not one. But he would do everything in his power to make this up to her, to win back her trust. She was angry, yeah, but she was hurting, too. And she loved him.

Chapter 22

Iain was in a foul mood the next morning. He'd spent all night at Marc's, twisting his brain into knots, trying to come up with a way to get his wife back. So far, he had zero ideas. Not a very promising start as far as plans went.

Several people smiled at him and Paul from data insisted on performing some complicated handshake. "Chap. Good morning, my man."

Iain pressed his lips together to keep from snapping. He greeted Amelia and nodded at the new girl. "In my office, Ames."

She followed a moment later. "What's wrong? Yesterday, you seemed like a normal person. Today, we're back to business as usual."

True enough. He used to be grumpy every morning, before Brynn. "My wife left me. Marc's becoming a full-time drunk. I need to win Brynn back, and he needs to sober up. Thoughts?"

"You and Brynn got married?"

"That's what the word *wife* usually implies, yes."

"She left you already?"

"Yes, Ames. Do keep up."

"Why?"

"She came here yesterday?" he asked.

"Yeah, looking for you. She came in here to leave you a note and checked her email."

That's where she must have seen the files, on his computer. He'd figured as much, but honestly, did it really matter how she found out? The point was, she wanted out of their marriage.

Seeing Brynn with her tearstained face, knowing Iain was the cause of her pain, nearly destroyed him, it did. Yet in spite of her broken heart, Brynn had confronted him. Stood toe-to-toe with him and told him what she thought. *Disgusting*. *Go fuck yourself*. No couching her phrasing this time—just straight to the point.

Iain clicked a few keys, opened the file, then swiveled the screen so Amelia could see it. "Because of this."

She read the opening page. "You had her investigated?"

Iain said nothing.

Then Amelia glanced up at him. "When she arrived that first day, you weren't surprised. You planned it from the start, didn't you? Why?"

"Her brother-in-law is Trevor Blake. Don't look at me like that. I wanted Brynn, too."

"So you used her on two levels. For business and pleasure. That's so disturbing, Iain. I don't even have words to describe… God, what were you thinking?"

"I just wanted to meet Trevor Blake. I didn't set out to seduce her, right. It just happened. I didn't mean to fall in love with her, either. I *am* a horrible person, but not that horrible."

"Brynn must be crushed from all this," she said.

"She is. But I plan on getting her back and making things right. Now tell me how to do that, would you?"

Ames stared at him with round eyes. "How should I know? How do you make up for something this monumental?" She nodded at the computer screen. "Some things can't be fixed."

"I have to fix it. I'm lost, Ames. I need her, don't I? Nothing means anything without her."

"You're such a stupid man. You and Marc both."

Iain rose from his seat and reached for the dice. "I understand that. But I've apologized. She won't listen."

"Of course she won't. An apology isn't going to cut it. You're going to have to give her some time, Iain."

"How much time? If I give her too much, she'll start to hate me."

"I know you're the ruler of your little universe, but you can't dictate how long she'll need. And if she hates you…" Amelia lifted one shoulder. "Call her. If she doesn't take your call, leave a message, but don't bombard her. Give her some space."

"That's it?"

With a sigh, she drummed her fingers on the file. "Prove to her that you're not a totally despicable human being. Show her your good side. Remind her that you're a decent person, Iain."

He sank into the leather seat. "But I'm not, am I? I'm a crap person. Until a few weeks ago, every employee hated me, and now my best mate doesn't want to be my partner anymore because he thinks I'm a twat. I'm ruthless. I'm hard."

"You hide your caring side, but it's there. Find what matters to her the most, and show Brynn how much you love *her*. Not her brother-in-law, not her vagina, just her. If you put your mind to it, I know you can come up with something."

When she left, Iain thought long and hard about what

mattered to Brynn. Her family, obviously. Her friends. She liked to rescue broken things and make them whole. She'd done it with him.

Still out of ideas, Iain called Brynn and left a message. Stilted. Awkward. He didn't say he loved her, only that he worried about her.

The second day, he called to say he missed her.

Day three, he apologized again.

Day four, he pleaded. She didn't bother to reply—not that day or the next or the next.

After a week and a half, Iain decided he needed a new plan. Brynn's friends and family. That was the key.

Brynn put the finishing touches on a proposal for a new client, a family-owned microbrewery. Eleven of her TDTC clients had followed her immediately, and her new salesperson, Tash, had just signed up three more. Business was booming.

She worked in the dining room while Tash and Paige took the living room. Paige was ruthlessly efficient. Though Brynn absorbed most of the start-up costs for a new computer and all the software she'd so desperately needed at TDTC, she and Paige were equal partners.

Tash sort of pushed her way in. She was good at that.

Brynn couldn't stop yawning despite all the coffee she'd drunk that morning. She hadn't had a full night's sleep since she'd found out Iain was a no-good, lying sack of crap. Instead, Brynn spent every night crying her eyes out and watching infomercials and old movies with happy endings. Too bad Brynn wouldn't have one of those. Iain had crushed her heart, destroyed her belief in people. She'd never let another man come near her. Besides, she didn't want another man. Ever.

Why did she miss Iain like crazy? His smile. His scowl. That deep dimple in his right cheek. The sex. She missed it so much. Yeah, she was pitiful. Her husband had gotten her hooked on his primo sex skills so he could get his hands on Trevor's money. He was a user. A manipulator. A liar. And she missed him with an ache that wouldn't go away. Every morning, she was bleary-eyed, exhausted from too many tears and a serious lack of zzz's.

Brynn thought she'd feel better after confronting him that night, using her words in an effort to hurt him. But she felt worse. Besides, she couldn't hurt someone who didn't have a heart to begin with. *He has a heart—Davy, Marc, Amelia.*

Iain had affection for a few people, that was undeniable. But *not* for Brynn. It had all been an act. And knowing that was so torturous, she almost couldn't stand it.

Iain's daily phone calls weren't helping either. What was his endgame? The jig was up. She knew the truth, so why did he keep trying?

At first, she listened to the messages, replaying them, trying to find a nuance in his words. He sounded concerned, sincere. But she couldn't trust it. So Brynn started erasing the messages without listening. She didn't want to hear his meaningless apologies. Because even though she knew it was bullshit, Brynn wished they were true—that he was sorry. That he loved her. That he wanted her back.

Her thoughts lapped in circles until she shut her laptop and wandered into the kitchen. Time for more coffee.

Tasha and Paige stood near the sink. They stopped whispering the minute she entered.

"What?"

"Nothing," Tasha said, leaning against the counter.

Paige shook her head. "Nope. Nothing going on here."

"Tell me." After setting her mug down, Brynn crossed her arms and gave them each a stony glare.

"Iain bought plane tickets for Tasha's family to come and visit." Tash elbowed Paige in the ribs. "Ouch. What? She'd find out anyway."

"I do not wish to tell you this," Tash said. "Your Englishman crush your heart like tank rolling through village. He is asshole and on my long list of shit."

That was surprisingly accurate. Again, why was Iain going to these lengths? So Brynn would think he was a good guy? That ship had sailed. She knew exactly who he was. *Unless he's trying to show you how much he cares*. Huh. Right.

"That's not all." Paige grabbed a phone and pulled up a text. "Read this."

It was from Cass. Iain had bought TDTC.

Brynn stepped backward until she fell into a chair. "She sold the business? To Iain?"

"Apparently." Paige shrugged. "I called Peanut Allergy Brandon and got the lowdown. Cass is now the figurehead and gets a yearly salary."

Tasha pursed her lips. "He try to win your affection. On me, this may work. I have romantic side. Zeke could use lesson from your Englishman."

He *was* trying to get her back. Well, it wasn't going to work. Brynn hated him. With a passion. A strong, deep, yearning passion. *Give it up, jellyfish. You still love him.* Yeah, she did. But so what? Love didn't conquer shit. All gestures aside, love wasn't going to turn Iain into an honorable man. Her instincts had been wrong. He wasn't good. And he wasn't decent. *He's not perfect, but he's trying.*

Feeling exhausted and conflicted, Brynn stalked to the living room and grabbed her bag. "I'm going out for a while."

Brynn left the house and started the car. Without conscious thought, she headed for Allie's place. Brynn had only stayed at the mansion one night. The next morning, despite Allie's pleas, Brynn had gone home and gotten to work. She had a new business and Paige was depending on her. She refused to sit around and mope over Iain and the destruction of her short marriage.

But now she needed her family—the comfort of Allie's fussing, the shouts of her rowdy nephews, and Trevor's cutting wit. Also, Brynn could use a scone. Or six. She wanted to stuff her feelings with carbs and fat.

When she pulled through the gates and around the curved brick drive, Monica's Mustang already sat in the driveway. As Brynn turned off the ignition, something in the corner of the floorboard glinted in the sunlight. Her wedding ring. Brynn leaned over the passenger seat and snagged it. It was a really beautiful ring. *I wanted to buy the biggest bloody diamond they had, but I thought this would suit you better.* He knew her. Not just the facts in the background report. Iain understood things about her no report would ever be able to tell him.

She made a fist around the ring, letting the prongs dig into her skin. Brynn didn't like this new pessimistic streak she'd developed. It wasn't her. The truth was Iain Chapman had brought her joy. She may have made a terrible mistake by trusting in him, but while they were together, she'd been blissful. She couldn't regret that. She wasn't sure how she was going to make it another day without him, but eventually, years down the road, she'd look back and be grateful for the lessons Iain had taught her, like how to stand up for herself and ask for what she wanted. Those were good things to take away from this.

She didn't put the ring back on but stuck it in her pocket as she walked into the house without knocking. She felt it through her jeans, like a hot secret, burning a hole through the denim.

Voices carried from the drawing room, so Brynn started down the hallway. But when Monica mentioned Iain's name, Brynn drew to a halt outside the door and eavesdropped.

"Can you believe this guy? He bought three mobile compact mammogram machines. They can literally drive these vans to a village, give breast screenings, and then move on to the next location. We're sending two to Africa and one to India. I'm still in shock."

"He donated a million dollars to the foundation," Allie said. "In Brynn's name."

Did Iain really believe this would work? He'd throw some money at her friends and family and she'd go running back? He couldn't buy her forgiveness.

Turning on her heel, Brynn walked out to the garden. The day was stifling and oppressive. Normally, she loved the floral aroma, but today the blooms reminded Brynn of her wedding day, when Iain had filled the bedroom with flowers. Brynn had felt so close to him. All those promises—he had never meant a word of it. *Did you mean it, jellyfish? In good times and bad, till death and all the rest?* At the time she had.

She sat on a bench beneath an arbor, bent in half with her face in her hands. The fountain burbled softly, breaking up the quiet. When she sensed someone next to her, Brynn glanced up. "Hey, Trev."

"Mind if I join you?"

"It's your garden."

He sat and crossed one leg over the other. He wore an expensive suit, which reminded Brynn of Iain. Everything reminded her of Iain.

"Are you as miserable as you look?"

"Probably," she said. "How miserable *do* I look?"

"Very. And how am I, you ask?"

Brynn straightened and stared at the fountain. "I didn't ask."

"An oversight on your part, I'm sure. My sex life is suffering because my darling wife is worried about you."

"The trickle-down effect?"

"Indeed."

"Sorry my failed marriage is keeping you from getting laid." Brynn loved Trevor, but every once in a while he was a pain in the ass. Today was shaping up to be one of those times.

"Pity, that." His quick glance took in her face, her uncombed hair. "If it's any consolation, I believe he loves you."

"Iain?"

"No, the postman. Of course Iain."

"What makes you say that?"

"He never actually came to me for an investment. Didn't contact me at all. He had his chance to, that night after the family dinner. But instead, when he saw you were blind drunk, he took you home. The way he cared for you, touched you—well, I knew then how he felt."

A tiny spark of hope flickered to life, but Brynn squashed it. "Even if you're right, it doesn't matter. It's over."

"Excellent." Trevor patted the top of her head as if she were still a child. "You can do miles better. He's a working-class upstart who's so far beneath you, his interest is an insult. That he was presumptuous enough to touch you, let alone marry you—well, you'll do better the next time, I'm sure."

With her upper lip curled into a sneer and hands fisted at her sides, Brynn leaped to her feet. "That's a really horrible thing to say. Even for you. Iain didn't start out with all of your advantages. His home life was brutal. You have no idea. He's worked hard to get to where he is, and I'm not going to sit here and listen to you put him down. Just because he wasn't born with a silver spoon in his mouth doesn't make him any less of a person. You're a classist snob, Trevor Blake. And might I remind you, Allie's from a working-class family? *My* working-class family." Brynn thumped her chest. "So what does that make you?"

"Terribly fortunate." Trevor stood and peered down at her. "Sounds like you still care for the bloke after all."

Trevor had been trying to provoke her, and Brynn had taken the bait. She rolled her eyes and unclenched her hands. "Congratulations, you got me to admit it. I can't just stop loving him overnight. It doesn't work that way."

"No, it doesn't."

Iain spent the morning in a very morose and unproductive way, by ambling through the building near Fremont Street. When he'd taken Brynn there, Iain had been so full of pride, so certain of his future success. But as he ripped a board from the window and stared out at the property across the street, he was ready to let it go. Let it all go. None of it mattered. Not without her.

Brynn softened his razor-sharp edges. She centered him, gave him peace and comfort. If she weren't here, what was the bloody point of it all? He tried to show her that he loved her by helping Tasha, by giving to Allie's and Monica's charities, buying Cass's business. It made no difference. She still hadn't contacted him. Brynn was through.

Iain usually looked at a problem and came up with six different solutions simultaneously. But now he was rudderless. That old feeling of desperation reared its head.

Iain replaced the board and left the building. He wouldn't come here again. His ambitions for this place had cost him everything.

On his way back to the office, he stopped by Marc's house. Though he didn't smell of alcohol, Marc's gaunt frame was worrisome. His hair was longer than he normally kept it, and he hadn't shaved in days, possibly weeks. But at least he was sober.

"You again, eh?" Marc turned and left Iain on the doorstep.

Not the friendliest welcome, but Iain would take it. He trailed Marc to the living room.

"If you're going to harass me about coming to work—" He flopped onto the sofa.

"I'm not," Iain said. "I just popped 'round to check on you."

"Oh. Well, as you see, I'm fine. Go away, your conscience is clear."

"Hardly. Look, if you want out of the business, we'll sell everything and divide it. If you'd rather be a silent partner, that's fine too. Whatever you want, mate. And for what it's worth, I'm sorry."

Marc propped his bare foot on the coffee table. "Don't just stand there like a twat. You're giving me a crick in me neck."

Iain unbuttoned his jacket and sat in the chair. He gazed around the enormous room and up at the cathedral ceilings. "This house is far too big for one person. What are you going to do now, sell?"

"I don't know. I may just sit here, watching telly, until I keel over. What are you sorry for specifically?"

Iain rubbed his forehead and sighed. "Everything. That you lost her. That I didn't treat you as an equal partner. That I'm a know-it-all prat."

"Yeah. You are a prat. But I let you take charge, didn't I? Easier that way. Less worry for me. I put it all on your shoulders."

"I thought I had it all figured out. Turns out, I'm a bloody fool."

"We both are," Marc said.

"Do you still want to sell off the downtown properties?"

Marc studied him. "We'll probably take a loss, what with the taxes we've paid in the last couple years and the market being what it is."

"I know. But I don't care anymore, do I? I've lost Brynn. She won't talk to me. Not a word."

"Look at us, making a total bollocks of it all. Mel went to stay at her mum's and told me to respect her choices. Says she needs 'head space.' What the hell does that even mean? And how long do I give her?"

"Exactly. How long is too long?" Iain stood. "And I'm tired of waiting for her to call. She's still me wife. I'll give her anything she wants, except a divorce. But she has to talk to me at some point, yeah?"

Marc lowered his foot. "Spot on. And I should go get Melanie. Bring her home. I love her, right? She belongs here with me. If I didn't want to be rushed into marriage, we should talk it out. Like two rational adults."

"Cheers. This is what I've said to Brynn." Iain nodded and began pacing the room. "Listen to the pair of us, moaning like old women. When did we lose our balls, mate? You should bring Mel back to Vegas."

Marc stood. "I've been whinging for weeks. Like a schoolgirl. What the bloody hell?"

They looked at each other and grinned. Iain walked forward and lightly smacked Marc on the side of the head. "Bring her home, yeah?"

"You too. Even if it takes the rest of your life, you'll get her back."

"The rest of me life?" he echoed. Still, what kind of life did he have without Brynn? Not much of one. Work. Sleep. Snarling at people. That was hardly an existence.

"Come on, now. You're Iain Chapman. She won't

be able to resist your charms for long. I'm going to fly to Arkansas and get Mel. I'll be back by next week, I guarantee it."

When Iain left the house, he felt lighter, but once he glanced at his phone and saw that Brynn hadn't called, stark reality set in once more. He looked at the dice in his hand and shoved them in his pocket. Despite all his big talk in front of Marc, for the first time since he was a lad, Iain didn't know how to go about achieving his goal. *Desperate*. He couldn't force Brynnie into taking him back. He couldn't seduce her or use flowery language. So how could he convince her to give him another chance?

Iain called her again and left a message. Was she even listening to them? Maybe she was ignoring him altogether. Bloody hell.

Back at the office, Iain tried to put on a friendly face for the team. He nodded at a few people, said hello. As he passed the conference room, he noticed Amelia's lad, Tyler, sitting at the table. Iain poked his head in the doorway. "Why aren't you in school?"

Tyler glanced up from his tablet. "Teacher's conference. Mom said you wouldn't mind if I'm here."

"I don't mind." He started to walk away.

"Hey, Iain."

He turned and walked back. "Yeah?"

"I did that thing you said. I found my enemy's weakness."

"How'd it go?"

"Adam, the kid who makes fun of me the most, he has this blond hair that he's always messing with. He uses a lot of gel and stuff. Anyway, he was making fun of me at lunch and I called him Goldilocks. Everyone laughed."

"So it worked then." Always did. Everyone had a fatal flaw. *And yours is overconfidence. Too much damned pride.*

"Yeah, but I feel bad. He got his hair buzzed last week, but everyone's calling him Goldie."

Iain walked into the room. "Well, maybe it's good that you feel bad. Means you're an honest person, yeah? That you care about other people." That's what Brynn had been trying to tell him, but Iain had been too bull-headed to listen. If he could go back, he'd do things differently. Iain rapped his knuckles on the table. "Now, stop playing that video game and do some studying, yeah? Your mum's worried about your maths."

He walked to his office suite, stopping in front of Amelia's desk. "Marc is going to Arkansas to get Mel."

"I'll book him a flight. Your brother-in-law is waiting in your office. He's been here for an hour."

Iain's brows slammed together. "Trevor?"

"Yep."

"You just let him into my office, did you?"

"What was I supposed to do, tackle him?" She looked down and started tapping on her keyboard.

Iain braced himself, adjusted his tie, and strode into the room. "Trevor."

The toff was sitting on the couch looking quite at home as he jabbed at his phone screen. "About time."

"Why are you here? Is Brynn all right?" Did she send him?

"Quite well. Saw her a couple of hours ago."

"Does she know you're here?"

"Doubtful." Maddening, he was.

"So what's this about, then?" With his hands in his pockets, he lowered his head. Trevor wanted something. Iain could feel it in his bones.

"I'm here to make you an offer."

"Are you now?" Iain didn't trust any offer coming from Trevor Blake. The man hated him. And he had every right. Iain silently waited him out.

Trevor stood and glanced down at his phone one last time. "I'll invest in your downtown properties. All of them." He sauntered to the middle of the room. "Give you seventy-five percent of the money up front."

"Will you now? That's very generous."

"I want something in return." When Trevor smiled, he flashed his teeth. Like a shark.

"Course you do," Iain said. "Can't wait to hear this caveat of yours."

"In return for my investment, you'll divorce Brynn and agree to never contact her again."

Iain laughed, but it wasn't funny. The nerve of this knob, waltzing into Iain's office and laying down impossible rules. Never see Brynn again? Not an option. "Fuck off."

Trevor raised one brow and appraised him with those chilly, gray eyes. "I thought this was what you wanted. It's a sound plan, converting those old buildings into livable space. Fremont is expanding, and it's just a matter of time before someone else pounces on the idea. Brynn's too good for you. Let her get on with her life and find a man who's worthy of her."

Iain very carefully removed his hands from his pockets. His body hummed with anger. With his jaw clamped tight, Iain took three steps forward until only an inch separated him from Trevor. "Oh, I know I'm not good enough for her. Not even close. But I love that woman, and I'm not giving her up. Now if you don't get out of here, I'll—"

Trevor waved one hand. "Do calm down. I left her in my garden. Defending you. If you hurry, she might still be there."

"Wha'?"

"Quite."

Iain stood frozen to the spot. Had that been a test of some sort?

"Are you planning on standing here all day, or are you going to go get her?" Trevor asked.

What would he say to her? Perhaps he should start by being honest. Then get on his hands and knees and beg her to come home. Tipping his head to Trevor, Iain spun and nearly ran out of his office.

"Go get her, tiger," Amelia called after him.

Brynn dangled her feet in the cool water, and even over the splash of the waterfall, she could hear Monica and Allie arguing, their voices raised. Life as usual.

"I can hear you fighting," she called. "Don't make me come over there." Truth was, Brynn was tired of playing the peacemaker. It didn't do any good. Al and Mon snapped and growled at each other and probably would for the next sixty-five years.

"I do love those blue toes."

Iain.

Brynn snatched her feet out of the pool and stood, but in

her haste, she slipped against the slick tile. Iain reached out and grabbed her elbow to keep her from tipping into the water. She didn't pull away immediately. And he didn't release her arm right away. His touch sent shivers across her sun-warmed skin. She'd missed his voice. *That accent*.

"What are you doing here?" She finally extracted herself from his loose grip, her gaze eating him up, searching for any changes. It had only been a week and a half, but she noticed a few. Dark half circles shadowed his eyes, and his chin bore a small cut. A shaving accident, most likely. His hair was a little too long. He got it trimmed every three weeks, whether he needed it or not, but he must have missed an appointment. As he squinted against the sun, the lines fanning his eyes seemed longer, a little deeper. He wore a suit, of course—ivory linen. Brynn stifled a sob. He looked like her Iain, the man she'd fallen in love with, but that man didn't exist. Not really.

"Trevor said you were here." Iain wagged a thumb over his shoulder. "Your sisters were trying to keep me from you. Foolish, yeah?"

Iain had been talking with Trevor. That could only mean one thing. Brynn thought her heart couldn't hurt worse than it already did, but with a few words, Iain had broken it a little more.

She tried to hide her disappointment by glancing over his shoulder. Monica and Allie huddled together near the delphiniums, confabbing. While Monica frowned, Allie's scowl was downright scary. "Trevor, huh? I guess your downtown plans are going through after all. Congratulations."

"Brynn Campbell Chapman, I did not take money off your wanker of a brother-in-law. Nor would I. I was wrong not to tell you what I'd done, I'll freely admit it, but Brynnie, if I hadn't, we'd have never met. So while I'm not sorry about setting you up, I should have come clean a long time ago, and for that I apologize."

"I trusted you." She barely uttered the words, but Iain heard her.

"I know. I'll do whatever it takes to earn it back. Anything, Brynn."

She shook her head. "I can't." Brynn started to walk toward the house, but Iain blocked her path.

"No, I don't accept that. I'm selling the downtown property. We'll get a house near your sisters if you like. Whatever you want."

"I just wanted you. Only you. Nothing else mattered." Brynn bit her lower lip. She wanted so badly to take him back. But she'd always second-guess everything he said. *What about you, jellyfish? Your promises don't hold much weight.*

"You had me, love. You still do. Please, Brynnie. I'm begging you." He was hurting—she could see it in his eyes. They probably mirrored her own.

Brynn wanted to step closer, erase the distance between them, but it was the emotional distance keeping them apart. "You had your chance to tell me so many times. Why should I believe you?"

Iain grabbed her hand and lifted it, pressing his lips against her palm. A small cry escaped her then.

"Brynn." His voice was raspy as he placed her hand on his chest. "I'm standing here before you, baring me heart, love. What more can I do?"

"I don't know. Maybe not everything can be fixed."

"No, I don't believe that." Then he dropped her hand

and started pulling the jacket from his shoulders. He yanked it off and threw it on the ground.

"What? What are you doing?" There went his vest. He dropped it on the flagstone tiles. Then he ripped at his blue-and-tan striped tie.

"I'm baring me heart, me soul, and the rest of me. Trevor's going to come back, see me bare bum, and I'll have completely humiliated meself in front of a man who will never let me live it down. I didn't lie to you, but I didn't tell you the whole truth either. Just you and me, Brynnie. Nothing between us. Not even me goddamn trousers." He kicked off his shoes and whipped off his socks.

"Iain, stop. Right now. I mean it. You're insane." She glanced back at her sisters. Allie appeared horrified, but Monica angled her head.

"Nope. Not stopping." He began unbuttoning his shirt.

"What does this prove?"

"That I'll do anything for you. Go to any lengths. That I'll make an ass out of meself for you. You want me to get on my knees and beg? Because I will. I have no pride left. It's all gone to hell without you." He lowered himself to his knee. "Take me back. Please."

All the money, all the trappings—they meant a lot to Iain, but they were just symbols. His pride was his Achilles' heel, and he'd just laid it down for her. She jerked on his arm until he stood once more. "No, that's not what I want."

"Then tell me, Brynn. I'm so sorry, pet. I shouldn't have given you an ultimatum that night or said our marriage was through. I'll regret it till the day I die. It was the first time since I was ten that I said something I didn't mean."

He'd finished unbuttoning his shirt and as he slipped it from his shoulders, Brynn sped forward. "Stop. Don't take off anything else." Her hands latched on to his warm biceps. She'd missed seeing him like this.

She peeked around him to glance at her sisters. "That's enough, you two. Go inside. Show's over."

"We'll stay for moral support," Monica said. But Allie grabbed her arm and dragged her to the house.

Once they left, Brynn glanced back at Iain and dropped her hands. With a deep breath, she forced her gaze away. "Do you think that after one glance at your magnificent body I'll forget everything—all the times you asked about my family, my mom? And you already knew the answers?"

To Brynn's relief, he shrugged the shirt back on. "I looked at your credit card history and saw that you buy all those gadgets at that fancy crockery store. But I didn't know how great of a cook you are. I was aware you had two sisters, but I didn't know that you were the peacemaker, or that Allie protected you and Monica has a mouth like a lorry driver. I read the facts, Brynn, but they didn't prepare me for *you*.

"Trevor came to the office today. Offered to partner up on the downtown project, said that he'd make all my dreams come true if I agreed to never see you again. But I could never agree to that. I don't have any dreams without you.

"I could have pressed you for an introduction to Trevor. I didn't. I could have insisted you tell your family about our marriage and pushed my advantage. I didn't do that either. I love you, goddamn it."

Brynn flinched at his words and walked a few feet

away, rubbing her forehead. She turned back to face him. "Trevor sent you here. Why?"

"After I turned down that offer, he told me you were here, in the garden. You can send me away today, but I'll be back tomorrow. And the day after that. I'll keep coming back, Brynnie. I made vows and I intend to keep them. What about you, love?"

She believed him. God help her. "What happened when you were ten?" At his confused expression, she took a step toward him. "The last time you said something you didn't mean, you were ten years old."

Iain glanced away. "I never told anyone this. Not even Marc. But one night, me dad came home, drunk as usual. I tried to stop him, promised my mum I'd protect her. But I was too scrawny and the old man was too mean. I made a promise I couldn't keep. He beat the shit out of both of us that night."

This was the Iain she'd come to know. He wasn't lying about this. From that frightened little boy, he'd worked hard and remade himself into this complicated, smart, proud man. Now he'd shared this painful memory with her because he trusted her. Because he loved her.

Brynn ran toward him then and jumped. Iain caught her and held on tight. She loved him. With her entire being, she loved him. She couldn't help it. He'd always had her heart.

"You won't regret giving me a second chance, I swear it." His voice was tight, emotional. As he kissed her, Brynn wrapped her legs around his waist. "Tell me," he whispered against her lips. "Tell me you still love me."

"I do. And I'm going to keep my promise this time.

I'll never run again. From now on, I'll stay and fight it out with you."

Iain angled his head away and he wore a grim expression. "Don't say it unless you mean it."

"I mean it." Brynn unhooked her legs. "Put me down, just for a second." As soon as Iain lowered her to her feet, Brynn dug the wedding ring from her pocket. "Let's have a do over."

"Wha'?"

"Let's make new vows." She handed him her ring.

Iain tugged the band from his finger and placed it in her palm. "You go first, yeah?"

Brynn felt the gravity of the moment. The wedding had been outrageous and fun, but this time, it felt different. The smell of the garden mixed with Iain's bergamot cologne. The sky was bright and cloudless. His shirt was still open, and she could hear the splash of the waterfall behind her. She gazed into his cyes and saw only vulnerability. "I, Brynn Chapman, swear that I won't run away, that when I'm feeling cornered, I'll talk to you. I'll confront you when I'm angry. I'll always be honest with you. And I'll never take my ring off again." Fine tremors caused her hand to shake as she slid the heavy gold band on his finger.

Iain's mouth thinned and he cleared his throat. His bare chest expanded as he took a deep breath. Brynn had never seen him this emotional and it touched her heart. "I, Iain Chapman, swear that I'll never do anything behind your back. I'll never lie to you, even by omission. And I'll try my utmost not to be a dickhead."

Brynn couldn't help it—she laughed.

"Stop that." He lightly squeezed her hand. "This

is a serious moment." He waited until she sobered. "I promise to spend my life making you happy. I pledge my love to you, Brynnie Chapman, until the day my heart stops beating."

Tears filled her eyes as he leaned down and kissed her. "I missed you, my beautiful, sweet Brynn. Let's go home, eh? To your house."

Brynn blinked up at him. "Are you sure? You don't like my pink kitchen."

"Who gives a toss about a kitchen? I only want to be with you."

Brynn reached up and caressed his cheek. "Okay. But before we go home, you should know this garden has a lot of private spots."

"Is that right?"

Brynn shrugged. "Seems a waste not to find one, since you're half-naked."

"That would be a terrible shame. Very resourceful, you are. It's one of your many skills." Iain shoved one hand into her brown waves. "Do you really think my body's magnificent?"

"Mmm hmm." She nodded. "It's spectacular."

Then Iain swooped her up in his arms and carried her past the rose bushes. After a few steps, he glanced down at her. "Thank you, love, for taking me back. You utterly changed my life, you know."

"You changed mine, too. *I* believe this is a win-win scenario, where each party can reach a satisfactory outcome."

"There's one thing you can bet on, love—*I* plan on spending the rest of my life giving you multiple satisfactory outcomes."

Epilogue

The flowers' sweet perfume rode the air. Brynn breathed it in as she slowly made her way through the garden, past the rose bushes. A soft breeze lifted her curls and she brushed them back with one hand.

She rounded the corner, and there was Iain, wearing a black morning suit and a charcoal vest. She'd *never* get tired of staring at him. Just a glimpse of that face made Brynn's heart race. But seeing him in the traditional British suit left her knees a little wobbly. She might just make him wear it around the house for kicks, because, boy, he was something else.

A string quartet played softly in the background, That was Allie's doing. She claimed you couldn't have a wedding without music.

When Iain's gaze lit on Brynn, his jaw tightened and he nodded. He wore his emotions openly. Desire shone from his intense, glimmering eyes. His torso leaned toward her, as if he were about to rush up the aisle, drag her off to have his big, bad way with her. Brynn suppressed a delighted shiver at the thought.

She grinned as she slowly advanced toward him. This was it. Their big moment. Well, their second big moment. This time, there was no Cher. No Hummer. Just a simple ceremony with their families. Iain always claimed he didn't have one, but Marc, Ames, Tyler—they were *his*.

It was a perfect Vegas afternoon, the sun bright and hot overhead. When Iain had first seen Brynn in this garden all those months ago, she'd been hiding in a dark corner. Those days were long gone. Brynn wanted to remarry Iain in the sunshine, so she didn't miss a thing.

She carried a bouquet of peach roses, just like in her first wedding. In lieu of a veil, she wore a wreath of freesias in her hair. And she'd picked out a real wedding dress—a vintage gown from the twenties with aged lace. It went beautifully with the necklace Iain had given her on their original wedding day.

Every eye was focused on Brynn. She found she didn't really mind. These were their people—hers and Iain's. They were here to wish her well. Being the center of attention once in a while wasn't such a bad thing.

Paige and Tasha sat in the last row. Paige even had a date—Peanut Allergy Brandon. Go figure. And Tasha had dragged Zeke along. He sported a tuxedo shirt. Tasha pointed at him and rolled her eyes.

Ames sat on Iain's side and was beautifully dressed in a classic navy suit. Her red hair was bright in the sun. Next to her, Tyler kept tugging on his tie.

Marc and Mel sat stiffly, side by side. They hadn't worked out all of their problems, obviously. Brynn didn't know the particulars, and she didn't ask. She just hoped they would find their happily ever after, as she and Iain had.

Monica and Cal sat huddled together. Those two couldn't keep their hands to themselves. They were in a constant state of foreplay, even when they stood across the room from each other.

Allie and Trevor flanked the twins. Trevor stretched his arm across the backs of the chairs so he could stroke Allie's shoulder. The glances he sometimes gave her were intense enough to sear Brynn's eyeballs. It was nice to know they were still hot for each other after all these years.

The twins squirmed in their seats, unable to sit still for much longer. Allie had threatened to hold their game consoles hostage if they didn't shape up, but Monica had been sneaking them chocolate for the last hour. Consequently, their little bodies were twitchy from all the sugar.

Cal's mom, Pixie, sat next to her husband, Paolo. For some reason, Pix thought a red leather bustier and a gigantic poppy fascinator made for appropriate wedding attire. Brynn didn't care. She loved it. It added a touch of the whimsy to the proceedings. Pix waved madly as she passed. "You look stunning, darling," she whispered loudly.

Trevor's parents, Mags and Nigel, were there as well, both looking chic. Mags sobbed into an embroidered handkerchief, but Brynn had yet to see any actual tears coming from her eyes. But Mags did love a good wedding. She'd had five of her own to prove it.

In the front row, Brynn's dad, Brian, and his wife, Karen, looked perfectly normal. Her dad was tan from spending so much time outdoors. He was happy in his new life. Karen looked content, too.

Brynn missed her mom. Still. Always. But as she reached the end of the aisle and stood next to Iain, she realized she had a new family—a fresh start, in more ways than one. Brynn belonged here, with this group of people. And she was grateful for all of them. Most of all, she was thankful for Iain. Together, they strengthened one another. That was the way it was supposed to be.

Iain bent down, his lips touching her ear. "Don't even have words for how beautiful you are."

She handed off her bouquet to Karen, who sat closest to her, and squeezed Iain's hand. It felt warm against hers, so big and strong.

An officiant presided over the ceremony this time. Their vows were traditional. She and Iain had made their own vows in this garden the day they'd reunited, and those promises mattered the most.

Iain glanced down at her as if she were precious. "I love you, Brynnie Chapman." He placed a plain, thin band on her finger this time. She refused to take off the diamond band. She didn't want to be without it, even for a few hours.

"I love you too." Then she repeated the vows.

When they were pronounced man and wife—again—Iain kissed her with a fierce possessiveness that made her blush. And she kissed him back, curling her arms around his neck and holding on tight.

When they came up for air, everyone stood and clapped. The quartet began playing a medley of Cher's greatest hits, a nod to their first wedding. It had been Iain's idea, and a damned good one.

The twins jumped out of their seats and rushed toward them. "Happy wedding, Aunt Brynn." They pelted her and Iain with handfuls of birdseed.

Iain calmly brushed a pile of sunflower seeds from his shoulder before clinging to Brynn's hand and tucking her into his side. "Feel any different, Mrs. Chapman?"

Brynn smiled up at him as tears pricked her eyes. “Everything’s different,” she said. And that was as much a vow as anything that had come before.

Keep reading for a sneak peek at the first book in Terri Austin's Irish Brawlers series

The Rules of Engagement

"It's not too late. We can still turn back." In the last hour and a half, Jessica McIntyre had voiced those words more than once—at the "L" station, during each train line transfer (pink, red, *and* blue), and again in the cab as it crawled along this dark, lonely stretch of road. Now watching the taxi drive away, its tires pinging and popping over large chunks of gravel, Jess felt the need to repeat herself. "Are you sure this is the right address? Where are all the cars?"

Her friend, April Robertson, didn't reply. In fact, for the past thirty minutes she'd been blasting Jess with silence—the hostile kind. That, combined with her long-suffering sighs, said she'd run out of patience with Jess's nervous babbling. Too bad. She should be used to it by now. Jess was a worrier, always had been, and getting stranded in the middle of nowhere didn't exactly ease her anxiety.

Though there were no signs of life in the empty lot, Jess heard a low-pitched rumble from the warehouse on her right. Voices. Male voices. Which would make sense. How many women attended a fight club in an abandoned industrial graveyard? Not many smart ones she'd guess, yet here they were.

The night air, heavy with humidity and dank from the nearby lake, had Jess plucking the front of her blouse in an attempt to catch a small breeze. As she tore her gaze away from the cab, she glanced down at her phone. A sense of unease sliced through her. "I'm getting zero reception. How about you, any bars?" April still didn't respond. Huffing out a breath, Jess hung on to her composure by a thread. "So how the hell are we supposed to get home? Hitch a ride? Not happening."

April rarely worried about life's boring little details. She left that to everyone else—usually Jess.

When April finally spoke, her words dripped with bored sarcasm. "You can click your heels together, Dorothy. Maybe that will do the trick." Uh-oh. *Wizard of Oz* jokes. Jess ignored the remark, refusing to take the bait. April liked pushing buttons, forcing a reaction. Jess had learned long ago to choose her battles wisely. Even then, she rarely won. Take tonight for example. April had been adamant about coming to an illegal boxing match, though Jess repeatedly tried to talk her out of it.

Jess was *that* friend—the level-headed one, the sober driver, the emergency contact. She couldn't, in good conscience, let April fly solo. Now here they both were, stranded, without a ride home. Great.

Jess turned her attention to the looming two-story building. One security light dispelled the darkness, providing enough illumination to highlight spindly weeds framing the concrete foundation. Without windows, the warehouse was a massive black hole, sucking in what little moonlight trickled through the swollen clouds.

"Looks like it might start raining soon. No umbrella, no ride. *No bueno*." Jess should have had a pre-planned exit strategy in place. Normally that would have been a no-brainer, but she hadn't been on her game lately. A better plan would have been hauling April to the nearest bar, plying her with shots, and pointing out every hot guy in the room. Damn, why hadn't she thought of that earlier?

Making a last ditch effort to return to the safety of her apartment and all of its wireless capabilities, Jess wagged a thumb over her shoulder. "The cab's not that far. If we run, we could still catch it. Maybe grab a pizza and call it day? What do you say?"

April pursed her lips and tipped one brow. With her sheer ivory blouse glowing in the darkness and every flat-ironed strand of hair perfectly in place, she appeared effortlessly chic, despite the heat. "There's an entire warehouse full of men in there who will be happy to give us a ride, but if you want to go, I won't stop you." Crossing her arms, she took a step closer to Jess. "Seriously though, if you bitch just one more time, I *will* go south side on your scrawny ass."

Jess knew the threat was all snark and no bite. From the moment they'd met all those years ago, Jess had immediately seen past April's armor-like exterior to the gooey marshmallow heart she tried to hide. "You won't touch my scrawny ass. You love me. Admit it."

"Huh." April dropped her arms. "What did I tell you? Admit nothing. You're never going to make it on your own if you don't learn some survival skills, girl."

"Actually, I learned *that* lesson a long time ago from my father. Politicians never admit to anything. Telling the truth is considered professional suicide." Jess cast a final glance over her shoulder. The nervous tension fluttering in her belly increased as the cab's red taillights receded, then disappeared from view. There went her last chance of escape. "Why did I agree to this?"

"Because you're a good friend."

"Yeah, you remember that." Jess shoved her phone in her purse. She wouldn't be needing it for a while.

"As if you'd let me forget. Besides, you needed to get out of the house."

"I get out every day. It's called a job." Working for the admin department of UIC wasn't the most thrilling gig in the world, but Jess liked the routine. It wouldn't satisfy her forever, but it worked for right now.

April snorted. "Let me be more specific. You need to get a life. If you didn't come willingly tonight, I was going to *drag* you out."

Irritation had Jess frowning—then her mother's tight-lipped words echoed through her head. *Never frown, dear. They'll smell blood in the water*. In defiance to that annoying voice, the corners of Jess's lips dipped further downward, and she refocused on April. "So you orchestrated this whole thing? Lured me out to bum-fuck nowhere on purpose? And I was stupid enough to fall for it." *You really are off your game*.

"I hate to tell you this, but you're only a couple of posted cat memes shy of pathetic."

Jess winced.

So what if she'd been a little reclusive lately? It was only natural under the circumstances. Calling off a highly publicized political merger—her wedding—had been traumatic. Now, with her personal and professional life in turmoil, Jess was in the throes of an existential shit storm. April could be a little more supportive. "That attitude's not helpful. I'm not exactly a hermit, you know. I'm simply taking time to decompress and think about my life." Or avoid thinking about it. Jess had changed the shelf paper in the kitchen three times and her clothes were no longer organized by season, but by shades. Last night, she'd hung everything according to the color wheel. Okay, maybe she did need to get her ass out of the house.

But until a short time ago, her entire future had been mapped out. *By Derek and your parents. You just went along for the ride*. That was the uncomfortable truth—one that kept her awake late into the night. But at least it had been a plan. Jess liked structure. It made her feel secure, if boring. She wasn't meant for spontaneity.

"I think you're hiding," April said. "You're scared because you're a by-the-book person, and your life is a crap pile right now. I get it, but this loner act needs to stop."

Jess kicked a piece of gravel with the toe of her shoe. "Have you ever thought of becoming a life coach? No? Good, because you'd suck at it."

April's brow lifted to new heights as she jabbed a finger at the warehouse. "No one in that building knows who you are, and if they did, they wouldn't give a shit. It's time to live your life and stop being so damned worried about what other people think."

"Easier said than done." Jess had been instructed from the time she could talk to weigh her words carefully, to think twice about every decision. One slipup—a drunken moment caught on a cell phone or an inappropriate text sent to the wrong person—could cause serious repercussions for her family, meaning her dad's career and her mother's reputation. Those ingrained habits didn't disappear with a new address.

"Jess, my grandmother wheels around an oxygen tank and is recovering from knee replacement surgery. *She* has more of a social life than you. Your dad's name doesn't carry any weight here. You're finally free."

Free. As the word sank in, Jess took a deep breath, releasing some of the tension running through her shoulders. She didn't feel free. She knew she'd made the right choice when she broke off her engagement, and while she didn't feel guilty, she didn't exactly feel liberated either. Jess continued to live her life as if she were under a microscope—every move open to criticism and censure. Some days, it seemed like an invisible entity was always peeking over her shoulder, waiting for her to screw up. God, was it exhausting. That's why she'd left Kansas in the first place, to gain a little breathing room, but it didn't seem to be working. So when was she going to cut the strings already, start living on her own terms? She'd already blown up her life, had disappointed her parents to the point that her father wasn't even speaking to her. What more did she have to lose? *Not a damned thing*.

"You know what? You're absolutely right."

"I always am," April said.

There was no one here to impress, no one waiting for her to fail, to point out every flaw. Jess was free. So when was she going to start acting like it? "I'm an adult. A grown-ass independent female."

"Yes, you are." April bobbed her head in affirmation.

"I can do what I please, and I don't have to answer to anyone."

"Preach."

Jess fussed with her purse strap, jerking it higher onto her shoulder. "And maybe I could stand to loosen up a little. That wouldn't be so terrible, would it?"

"What are you going to do, have *two* glasses of pinot? It's going to take a lot more than watching a fight to tarnish that shiny halo. And for your information, we didn't haul our asses out here just for you. I want to hook up with that boxer I met the other night. He was very hot, and my needs are *real*. I know you'll never admit it, but under all those Girl Scout badges, you have needs too."

For the first time all night, Jess laughed. "Yeah, well, I could easily fulfill my needs with a vibrator." After all, that's how she'd managed to get through the past year—and that was before the breakup. Derek had been so stressed over his own political future, their sex life had dwindled to one perfunctory lay every few weeks. The kind that didn't even mess up her hair.

April wagged her finger. "Go in there, find yourself a hot guy. It's time for *you* to do *you*." She shoved her hand into her purse and removed a string of condoms. Ripping off a couple, she shoved them at Jess. "Here. Now go forth and be safe."

"You know I'm not going to do that." Jess tried to hand them back to April, who refused to take them. With a sigh, she wound up tucking them into the front pocket of her jeans. Hooking up with a random guy had never been Jess's thing. She wasn't programmed for casual. She and April had different definitions of cutting loose. To Jess, it meant drinking a shot of straight tequila instead of a light margarita. "Why couldn't we have scratched your itch back in civilization? I still think coming out here was a mistake. This place is a perfect dumping ground for a serial killer."

"Do you see any chainsaw-wielding psychos?" April propped her hands on her hips. "I thought you moved to change your life, get a fresh start. In order to do that, you need to lighten the fuck up."

April was right, though it pained Jess to admit it. After canceling her wedding, she knew she needed to make some serious changes. She just hadn't figured out the details yet. But being the dutiful daughter, taking the road most traveled—it'd made her miserable. The truly tragic part was that she had barely even noticed how unhappy she'd been.

Moving to Chicago was supposed to be a bold, new adventure. So far, the old cautious Jess had been in charge. She'd spent the last twenty-five years sleepwalking through her life, and she was tired of it. She may not have any answers about her future, but she could be in control of this moment. Right here, right now, she could let go of the past and take charge of her life.

With only the briefest hesitation, she strode to the warehouse. When she yanked open the metal door, grainy, yellow light spilled out into the night, cutting through the darkness. A bellowing roar from the crowd rushed over her. *No turning back*. She glanced at April. "Are you coming or what?"

"Now there's my brave bitch. I knew she was lurking in there somewhere." April crossed to the threshold and lightly patted Jess's cheek, before strutting into the building.

Jess followed, letting the door clang shut behind her. Inside, the temperature dipped only a few degrees, but humidity clung to her skin, making her arms and neck sticky. Despite enormous ceiling fans circulating the ripe air, condensation coated the steel walls and concrete floor. Scrunching her nose, Jess tried to block out the combined stench of alcohol and testosterone. It smelled familiar, reminding her of the frat house parties she'd attended in her college days. But there was nothing collegiate about this crowd.

A few hundred men—blue-collar casual, tatted up, and soaked to the gills—gathered around the raised ring in the center of the room. Holding clear plastic cups of beer, they cheered, booed, and hurled obscenities at the two men fighting.

The boxers didn't use gloves. They bare-knuckled it, with only white tape wrapped around each hand for protection. That *had* to hurt.

Fighting of any kind made Jess uncomfortable. But as she watched the men box, she was fascinated. She took a few steps toward the ring, her gaze fixed on the fighters. With each brutal punch, she winced in sympathy, yet couldn't look away.

The energy in the room felt dangerous—violent and unpredictable. Nevertheless, Jess found herself intrigued by the way the two men moved, bouncing from foot to foot, their bodies coiled and ready to spring. There was power and purpose behind each hit.

The boxer in green shorts had a cut above his right eye. Bloody rivulets mixed with sweat and coursed down his face, staining his opponent's taped knuckles. Jess's stomach muscles formed a tight knot. She *hated* the sight of blood, but she had to admit, there was something primal about it all. Something honest.

She watched the fighters circle each other until April grabbed her wrist and pulled her forward. Together they made their way through the crowd, weaving through throngs of men, not stopping until they stood ringside.

While the fight continued, Jess tried to subtly glance at the men closest to her. Most were nearing middle age. A bearded bald man to her left openly leered at Jess's breasts. She did her best to ignore him, edging a few inches closer to April. Eventually, he turned back to the fight.

Jess realized he wasn't the only one ogling. She and April seemed to be the only women present. That fact garnered a fair amount of unwanted attention, and while April took it in stride, it made Jess's skin crawl. There was nothing respectful or even flirtatious about the way these guys eyed her. It was more than sexual interest—there was something predatory in the way they stared.

She crossed her arms in an attempt to discourage anyone's gaze from lingering too long on her chest, and tried to concentrate on the fight. For the next ten minutes, the boxers circled each other, trading jabs. As they sparred, their biceps flexed and their abs contracted in a graceful, brutal dance.

Finally the one in green shorts, with the cut above his eye, ran out of steam. After his opponent delivered a solid punch, he face-planted in the center of the ring, tipping over like a felled spruce. He lay on his stomach, blood spurting from his face and pooling onto the canvas. *Oh God. So much blood.*

April shook her head. "Ouch." She glanced over at Jess and did a double take. "Oh no, you're freaking out, aren't you? It's the blood thing?"

Jess waved her off. "I should have braced myself. I'll be all right. Really."

April gave her arm a squeeze. "It's almost over. It'll be okay."

Of course it would. It was only a little fluid. Nothing to panic about, right? After a few deep breaths, Jess raised her eyes and focused on a dark-haired woman she hadn't seen before. Wearing a pair of blue scrubs and matching latex gloves, she entered the ring and rushed to the unconscious man. She knelt next to him, completely oblivious to the red puddle forming around his head. Then she whipped out a pen light, peeled back his eyelids, and checked his pupils.

"I hope he's all right," Jess said. "I wonder if he has a concussion."

"I'm sure he'll be fi… Hey, watch it, asshole." The man next to April had gestured with his cup and splashed beer over the hem of her jeans, dousing her purple faux snakeskin heels. He shrugged instead of apologizing. "Goddamn it," she said, "look at this. Now I'm going to smell like I'm on tap for the rest of the night."

Jess immediately rooted through her purse and pulled out a tissue. "Here. We should find the restroom, get you cleaned up."

April bent over and dabbed at her foot. "No, you stay here. I won't be gone a minute." Without waiting for a reply, she took off at a quick pace, melting through the crowd and leaving Jess alone. With all these men.

Shit.

Jess thought about traipsing after April, but curling her toes in her pointy black pumps, forced herself to stay put. Surely she could handle being on her own for a few minutes—even in this crowd. The cautious, predictable side of her personality needed to take a backseat tonight. There was a new Jess in town, and she wasn't afraid to take chances. *Yeah, right.*

Throwing her shoulders back, she glanced around the room, not making eye contact with anyone in particular. Too bad all that self-talk about embracing new adventures hadn't covered this kind of testosterone-fueled situation. The men on either side of the ring—not to mention the perv standing next to her—ate her up, their heated gazes ripping through her bravado like it was tissue paper. Maybe she should have listened to her instincts and followed April. All this lust-filled attention was making her very nervous.

In an effort to shut them out, Jess whipped out her phone and checked for a signal—still no reception. The anxiety she'd felt earlier slammed into her once again. Which one of these unruly horndogs could she trust to give her a ride home? None, and it was a long, dark, bumpy five-mile walk back to the train station.

Jess cut a glance to the left. The bearded asshole stared at her and slowly licked his lips, leaving them wet and slick. *Gross*. When he made a rude gesture with his tongue, she angled away from him and surveyed the men standing on the opposite side of the ring. That's when she saw *him* for the first time.

He stood near the back of the room, head and shoulders taller than everyone around him. He stared at Jess with an unyielding, narrow-eyed intensity that caught her off guard. Easily six-and-a-half feet tall, his shoulders were so broad each one needed its own zip code. The sky-blue T-shirt he wore not only clung to his torso, outlining his solid chest and bulky arms, it also matched his light blue eyes. Thick, burnished waves framed his face and brushed his square jaw.

More rugged than handsome, his angular cheekbones were sharply chiseled, not molded. The flat, blunt bridge of his nose blended with the ridge of his brow line. It had obviously been broken more than once. But none of that rendered him unattractive. Instead, it made him seem rock solid. Manly. Rough around the edges, and unapologetic about it.

He studied Jess just as thoroughly, but not in a sexual way. In fact, he seemed almost detached. Aloof.

Everything about him, from his casual posture to the upward tilt of his strong chin, made it clear that he was in charge of his own world. Powerful. Intimidating. Not Jess's type at all. She'd lived her life around men who'd do anything to get their own way—first her father and his political hack friends, then Derek. She'd had her fill of alphas, thank you very much. Not that this man seemed particularly interested in her. Still, he didn't look away. He trapped her with those blue eyes, refusing to break contact.

If there was one thing Jess knew about alphas, it was that they didn't like to be challenged. She should drop her gaze first, which was exactly what she'd done in the past. When her father lectured her for not smiling enough in photo ops or ditching Derek three months before the wedding, Jess would lower her eyes in defeat. It was a useful tactic, and at the time, seemed a small price to pay for a little peace. But it'd cost her dearly. Every time Jess conceded, she'd lost a bit of herself.

Old, careful Jess would submit to this man. She'd

lower her head and back away slowly, then scamper off to find April. But that Jess wouldn't be at a fight club in the first place. That Jess would be back in Kansas, married to a candidate for the state senate, using her vibrator, bored out of her mind. *This* Jess was bold and brazen, open to new experiences. So instead of letting this man win, she quirked a brow, daring *him* to look away first.

That move earned her a scowl, causing the lines bracketing his mouth to deepen. Nope, he didn't like that at all. *Too damn bad, hotshot.*

To add to her rebellion, Jess lifted her chin and angled her head just a fraction. *You're not going to intimidate me, tough guy. I'm a grown-ass independent woman.*

His eyes widened in surprise, then his brows slammed together in irritation. *How* dare *you not cower before me?*

She smiled at his reaction. Oh, she was starting to like this brave new side of herself. It was fun. And reckless. In a sea of men, she found herself in a pissing contest with the biggest shark. What the hell had gotten into her?

Then the perv on her left shuffled a few inches closer, brushing his arm against the side of her breast, bringing Jess back to reality with a thud.

For the last ten minutes, Aidan O'Shea had been watching the beauty across the room. She was out of place among these shitfaced savages and far too posh for this event. That lovely face was so terribly expressive. Every time Byron had taken a hit in the ring—and since he wasn't an experienced fighter, he took quite a few—she cringed. When he finally went down, she couldn't bear to watch. Obviously, she wasn't used to violence. So all this begged the question: What the feck was she doing here in the first place?

Without shifting his gaze away from her, Aidan reached out and grabbed his brother around the back of the neck, pulling him close. "Who is she?" he yelled in Liam's ear.

"Who's who?"

Aidan gripped Liam's neck a little tighter. "Across the room. Dark hair, blue eyes." *Bleeding gorgeous.*

Liam scanned the crowd, then found her. "Don't know, but she's well fit, isn't she?"

Aidan growled and shoved Liam away. "You'll steer clear of her." Even as he gave the warning, he still couldn't take his eyes off her. She moved with an innate grace, right down to her delicate pale pink fingertips. There was something innocent about this woman. Sheltered, maybe. Refined—definitely.

Her presence here drew too much attention. Aidan could feel it in the air, a restless mood that rippled through the crowd. He could see it stirring in the eyes of the other men who also watched her, and it brought forth something he hadn't felt in a very long time—a protective instinct. Which was rubbish, of course. If she should be protected from anyone, it was Aidan himself. He'd shag her in a heartbeat, given half a chance.

"What about her friend?" Liam asked. "Can I have a go at her?"

"Don't care." Aidan had barely noticed the friend. But the brunette…now she was captivating. Her large, blue eyes were made brighter by her pale skin and long, dark hair. She probably smelled like heaven—rich and expensive. *She's out of your league, ya mucker*. That she was. It didn't stop him from looking his fill, though.

She began scanning the crowd, her restless glance not lingering on anyone or anything for very long. Then out of nowhere, she flashed those blue eyes on him, and Aidan found himself completely ensnared. They locked gazes for a long moment, before hers flickered over him. She didn't look impressed by what she saw. In fact, she quirked her brow in a move that said *what the feck are you looking at?*

It was one thing for Aidan to admit she was above him in every way. Another thing altogether when *she* acknowledged it.

When she inclined her pretty little chin, looking down her nose at him, it raised Aidan's hackles. Who did she think she was, coming into *his* house and acting all superior? She didn't belong here in the bleeding first place.

And he was more than happy to show her.

Acknowledgments

There are so many people that help a book get from my computer to your hot little hands. First of all, the Sourcebooks team. You guys are amazing. Cat, Rachel, Dawn, Becca, Morgan, Amelia—you ladies are lovely and wonderful to work with. A big special ginger hug to Mary Altman, my editor. I can't even tell you how much I love working with you. You are a joy and a delight. Thank you!

My sweet husband, who grocery shops and cooks without complaint. Thank you!

Sherry, Kathy, Larissa, Sara—thanks so much! You are always there. I love you guys!

About the Author

As a girl, Terri L. Austin thought she'd outgrow dreaming up stories and creating imaginary friends. Instead, she's made a career of it. She met her own Prince Charming and together they live in Missouri. She loves to hear from readers. Visit her at www.terrilaustin.com.